SHE LOVES ME, SHOW LOVES ME NOT

A PACIFIC NORTHWEST LOVE SERIES

BOOK 4

SHANNON MORSE

ISBN: 979-8 234-03646-9

Cover by: Lopez Designs

1st Round of Editing: Ramona Mihai

2nd Round of Editing: Samantha Talarico

Formatting: Kalie Gerwig | Good Girl Author Services

TRIGGER WARNINGS

Death of an animal (not on page)
Assult
Arson
Stalking
Bullying
Manipulation

ALSO BY SHANNON MORSE

A Pacific Northwest Love Series
Broken Luck: Book 1
Fairytale in a Big City: Book 2
Stop Drop and Run: Book 3
She Loves Me, She Loves Me Not: Book 4

Standalone Contemporary Romance:
Flour, Sugar & a Tiffany Ring

Standalone Dark Paranormal Thriller
Absinthe (S.M.M)

To all the crazy plant ladies & flower dudes:
Plant your love and let it take root.

PROLOGUE

Pro Tip: *Success for a plant and flower shop depends on visibility, foot traffic, and having a strong social media presence. A following can help drive repeat sales, and remember, beauty sells.*

Pussy, that's all Broc loves, and their sweet nectar; an elixir that all women possess. It doesn't matter how they look, taste, or smell. Their perfume could smell like the wet dew on grass or have the aroma of the sweetest orchid. To Broc, the feel of his thick pulsing stem sliding inside the slick waiting pussy has him addicted to their flavor as much as Adderall. The sensation of every smooth thrust has him wanting and dreaming of his next score. And there will never be enough for this young, attractive, popular man. As far as this addiction goes, every ripe legal-age fruit isn't enough; he's always craving juicy peaches, strawberries, or nectar. Doesn't matter to him if it's connected to a pair of caramel, pale, or dark chocolate thighs. A flower is a flower; a pussy is a pussy; each is beautiful as the petals they bloom from. And every time, he thrusts in and pulls back, staring down at the creamy silk covering his veiny cock or with his neck straining to the heavens above while the fireworks light up behind his eyelids. He fucking loves the feel of each wet pussy, his balls slapping against those creamy or dark chocolate thighs. Not only does he love it, but he's fucking obsessed with sex, clearly, and all the women he fucks know it. Like a cut flower, the girls he's pumped his seed into can only be used once. A cut flower eventually wilts away. Yeah, he's a fucking asshole. He dips his stick like he works for Oil Can Henry.

But...there was that one time. That one time years ago, he regretted pumping and dumping, but that was a long time ago.

Sometimes a little love & care can make a flower blossom....

1

A FEW YEARS AGO

HIGH SCHOOL SENIOR YEAR

Pro Tip: When using peonies in a floral arrangement, be sure to use mostly closed petals because at the slightest touch, the flower will drop petals, leaving only the stem.

"Broc! Toss the ball over to me!" Adam shouted, his voice echoing off the high ceiling of the gymnasium. A football spiraled through the air, spinning under the fluorescent lights as it flew across the gym. Broc, carefully balancing a bouquet of orange gerbera daisies and white lilies, navigated through the bustling crowd of students while keeping an eye on the approaching football. Groups of students chatted and laughed, backpacks slung over their shoulders, while a few kids took some final shots at the basketball hoop. The sound of bouncing balls thumping around Broc had him pick up his pace, his eyes darting between his hands and the flying football.

"Fucking Adam," Broc mumbled as he jogged carefully to the center of the gymnasium. The football landed right in front of him, bouncing high and then rolling across the shiny wooden floor. He pressed his lips together in annoyance, only stopping to step over the football as it rolled closer to his feet.

There were card tables which were set up in the middle of the gymnasium, ready for all the contestants' floral displays, which would be judged during tonight's event. Ferris High School was hosting a special competition that could possibly change Broc's future path if he won. He refocused on the flowers, knowing that every detail was crucial for the contest. "God damn it, Adam!" Broc shouted, frustration creeping into his voice as he glared at his friend. Carefully, he set his floral arrangement next to his name tag on the card table, adjusting the vase so that every petal was perfectly displayed.

Adam stood across the gymnasium, hands on his hips, a mischievous grin spreading across his face as he watched Broc's face turn red with anger.

When Broc finally straightened up, he yelled, "You're so immature!"

Adam chuckled, shaking his head. "Come on, Broc! You can't seriously think this is how you're supposed to catch a football! What would the coach think!" He leaned against the wall, clearly enjoying himself.

In an exasperated stare, Broc glowered at him, trying to keep his composure. "I'm not on the football team, you fucking idiot! Maybe if you helped me instead of just trying to nail me with a football, I wouldn't be pissed off!"

Adam wiped away a tear of laughter. "But it's so fun to watch you dodge my balls!" He leaned back against the wall, chuckling. "Alright, alright, I'll help. But only if you admit that you like my balls flying in your face!"

"God damn it, Adam! You're a shithead, so immature!" Broc yelled back, but the sound drowned out in the already loud gymnasium as more students pushed through the double doors, filling the space, hoping to get seats in the bleachers.

Another football soared in the air as Broc jogged along the

polished wooden floor, his gaze instinctively following the trajectory of the ball. He squinted slightly, trying to gauge its path.

"Adam! Where the hell did you get another ball?" he shouted.

Adam stood with a sheepish grin spreading across his face. At his feet lay an open duffel bag filled with footballs from the school's football team. The football Adam had just thrown flew over Broc's head, just out of reach, before landing with a soft thud. Frustration simmered beneath Broc's skin. Again, another ball was flying towards Broc; instinctively, he pivoted to intercept the ball. He deftly weaved through clusters of students, focused solely on the prize that was just out of reach. "Adam! Seriously, how many balls are in that fucking bag!" Broc yelled, then added, "Stop throwing balls in my face!"

"That's what she said!" Adam replied with a laugh.

Once Broc realized that the football would be out of reach, he gave a halfhearted jump, then skidded to a stop, his eyes lazily following the football's descent as it hit the polished wooden floor with a thud, bounced back up, and wobbled away. "You overshot the pass, idiot!" Broc said with a smirk, shaking his head and raking his hand through his thick mop of black curls.

"Well, if you had jumped for it, you could have caught it!" Adam argued back at Broc, his eyes wide and arms flailing, as if it were obvious.

"I did jump for it, moron!" Broc shouted back, walking over to where the ball had landed to pick it up. Looking over his shoulder, Broc saw Andy walking in from the field, his sneakers squeaking against the gymnasium floor. He stood next to Adam who was lost in his laugh, dropping his worn backpack next to his feet.

"Come on, toss that old pigskin!" Adam called, elbowing Andy as he nodded toward Broc who stood with his arms crossed, scowling. He bent down to palm the football, and when he looked back up and slapped it, he noticed a few members of the Dance Team walking into the gym after their outside practice. Each girl flipped her hair and sucked in her stomach as soon as they spotted Adam and Andy, who stood at the edge of the basketball court, radiating confidence and sex appeal. The immediate change in the girls' behavior made Broc roll his eyes, but he couldn't look away from their little show of attention, which Adam and Andy were also participating in like peacocks. The young women's obvious attraction to the two boys did not go unnoticed either. Eager teenage boys watched their next meal with an intensity that suggested they were savoring every moment, like it was an ordinary Tuesday filled with eagerness, boobs, and lots of kissing. The young women, mirroring their radiating confidence, walked with a playful flirtation in their step, each sway of their hips catching the eye of the guys.

The girls took their time, allowing their eyes to roam over Adam and Andy's toned bodies, fit from their long runs and time spent in the gym lifting weights; they were undeniably attractive and widely known as single. The guys reciprocated by admiring the women's bodies unabashedly. The unmistakable chemistry crackled in the air, bouncing off both the girls and the guys, making the moment feel static as all of them reveled in the thrill of the chase. Adam, unshy with his actions, slid his hand down his body and adjusted his hardened length, uncaring who saw what he was concealing.

Lexi, Sara, and the other girls flashed their best smiles, eyes following Adam's movement, each one fluttering their long lashes and playfully licking their lower lips before gently biting them, showing their eagerness to see who might take the bait. Most likely, it would be Adam. While these guys were just as attractive as any of the football stars, it was Adam who had the bulkiest shoulders and washboard abs that attracted the attention of the girls around him like bees to honey. Naturally, those girls' thoughts began to wander to the idea of feeling his strong abs, while Adam was only thinking about how those girls would feel naked against his skin—maybe he would even feel two of them. This thought made his smile widen and his cock thicken even more.

One factor that contributed to Adam's greatest asset was his charisma and, of course, attracted girls throughout high school. He often joked that he should hand out coffee punch cards to the girls who wanted to date him, saying, "Buy one date, get one free!" Like a coffee-obsessed teenage girl, Adam breezed through one-night stands as if he were sampling different brews of the day. Soon, he would need to start working on actual conversation and not rely on his washboard abs, but with the way things were going, he might end up with more than he bargained for. Like he cared at the moment. The school year had just begun, and Adam was already treating dating like a daily caffeine fix; it was something quick, intense, and definitely left him wanting more. He was more than willing to accept any girl's offer.

Lexi, one of the Dance Team girls with long, flowing blonde hair, stopped in her tracks and turned to fully face Adam and Andy, who were still gawking openly, probably making it weird but not giving two shits. Lexi stood out not just for her striking appearance, but also for her Dance Team Captain uniform. The outfit consisted of a very short black skirt, tightly fitted and adorned with bold red and white trim along the hem, paired with a matching midriff black top that prominently featured a large red letter "F" sewn across the front, signifying their school's initial. Every horny boy's wet dream, literally standing in front of two guys who were ready and eager to make her scream their names in a very intimate horizontal dance.

With a playful twist of her hair around her finger and a naughty glint in her eye, Lexi called out, “Hey, guys! Are you two coming tonight to watch the floral contest?” The tone was sultry, and the sound of her gum smacking echoed slightly, drawing even more attention from Adam and Andy.

Across the gymnasium, Broc watched the unfolding scene with interest and slight jealousy. He palmed the football in his hand and decided to jog across the gymnasium, weaving through the throngs of students. A sudden wave of FOMO washed over him, propelling him forward. From behind Lexi, Broc watched how she interacted with his friends. It was also the perfect view of Lexi's figure; her hourglass body had him biting his lower lip and squeezing the football tighter. He couldn’t deny how attractive the girls looked in their uniforms. The sight of her in that short skirt stirred something within him, igniting a flame in his core and filling his cock with all the blood in his body; the tightness in his pants had him adjusting himself slightly. But it wasn't what he really wanted, and the tightness eased. In the whole scope of things, Broc was a young man with certain interests: flowers...and pussy. He was a flirt, and he knew it, but there was one person who seemed to hold his interest more than others.

When the gym door swung open, a chill from the crisp fall air swept in, but it wasn't just the temperature that halted Broc's thoughts. It was who'd opened the gymnasium doors. Standing in the entrance was Rosie Clark, a young woman whose presence immediately captivated him. Her black hair hung down her back in a long braid, with strands that fell to frame her delicate face. Broc found himself entranced by her creamy skin, which seemed to glow under the gymnasium lights, and the way her bright bluish-purple eyes sparkled with shyness. Her petite features, highlighted by a cute button nose and bowtie-shaped lips, only added to her beauty. A well-worn backpack slung casually over one shoulder, Broc watched as she carefully stepped through the double doors; he couldn't help but feel a flutter of excitement as he followed her with his eyes.

This wasn't the first time he'd seen her though; they did in fact share a horticulture class. Broc had always admired her from a distance. Today, however, she walked confidently toward the center of the gymnasium, where the folding tables were set up. Broc's heart raced as his eyes flicked to the table where he saw that her name stood prominently near his floral arrangement. He had been so focused on carefully arranging his own floral display that he hadn't realized Rosie was also participating in the same competition. Now, the thought of sharing this experience with her sent a rush of adrenaline through him, a vibrant sensation that tingled just beneath the surface of his skin.

Just hours earlier, Broc had been with Rosie in the greenhouse. His unabashed stare continued to watch Rosie as she approached the folding table and dropped her bag beneath her name plate. She scanned the open space, glancing over her shoulder to catch Broc's gaze. A light blush crept up her neck and settled on her cheeks, revealing her embarrassment. The memory of their intimate kiss, his body pressing into hers, flooded her thoughts, and she couldn't shake the feeling that he was still in her mind just as vividly as she was in his. The subtle rise and fall of her chest suggested she was lost in those memories, caught between shyness and the warmth he'd evoked in the autumn air.

In the school's greenhouse, only an hour before, the connection between Broc and Rosie had taken a turn and their subtle flirting had taken on a life of its own, reaching a pinnacle between their shared glances across the classroom, light teasing, and innocent touches. But it was in the quiet solitude of the greenhouse that the tension heightened. With only the soft sound of water spraying, Broc found himself drawn to Rosie like a magnet. He'd seized the moment and stepped closer, his hand gliding gently up her arm, feeling her skin tingle beneath his fingertips. Then, slipping his hand to cup the back of her head, he'd threaded his fingers through her silky hair, which had been down at the time. He'd drawn her gaze to meet his, and time seemed to stand still as they'd locked eyes. In that moment, a flush had crept up Rosie's chest and neck, blooming into a deep crimson that mirrored the vibrant colors of the poinsettias nearby. Her cheeks had radiated a rosy embarrassment, and Broc had interpreted her blush as his invitation. Nervous excitement seemed to swirl within her and he'd leaned in, closing the distance until his lips met hers, pressing softly. He wanted Rosie and, in that heartbeat, everything else had faded away.

The attraction to Rosie had grown too intense for him to resist any longer. The fogged windows of the greenhouse muted the world outside, and he'd felt a surge of adrenaline. With a swift motion, he'd unhooked the straps of Rosie's overalls, his hand gliding down her flat stomach, feeling the silky smoothness of her skin under the palm of his hand, but then he'd paused, staring into her bright blue-violet eyes, before continuing. "I'm going to make you feel good, Rosie," Broc had told her. His breath wrapped around her ears as he'd added, "Are you ready for me?"

In an instant, he found himself back in the gym, the chatter of voices snapping him out of the moment. No longer lost in the intimacy of that greenhouse moment, he was now surrounded by the vibrant energy of the dance girls and laughter from his buddies. Broc's gaze swept away from Lexi's backside and back across the gymnasium; the sight of her and not Rosie instantly deflated his cock. But when Broc slid his eyes across the gymnasium, they landed back on Rosie, who was now gingerly making her way back to the double door exit. A quick flick of her eyes darted in Broc's direction, uncertainty passing over her features. The energy in the room shifted as their eyes met, a silent connection sparking in the bustling crowd. The flashback of when he'd lined up his condom-wrapped length against Rosie returned. She'd been sitting on the wire watering table in the greenhouse, fully exposed from the waist down, and how she'd cried out. The moan echoed in the recesses of his mind, bringing back the memory of that moment when he had looked down at their connection and seen the deep red stain on his cock, as vibrant as a rose. Broc's eyes quickly shifted to his hand, which was now clean as he held the football. But the soft whisper from Rosie still haunted his mind.

"Sorry."

While Broc stood with Lexi, Sara, Adam, and Andy, his thoughts drifted back to Rosie. The delicate way her fingers had brushed against the petals of the flowers pinned him in place like a pressed flower on display. Each moment they'd shared made it hard to focus on anything else. His stomach still flipped as he replayed her whisper in his mind. Back at the greenhouse memory, Broc had cupped her cheek, his thumb rubbing across her lower lip and then caressing her jaw. He had whispered in response, "Had I known this was your first, I would have done this differently. I'm the one who should be apologizing."

The grip on the football tightened, his knuckles turning white, as he watched Rosie walk away. He wished he could reach out, call her back, but he knew the moment was theirs alone. It was a secret hidden in the corners of his heart, buried deep in the dirt. Rosie had this way of breaking down his defenses, exposing the vulnerability he rarely acknowledged. Once he'd seen the blood on the condom, she had told Broc, "This is perfect, Broc, among the poinsettias, with you, this is perfect." Her words echoed in his mind.

When she turned back to glance at him, her eyes sparkling with unspoken sadness, it sent a rush through him. He wanted to be the one to tell their story, to share the secret that brought them together, but for now, he stayed silent, hoping for another moment, another chance to bridge the distance between them. Even if no one else understood, he knew in his heart that what they had was anything but ordinary.

But now, Rosie was only a memory.

To maintain his playboy status, Broc pushed down his feelings deep inside his body. Instead of listening to his mind, he chose to heed the impulses typical of a young, horny teenage boy. To keep up the facade, he forced a broad smile that stretched almost from ear to ear, an overly enthusiastic gesture. The dance girls noticed, licking their lips and popping out their hips for attention. However, no matter how hard he tried to forget, the memories of Rosie lingered, only intensifying his desire to be with her. Everything about Rosie was delicate; he'd witnessed her blossom right before his eyes, pulling the shyness from her.

Puffing out his chest and folding his arms to make his biceps look bigger, Adam stood tall—about a foot taller than all the girls. He winked and plastered his prize-winning smile on his face. "Of course, I'll be watching my boy here!" Adam said to Lexi, slapping a hand on Broc's shoulder, which made Broc's eyes snap back to the group, tearing his gaze away from Rosie.

Lexi flipped her hair off her shoulders and placed her hand on her hip. Sara Peterson stepped closer to Andy, raised her hand, and rested it on his chest. She tilted her head slightly and gave Andy a coy smile, waiting for his reaction. It didn't take long for Andy to flick his eyes to the touch resting on his chest. Although Sara and Andy didn't have an official relationship, they often used each other to relieve any sexual tension. It seemed like someone might be feeling stressed tonight.

Rosie walked out of the gym, feeling anger and shame surging through her body. She made her way back to the horticulture room to retrieve her floral arrangement. Once she had it in her hands, she braced herself to re-enter the gym, knowing she would have to face Broc. With care, she walked back inside the gymnasium, holding her beautiful arrangement. Broc's gaze found her again and followed her. He noticed the slight unease in her stride. The moment he dropped his gaze at her floral design, which was unique and far from the typical arrangements taught in class, his heart sank; he immediately knew she would be the winner.

Broc casually removed his arm from around one of the other girls and ran his fingers over his lips, still inhaling the sweet floral scent that lingered on his fingers from her body. One of the girls from the now-growing group was leaning against him; her presence faded from his mind entirely, as it was only Rosie who seemed to capture his full attention.

While Broc watched Rosie glide across the polished wooden floor, carrying the most amazing peony floral arrangement, his eyes roamed down Rosie's slender, long neck to her perfect, slim figure and to her long, black single braid slung over one shoulder, and then back to that beautiful flower arrangement once more. Even though her overalls covered the most central part of her body, Broc wanted to feel her against his body once more. While he had already marked her into a mumbling mess, he hadn't been able to get a clear glimpse of her body as they'd quickly reclothed and watered the plants, as if nothing had happened inside the greenhouse.

Were her hands soft?

Were they rough from gardening, or did she protect them with gloves?

Rosie's steps faltered briefly as her eyes once more landed on Broc's. The dance girls flocked under Andy, Adam, and Broc's wingspan. Yes, for him, it was clear that his heart beat a little faster, but it wasn't from these girls. But Rosie was confused; how could weeks of feeling like she meant something to Broc be wiped away so easily? For her, just thinking about what they had done in the greenhouse made her stomach flip. Now it flipped with raw disgust. With a glower at Broc, feeling nothing but regret, she quickly turned away and walked to the card tables.

A girl who was usually just as quiet approached Rosie; this was the same girl that Broc's buddy, Davis, loved to play "where is Sammy today," a hide and seek game that only Davis was playing—yeah, kind of creepy. The girl with long mousy-brown hair and pale skin pushed her glasses up the bridge of her nose and blushed as she placed a hand on Rosie's shoulder. Her movement was trying to prevent being pushed into Rosie by a random kid with a large backpack. The redness rose up Sammy's neck as she mumbled something before adjusting her glasses and walking away with her head down.

Just then, Davis slipped into Broc's group, adjusting the strap on his backpack and leaning in like he was about to drop some significant intel. "Look who it is: Sammy. Finally spotted her today," he announced, his lopsided grin morphing into a proud smirk.

"Dude, your game is so weak! Just go say hi to her already," Broc replied, shaking his head.

"Can't—Camille, remember?" Davis shot back, his grin slipping just a little.

One of the girls rolled her eyes dramatically. "Seriously, dude, Camille is such a turd! Why are you still with her?"

Adam turned to Davis, a playful look on his face. "Yeah, man, spill it! What's the deal?"

Davis ran a hand through his dark, wavy hair, smirking as he joined in. "Loyalty, I guess. Or maybe I just like the drama?!" The laughter that followed made Davis blush a little, but he just shrugged it off, pretending it didn't bother him, when Broc knew it did.

"Pussy whipped more like," Adam mumbled. "Hey, Broc, go long!" Adam suddenly yelled, pushing his shoulder. The sound of two girls squealing as Broc shoved them aside and sprinted down the gymnasium caught Rosie off guard. Adam tossed a football across the room, and her eyes followed it. Davis began running alongside Andy, while Broc also picked up speed; all three of them headed towards Rosie.

Unsure of which direction to take, Rosie felt pinned in place. She quickly glanced back just in time to see the football heading straight for her head. With Broc turned while pursuing the football and Davis closing in quickly, Broc collided with Rosie. The shock of the impact caused her to lose her grip on her floral arrangement. And a shocked yelp left her lips. In slow motion, she watched in horror as her arrangement fell to the gymnasium floor, almost as if it were happening in another time zone. She wished time would stop or that she could be like Neo from *The Matrix*, reaching out to catch the bullet or, in her case, her flowers. Instead, she was shoved backward with a loud "oof!" and landed on her butt, crying out in pain as she watched her vase of peonies shatter against the polished wooden floor. The broken crystal vase, once her deceased grandmother's, was scattered across the floor, along with the beautiful ombre of peonies she had handpicked the day before.

Instagram had teamed up with Kerry from Seattle to find a new apprentice for an upcoming floral Netflix TV show called 'Battle of the Floats and Flowers.' This show would take the top horticulture students to the Rose Bowl Parade in Pasadena, California at the end of the year. The students would assist Kerry in designing and decorating a float with flowers. The winning float would earn a creator's job at Kerry's floral shop in Seattle, along with over $500,000 in living expenses, $10,000 in free marketing from Instagram, and opportunities to help with the Oscars and Fashion Week in New York City.

This was one of Rosie's best chances to escape Spokane and her foster home. However, as she watched her floral arrangement shatter, her heart broke with it. Silent tears streamed down Rosie's cheeks. For Broc, tonight's floral contest would set him up. Unlike his buddies, Adam, Andy, and Davis, he had an eye and love for plants. Landscaping had always been his summer job. He'd always wanted to own his own greenhouse or flower shop. While Broc wasn't poor and didn't live in the foster system, like Rosie, college would still be expensive.

The crowd in the gymnasium hushed as a screech echoed, followed by gasps of surprise. "Oh shit!" Broc exclaimed as he knelt beside the card table, while Davis lay on his side, cradling the football and looking up from where he was sprawled on the floor.

"Fuck. You okay?" Davis asked Rosie, planting his hand on the ground, pushing himself into a seated position. Rosie sat frozen, her eyes fixed on her ruined future. Her lungs burned, reminding her to take a breath. Andy rushed up to Broc, Rosie, and Davis, offering them a hand to help them stand and move away from the broken glass.

Meanwhile, Adam jumped up and down on the side of the basketball court, shouting, "Touchdown!" Lexi and Sara giggled as Adam continued to clap and pump his fist in the air, yelling, "Woo-hoo! Touchdown!" Then he ran in circles around the girls.

At that moment, Kerry, the floral legend, entered the gymnasium and glanced over the scene. Disappointment flickered across his face for a moment, but then his smile, the one that won over so many on Netflix, slid into place. With a quick clap of his hands, he waved to a few cameramen who had just stepped into the gym.

"Hey, Lars, think you can help clean up this mess before we start shooting?" Kerry asked.

A man in a dark suit approached Rosie. "Unfortunately, you must forfeit today's contest due to the absence of your floral arrangement. All of us here from Instagram, along with Kerry Robinson himself, want to thank you for your time and apologize for what happened. I'm sure it was just a simple accident," the man said, casting a glance at Broc and Davis.

Rosie felt as though she were standing on stage, with pig blood dripping down from her head onto the floor. She could hear her heart pounding against her chest as her skin flushed crimson with anger. All of her hopes were dashed. Rosie's bluish-purple eyes narrowed in rage, her face burning like the reddest rose.

Meanwhile, sadness washed over Broc as he looked at Rosie, more tears welling up in her eyes and threatening to spill over. When her gaze shifted to Broc, fury overtook her heart, blackening it like the rich soil covering the earth, wishing he was six feet under that soil, pushing up daisies.

2

A FEW YEARS LATER

Pro Tip: When propagating a leaf, let the cutting dry for one day to prevent any rotting. When planting the leaf, make sure its cutting is in a moist, well-drained soil and place it in indirect light.
Don't let the soil dry up.

The trendy Little Café, with cozy outdoor seating, was nestled on a bustling street corner in the historic section of downtown Spokane. With its exposed brick walls and rustic wooden accents, it was one of Rosie's favorite places to stroll to every morning before starting her workday. Located just a short walk from her plant shop, both businesses were proudly owned and operated by two young women, who happened to be best friends. The key difference, however, was that while Little Café thrived and boasted a steady flow of customers, Rosie struggled to keep her plant shop afloat. Despite the low sales and customers, Rosie found joy in owning her business. She loved venting about her life to her plants and cherished the quiet moments spent among her colorful clippings and affectionate potted friends. After all, they never talked back to her, nor did they get high, break into her shop and steal money, or screw any walking woman while under the influence.

Little Café quickly became the go-to spot for locals and visitors alike, with friendly conversations and the latest gossip; it was the ideal place to "spill the tea or coffee." The café's popularity soared after it was featured on social media, drawing the attention of numerous Instagram influencers and food bloggers who helped elevate their own personal profiles while simultaneously turning it into a local hotspot. While longtime residents initially loved having such a quaint café in their neighborhood, they'd had to come to grips with the new local fame of their favorite café. Adding to its accolades, Little Café had proudly won the prestigious "Best of" award in the Inland Northwest Inlander Newspaper, marking a significant milestone for Alessandra Lopes, Rosie's best friend and the café's owner.

Alessandra, always the bubbly, happy friend, was the voice of reason, which was aggravating for Rosie because she was usually right, and it was always with a smile. But the good thing for her was that when she was right, her smile always made Rosie feel better, and for some reason, it was often contagious. Even standing in line right now amongst the crowded coffee shop, Alessandra's warm greeting could be heard floating in the air as each new customer gave their order, and she greeted them with a genuine smile every time. Patiently waiting, Rosie's eyes wandered over to the new décor on the wall just to the left of where she was standing. The art display hadn't been there yesterday when she'd stopped in for her usual cup of coffee, so it seemed Alessandra must have had it installed only last night.

While Rosie stared at the new wall display, the memory of how they'd met floated into her mind just as the next breath filled Rosie's lungs. It just so happened that about two years ago, Rosie was walking down the sidewalk, collecting dandelions to make her dandelion jelly, when she'd seen movement inside the once-vacant shop. Rosie had knocked on the window. That was when Rosie had spied Alessandra alone, doing her best to prepare her new shop for her grand opening. Rosie and Alessandra had been inseparable since that fateful day. Kindred spirits and souls, it was a certainty that these girls were fated to meet and become friends.

The queue started to move forward. The heavy feeling of someone standing almost too close to Rosie didn't go unnoticed; the sense of claustrophobia covered her body like a rough blanket. Pushing her annoyance aside, she stepped forward, trying to avoid the intense reaction from her inner thoughts as the line continued to advance. Taking a calming breath, Rosie tried to focus on the chatter around the café. The Little Café was loud, even with its tall ceilings and open industrial concept; everything echoed, from the slightest whisper to the loudest sneeze. Not having a drop ceiling hadn't been the first choice for Alessandra. But it turned out that the people of Spokane loved the feel and look of her trendy coffee shop. Each wall had been painted a deep forest green, with pink and gold velvet cushioned chairs and navy-blue accents. The countertop was a beautiful pink marble, and her sleek matte black espresso machine whirred to life as Alessandra lifted a paper cup and started to write the customer's order on it, then set it down next to the barista.

Behind the counter, on the wall, were rows of thin slats of wood with large Scrabble game pieces, which displayed the coffee prices and sizes. Under those Scrabble game pieces were three large oak-framed black chalkboards with delicate handwriting explaining the coffee choices, non-coffee menu items, added flavors, and milk types. These days, whole milk wouldn't cut it anymore. The ever-loving millennial couldn't live without their need to *milk* everything, with tits or without tits. Whether it was almond, cashew, soy, oats, cow, or goat, they wanted it until CNN came out with the latest information that could encourage or discourage the use of milked products. Rosie's eyes slid over to the new art display to the left of the counter. From floor to ceiling, Alessandra had placed about a hundred open books and nailed them to the wall, exposing all the pages in a beautiful display of art.

Rosie loved it.

The pages brought a smile to her face. Placing a finger on her lips, her mind wandered back to work-related stuff. One task she dreaded was a letter she needed to write. It was to the soil company in Portland, Oregon, to whom Rosie had just paid over four hundred dollars, only to tell them she had been sold tainted soil. Their guarantee of pure black gold was, in Rosie's mind, just a bunch of shit.

A throat clearing from the man standing too close to Rosie indicated that the line had moved forward. Not looking back, Rosie, who was already annoyed by the rudeness, reluctantly took a step forward. Reaching for her long, now dyed purple hair, she grabbed her braid and slung over her shoulder; she started to play with the end of her hair, brushing it lightly over the outside of her cheek as she bit the inside of her mouth. The thought of writing that letter was something she hated to do, but she also knew she at least needed to try to get her money back. The reason: Money was already tight with her shop; it wasn't doing as well as Alessandra's café, and she didn't know why. Plants were the best companions; they listened to you complain about living friends and never talked back to you. Sometimes, they showed their affection by blooming like bud blossoms or making little babies, so you had more friends to talk to, and they never judged you.

Rosie had spent money she really didn't have on the supposedly "Black Gold" from this prestigious soil company. She hoped to increase the growth of the cuttings she needed to transplant, which would help her store. However, when the bags arrived, they proved to be contaminated. They were full of white roots. Now, for those who weren't gardeners, finding roots in clean dirt was not good, not good at all. While 'clean dirt' might be an oxymoron, using dirt rich in nutrients, minus the roots, was necessary to achieve the best plant growth ever.

Earlier that morning, Rosie had carefully tried to feel her way around the soil to find the source of the white roots, dumping the entire large bag on the floor in the back of her shop. Just as she suspected, it was from a seed; most likely, it was from ryegrass. One of the worst invasive weeds a garden could get. ryegrass would destroy and suffocate a garden or plant. Rosie hated confrontation, and writing the letter asking for her refund would not be fun, but that was the least of her concerns.

Another clearing of the deep throat broke Rosie's thoughts,

instantly sending a wave of annoyance through her body, only to settle in her spine. Sure, she wasn't paying full attention, but it wasn't like she was standing at the back of the room refusing to move; she was just moving a little slower. Resisting the urge to turn around and scowl at the throat-clearing jerk, Rosie stepped forward, closing the gap between her and the man standing before her and moving away from the jerk behind her. Out of habit, Rosie ran her fingers through the stubble on the side of her partially shaved head, making it hard to resist the urge to glance over her shoulder, but she did resist.

Another one of Rosie's concerns, besides the money lost on her dirt, was a new leak in her building, and she needed to figure out where it was coming from before something catastrophic happened. There always seemed to be something going on with that old, derelict building Rosie liked to call home. Tracing her finger up to the top of her head, she ran it down the center of her French braid and then over the long braid below her shoulder again. Taking in a deep inhale, she bounced from heel to heel as she waited in line, trying to pay attention this time as the line moved. Adjusting the strap on her denim overalls, she smiled when she took another step forward, proud that she didn't need the jerk behind her to clear his throat again. The man right in front of Rosie placed his order. Finally, walking up to the counter, she greeted Alessandra with a pleasant smile. Looking at the barista, Rosie gave a slight wave to Basil, who was making the beverages.

"That's a twelve-ounce caramel macchiato, Basil, whole milk foam, got that?" Alessandra said right before she turned to give Rosie her full attention, complete with her lips tipped up into a wide smile.

"Yep, whole milk foam, caramel macchiato coming right up," she repeated. Basil had only started working with Alessandra about six months ago; she split her time between Rosie's plant shop and the café. "Best of both worlds," she would say. It was a place for her to go, while her wife went to work at one of the law firms downtown. Basil was tall and beautiful, with short, spikey dyed blonde and green hair, a bull-nose ring, large painted floral discs in her earlobes, and a chain around her neck with a heart lock, symbolizing her love for her wife.

Many wouldn't know it, but she was in the process of becoming a woman. Basil's wife had known for a while that her then-husband wasn't happy with life, and after a heart-to-heart, Basil had told her wife that she was meant to be a woman.

Although it was a shock, Basil and her wife's love for each other overcame this little bump in the road, and now their devotion was more profound than the ocean. Witnessing their dedication to each other was an honor for Rosie. Basil was heavily involved in the transgender community and would often ask if a youth from the local community center could come and assist at the farmer's market that Rosie sometimes attended. They would also help plant seeds for the vegetable plants Rosie tried to sell. The help was always excellent, and Rosie enjoyed the teaching aspect whenever a new volunteer came into her shop. She thought all the kids were terrific, and she admired how compassionate Basil was.

"Eh-hem," came another grunt from the jerk behind Rosie. Inhaling a deep breath, she shook off the annoyance and stepped forward, leaning in closer, making it known to 'said jerk' behind her that she was known here at this café.

Right on cue, both Alessandra and Basil looked up and greeted Rosie with a smile, "Hey, girrrl!" from Basil and "Hi, hon!" from Alessandra at the same time.

Returning their hellos, the man in front of Rosie stepped away from the counter and moved over to the side, waiting for his coffee, which allowed Rosie to step up. Without asking Rosie's order, Alessandra reached out, plucked up a paper cup, and handed it to Basil, who started making Rosie's usual non-fat vanilla latte. Turning back to Rosie, Alessandra wiped her hands on her pink apron and smiled.

"So, what do you think of my new display?" Her smile was hopeful as she waited in anticipation for Rosie's response.

Swiveling her head and thumbing over to the open book display, Rosie placed her hands on her hips, turned slightly more to face the artwork, careful to avoid looking at the man standing behind her, and made a show as she admired the books on the wall a little longer than she needed to just because she could. "I love it!" Rosie finally said, clapping her hands together. Then she turned, faced Alessandra, and slapped one hand on the counter. "By the way, I'll be back this afternoon. It's gonna be a two-cup coffee day."

"That bad, huh?"

"Yeah, I found roots in my soil," Rosie mumbled. Basil and Alessandra hissed as soon as she revealed her already destroyed morning. They knew how much money she'd spent on the soil and how much potential she put into those black bags of dirt, hoping it would help turn her business around.

Three years ago, while shopping for a small plant to put into her tiny living space, Rosie had stepped inside Miss Marigold's Plant Shop, and the two women had struck up a fast and comfortable friendship; she'd even taken Rosie in with open arms as her mentor. They'd shared their pasts and talked about their dreams. Although Miss Marigold was well into her nineties, she'd explained she had nothing else to do; with all her friends gone, she only had her plant friends left. She hadn't had anyone to take over her shop, and she'd wanted to leave it with someone whose heart would be in it as much as Rosie's was. It was the fateful day that Miss Marigold had taken Rosie fully under her wing and trained her to run the plant shop, Miss Marigold's Plants. It had been Miss Marigold's wish to give the shop over to Rosie when she passed away, and when she'd died only a year ago at the ripe age of ninety-six, it had become Rosie's, along with a pet chicken and a cactus named Spike.

Losing someone who'd treated Rosie like a granddaughter, or even a daughter, had broken her. She had never had anyone love her as much as Miss Marigold had. Growing up in the foster care system had hardened her heart, made her feel like she'd never belonged, and Rosie had always been waiting for the next case worker to come and take her away to a new home. Living like that, it had always been hard for Rosie to make attachments or trust people. There'd been a time when she had let her guard down, when the family she'd been living with had made a promise to Rosie, saying they would adopt her and make her their own. But all that ended the day the wife had become pregnant, and they'd instead wanted to traverse their new miracle, with only just the two of them. Rosie had been once again cast aside.

"I think it's rye," Rosie said flatly, shaking the memories from her head as she returned to reality.

The deep voice behind her cleared his throat again, but this time, he spoke words that were not right either. "Why don't you just spray Round-up on the roots? Problem solved, and if you're done with your order..." he said, making a hand motion for her to step aside. Rosie stared at his hand with abhorrence and even more disgust when she realized whose body it was attached to. Both Basil and Alessandra's eyebrows rose almost to their hairlines; Alessandra covered her open mouth to stifle a giggle, knowing Rosie hated chemicals. Twisting to direct her attention fully at the man, Rosie narrowed her eyes, her arms crossing firmly over her chest as she stood her ground. Her gaze traveled over his powerful, steel-like arms, each muscle defined and accentuated, conveying strength and resilience. The warm glow of his sun-kissed skin highlighted intricate vine tattoos that meandered across his forearms, showcasing delicate blooms of Japanese lantern flowers. These blossoms, with their rounded petals, bore a striking resemblance to Jack-o'-lanterns, infusing a touch of whimsy into his rugged appearance. They were beautiful, all of his leafy tattoos and vines that twisted up his arms were, and if Rosie wasn't so pissed off about his throat clearing already, she would have reached out to touch the beautiful canvas painted on his skin, the ones that almost matched the flower and strawberry vine tattoos that she had snaking up her own arms. But she was pissed. Her eyes flicked away from the stunning tattoos to the man's bulky chest, which was covered with a tight-fitting gray cotton tee. The vines continued up his body and snuck out from the neckline to circle around his neck. As Rosie's eyes landed on the man's face, her eyes widened.

Pressing her lips together as soon as she confirmed that she did, in fact, recognize the man standing behind her, she blurted out, "No."

"No?" he responded, questioning her. Her response intrigued him. Usually, women would either climb his body wanting to touch and fuck him, or they would run and hide. The woman standing in front of him did neither. The closest reaction was disgust, so he thought climbing on his body was probably a no-go.

Basil and Alessandra looked at each other briefly before their eyes landed on Rosie.

"No. If you spray Round-up, it will kill anything that you plant in it afterward. You, of *all* people, should know that, *Broc*," Rosie explained with a sneer. She crossed her arms and took a step away from him.

"Do we know each other?" Broc asked. It wasn't out of the norm to have a beautiful woman recognize him; he, after all, had been on the A-List for the past few years since winning the Floral Contest that Instagram and Netflix had sponsored years ago, and where he'd gotten his big break. Winning had changed his life; as Broc saw it, it was for the best. He'd gotten his name behind some of the best A-List actors and influencers, landscaping their mega-mansions, decorating their weddings, and helping with Fashion Week every year in New York City. He'd made a name for himself and had even modeled in the nude for People Magazine, being as tasteful as possible with plants and flowers covering his bits.

"Seriously?" Rosie responded bluntly, knowing that the competition all those years ago was something she should have won, and the life Broc was living right now should have been hers. And it irked her.

"Yeah, just asking because if I'd ever bumped into you, there's no way I would have ever forgotten a beautiful face like yours," he replied, lifting his lips to his trademark panty-dropping smile. That remark only infuriated Rosie further, a jolt of anger coursing through her as memories flashed in her mind. Broc was the one who had taken her virginity, a moment that had once felt sacred, quickly tarnished by the sight of him mere hours later, enveloped by two classmates under his charming, misleading wingspan; that betrayal still stained their intimate encounter of over five years ago. In that moment, Rosie had understood she'd meant nothing to him. Just another plot in his endless garden of conquests.

Asshole.

With a deep breath, she lifted her hands, allowing them to float softly before her as she closed her eyes, trying to center herself. She turned around in defiance, her gaze steady as she awaited her latte. "No, I'm not doing this, Mister Influencer." The words slipped from her lips; each one laced with the sharp edge of her resolve.

"Ahhh, so you're a fan, huh?"

"Uh, no. Not at all," Rosie called over her shoulder, crossing her arms over her chest and waiting impatiently for her drink to magically appear on the counter.Taking a deep breath, Rosie lifted her hands, allowing them to hover gently before her while she closed her eyes. When she opened them, they were ablaze with unexpressed frustration as she fixed her gaze on Broc, who stood casually at the counter, a smirk playing at the corners of his mouth. "Nope, I'm not wasting my time on you." Her voice cut sharp and clear.

Broc chuckled. "Oh, come on. Just give me a hint. It's killing me not knowing where I've seen your face before," he replied, leaning in playfully. "Was it at that art gallery? You know, the one with the weird giant inflatable octopus?" He raised an eyebrow, his grin unwavering despite her steely expression.

Rosie stared at him, unmoving, an eyebrow arching defiantly. "As if I'd hang out at a place filled with so much...pretentiousness. I have standards, you know."

Broc feigned a gasp, placing a hand over his heart. "Wow, I didn't realize I was speaking to royalty! Should I be bowing right now?" He leaned closer, still teasing, as if he were on a quest to draw out a smile. That made Rosie hate him even more.

"Yeah, well, you might want to save that for someone who wants to play along," Rosie shot back, her voice with a definite edge, "because I'm not here to entertain you or your ego."

"Just trying to jog your memory, sweetheart. You know, I think I could make a pretty captivating character in your next novel," he countered with a wink. "After all, what's a good story without a charming antagonist?"

She remained resolute. "You're not a character, Broc. You're a distraction. And I have enough of those in my life."

Undeterred, he chuckled. "Distraction? I prefer to think of myself as an adventure waiting to happen. Come on, what's life without a little hiccup?"

"No hiccups today," she said firmly. "You're more like the weed I need to kill with vinegar. Today is about focus, and right now, I'm trying to figure out if you're somebody I should dread or someone I can ignore."

"I vote for the second option," he replied, his smile infectious. "But for what it's worth, if I've crossed paths with you before, I'm pretty sure I'm the one who would never forget someone as stunning as you."

Rosie couldn't help but let a small scoff followed by a thin smile slip through, but she quickly masked it again. "You may want to reconsider that, Mister Influencer. The last thing I need is another bad decision."

"Challenge accepted," he responded, leaning casually against the chic counter. He had no intention of leaving just yet. Not with this gorgeous blue-violet eyed, purple-haired, beautiful woman standing right in front of him.

Rosie poked a finger on his broad chest, something she regretted once she felt how strong he was under his shirt. "I paid a steep price for that soil," Rosie told him. "I won't introduce any chemicals into it. You should know better than anyone."

Alessandra and Basil raised their eyebrows again, watching the banter between Rosie and Broc, unsure what was happening. "Hey, here's your latte, Ro—"

"Great!" Rosie exclaimed, her voice cutting off Basil. She was determined to keep her name from escaping her friend's lips. "And here I thought the hippie, pot-loving state would boast rich, vibrant soil," she mumbled to herself, the thought nudging her that she still needed to write that letter. With a flick of her long, purple hair over her shoulder, she pressed her lips together in a moment of contemplation, preparing to pivot on her heels when she felt an unexpectedly firm grip on her elbow.

Glancing down, she saw Broc's hand wrapped gently yet firmly around her upper arm. The instant connection of his fingers against her skin sent a shiver racing down her arm and spine, igniting a spark of unfamiliar electricity that left her momentarily frozen in place. Rosie's eyes fluttered shut involuntarily, surrendering to a fleeting moment of weakness.

The sudden gasp of a woman from the front door snapped Rosie back to reality, providing a jolt of clarity as she instinctively pulled her arm free from Broc's grasp. Both Broc and Rosie turned to face the source of the commotion, their eyes wide as every gaze in the cozy café shifted to follow the direction of the gasp, creating a heavy atmosphere of curiosity. In the center of the bustling café stood Mindy Harper, once the shimmering beacon of Hollywood glamour and the quintessential IT girl. However, since her last film, *The Farmer's Song*, had graced the big screen, her star had dimmed significantly. Whispers and scuttlebutt swirled through tabloids like autumn leaves, detailing her tempestuous nature on set and the exorbitant costs of her unpredictable outbursts, all rumored to have spiraled into the hundreds of thousands, much to the dismay of film production companies. Adding fuel to the gossip mill was her alleged pursuit of the leading actor, who, unbeknownst to many, was deeply entrenched in a clandestine romance with his now-wife, a former waitress and mother of a young boy from a previous marriage, which was said to have ended in heart-wrenching tragedy.

Mindy glided across the café floor. She moved with an exaggerated grace reminiscent of a runway model, dropping effortlessly to the side of Broc. Her meticulously curated Hollywood smile, a flawless mask devoid of authenticity, was plastered on her face. An unmistakable territorial glare flickered across her features when her eyes raked over Rosie, taking in the eclectic ensemble: Birkenstocks, faded overalls that spoke of years of neglect, and a stunning array of tattoos adorning her arms, a vibrant tapestry of strawberry vines and orchids that danced up to her facial piercings. Those large white discs in her lobes and the striking purple of her Viking hair painted an image of rebellion, an exhilarating contrast to Mindy's polished façade.

With a self-satisfied smirk, Mindy reveled in her supposed superiority, leaning into Broc's solid frame and waiting for his muscular arm to encircle her delicate waist. Her tight Lululemon attire clung to her like a second skin, perfectly calibrated to give the illusion of 'toned,' while her silky and blonde hair was pulled back into a taut ponytail.

Rosie's latte in hand, she took a sip and quietly watched Mindy slip her arm through Broc's folded arms across his chest. The look on Broc's face changed from one of intrigue while talking to Rosie to annoyance as he flicked his gaze over to Mindy. "I thought I told you to stay in the car," he said in a low, irritated tone. Rosie rolled her eyes, but she was also pleased that he was annoyed with the fake and plastic woman just as much as she was. She took another small sip from her latte.

Not wanting to squander any more precious time away from her daily duties, Rosie pressed her lips together in determination and pivoted on her heels, deftly brushing past the two most infuriating individuals to cross her path that morning. The muffled sounds of Mindy's cooing complaints cut through the atmosphere but grew softer as Rosie made her way to the front door. Mindy was whining about Broc's evident lack of affection.

"But you were taking too long. I wondered if you had already replaced me, so I needed to make sure I staked my claim," Mindy purred. The nauseating thought that Broc's hands, likely still warm from touching Mindy, had dared to brush against Rosie's skin. *How dare he touch me,* her mind raced, *with the same hands that had probably been slithering all over her body just moments before he began this charade of clearing his throat to get my attention*. Visibly shuddering, she opened the glass front door and walked out of Little Café without looking back.

The burn in the back of her head seared as Broc marked her like a target. Rosie knew Broc's eyes were trailing after her. He was watching her. Breathing became difficult, knowing Broc was most certainly staring at her as she walked away; her nose and eyes burned with the same heat that ignited on her back, causing her chest to redden as the whispers of her past floated in the air, crushing her confidence.

3

Pro Tip: Some plants, like succulents, prefer dry soil in-between watering.

The rest of the day unfolded quietly for Rosie with the rhythm of routine. She carefully re-potted a few of her delicate orchids, their roots nestled in bark chunks and partially exposed to capture air, no longer in that nasty soil that rots roots. In the back room of the plant shop, she tackled the potting mix mess that seemed to multiply overnight. It was like plant confetti from a party she was never invited to. "Next time," she chuckled, "I'm getting a tiny bouncer to kick out all this soil!" When she was done, she turned her attention to her snake and ZZ plants, the hardy green foliage a staple in her shop. Their glossy leaves were her favorite part, and the tall striped patterns on the snake plant was also another favorite. Rosie couldn't help but smile as she wrapped her fingers around the tall stalks and gently ran her hand over those stiff shoots as she walked by them. Most of her customers would stroll into Miss Marigold's with their phones extended, showing her photos from Pinterest. While these images were a treasure trove of inspiration, customers often didn't understand what the proper plant care would be for their dream room, which Rosie would destroy for one reason or another.

For example, fig trees, with their impressive height and lush, pear-shaped leaves, were particularly trendy at the moment. Rosie knew that these popular plants demanded attention and lots of sunlight. They often caught the eye of eager buyers, but she always delivered the bad news, like a grim reaper of plants: the plants the customers wanted would eventually die in their chosen locations. The irony was not lost on her; many customers longed for the grandeur of a six-foot fig tree, but she was dedicated to the lives of each plant, even if it meant forgoing a sale that exceeded $300. If they lacked the vital east- or west-facing windows that poured in sunlight, she would guide them gently toward the more resilient snake, pothos, or other partial shade-loving plants instead.

Feeling a sense of happiness from having cleaned up her shop and moved plants around for better lighting, Rosie surveyed her space, which was nearly spotless aside from the confetti-like soil in the potting room and her beloved plants scattered throughout. A satisfied smile spread across her lips as Rosie stood proudly among the greenery, her hands resting on her hips. She took in the beauty of her orchids and the vibrant shades of rich greens and purples from her plants' foliage. A light creaking sound drew her attention to the back door, and she turned to see her best friend, Fluffy the chicken, flouncing in from the backyard through the small doggie door that had been installed years ago. Fluffy, with her soft black and white feathers in a mop of a mess on top of her head and her sleek black body glistening in the light, began to scratch at the loose dirt scattered across the floor, emitting a series of bocks and clucks that brought a smile to Rosie's face. Unable to resist the charm of her feathered friend, Rosie knelt down and offered gentle strokes along Fluffy's back, then scratched under her beak affectionately.

The chicken was a bittersweet souvenir, an endearing remnant of Miss Marigold's legacy. She had been one of Miss Marigold's last pets who truly knew her, and that connection meant everything to Rosie. Every day, as she looked at the chicken, she felt an ache in her heart because, in quiet moments, Rosie missed Miss Marigold terribly, and the presence seemed more distant with each passing day.

"Come here, Fluffy," Rosie cooed, her laughter ringing softly as the playful chicken flapped her wings before plopping down for a dirt bath, sending tiny clouds of soil flying, adding more confetti throughout the nooks and crannies as she joyfully rolled about in the soil. Fluffy soon popped back up on her feet, resuming her search for hidden treasures beneath the dirt. "Sorry, little one, only rye-seed roots in this soil; no bugs," Rosie whispered with a giggle, watching as Fluffy scratched at the floor, oblivious to the lack of worms. While she was lost watching her little chicken, the front door chimed. Carefully standing up and dusting off her dirty hands on her overalls, Rosie walked out from the back room and into the front.

“Good morning, Miss Rosie! How’s your day shaping up?” the middle-aged woman inquired with a smile. The mail-lady was a beacon of friendliness, effortlessly sharing tidbits about the neighborhoods on her route. With dreams of one day becoming the Postmaster of Spokane, her positive attitude led Rosie to believe that she would surely reach her goal someday.

“I found rye-seed in my soil,” Rosie responded, biting her cheek.

“Oh no, Miss Rosie! Rye-seed?” Mail-Lady replied, aghast. Over the past few years, the two of them had come to know each other quite well. Yes, they’d gotten to know each other, but Rosie had failed to ask her what her name was, and since then it had just always been Mail-Lady.

“Ye-p!” Rosie responded, popping the ‘p.’ She moved closer to Mail-Lady and reached out for the little bundle of envelopes she was holding in her hand. “Anything good?”

“I don’t know. It’s probably bills, and this one looks a bit suspicious.” Mail-Lady flipped the envelope over, scrutinizing its contents before returning it to the stack of mail in her hand. “It’s from the IRS. Are you holding up okay with the shop?” Mail-Lady asked, her gaze flickering up from the stack of envelopes, trying to read the unspoken words coursing through Rosie’s expression. The muscles in her jaw tightened as Rosie took the envelopes from Mail-Lady’s hands and then pressed her lips together in a thin line. It was curious how a small piece of paper could feel like a rock. A jolt of stress surged up her arms and settled heavily in her stomach.

“Yep, all good!” Rosie replied, her tone coming out just a beat too fast and a note too high, as if attempting to convince both Mail-Lady and herself of a truth that felt increasingly precarious. She needed a distraction from the boulder of a letter in her hands. Before Mail-Lady could say anything, Rosie walked over to a small shelf beside the register and plucked up the small potted plant, anything for a distraction. “I was able to re-pot your String of Hearts for you. Now remember, this little girl needs lots of sunlight and fertilizer at least once a month, and try not to overwater her this time; just once a week.”

“Oh! Thank you so much,” the mail-lady exclaimed, her eyes sparkling as she reached for her newly potted plant. Distraction achieved, a small smile crept onto Rosie's face. “Alright then, I really must be on my way." She smiled and then shrugged. "Mail to deliver and all that,” she added, casting a glance at the cute little plant, gently poking its leaves.

“Yep, back to the grind! I understand completely. See you tomorrow!” Rosie said, waving off her friend.

“You too, hon, and...” There was a pregnant pause, as she contemplated how to finish her thought. “Just have a good day, okay? And don’t forget to give that chicken a kiss for me, alright?”

“I will, thank you,” Rosie replied, watching the mail-lady step out of the plant shop and down the sidewalk toward Alessandra’s Little Cafe.

Once Rosie found herself alone, a weight settled on her shoulders, and she just stared at the envelope in her hands. The thought of opening a letter from the government filled her with a lingering sense of dread; she knew that ignoring it rarely resulted in anything pleasant; more likely, it was a storm of complications than a bouquet of roses.

With a frustrated internal groan, her thumb brushed tentatively against the delicate flap. She paused, her heart racing as she fought to steady her thoughts and compose herself. "Fuck it," she muttered under her breath. In a sudden surge of resolve, she tore open the envelope. The crisp pink letter slipped out; carefully unfolding it, she took a deep breath and began to read, the words blurring as her mind raced.

Notice of Intent to Levy and Notice of Your Right to a Hearing

Intent to seize your property or rights to property

Amount Due in 60 days: $44,922.25

***Please note that the IRS has repeatedly tried to address your overdue taxes. The IRS may seize (levy) your property on or after December 25th of the current calendar year**

Property includes the following:

- **Wages and other income**
- **Bank Accounts**
- **Business Accounts**
- **Personal Assets (including car/home/property)**
- **Social Security Benefits**

Billing Summary:

Amount you owe is $44,922.25
Additional Penalty Charge of $500/week if late
Additional Interest Charges $115.25/week if late
Bill due December 25th $44,922.25
(subject to change – pending additional late fees)

If Rosie ever thought she was strong, a hardened soul, this was the one thing that broke her down. The pain and stress that followed reading the letter that she held so tightly in her hand was like a storm filled with fury and silence all at the same time. Just a quiet tornado. She lifted her hand to rub at the pain in her chest that suddenly appeared. At this very moment, she wished that Miss Marigold was here to help guide her or to ask her why she'd left her with so much debt. How could this happen? The thought of hiring a lawyer felt absurdly comical to Rosie; it was a luxury she simply couldn't afford. Four hundred dollars on contaminated soil had already drained her finances, leaving her feeling defeated. "Fuck my life," she muttered under her breath, tipping her head back and closing her eyes. It was the weight of her circumstances that kept pressing down on her like a sledgehammer.

The familiar chime of the door awakened her through her spiraling thoughts. With a sigh, she set the letter back on the counter. Then she looked up and saw it was the unwelcome sight of whom she liked to call 'Tactless Oxygen-Depleting Asshole,' also known as her ex-boyfriend, Orson Ryes. Rosie turned her body away from him, "No, Orson, I don't have time for this—you," Rosie said, her voice laced with frustration as she slumped against the counter, feeling drained.

Orson emitted a soft tsk, prompting Rosie to glance over her shoulder at him. "Naw, come on," he exclaimed, a playful lilt in his voice. He waved his hand in a dismissive gesture, his posture relaxed and carefree, as if they were simply two old friends meeting on a normal Thursday evening for a game of poker. "You know nothing happened between me and that girl. We were just old friends catching up," he insisted, leaning in slightly, his arrogant grin causing an unwelcome tightening in her chest. He was too close to her, his body was drenched in cologne, and it assaulted Rosie's senses; once a pleasant smell, now a rude attack. Rosie fought the urge to roll her eyes, striving to maintain her composure in the face of his unyielding lies.

Irritation swirled in her chest as she pinched the bridge of her nose, while Orson sauntered around her body, his movements slick and calculated. He leaned in, pressed his hand against her hip, and planted a quick, almost rehearsed kiss on her forehead. "No, Orson, that's not what it was, and you know it. I saw that girl's Instagram account, and just by looking at the photos, it's clear your little *chat* included the early morning hours spent with your dick in her cunt...in her bed. Look, you know what? We're done. That's it; I'm not going to rehash this fucked up...us. I've got too much going on—"

"Hey, wait a second," Orson cut in, feigning innocence as he reached behind himself and pulled out a small plastic container from his back pocket. "I thought Fluffy would love some grubs I picked up at the pet store for her." He offered up the container with a forced grin, in a desperate attempt to distract Rosie. "I know one way to get my girl's heart thumping, and it's not cut flowers; it's bugs," he stated with a wink.

It was a passive-aggressive skill that Rosie still appreciated, his kindness for her chicken, even while the truth about his cheating hung like a damn red flag between them.

Reaching out to grab the container, Orson seized her wrist. "I take this as you forgive me." He leaned in and kissed Rosie on the forehead again before she could pull away from his grasp.

"Orson, no, I can't do this anymore. I won't! Do you know how often your little 'slip-ups' cause a ripple in our relationship? I'm not just going to keep letting it happen over and over again. I'm done; we're done. We should have been done a long time ago."

"No, baby, we're done when I say you're done..." Orson growled through his clenched teeth, his frustration palpable as his grip tightened around Rosie's waist and pulled her closer, nearly pinning her against him. The possessiveness in his voice left no room for argument, while he nuzzled into the soft flesh of her neck.

There was nothing but a wave of anger that surged over Rosie. She was just supposed to endure his philandering while his thoughts of any man touching what he'd claimed or getting too close always made him more than seething.

"Why do you always try to pull away from me?" he muttered, the heat of his breath like poison against her skin. She squirmed in his hold, but he wasn't about to let her go. The front door chimed again as another customer stepped in; Orson's fierce gaze locked onto her, an unyielding reminder that he wanted to keep her, and also one for how badly she wanted nothing to do with him.

"Stop it, Orson, I mean it," Rosie hissed. "I'm not yours to use whenever your dick wants to get wet; you've proven that you've been able to dip it outside our relationship many times," Rosie whispered through her teeth. A clearing of a throat had Rosie glancing up. She recognized that throat clearing, and when she looked up to see that Broc had stepped into her little plant shop, she groaned. Finally shoving herself free, pulling away from Orson, and throwing her head back, she mumbled, "Can this day get any worse?"

"Hi to you too," Broc said with a broad smile as he stepped into the plant shop, shoving his hands into his designer faded jeans. He paused to admire the foliage on tables scattered around, gently stroking the velvety leaves and bending to read the little nameplates in each pot. Standing back up, he placed his hands on his hips, taking in the organized chaos of her shop. "Nice place you got here," he complimented. He moved through the narrow aisles lined with an eclectic mix of plants in teacups and quirky containers, ranging from butter tubs to old coffee tins, and even an old army boot. This wasn't just a shop; it was a living expression of who Rosie and Miss Marigold were.

"I don't have time for chit-chat, so if you see anything you like, just let me know, and you can look up the care instructions yourself." Rosie sighed after replying in a short quip.

"Well, if that's how you talk to all your clients, then I can see why this place is barren of customers," Broc responded, straightening himself up and folding his arms across his chest. He was still trying to figure out how he knew this purple-haired vixen. It was impossible to overlook the slimy punk man beside the mysterious purple Viking, who had been trying to pull her close in a possessive way. From the look on the shop owner's face, it was clear the purple beauty wanted nothing to do with that man touching her.

With a simple nod as he read the room, Broc turned his attention to the wiry young punk in an old, faded-black Metallica shirt and faded-black ripped jeans, complete with old, rugged black cowboy boots. Broc lifted an eyebrow at him, not willing to back down when he saw something not right, then he said, "Looks like she doesn't want to be touched; I mean, I'm not a body language expert, but the way you're trying to crawl up her body, she doesn't seem to want you using her like a ladder."

Orson narrowed his eyes; lifting his hand, he tried to pull Rosie into his side once more. Then switching tactics, he ran his hand over his already slicked-back hair. Douche move. Although Broc sported facial piercings and vibrant discs adorning his ears, the punk beside him boasted an impressive array of earrings, far more than Broc's collection. Unlike the distinctive discs in Broc and Rosie's lobes, this punk showcased a bold alignment of hoops in both ears. Two glinting lip rings enhanced his sneer, and from the subtle flash of metal within, Broc could see a tongue piercing. *At least she has a type*, Broc mused silently to himself. "She's my girlfriend," he asserted with possessiveness.

"Ex," Rosie corrected. "He's my ex, and he was just leaving." She pushed his body off of hers and stepped away from him. The movement had Broc stepping closer to the purple-haired vixen in a protective manner; he didn't know why, but he felt the need to be there for her. The urge to pull her further away from the slimeball was a protectiveness that he'd never felt before with any woman. A foreign feeling seemed to have sprouted in his core and grown into something fierce that crawled around his veins like a vine, entangling all his feelings and forcing him to protect what was his.

His?

Where did that come from, he wondered. But even as Broc questioned those thoughts, he gently touched the woman's shoulder and, with ease, pulled her slightly behind him, keeping the ex and her apart. The ex's face darkened with anger. The punk stood about four inches shorter than Broc, his frame slender and lacking the definition of pure muscle that characterized Broc's imposing stature. He had to weigh at least ten pounds less than Broc, which he thoroughly enjoyed. So, when Broc folded his arms, the movement served to accentuate his bulging biceps, a gesture more for show than substance. Recognizing Broc's silent challenge, the punk hesitated, then stepped away from Broc and Rosie. *Good choice,* Broc thought. Looking over Broc's shoulder, Orson narrowed his eyes. "I'll be seeing you around because I know you'll come bouncing back to me. No one wants a broken flower like you," he reminded her with a sneer.

Broken? Broc thought. Those words cut more than a knife. But for Orson, that man knew her secrets and past. All because he had been around for the past three years. And for each and every one of those years, he'd wandered off, fucked whoever was his latest flavor, and then would come back to Rosie. Orson knew she'd be back in his life because she wasn't going anywhere, and he knew it. He'd let Rosie win this round, but he would be back—to remind her who she belonged to.

Once the door chimed Orson's retreat, Broc looked at Rosie and tried to figure out where those beautiful bluish-purple eyes had once been in his past. Those eyes seemed familiar, yet at the same time unfamiliar. "You okay?" Broc asked, lowering his voice; feeling the pull to touch her, he reached out, placed his finger under her chin, and tilted her head to his. The intimate movement from Broc as he carefully eyed her had Rosie closing her eyes, her own breath quickening. His thumb glided over her silky skin, caressing the curve of her lower lip with a feather-light touch.

"I don't need your help," Rosie hissed quietly. A sudden chill swept through the room as the front door creaked open once more, the sound of a deliberate throat-clearing shattering their moment. With a rush of composure, Rosie instinctively stepped back, a flicker of uncertainty crossing her face. She shook her head slightly, her heart racing, and wiped her clammy hands nervously on her worn overalls; the fabric felt cool against her skin. Once again, she looked up to see that another woman had entered the plant shop. *God, was he collecting women?* Rosie thought to herself.

"Broc, would you still like to see the other properties?" A very polished woman had stepped into Rosie's plant shop. The look of confusion that initially crossed her face quickly faded when she noticed Rosie watching her. With a professional smile quickly forming, the woman came deeper into the shop, clutching her handbag tightly against her chest. She moved deliberately, trying to avoid touching anything that might possibly stain her shirt. Rosie's eyes flicked to the woman wearing a smart business suit with stilettos, a brave choice in Spokane's colder months. Her short blonde hair, styled in a way that reflected the importance of her career, gave the impression that she was deadly serious. "Sorry to interrupt, but I have limited time before closing another transaction." The lady walked over to where Broc and Rosie stood; she reached into her pocket, pulled out a dark blue business card with gold lettering, and handed it to Rosie. "This place has great potential; do you own this building?" she asked Rosie. With a simple nod, Rosie gave her the answer she sought. "Great. If you ever consider selling, please let me know. I can market this building and secure a phenomenal price for you. My name's Laura Catron. I work for Sotheby's. I'm not about a dog and pony show. I mean business. Keep me in mind." She smiled her perfect, nude-lipstick smile at Rosie and then turned to Broc. "You ready? Mindy is getting restless, and I won't babysit for you. I've already had to tell her not to post me on social media." Laura smiled quickly, then turned on her heels and returned to the front door.

Mindy was now standing and leaning against the open door with her hand on her hip, smacking her gum and twirling her hair like a cheerleader in high school. Already having been around Mindy for a short time, Rosie was not a fan. "What is this, a merry-go-round of women?" Rosie questioned with a snarky tone, her voice low but not low enough to escape Broc's ears.

He snorted, unable to contain a chuckle as he dipped his head and flicked his nose with his thumb. Inhaling a deep breath, Broc turned with an unsmiling face, his expression bleak as he walked back to Mindy. "Again, I asked you to stay in the car," he mumbled.

"Aw, baby. You know you can't hide all this from the public," she said, waving her hand down her body. "My fans, they need to see me in IRL." Mindy flashed her bright, fake smile at Broc and then quickly took a selfie of the two of them.

Rosie narrowed her eyes again, *Did she just say IRL out loud?* she thought to herself.

"Come on, baby. Let me just post this, and then we can get back to whatever you're up to with the suit," Mindy chirped playfully as she smacked her bright pink gum. With a teasing flick, she ran her hand down the front of Broc's broad chest, her fingers lingering for a moment.

He responded immediately, reaching to capture her wrist firmly, pulling it away from his body with annoyance. Broc's gaze darted back to the striking woman with the purple braid and half-shaved head. With a smirk, Broc gently loosened his grip on Mindy's wrist, allowing his hand to glide down to the small of Mindy's back, his palm pressing her forward as he guided her out of the plant shop. The scent of the plants was fragrant, with the earthy aroma of soil and blossoms, but his focus was elsewhere, caught up in intrigue.

Rosie slid her glance back to Broc's hand on Mindy's back, a personal and intimate spot to touch someone closer than a friend. Then anger filled her veins, and she realized the same hand had just touched her chin. Not even when Orson touched Rosie had she felt the same way as she did when Broc had. It was as if a force was winding through her body and grabbing hold of his soul, but the tendrils of the vine had slipped through the air, catching nothing.

The void of his presence didn't go unnoticed; as soon as he walked away, the door clicked shut, and all Rosie could say was, "What the fuck just happened?"

4

Pro Tip: Seeds should be started in good soil and any type of container that has drainage holes.

A few days had passed since Rosie's run-ins with both Broc and Orson, but the weight of it all still crashed down on her like a freight train. She was over it, and frankly, it just pissed her off. Seated on the cool, tiled floor behind Alessandra's counter at the Little Café, Rosie felt the suffocating reminder of the nearly forty-five thousand dollars she owed the IRS. Seriously, why did they choose now, three years after she'd taken over the shop, to drop this bomb?

"Are you just going to sulk back here all morning?" Alessandra asked as she gracefully stepped over Rosie's outstretched legs, snagging almond milk for Basil.

"Yeah, yep, no idea," Rosie mumbled, letting her head fall back against the cupboards in defeat.

Basil was busy preparing the coffee order when she took a second to glance in Rosie's direction. "Listen, sugar, what's really eating at you? Don't give me your half-hearted-nothing routine; I only see you hide like this when there's something on your mind. So, spill."

"Maybe?" Rosie replied, her lower lip jutting out like a sulking child.

"Someone or something?" Basil pressed, brow raised.

Alessandra wrangled a crinkling plastic trash bag. "C'mon, Rosie. At least bend your knees while I'm juggling this stuff," she requested, her cheerful energy aggravating Rosie's moodiness. "Did you at least get your latte?"

Rosie tightened her lips, wrapping her arms around her knees, curling herself into a protective ball. "Nope, Basil is withholding caffeine to pry out my secrets...so ironic," she murmured into her limbs.

Alessandra chuckled, her laughter intermingling with the rich, intoxicating scent of freshly brewed coffee. "Alright, if she brews you a sixteen-ounce latte, you'd better spill why you're taking up all this prime real estate behind my counter instead of doing your own thing over at the shop."

"Fine," Rosie relented, a hesitant smirk finally cracking through the scowl. "But it better be extra hot. My words will already be scorching my tongue on the way out; might as well join the boiling hot latte..."

Basil snorted. "You're so dramatic, Rosie," she teased, rolling her eyes while grabbing the nearly empty carton of milk. "If you need anything more than an ear, I can ask my wife for help. But if you've committed murder, we'll need a whole set of professionals for that."

"Trust me, I haven't murdered anyone...yet," Rosie shot back. "The only thing I've killed is my own spirit, but that's all under control now because it's dead and buried already."

Alessandra finished with a customer and turned her iPad around to process the payment, glancing back over her shoulder with a frown. "Did you even get all the rye out of your soil? And seriously, this floor is a disaster; why not mop it while you're at it...be more useful?"

With a groan, Rosie pushed herself up. "Fine, whatever. I should wash my hands anyway," she muttered and shuffled to the sink, turning on the warm water. Each second felt like a hammer pounding against her mind. Adulting was truly the worst right now.

Basil tossed a hand towel her way before handing her a steaming vanilla latte. "Talk to me, Rosie," she coaxed.

Rosie sighed, drying her hands and letting the towel drape over the sink's edge.

Just as she reached for the latte, Basil pulled it back. "The whole truth, Rosie."

"Fiiiiine," Rosie sighed again, rolling her eyes as she finally snatched the cup from Basil's grip. "Orson dropped by the shop, acting like we were still a thing, a couple. And that rye business? Just ridiculous." She bit her lips to keep her thoughts under wraps.

"Rosie...I meant everything," Basil pressed.

"Ugh! I hate how well you know me," Rosie mumbled, burying her face in her latte, craving comfort in its warmth and rich aroma.

Alessandra shot a quick glance over her shoulder, a playful smirk curling on her lips. "Please, we both do! Remember that other time you camped behind my counter? You were a total wreck after Orson cheated on you... What was it, oh right, the third time?"

"Don't forget when you found Tiger dead in the chicken coop," Basil chimed in. "Or how about that clay-filled soil you dragged in from New Mexico? Or—"

"Okay, I get it! This is my hideaway!" Rosie snapped, frowning deeper into her latte. "I just like to sulk in good company. Sue me." She took another sip, letting the liquid spread through her as she set her drink down with a soft, defeated thud. "Actually, don't, I've got no money." Goosebumps peppered her arms as she started to reach for the mop tucked away in the corner, but before she could fill the bucket, Alessandra stepped in. A gentle hand landed on Rosie's, pausing her thoughts, drawing her gaze.

"Hey, hon, it's not just Orson and his stupid games. What's really going on?" Alessandra's eyes bore into Rosie's, searching for what lurked beneath the surface. She caught the familiar sign, the way Rosie tugged at her braid like it was a lifeline. "There it is, your tell," she pointed out, a knowing smile softening her voice. "Look, we can talk after work. I'm not gonna push you to share; I just want you to know we're here when you're ready." She gestured to herself and Basil. "We're not going anywhere."

A wave of emotions crashed into Rosie, tears threatening to spill as she fought to keep them at bay. She knew that speaking her truth would mean exposing her failures, and that title she had fought so hard to bury since moving out on her own began to suffocate her. Lowering her head, she nodded, barely able to meet Alessandra's concerned gaze.

"Talk soon, okay?" Alessandra whispered, pulling Rosie into a tight hug, her fingers soothingly stroking over the braid before they reluctantly parted.

Biting her lip, Rosie nodded again and squared her shoulders, straightening the bib of her overalls. "I need to get going anyway. I haven't fed Fluffy, and she's definitely going to be ticked off at me."

Basil snorted, the sound mingling with Alessandra's gentle laughter, as he added, "Go on. We'll be here when you need another cup of coffee, alright?" Alessandra gave Rosie a sweet smile.

Rosie maneuvered past them, head down, until out of the corner of her eye, she caught a movement. When she lifted her gaze, she spotted Mindy strolling into the Little Café. With her designer handbag swinging from her forearm and hair perfectly styled, she looked like she had just stepped off a movie set. But in the cozy café packed with locals in their soft sweaters, Mindy looked like a mismatched puzzle piece, glaringly out of place. It was obvious she craved the spotlight like it was oxygen, desperate for attention and validation.

Rosie intentionally turned away; she caught the flash of anger that crossed Mindy's face, an icy chill settling over the room. Mindy's expensive perfume assaulted her senses, making Rosie's nose crinkle in disgust, as she saw the disdain settle on Mindy's features as her eyes narrowed, following Rosie's every move.

THE VACANT BUILDING wedged between the Little Café and Miss Marigold's Plant Shop had its front door wide open. For years, it had sat empty and forgotten, but something had shifted. Curiosity tugged at Rosie, and she slowed her pace, peering inside. There, in the center of the space, stood an older man in Carhartt jeans and a ragged white work shirt, sporting some faded logo. His arm was outstretched, phone in hand, like a lifeline to someone on the other end.

"Yeah, that's a good angle. Just take a few shots of the room and send me the measurements," the male voice crackled from the speaker, reverberating through the echoes of the vacant shop. "Verify you can send me the blueprints and check if the building has its original plumbing and electrical systems. Let's see if that's outlined in the plans. And how many 220-volt electrical outlets are there? If there's a 110 outlet, we might need to run more Romex wire, or hell, maybe just rewire the whole place..." The voice trailed off into thought.

The contractor turned, directing his attention back to the caller. "We should definitely consider new wiring. I'm pretty sure this is knob and tube," he said.

"Yep. Let me know. Thanks, Raymond. Just keep me posted when you get those plans scanned or mailed." The voice on the line had a tone that brooked no argument.

"Alright, I'll get on it," Raymond replied, sliding his phone into his pocket as his gaze landed on Rosie standing dumbfounded in the doorway. "Hiya, ma'am. Can I help you with something?"

"Oh, sorry," she stammered, shaking off her surprise. "Curiosity got the better of me. This building's been empty forever. Any idea what it's being turned into?"

"It's got good bones, but the wiring definitely needs an update," he said, absentmindedly rubbing his chin as he surveyed the room. "Heard it's gonna be a flower shop, though."

Rosie froze. "Flowers? Right next to my plant shop?" A frown carved itself onto her face, disbelief and irritation brewing. "Isn't that, like, a total conflict of interest?" It felt downright unfair that someone with cash could waltz in and set up a business that was basically a sister to hers. Just then, a sharp clicking of heels echoed on the sidewalk, pulling her attention away. She looked up just as Mindy strutted down the way, coffee in one hand, her designer bag swinging at her side and her loud red lipstick flashing like a warning flag. "Fuck my life" mumbled Rosie.

"Can I help you?" Mindy asked, her eyes narrowing as she approached, tone dripping with condescension.

"I was just checking out the scene." Rosie matched her glare, refusing to back down.

"Clearly, there's construction going on here," Mindy shot back, popping her gum and rolling her eyes dramatically. "This is gonna be the best shop ever. But you might want to spruce up yours a little. It's looking sad, and it'll totally ruin the look of my flower shop. I don't want to see those pathetic card tables with those ugly plastic containers outside. It's just...sad." Mindy sneered, her haughtiness more annoying than her designer bag.

"Don't you think opening a flower shop right next to mine is a bit risky?" Rosie fired back, blunt and defiant, purposefully ignoring Mindy's jabs. This was her turf, and she'd fight for it.

Mindy crossed her arms, a smirk plastered on her face. "Seriously? You really think your Instagram following will be enough to lure customers into your shop? And this is not just going to be a flower shop; I'm throwing in plants too!"

A surge of anger washed over Rosie, nearly boiling over. "What? Why would you do that? My plant store has been selling plants for decades, even before I took over ownership. That place has been a staple in Spokane for almost forty years! Why would someone like you want to come in directly next to my shop?" The heat of fury coursed through Rosie. After a moment, she forced herself to take a breath, regaining some composure.

Without another word, she walked past Mindy and over to her plant shop, unlocked the front door, and stepped inside. But she froze as soon as she spotted Orson leaning against her front counter, casually holding the letter from the IRS.

"What the fuck did I do in my past life to deserve this?" Rosie whispered.

"Well, hello there, my little broken flower. Just going through the mail," Orson said, an unsettling grin spreading across his face.

"Why are you here, Orson?" Rosie spat, marching toward the back room to unlock the door. Orson pushed off the counter and followed her to the small chicken coop. "I broke up with you, remember? Or rather, you decided we were done when you fucked that other girl. What are you doing back in my shop?"

"Aw, I thought I'd stop by and feed Fluffy since I drove by earlier and saw the shop was closed. Was worried...about Fluffy, you know." Insincere faux concern dripped from his tongue.

"Then why was Fluffy still in her coop?" Rosie snapped, flinging open the metal trash can lid to grab the chicken feed, scattering it over the ground. She glanced up to meet Orson's smug gaze before replacing the scoop and slamming the lid shut. As she brushed past him, she intentionally knocked his shoulder, forcing him to jerk back. But he quickly reached out, catching her upper arm and spinning her to face him.

"You really don't want to test me, my broken little flower. You seem to forget, I have just as much at stake in this 'shithole' as you do. How many months did I keep this shop afloat while it was struggling?" Recognition washed over Rosie. It hit her hard, leaving a bitter taste in her mouth. Months of him covering the bills from his trust fund, a supposed gift, never a loan. He had said it before: "Let me help you out, Roise." She had foolishly let his thumb press over her life, losing control of her inheritance. But for Orson, it had been a way to keep her around, all while he fucked different women behind her back. This was the invisible chain that bound them. And because the shop meant everything to her, she had accepted that handout. Now, the truth stung like venom: she was trapped, and he reveled in it. "By the way, looks like you've gotten yourself into a bit of a pickle, my broken flower." His grin sent chills racing down her spine.

Leaning in closer, he whispered, "I can make it all go away, but you won't be leaving me. You can't leave when I never gave you permission to. You seem to forget, I still own you." His gaze ensnared her.

"Orson, no, I'm not doing this. Our relationship is toxic," she finally managed to whisper.

"The only toxicity in our relationship is you breaking free. Trust me, bad things will happen if you're not in my bed where you belong."

The heat in Rosie's throat burned as she fought to swallow against the anger rising in her chest. "You've already filled it with another woman, Orson; there's no room for me," she responded. She was a nothing. Just a ghost in a shop that barely clung to life.

"My other distractions mean nothing to me, Rosie. Once you understand that, we won't have any further issues." His hand brushed softly against her jawline, and she recoiled, retreating into the shop, grabbing a watering can to fill with water for what had become a pointless morning ritual. Orson sauntered back in, leaning casually against the counter, his gaze fixated on the ominous letter from the IRS. "Ever think about how this ends? Or where you'll go?" He folded the paper and smacked it against his palm, a devilish grin forming. "Well? What's your plan?"

She shot him a glare, eyes blazing as she snapped off the faucet and marched back around the shop, watering can in hand. "Didn't you say I'd be warming your bed again? Or has your memory failed you?"

"I remember, but I wanted to see just how much you love this rundown place," he purred, his eyes roaming over her with a predatory hunger.

Her nostrils flared as her frustration boiled. "Are you really that desperate for a girlfriend? Trying to lure me into a loveless addiction?"

"Oh, clever words, Rosie. But I've been clean for months. Keeping you is non-negotiable. You're mine, and you owe me for this dying little shop. Looks like I have sixty—oh, wait—fifty-nine days to fix your mess."

Fury surged through her veins like wildfire. There was no mistake; she hadn't seen any letters, any warnings from the IRS. She paused, locking eyes with Orson. "You did this, didn't you?" She set down the watering can, fingers trembling as she pointed at him, her gut instinct screaming.

With a dismissive shrug, he leaned back, a smirk playing on his lips. That arrogant demeanor ignited an inferno within Rosie. Orson was a trust-fund brat, getting his way with a smile, leaving a tornado in his wake. "How could I have done anything? I don't know anyone in the IRS," he replied, his tone too smooth, the words slick like oil. Her breath hitched, anger filling her chest like a raging storm. "But you should pay closer attention to your mail. You never know when something important might show up. Seems a few letters made their way to your mailbox, and you overlooked them."

She gritted her teeth in anger. "You know damn well I didn't see those letters!" The gleam in his eye revealed the truth. He was the reason behind it all. That stifling weight settled in her throat, turning her lungs to lead and curling around her heart like a vice. She pressed her hand hard against her chest, feeling her heart pound against her ribcage as if trying to claw its way out. "You tipped off the IRS, didn't you? Did an anonymous call just to send them after me. You bastard." Her voice was a fierce whisper. "Why?" she demanded, advancing on him. There had to be a reason, but all she could see was the ruthless game he played. The plant store barely scraped by, and Rosie couldn't even afford a regular paycheck for herself. She made do with what little there was. Paying bills and buying just enough food was her reality. "Orson, why? I didn't do anything to you; I barely make anything. This isn't a Fortune 500 pharmaceutical empire. I'm a nobody in the eyes of the IRS."

The way he looked at her told her all she needed to know; he was already checked out of this conversation. He ran a hand through his hair, his body straightening to its full height as he moved closer. Pulling Rosie against him, he spun her around so her back was pressed against his front. His finger glided down her jawline, sending a chill down her neck. "I was bored with our relationship," he whispered, his breath hot against her ear. The cruelty in his tone seeped into her, raising every hair on her body. He was playing mind games, ones that would crush her, leave her homeless and jobless. Living under Orson's thumb wasn't even an option. "And your boldness needed to be cut at the legs because you're mine. And I keep what's mine, till I get bored."

"Get out, Orson, just get out. I can't believe you would ruin something I love just because you're bored. Jesus, Orson! Instead of destroying lives, go find a fucking hobby!" Rosie spat, wrenching her body free from his grip. "Or better yet, go get a fucking life and stop ruining mine!"

He slapped his palm on the counter, tipping his head in a mocking nod, then sidestepped her trembling form. "I have a fucking life, and while I sit and watch your sorrow, Rosie, I'll see your shop rot. It's been fun, my broken flower, but I have places to be and money to make. I could make this little mess disappear; all you have to do is show up at the courthouse." He lifted his hand and snapped his fingers, then rubbed his thumb against Rosie's ring finger. She recoiled, as if he'd burned her, a vile itch spreading where he'd touched her. "But don't take too long. You know I hate waiting. And don't even think about running to another man for help, because if anything happens to them, it'll be on you." With that, he sauntered out, throwing a look over his shoulder as the door swung shut. "Remember, Rosie, the devil doesn't bargain."

5

Pro Tip: Fertilize your house plants at least once a month and try to control the pests. Aphids, scale, and whiteflies are a common household problem. Regularly inspect your plants and treat when possible.

The cold air filled Rosie's bedroom and made it hard for her to sleep. Sighing, she finally pulled the covers down and groaned, knowing that it would be another unfun day as soon as her toes touched the floor. Rosie couldn't understand why she seemed to be the target of two men. One of them was someone she'd thought she knew, but now she saw it was just a façade—a man who had tricked her into loving him. Orson enjoyed playing games and being in control. Although he had more money than anyone could imagine, thanks to his wealthy father, his fortune differed sharply from her own dismal bank account, which held a mere hundred dollars, if that.

The other man was Broc Chase, the one who had taken something precious from Rosie years earlier. His behavior right after their intimate encounter showed that it had meant more to her than it had to him. That day, which was etched in her memory, had killed part of her spirit, knowing she'd meant nothing more than a weed to him.

Reaching over to the nightstand, Rosie absentmindedly tapped the top of the small table, searching for her cell phone. Not finding it, she started slapping the table until she felt it under her fingers. Tapping the screen, the bright display illuminated the time: 4:26 AM. *Damn*, Rosie thought to herself, groaning in frustration. Flipping through her apps, she clicked on the weather and saw that the temperature outside had dropped to 29°F. "Shit, Fluffy," she said, sitting up and throwing back her comforter. Jumping out of bed, she shoved her feet into her slippers and walked over to a pile of clothes in the corner of her room. Tossing clothes over her head, she searched for a sweatshirt, quickly pulling it on over her tank top. Desperately looking around again for pants, Rosie bent down on her hands and knees to check under her bed for a pair of sweatpants, anything warm, really. Pulling up the comforter that had slipped over the edge, she swiped her hand under the empty space and soon felt her fleece pants. Grabbing them quickly, she pulled them out, leaned back on her heels until she fell onto her bottom, then slipped her slippered feet into the fuzzy pants. Using the bed for support, Rosie rushed out of her room, down both flights of stairs, and outside to the chicken coop.

Wrapping her arms around her waist to hold in the slight warmth from her sweatshirt, Rosie increased her pace and headed toward the front door of the coop. With her hand outstretched, she flipped the latch, pulled the door open, and stepped inside. Rosie flipped on the heat lamp and looked around in the chicken boxes; Fluffy was snuggled in her box of hay. Bending down in front of Fluffy, Rosie ran a finger over the top of the chicken's head, watching as the little black hen snuggled deeper into her cozy nest. Satisfied that her pet chicken was as snug as a bug in a rug, Rosie checked the hook and heating lamp to ensure it was secure and wouldn't fall. Before the light became too hot to touch, she tapped the cage around the light bulb to confirm it was attached. With everything in place, Rosie took one final look at Fluffy and then walked out of the coop, latching it again before stepping back into the house and returning to bed.

By the time Rosie finally peeled her eyes open, the sun was whispering over the horizon, but that dream of cascading waterfalls still tugged at her. She sat up, stretching her arms in an exaggerated arch, severing her connection with the cozy embrace of her bed and feeling the cold air in her room.

Time to face the day; plants needed watering. She stood up, determined to keep her morning bliss intact; no Orson, no Mindy to ruin it. She quickly threw on a pair of jeans, a clean shirt, and the same sweatshirt once more, then sank back onto her bed to wrestle into some thick socks before slipping on her beloved Birkenstocks. But as she settled into the morning, a faint dripping sound snagged her attention. Curiosity piqued, she got up to investigate, padding over to the tiny bathroom off her bedroom on the third floor. But luck wasn't on her side, no leaks in sight under the sink, toilet, or bathtub. Next stop was the second floor. She peered under the kitchen sink and then checked out the back of the building where a half-bath lurked. The dripping persisted, and the realization clawed at her: a leak had to be lurking somewhere in her walls. Earlier that week, she'd duct-taped a leaky joint in the potting room, a temporary fix that now seemed to be the problem.

Sighing heavily, Rosie resigned herself to the fact that her day was about to spiral into another one of *those days* for her. Even without Mindy or Orson's interference, it promised to be a showdown with hardware stores, pipes, and torrents of water. Winter's bite in the air only served to make her impending handyman projects feel more like punishment.

Drip...

Drip...

Drip...

The sound was faint, yet it wrapped around her thoughts like a cold foghorn blaring in the distance. Grabbing a flashlight from the shelf by the crawlspace door, she knelt and pushed it open, dread pooling in her gut. With a flick of the switch, the beam cut through the darkness. What Rosie saw made her gasp, an exasperated curse spilling from her lips. "For fuck's sake, just give me a goddamn break."

Inside the crawl space, water pooled ominously on the floor. Rosie stood there, fists clenched, teeth grinding as frustration churned in her gut. Questions flooded her mind: How deep was that water? How long had that damn pipe been leaking? And, of course, what would Avista Utilities hit her with for the next bill? In her mind, she could almost see dollar bills bobbing happily in the murky water, disappearing into the rotting floorboards above her.

After a heavy sigh, she inhaled sharply and dropped her head against her chest, taking a moment to steel herself for the day ahead. She didn't bother to close the crawl space door as she stomped toward the back corner of her shop, where the main water line was. She turned off the water. Instantly, the dripping ceased, leaving her in an unsettling silence, a bleak hope lingering that the water might eventually seep into the ground below.

"Fuck," she muttered, leaning back against the cold wall, exhaustion weighing on her. She let her forehead thump against the rough surface, again and again, as if trying to knock some sense into her fraying nerves. It was a moment before she remembered how Miss Marigold had brought in the Spokane Neighborhood Action Program (SNAP) to winterize the crawl space years prior. They had laid down a thick plastic barrier that was supposed to keep moisture out. The irony wasn't lost on her: it had turned the crawl space into a damn swimming pool instead.

"Fuck my life," she grumbled, frustration spilling out.

She glanced back at the watery swamp beneath her shop; it now resembled a poorly planned Venice without the romantic gondolas. Rosie shuddered at the thought of wading through that murky hell to replace the split pipe with a PEX pipe. No way in hell was she crawling into that underground pond. So, like any reasonably sane person would, she turned on her heel and walked away.

The walk to the Little Café was usually one of her favorite parts of the day, but today was different. Today, Rosie found herself hurrying, practically jogging, a rare burst of energy that felt strange. Just before she rushed through the café's glass door, her reflection caught her eye: hair a mess from the morning and breath that...well, she hadn't brushed her teeth. Cupping her hands, she exhaled into them, then inhaled to check—the smell confirmed her fears. Ripe and disgusting, to say the least.

Forced to join the morning coffee line, her patience dwindled with every second. She pressed her lips together, smoothed down her sweatshirt, and brushed her hands against her jeans, her foot bouncing restlessly like a kid needing to pee. Finally, she stood in front of Basil and Alessandra.

Alessandra peered at her with wide eyes, a playful grin lighting up her features. "What stung you, Ro? You look like the devil ran you over."

"I need a wetsuit. Don't you have one? Didn't you scuba dive last summer?" Rosie shot back, desperation staining her tone.

Alessandra snorted. "What? No way! I'm terrified of going underwater; the idea of no air freaks me out worse than...well, flying."

Basil, already reaching for a paper cup to whip up Rosie's usual vanilla latte, chirped in, "I have a wetsuit, and so does my wife. We went to Aruba last year for our anniversary. Want me to call her and grab it for you?"

"Oh my god! Yes, would you?" Rosie turned fully to her, surprise lighting up her face.

With a casual wave, Basil brushed off the bizarre request like it was just another day in their oddly charming lives. "Sure, let me finish your drink, and then I'll text her." With a warm smile, she completed Rosie's latte with the care of an artist perfecting a masterpiece.

Sipping her drink, Rosie watched as Basil leaned over to grab her purse from under the counter. As Basil texted, Rosie couldn't help but admire her friend's eclectic style: white fishnet stockings beneath a black-and-white striped skirt, a vivid lime green shirt layered with a matching fishnet top. Each touch was uniquely her, from the rainbow-striped arm sleeve to the bold green spiky hair. No one else could pull off that look, and it didn't matter; Basil lived for herself, unapologetically. Just like Rosie wished she could, especially today.

"There, Becca said her assistant will bring it down," Basil said, waving her phone in front of Rosie.

Rosie's eyes widened. "Her assistant? Absolutely not. I'm perfectly capable of taking the bus to your place. Wherever."

Basil shrugged, nonchalant. "It's no biggie. Alyssa does this all the time. She's dropping the kids off at daycare and was heading back to their school anyway because they forgot their lunches. Hell, she even does our grocery shopping."

"That sounds more like a nanny or a housekeeper," Rosie replied, taking a sip from her coffee cup, hoping the aroma might inject a little energy into her bones.

"Jesus, Rosie, what's going on?" Alessandra asked, her voice soft but her eyes heavy with concern. Taking another long sip, Rosie forced a smile. She could say plenty, like how Orson was throwing down ultimatums like candy, but she chose to keep it light. No way in hell was she transplanting her troubles onto her friends.

"There's a leak in the building again," she said, settling on something simple. "So, I turned off the water, and now I can't water my plants. Could I use your water for that?"

Alessandra nodded. "Of course. Do you need help?" It was a kind offering, but Rosie knew better. Business was brisk, and the line behind her was proof enough of that.

"Thanks, but I've got it," Rosie assured her, taking another gulp of her latte, savoring the burn as it slid down her throat. "I'll just—" She glanced over her shoulder, noticing the queue creeping toward the door, and downed her coffee in a hurry. "I'll just get started. Oh, and, Basil, let me know when you grab that wetsuit, and tell Becca thanks."

"Will do, hon," Basil responded, waving her off as she reached for the next coffee order from Alessandra.

Stepping outside the Little Café, Rosie quickened her pace down the block, the winter air biting at her skin, waking her up even more. The chill swirled around her, prickling her arms with goosebumps, but she pushed through, finally arriving at her shop. She swung the door open and hurried into her potting room, ready to tackle watering her plants first. Rummaging under the sink, she pulled out a mop bucket, pleased with her find. But then she decided one bucket wouldn't be enough. She remembered the five-gallon Home Depot bucket she had shoved behind some pots on the bottom shelf of her rack. Crawling over on her hands and knees, she grabbed the bucket but paused, realizing it was stuffed with random junk. Rosie dug through plastic containers and fertilizer bags, feeling her annoyance rise. She pushed herself up, clutching both buckets tight before slipping out of the shop and racing back to Alessandra's to fill them.

By the time Rosie was on her fifth trip, Broc stood just inside his new blank slate of a floral shop with Raymond, finding himself caught off guard by the sight of the purple-haired girl from next door. She zipped toward the Little Café, then back, this time slower with buckets in hand, each step pulling at his curiosity. When the purple vixen walked past for the sixth round, Broc found it impossible to keep his focus on the conversation, his eyes glued to the mesmerizing routine. Finally, Broc held up a hand to pause Raymond mid-sentence, taking a step back to watch the purple-haired girl glide into the Little Café with her mismatched buckets. Moments later, she emerged, arms straining under the weight of the water.

Rosie stepped onto the sidewalk, head down and teeth clenched, willing herself to push through the pain radiating through her back and shoulders. Just a few more steps, she thought, nearly there. She didn't notice Broc blocking her path until she was almost on him, only seeing the pair of black Converse in her way. Her eyes traveled up from his shoes, weaving through the rips in his expensive jeans, across his tapered waist, and finally landing on his smug grin.

"Excuse me, can you move? These buckets are heavy," she muttered, trying to sidestep him. But Broc was captivated, refusing to budge as he took in her fiery determination and side stepping along with her. "Ugh, what the—please move," she said, frustration seeping into her tone. The water in her buckets sloshed dangerously close to spilling, and he couldn't help but smirk.

"Tell me, little vixen," he teased, arms crossed. "What's the deal with your little morning ritual? I've been watching, and I can't wrap my head around it."

"Move," Rosie insisted, muscles taut as she attempted to navigate around him, refusing to engage. Tension hung in the air as he casually reached out, brushing against her shoulder. "Don't touch me," she snapped, feeling a spark ignite where his hand connected. Captivated by her irritation and something that flickered in her bright blue eyes, Broc's gaze lingered on her. "Stop touching me," she hissed, but the warmth under his fingers sent a jolt through her, igniting dormant feelings she desperately wanted to bury.

Sliding his hand down her arm, he relished the sensation of her skin. So responsive, so soft. The gasp that slipped from her lips struck him hard, igniting a hunger that surged through him. "But I like the way you feel. Why would I stop?" he challenged, the draw to her undeniable. "The mystery that surrounds you makes me want to dive deeper every time we cross paths."

Rosie clenched her grip on the bucket handles, every muscle in her body straining. She shivered, hating and craving the tingle between them. He was nothing but an invasive weed, a threat to her carefully cultivated life, yet he had a way of igniting something inside her, something she wanted to cut off before it could bloom.

Nope. She needed to hate him.

Plain and simple.

Before a word could be said, a piercing voice behind Rosie cut through whatever electric tension had spun like a vine between them. It was enough to allow her to readjust her grip. Looking over her shoulder, she saw Mindy strutting up to Broc in her Patagonia jacket and Ugg boots paired with skintight black Lululemon leggings. Mindy's hair was pulled back in a severe ponytail, and her heavy makeup accentuated her model-like features. This only made Rosie feel self-conscious about her makeup-free face, which appeared paler and more basic in comparison.

Somehow, Mindy's appearance threw Rosie back to how she'd felt in high school, a feeling she'd thought she had overcome after all these years. It was a hated emotion that made her feel like someone had dumped a bucket of cold water on her. Oh, wait—Rosie looked down and noticed that as she'd sidestepped around Broc, more water had sloshed over the edge of the bucket, drenching her overall pant legs. Nope, that was just her being a fuck-up again. Rosie internally rolled her eyes.

"Fuck my life," she mumbled under her breath, quickly looking away from Mindy as she snaked up to Broc, wrapping her arm around him, leaning up on her toes, and kissing him on the cheek, completely ignoring Rosie as she placed her hand on Broc's chest, a straightforward way to stake her claim. It felt like she was pissing on him, marking her territory.

"Hey, baby, we have that GQ interview today. I already called Nordstrom to bring suitable outfits for both of us." His gaze traveled down to Mindy, his expression inscrutable, and he slowly reached up, encircling her wrist with a firm yet gentle grip, then pulled her hand away from his chest. A slight pout formed on her lips as Rosie saw the wave of embarrassment washing over Mindy. Undeterred, Mindy rose on her tiptoes, leaning closer, her voice a conspiratorial whisper meant only for Broc's ears. "Why don't we head back to your new place? I can help ease your nerves just like I did this morning," she purred, a sultry edge to her tone. Broc's eyes darted momentarily to Rosie before returning to focus on Mindy. She nuzzled against his shoulder, her fingers tracing delicate circles over his chest, a playful gesture laced with intention.

"Get inside; it's freezing out here." He nudged her gently aside with his elbow. A triumphant smile spread on Mindy's lips as she stepped through the door, giggling like a schoolgirl, but not before casting a smug glance back at Rosie. A clear message that echoed "he's mine."

Don't worry, thought Rosie.

"Broc, come with me," Mindy insisted. "I don't want GQ to see you with her; they might misinterpret the narrative, and you know how important appearances are, even if they mean nothing to her." Rosie felt a sharp sting from Mindy's words, a fleeting annoyance that quickly dissipated like leaves captured in a gentle breeze. It wasn't rocket science for Rosie to know that Mindy had no real heart, treating others as mere stepping stones on her climb to the top. Yet, upon reflection, Rosie couldn't help but see the parallels to her own past with Broc. He had stepped on her when she was down, literally, on the gym floor, staring at her broken floral arrangement. Now, she found herself looking at a world she felt she should have been living in, not Broc.

Broc's sudden movement caught Rosie's attention as he turned, shooting her a piercing glance. "Don't worry. I won't be seen with 'Jill fetching her pail of water,'" he replied. The barbed remark felt more sinister than hurtful. A tactic only to keep Mindy away from the purple-haired vixen because Broc knew how Mindy worked when she was jealous.

Asshole, Rosie thought and swallowed hard, her gaze flickering back to Broc's intense stare. There was a darkness in his eyes that sent a shiver racing down her spine. *Never mind*, she thought, *Words cut deeper than any slap.*

"Et tu, Brute?" Rosie remarked. Broc's expression hardened as he narrowed his eyes. He understood how harsh his glare could be; it served as armor for Mindy's sake. The last thing he needed was to put a target on the back of this enchanting little troublemaker who had woven her way into his thoughts, his feelings. She drew him in like no one else ever had, not even Mindy. Rosie squared her shoulders with quiet determination, holding his gaze with an unflinching resolve. "I always knew the devil would come for me one day," she stated, her voice steady. "But I didn't expect Satan's right hand would also be twisting his thoughts with venomous words. It's comforting to see that after all these years, nothing has truly changed."

He hesitated, two steps away from Mindy, contemplating whether to chase after the purple vixen and pour out a genuine apology. But he was rooted in place, caught in the fire of Mindy's penetrating gaze as it scanned him with judgment, sending a chill racing down his spine.

A particular phrase of hers echoed in his mind. There was a clear familiarity about this purple-haired, blue-violet-eyed vixen, and as the pieces fell into place, he couldn't help but let a small smile creep onto his lips.

They *had* met, and it was the only thought that consumed his mind.

6

Pro Tip: If you have overwatered a house plant in the past, try watering from the bottom of the pot instead of the top. Allow the pot to sit in a saucer of water for 20-30 minutes before removing the pot.

"Hey, are you actually going to join this meeting with Davis, or should I just let the princess take the lead?" Raymond leaned against the entrance of Broc's building. The planning session had stretched on, with Broc, Davis, and Raymond lost in a whirlwind of ideas for remodeling the space. The main floor stood bare and echoing, as Raymond gripped his cell phone. In contrast, Broc wandered through the emptiness like a predator surveying his territory. His hands sank deep into his worn jeans, brow furrowed in concentration as he bit his lower lip, lost in a vivid daydream of floral refrigerators and cozy seating arrangements. Details flooded through his mind, melding seamlessly with Davis's enthusiastic suggestions as he detailed some of the incredible layout possibilities.

Then came the strings attached. Two of them, to be precise.

Mindy and the purple-haired vixen.

And one was casting a shadow over every dream he had for this space. Mindy clung to the idea that Broc's creative sanctuary was her ticket to Hollywood stardom, an argument he wouldn't bother disputing, fearing the Twitter storm that might ensue. Mindy was in trouble. Her past was a swirling storm cloud over her acting career, her personal life spiraling. Her agent was practically begging her to get it together, to bury her wild impulses and sort out the mess. Mindy needed to disappear and lay low.

But Broc had another complication, one that made his pulse quicken with heat. That infuriating, alluring little purple-haired woman, whose mere presence drove him to distraction. Broc stood in his empty shop, trying to focus, but his mind refused to cooperate, drawn like a magnet to the sight of her running back and forth on the sidewalk, water splashing around her. *Why isn't she using her own water?* he thought. His fingers absently rubbed the stubble along his chin, caught in a web of conflicting thoughts. Just when he thought he could shake her from his mind, Mindy stepped closer to him, that trademark confidence radiating off her. She slipped her fingers into his, weaving an intimate, unwanted connection. His heart sank as their hands intertwined, an unsettling reminder of everything he wished to escape.

Mindy's touch felt wrong, an emotionless, empty sensation that clashed with the fire he craved. With her, everything was suffocating; it felt like he was being closed off from the world, like prey ensnared in a trap. But with the little purple vixen, it was electric. The yearning was real and fierce within him, a bittersweet ache that spoke to everything he truly desired. Mindy's warmth was devoid of that spark he desperately craved.

"Hey, babe, can we throw in a little seating area over here? Maybe a cute shelving unit to showcase those handbags I found? I spotted them the last time I was at Rodeo Drive, and seriously...oh my god, they were..."

"No." That was all Broc said before he pulled his hand away from Mindy, striding back over to Raymond, who was already on the line with Davis.

"Really, Broc? Just a few charming touches?" Mindy huffed, her hips swaying slightly as she followed him. "What's so wrong with making this place feel inviting?"

Broc rolled his eyes, shooting her a glance over his shoulder. "Inviting? You mean like a boutique that screams 'I'm way too high maintenance for this world'? This isn't your personal playground, Mindy."

"Oh, please. Every successful business needs charm! Don't you want to draw in customers?" Mindy asked, crossing her arms like a defiant little warrior. "Or are you too busy transforming 'charm' into 'bare bricks and bad vibes'?"

"How about we focus on what really matters? Like, I don't know, actually making money instead of wasting it on your shopping sprees? Not everything has to revolve around your latest 'must-haves' from Rodeo Drive."

Her annoyance shifted to frustration. "You think I'm just some spoiled princess? I'm trying to make this place better!"

"Better?" Broc smirked, leaning against the exposed brick wall, arms crossed over his broad chest. "Sure. And while you're at it, why not add a lip-filler bar with overpriced smoothies?"

"Oh, come on! Just admit you like my idea but can't bring yourself to say it!" she quipped, but Broc didn't have the energy to deal with her antics right now. He shook his head and turned away, leaving her seething.

"Mindy, just give me a minute; why don't you head back to the hotel and wait for me?" Broc suggested.

"Arg, fine! Only because I have a hot stone massage scheduled," Mindy replied, crossing her arms, with her handbag swinging on her forearm. After a few taps on her cell, and one Uber car scheduled, Mindy was gone.

Raymond strolled over and handed Broc back the cell phone. Broc greeted Davis like they were old pals catching up after a long time apart. "Hey, Davis, what's up, man? You've got some plans brewing for this space," Broc said casually. Davis's face lit up the screen of Raymond's cell.

"Welcome back, dickhead! Been a while since I saw your ugly

mug." Davis grinned. "Hold on a sec, Sammy just walked in." Through the screen, Broc watched as Davis turned to speak softly to his wife, who had just entered his home office. With a resigned sigh, Davis bent down to scoop up his little boy, Archie. The kid looked just like him, with tousled hair and mischief lurking in his lopsided grin. But those striking bright green eyes? Total dead ringer for his mom. "Sorry, Sammy had to take a call and didn't want to juggle this little tornado," Davis explained, his broad smile evident as he held Archie closer. "Looks like it's just us on toddler duty for now."

"What?! Sammy didn't think this was important?" Broc pretended to be hurt, grinning down at Archie. "Hey, buddy, how are you doing?"

"Good as can be," Davis chuckled, speaking for Archie. "Sammy's on the line with the Spokane Sheriff about some crime scene results, which probably means someone's going to jail."

"Well, in that case, don't sweat it, man. You guys doing alright?" Broc replied, genuinely concerned.

Raymond stepped up next to Broc, cutting in. "Let me grab my plans for this place. We can lay it all out and go over it together. I'll be right back."

"Yeah, sounds good." Broc nodded, turning back to Davis on the screen. "So, everything good with Sammy?"

"Yeah, she's amazing," Davis responded, turning to plant a kiss on Archie's head, who was grabbing at his curls. "You know, I've been mulling over your latest purchase," he said, leaning in closer to the screen. "How do you feel about stainless-steel countertops in the back? We could hire a decorator to whip this place into shape because, Jesus, if I have to respond to another text from Mindy... Is she there?" He lowered his voice.

Broc chuckled, leaning back as a smirk played on his lips. "She's gone." He glanced over his shoulder, the tension in his shoulders easing ever so slightly. "Mindy's been squatting in my space way too long. I just need her to land a role in some movie so we can cut the cord. Without that, she's just...always here." He sighed, half-exasperated.

"She's all over you like a bad rash. What's going on there?" Davis teased.

Broc sighed dramatically, pinching the bridge of his nose. "I'm just trying to make her see this whole relationship thing isn't what she thinks it is. It feels like she's setting up camp in my life, and let me tell you, I'm not ready to pitch tents just yet. Honestly? There's someone else who's caught my eye."

"Jesus, Broc, you're diving into the deep end, and you didn't even take a moment to breathe. What's wrong with you?" Davis huffed. "And please, for the love of all that is good, don't sell romantic bouquets. That'll only fuel Mindy's delusions."

"Deal. I'll stick to the forget-me-nots," Broc quipped, a smirk creeping back. "Those should at least keep her at bay until I can figure out an escape plan. And don't worry about the other girl; she can't stand me."

"HA! Finally, a smart woman! I need to meet her!" Davis burst out laughing.

"Da-da-da-da-Ad-Ad-Ad-Adam!" Archie chimed in, holding up a photo frame that he must have grabbed off Davis's desk.

"Yeah, that's right, Adam," Davis replied softly, running his hand over the top of his son's head. He chuckled, shaking his head. "It's like he loves Adam more than me sometimes. Sammy is always first, Adam follows closely behind, and as for me? I'm way down the line. But with Adam in Spokane, well, Archie's stuck with me."

"Adam's around?" Broc asked, raising an eyebrow.

"Yep! His girlfriend is running at the West Coast Championship inside the Spokane Podium. I thought he would've called you."

"It's Adam," Broc reminded him.

"True enough," Davis laughed.

"So, he's tied down now?" Broc inquired.

"Yep! She runs circles around him. Adam met her at Andy and Liz's wedding. You know, the one you skipped out on?"

"I know, I wanted to be there," Broc mumbled, a hint of regret surfacing.

"I'll never let you live that down; you're lucky my wedding was just at the courthouse," Davis said, bouncing Archie on his knee as the toddler dribbled drool. Broc laughed at the sight, especially when Archie decided to take a playful bite out of Davis's hand. "Kids and their teeth," Davis remarked, feigning annoyance. Then, when Archie let out a triumphant squeal, Broc quickly adjusted the volume on his speaker.

"Looks like he also laughs when someone's in pain, just like Adam," Broc commented, smirking. "Teething sounds rough. But seriously, man, dad life looks good on you. What happened to Camille?"

"You should've made it to Andy's wedding so we could catch up!" Davis replied, giving Broc a pointed look.

"I know! I was trapped in a Netflix contract, shooting another Hollywood A-lister's wedding," Broc explained, brushing it off.

"I get it, but we miss you, man. Adam misses you a lot," Davis said, his voice earnest. He bounced Archie, who was now fighting sleep.

"How's Adam doing since... You know?" Broc probed, concern slipping into his tone.

Davis leaned forward, wrapping his arms around Archie's tiny frame, lifting him close. The little one nestled against his neck, eyes fluttering shut. Davis's hand stroked Archie's back softly. "Daisy is perfect for Adam; they've got this natural chemistry. Plus, he's back on rotation with the fire department, with his chief being cautious about how much to pile on until he's fully healed. He's also taken on a side gig doing False Alarm Certifications for businesses across Washington. So, there's a good chance he'll swing by your place soon."

"Good, good. Raymond's back...let's get back to work," Broc stated, pulling everyone's focus back. An hour later, after wrapping up the call, Raymond shook Broc's hand firmly. But then, the sharp sound of heels clicking on the cement floor pulled him from those thoughts. It was Mindy, back from her massage, her face lit by the glow of her phone screen, completely lost in her own digital world. The constant tapping and giggling from her phone grated on his nerves, each click only heightening his annoyance.

Suddenly, Broc's phone pinged, and he glanced down at the screen. Of course, it was Mindy tagging him in her latest barrage of posts. "Fucking hell," he groaned, rubbing the back of his neck. Mindy was supposed to be a quick escape. Just a little fling to let off some steam, no strings attached. But somehow, those late-night encounters had morphed into months of this...whatever it was they had. He wasn't proud of it. Mindy was too much. Too much makeup, too much drama, and definitely too much jealousy. With the business call officially ended, he walked over to where Mindy was standing and reached out, tugging gently on her arm in the universal sign that he was ready to bounce.

"Yeah, okay, babe, hold on, smile!" she chirped, snapping a picture of her overly practiced grin beside his scowl. As they trudged toward the front door, he noticed she was already buried in her phone again, scrolling and posting as if the world depended on it. Rubbing his temples in frustration, he heard the door creak open.

"Yo yo yo! Adam is here, you fucker!" Adam burst into the room, arms wide and beaming like he was about to drop a mixtape.

The irritation on Broc's face evaporated, replaced by the biggest grin he'd worn in recent years. "Dear god, what brings the devil himself to my humble abode?" he laughed, walking over to Adam, who pulled him into the kind of bear hug that reminded him of the good ol' days.

"Man, I love what you've done with the place. Minimalist chic, right?" Adam said, spinning around comically, his arms gesturing like he was directing an orchestra.

"Shut up, you idiot," Broc replied, unable to suppress his smile. Just then, Mindy cleared her throat, shooting him a look that screamed attention.

"Why, hello there, beautiful," Adam greeted, pivoting toward Mindy with that signature charm of his. "I see Broc here has snagged quite a pretty little filly. I'm Adam, and some might call me a unicorn. Or a stud, if you catch my drift." He winked at her, the confidence just rolling off him.

Broc raised an eyebrow and put his hands on his hips. "How's

Daisy?" he cut in, hoping to steer the conversation away from any potential sparks between Adam and Mindy. He wanted to keep Adam's attention intact; he'd heard enough about Daisy to know she was a keeper.

Adam flashed a grin. "God, she's amazing. A total goddess. I'm down here for her indoor meet tomorrow. Her coach has her out for a shakeout before the big day. Thought I'd take a little tour of Spokane, and lo and behold, Davis texts me! Like he knew I was thinking of you. Can you believe that?" He chuckled, hands on his hips, his muscle definition on full display, even as the new prominent scar on his left cheek added a rugged allure. Adam turned back to Mindy. "Unless you're into that kind of thing," he teased, punctuating it with a wink.

"She's not," Broc interjected, his tone cutting off Mindy's thoughts. He knew Mindy well enough to anticipate where this could go.

"Sure, whatever. Anyway, fate brought me here because of Davis's impeccable timing," Adam said, now back to focusing on Broc, using his thumb to flick his nose.

"Glad you came," Broc replied, about to say more when something in the street caught his eye. A tall woman tiptoeing down the sidewalk, with short, spiky green hair bouncing as she dashed by, cradling something black in her hands. "What in the world?" Broc mumbled, moving further away from Mindy, who was still absorbed in her phone, flashing peace signs for her selfies. The grin that split Adam's face was nothing short of contagious.

"Damn, Spokane doesn't hold back," Adam commented, then swung his gaze back to Broc. "Show me what you've got planned for this place." For the next twenty minutes, Broc showed Adam around the shop, while Mindy seemed to fade into the background, barely registering. Just as Broc wrapped up his enthusiastic pitch, that same lady with the wild green spikes darted past the front display windows and hustled down the sidewalk back toward the café.

Broc raised an eyebrow at Adam, a teasing glimmer in his eyes.

"Wanna meet my neighbor?" he asked, earning an audible scoff from Mindy.

Adam tilted his head, intrigued. Mindy's unamused groans only piqued his curiosity further. "Uh, after what I just saw? Yeah, color me curious," he said, a cheeky grin breaking across his face. "After you, my liege." He performed an exaggerated bow, arm outstretched as if inviting Broc to lead the charge.

"Such a dick," Broc chuckled, shaking his head.

The purple-haired vixen's plant shop sat snug against Broc's new brick façade; while his building was plain with red bricks, the plant shop next door was filled with a riot of color and life. Mismatched cardboard tables outside showcased an eclectic mix of recycled plant containers, their sun-bleached tablecloths curling with age and from the weather. Adam ran his fingers along the leaves of a few plants before he pushed through the door, stepping into the vibrant oasis of greenery. The earthy scents wrapped around him. For Broc, the familiar aroma of dirt was soothing. Here, in this chaotic haven, it felt welcoming.

"Ugh, it smells like moldy dirt in here," Mindy groaned, trailing after the two men, scrunching her nose in distaste.

"Of course, you'd say that," Broc muttered under his breath. Adam heard Broc, then coughed to keep his scoff hidden.

"I'll be right with you!" a voice called from deep in the shop. Adam turned to Broc, who wore a Cheshire cat grin, enjoying this little scene playing out before him. Just then, a chicken flapped down from one of the towering racks in the back of the store.

"Ahhhhhhh!" Mindy screamed, hands shooting up protectively over her head as if she could ward off flying snowballs.

"Shit! I'm so sor—oh for the love of—what do you want, Broc?" The purple-haired vixen eyed him as if he'd just crashed a party he wasn't invited to. Adam's expression was pure gold; a cocktail of shock and amusement painted across his features. Standing before them, unfazed, was Rosie, wearing a black wetsuit and with a knife in one hand, like a weapon of choice.

"What! Isn't it enough that you're taking over next door? Why are you in my shop?" Her tone dripped with annoyance, every word like a razor's edge.

"Wh-what? No...I just..." Broc stammered, trying to decipher if she was about to commit murder—either to him or that poor chicken, now pecking curiously at Adam's sneakers.

Adam stood there, eyes wide with delight and a smile that could rival the sun. "I fucking love Spokane," he remarked, leaning casually against a small bookshelf. "Hi, I'm Adam, Broccoli's best friend," he introduced himself, extending his hand toward Rosie with an earnest grin, gesturing back at Broc with the other.

Rosie's eyes narrowed. "I know who you are, and I'm shocked Broc still has friends." The irritation dripped from every word, her teeth gritting tight. Confusion flickered across Adam's face, mirroring the bewilderment on Broc's. *What the hell?* Broc began reevaluating his entire social circle.

Mindy sidled behind Broc, quick to snap a picture of Rosie in her absurd ensemble, complete with a knife in hand. "Broc, that thing is getting closer!" she shrieked, kicking at Fluffy in a desperate attempt to keep her distance from the chicken.

Adam's gaze hardened as a smile curled at the corners of his mouth. He tilted his head, a calculating glint in his eyes. "Aren't you... Rosie? Rosie Clark from Ferris High?"

Broc's eyes darted between them, but they lingered on Rosie, tracing the defiance in her posture before snapping back to Adam. He stood there, chest puffed out and arms crossed, his confidence radiating like he owned the whole damn room. A bittersweet memory flickered in Broc's mind: Rosie sitting atop the wire table in the Ferris High School greenhouse, her delicate form exposed from the waist down, revealing the soft blush of her pink puffy pussy, wet with her cum, and his condom-covered cock so deep inside her pussy. That glorious memory flooded his cock to concrete status. The fabric of his pants stretched tightly over his hardened member, his zipper pressing firmly against his skin, an excitement he'd not felt since that very day so many years ago.

"Rosie," Brock whispered.

7

Pro Tip: When you can't be a pansy be a cactus.

Mindy clutched the back of Broc's shirt, her petite frame barely peeking around his broad shoulders. "Tell her to put that thing away!" she screeched, coloring her voice in pure distaste. "The only time I want to see a chicken is when it's skinned and drowning in white wine sauce!" She gestured dramatically toward Fluffy, the offending bird strutting just a few feet away.

"Name of your next sex tape!" Adam chimed in, stifling a cough with his hand. The half-hearted *Brooklyn Nine-Nine* reference earned him a narrowed glare from Rosie, a look that could cut glass.

"Rosie," Broc whispered again. She was the only one who'd left him feeling this way; it was electric, it was also guilty, and he was all too aware of the tautness he felt that pulled from her body to his. He hated the shame of pumping and dumping; it echoed in his gut like a bad hangover. The pull he felt toward her was magnetic, igniting something deep within him that he couldn't quite suppress. It was nothing he experienced with Mindy.

Rosie shot them both a dangerous look. "I'm kind of busy here, so why don't you all just get out?"

"Yep, totally agreeing with the freak holding the knife over there," Mindy added, still half-concealed behind Broc like he was some kind of human shield. She squared her shoulders, determination flickering in her eyes as she pulled at his shirt, making the fabric pull tight around his thick and rounded shoulders, trying to drag him away. But Broc stood firm, rooted not by Mindy's weak tug, but by Rosie's withering glare.

A bemused Adam shrugged, playing the charming fool. "Aw, come on, Rosie, I just got here! You don't have to kick me out. I'm not the one who destroyed your future," he pointed out, strolling closer and slapping Broc's chest with a smirk. Broc shot him a look, half frustrated, half amused; the trademark Adam betrayal always seemed to come at the worst times. Rosie flinched, her expression darkening further at the guys' banter. With a slap across Broc's chest, Adam said, "That was Broccoli here." His smile grew wider, his stance just as proud.

It had been years; was it five, maybe six? And yet, Rosie still felt the sting of being just another notch on Broc's bedpost. The old feelings crept back, and they were still just as suffocating. "Shop's closed anyway," she snapped quietly, wrestling with memories that refused to fade.

"Wait!" Adam exclaimed, stepping toward her, lifting a hand as a white flag, which almost meant nothing because of his mischievous stare. "I need to buy my girl a cute little plant...how about—" He planted his hands confidently on his hips, glancing around like a treasure hunter. When his gaze landed on a small violet nestled in a chipped teacup with whimsical designs, he grinned. "This! My Daisy would absolutely adore this...uh, thing." He held the dainty flower inches from Rosie's nose, the sweet scent wafting toward her.

She sighed, a defeated sound, and rolled her eyes. "Fine, it's twenty dollars. Cash or card?"

"Card—no, wait, cash...hold on..." Adam fumbled, patting his pockets in a frantic search. "Yo, Broccoli, can you spot me?"

"How convenient; it seems like nothing has changed," Broc muttered, eyeing his friend.

"You love and miss me," Adam responded, grinning like the Joker.

With a resigned roll of his eyes, Broc stepped slightly away from Mindy, retrieving a fifty-dollar bill from his back pocket. "Here, and I'll take one too," he said, nodding toward another teacup on the shelf. He walked over and picked up a second miniature violet in a sunny yellow cup.

"Ew, Broc, those aren't trendy. You need one of those cool plants from Pinterest. Like a fig tree or one of those tall spiky things."

"Figures," Rosie mumbled under her breath.

"What? Are you mocking me?" Mindy snapped, jutting her hip defensively. "You know the customer is always right," she said, channeling her inner mean girl.

Before things could escalate, Adam clapped Broc on the shoulder. "Cool, thanks, Broccoli! So, Rosie, this is your place?" Ignoring Mindy's indignation, he turned the focus back to himself, an expert at redirecting conversations. Rosie eyed him warily but stayed silent, so Adam continued his one-sided conversation. "Yeah, it's great. You did a fantastic job here. By the way, I LOVE the uniform," he added, giving her a slow, exaggerated once-over. "Are you going for a sea theme? Bringing out the whole Nemo vibe?"

Rosie's expression hardened, but there was that flicker of a challenge in her gaze, drawing Broc's attention even more, like a moth to a flame. She set Fluffy down on the unforgiving, cold floor behind the counter, rubbing her temples as a headache brewed. "No, it's not. A pipe broke last night with the cold snap, and now my crawlspace is a damn swamp," she snapped. "I asked a friend for their wetsuit so I could go in there and stab that stupid plastic barrier that SNAP laid down a few years ago. It's supposed to keep the water out, but I didn't think about a leak. Now it's just trapping the water in. If I don't fix this now, I'm going to have a mold party down there."

"You're handling the leak by yourself?" Broc asked, disbelief etched on his face.

Rosie fixed him with a sharp look. "Not everyone can just destroy their competition and rake in millions, then snap their fingers to have someone else clean up their mess. Oh wait, that's just you." Her voice dripped with biting sarcasm. "And I'm fully capable of fixing something with my own hands."

Adam leaned against the bookshelf, a grin creeping across his face. "HA! She's got you there! I swear, I wish I'd spent more time with you in high school, Rosie. Why didn't we hang out more?" His hand rested on his chin, feigning deep thought.

Rosie turned to him, unamused. "Probably because you were too busy sleeping your way through the entire junior and senior class to notice anyone who actually wanted to be your friend."

He clicked his tongue, mimicking a gun with his finger. "Yeah, that checks out. But I totally would've remembered you. Oh wait, I DID!" Adam says. Another glare from Rosie silenced Adam's laughter.

"This day can't get any worse," Rosie muttered, frustration bubbling to the surface as she threw her hands up, tilting her head back in disbelief. "Are you two done reminiscing? Because I need to get out of this wetsuit and return it to my friend. And not to mention, which I will say, since you're still here, I need to hit the hardware store before they close to fix this mess." She gestured over her shoulder.

"Oh snap! Yeah, done." Adam replied, flicking his wrist to check his Garmin. "Shit, look, I don't have to pick up Daisy for a few hours, and she has her cool down run after practice. Yes, I know what you're gonna say, Broccoli..." Adam rolled his eyes, directing his gaze at Broc, who was too busy brooding to even respond. "Daisy's totally chill with me, and I wouldn't dare cheat on her because she'd hand me my balls in a plastic bag." He snorted, a smirk creeping across his face. "Fuckin' love that girl." With his fingers wrapped around the small teacup, Adam turned his attention to Rosie. "Let me help you with your pipe issue. Not the lady pipe issue—the actual pipes." Adam winked, a playful glint in his eye, and to his amusement, Rosie couldn't suppress a snort and even cracked a small smile. Slowly, a few bricks tumbled from around her heart.

"Do you even know anything about pipes?" Rosie shot back, arching an eyebrow. Adam's smirk deepened as he made a show of grabbing his crotch. "Jesus fucking Christ," Rosie muttered, rolling her eyes. Adam had the mind of a twelve-year-old boy, but the unfun day was starting to wear Rosie down, so she tried to ignore him. She didn't have the energy to fend off Adam's antics. Turning to Broc, she asked, "Is this the shit you always had to deal with?"

"Just wait till he drinks," Broc replied, a hint of amusement in his tone, while Mindy scoffed to make sure Rosie was still aware of her.

Adam leaned in, ignoring Mindy, then draped an arm around Rosie's shoulders like he owned the place, daring Broc with his gaze. He whispered conspiratorially to Rosie, "Why don't you get out of that seal suit? I'll take you to Ace Hardware just up the hill by Huckleberry's Natural Market." He pointed dismissively in the general direction, as if that made it more enticing.

"Fine. But don't touch me," Rosie responded, shrugging off Adam's arm.

Slowly, Adam raised his hands, feigning innocence as he backed off. "Got it, no-touchy, but I can looky," he sang, his tone teasing.

"God, you're such a child," Rosie remarked, exasperated but unable to hide her smirk.

With a dramatic flair, Adam shoved his teacup into Broc's chest and grabbed Mindy by the hand. "Come on, Model-Mindy. Let's leave these two lovebirds to sort out their plumbing problems."

"What? No, that's my boyfriend!" Mindy yelped, her voice high and startled as Adam effortlessly scooped her up, tossing her over his shoulder like she weighed nothing. His casual display of strength was both impressive and infuriating, especially when Mindy looked so tiny in comparison. With a playful grin plastered across his face, he took long strides out of Rosie's shop, tossing a cocky glance back over his shoulder. "Not for long! You work out?" The sound of his laughter mingled with the soft chime of the shop bell, creating a tension thicker than mud between Rosie and Broc. Rosie felt a chill that had nothing to do with the crisp breeze sweeping through the open door.

"Of course, I work out!" Mindy piped up.

Adam chuckled again and gave Mindy a playful slap on the butt before pivoting back toward Rosie and Broc. "Huh, guess you don't fart yourself thin then..." There was silence once Adam walked out of the shop, and when the door closed with a soft thud behind them, Rosie was left staring at Broc. Adam had made it weird for sure.

"Rosie, hey. I—"

Rosie could hardly breathe, her heart heavy as she slowly lifted her hand, fingers trembling as she focused on Fluffy scratching at her feet. She squeezed her eyes shut, desperate to block out the world, turning her face away from Broc. Her voice wavered, a raw quiver lacing through her words as she fought against the pain that twisted within her. "Broc, no. Just save it. You can't change the past or heal what you took from me." The bluntness of her words cut through his skin, her hands raised as if to create an invisible wall, pleading with him to stop. Then, the door chimed again, its tinkling tone echoing in the suddenly claustrophobic shop. Broc assumed it was Adam coming back, Mindy nowhere in sight. But before he finally glanced over his shoulder, the anger and hardened glare from Rosie almost made him freeze. Her jaw was clenched, lips pressed into a thin, furious line. A rush of realization hit him; subtle changes in her stance told him everything he needed to know. She was rigid, her gaze darting past him, shadowed by the figure stepping into the shop. Heavy thuds of boots hit the floor, and he instinctively braced himself.

The wiry punk, Orson was his name—the ex, if Broc remembered correctly—slouched against the front desk, the same man who he'd seen in the past. "Shop's closed, man," Broc said, while Orson, completely unfazed by Broc's presence, swaggered over to Rosie, leaning in way too close, and Broc didn't like that. Orson swiped his thumb across his nose, wiping something white from his nostril.

"He was just leaving, and so are you," Rosie stated. She tried to show her bravery, but Broc noticed a hitch in her tone which said anything but.

"What's with the suit?" Orson asked dismissively, ignoring her as he nodded at Rosie's black wetsuit she was still wearing.

A cold shiver ran through Rosie, amplified by Orson's unwanted scrutiny. “I had a leak in the crawlspace. I’m going to fix it, so both of you need to leave,” she answered.

“Huh, so you’re suited up like a diver? Most people just call a plumber,” Orson retorted, his gaze drifting not to Rosie, but to the chaotic pile of papers on her counter. With a bored flick of his wrist, he sent the documents cascading to the floor, where they fluttered like butterflies. Fluffy paused her search for bugs to inspect the fallen papers, then flitted off, uninterested.

Rosie ran her fingers over her eyelids, trying to shake off the unease. “Just a quick reminder,” she said, her voice low but firm, “when you water this plant, fill a bowl and put the teapot inside, please don’t drown it. I drilled a hole in the bottom for a reason. It needs lots of sunlight, and a west-facing spot is best. Make sure you tell Adam… Have a wonderful day.” With that, she pressed two more violet teacups into Broc’s hands, knowing that Broc was already holding one and had taken Adam’s when he’d scooped Mindy out of her shop. Rosie turned and walked into the back of her shop.

Orson, still leaning against the desk, noticed Broc’s gaze following Rosie, and he didn’t like that, but Orson did like how Broc was being kicked out. A smirk curled at the corners of his lips as he leaned in. “You heard her; she’s busy,” he said, feigning a nonchalance that dripped with possessiveness. “By the way, I’m still her boyfriend.”

“EX!” Rosie called out from the back room. “You’re my ex, and both of you can just leave because I need to get things fixed before the temperature drops tonight.”

“Careful, my broken flower. This guy might get ideas about claiming something that’s not his,” Orson warned, his gaze fixed squarely on Broc.

Rosie stepped into the light, a chunky cable-knit tan sweater layered over her denim overalls, the wetsuit tossed over her arm. She scanned the floor for her shoes, finally retrieving them from beneath the plant shelves, slipping them on over her wool-socked feet. “Orson, he’s already dating someone. And don’t you have a life to disrupt somewhere else? I’d like to remind you that I’m *still* not interested.”

But Orson remained, unfazed, a predator sizing up its prey, arms crossed over his chest. He tilted his head and glanced back at Rosie. "Might I remind you about your little—"

"Orson, NO," she interrupted. "We're done. I have things to do, so if you don't mind, take your alpha caveman routine and get out of my shop."

Delicate teacups cradled in Broc's hands, Rosie's eyes flicked to him, as he stood frozen. There it was, the resentment towards her ex, the animosity that had shifted from him to Orson, and Broc would take that—gladly.

8

Pro Tip: You must ensure each plant doesn't get too thirsty; watering is essential to prevent stress.

"I really appreciate your help, Adam," Rosie said, her fingers pulling the wrench from her gardening apron and placing it carefully on the potting room's rickety shelf. From around the corner, Adam peeked out from the dimly lit crawlspace. He maintained a broad smile that seemed almost fixed on his face like a stain. "Do your eyes actually twinkle when you talk to women?" Rosie asked; his response was a snort, which only made her glower again.

"Not entirely convinced I'll sparkle like some Forks vampire, but I'm a man of my word!" he declared, standing tall with a bravado befitting him. Then, he winked at Rosie. The crawlspace door was quickly pulled closed behind him, creaking as a reminder of how old Miss Marigold's building was. "Really a fucking mess in there; too bad it wasn't a bigger space, I could have watched a little mud wrestling...got any friends who'd stop by?"

"God, you haven't changed a bit." Rosie snorted. Yes, she was annoyed, but despite her irritation, there was a kindness that Rosie felt, brought on by Adam's flirtatious charm. "Just toss that coverall in the trash... I swear, I'll have to burn it," she laughed as she began to remove her mud coveralls as well.

"First time I've seen you smile since I got here. What's got your feathers in a ruffle?" Adam asked, pulling down the disposable coveralls and stepping out of them. He balled up the paper coverall, then cast it into the wastebasket. Rosie couldn't tear her gaze away from the way his fireman's t-shirt clung to his form, the fabric stretching distinctly across each defined muscle, as if each movement was a note being elegantly played on a grand piano. Adam was undeniably stunning; the way his scars marred his face and ear only added to his ruggedness. "See something you like?" he teased. Flustered, Rosie quickly averted her eyes, her cheeks warming under his gaze. "Naw, it's okay. My girl's confident in our relationship. Took her cherry, too! God, it was beautiful."

"Jesus, Adam! TMI, fucking Christ TMI," Rosie scolded, squeezing her eyes shut and lifting her hands to cover her eyes.

Adam laughed. "Hey, I just wanted to let you know that she's mine now, and I'm not open to sharing...not anymore. Those were some truly fun days, full of—"

"Wow, Adam, so deep. Are you going to start writing poetry next? Because I'm just loving this journey through your sentimental scrapbook," Rosie remarked sarcastically, rolling her eyes. "But really, it's good to know you have a new 'mission' now. Can't wait to see how that goes for you."

He ignored her and continued with his thought. "But those times are behind me," he said, placing his hands on his hips, purposely flexing his chest and biceps. "I'm a kept man."

"Are you done talking to yourself?" Rosie questioned, raising an eyebrow. "Because I'd hate to interrupt your little self-admiration session."

"Yep, all done," he announced, smiling.

"Great. Now maybe you can give that ego a break. You want to talk about your new trophy on your face?" Rosie pointed to the scars.

He lifted a shoulder. "Eh, not much to tell. I just lost a battle with a fire I was fighting one summer. It's still pretty tender, and oh look!"

He reached up with one hand to pull his hair back and then flicked off his prosthetic ear using his other hand. "I got myself a trinket to talk about in the bars. Ladies love it." Adam winked.

"Oh my god," Rosie gasped, her hands flying to her mouth to hide her shock.

"Yeah, I know; trust me, if my buddy Broccoli wasn't so infatuated with you, then—wait, never mind, I'm still dating Daisy. Ugh, woman, you really need to stop making passes at me. It's incredibly confusing! And I'm a kept man!" he exclaimed, running a hand through his hair in exasperation.

Rosie snorted in response. "You're delusional," she retorted. "If you think that Broc over there," she said, gesturing toward Broc's new building, "has any interest in me, you've seriously lost touch with reality." With that, she leaned back against the worn, stainless steel work sink, crossing her arms defiantly over her chest. "And besides, he's with Mindy," she continued. "And that woman doesn't like Fluffy! Anyone who can't appreciate a chicken and makes snide comments about eating a pet should be kicked to the curb!" As if summoned by Rosie, Fluffy made her grand entrance, walking through the doggie door flap without a care in the world. Her glossy black feathers shimmered like polished oil in the warm light. With a one-track mind, Fluffy began scratching and pecking at the floor, where a mess of dark soil had spilled out from an open bag, revealing tangled roots of ryegrass that still tainted the bag Rosie had yet to tackle. Gently bending down, Rosie's fingers wrapped around the plump chicken, turning her over onto her back with affectionate care. Adam watched as Rosie began to scratch gently under the soft, downy chin, eliciting a series of soothing coos from the bird. The chicken nestled with her eyes fluttering closed as she fell under Rosie's spell and went to sleep.

"You're like a whispering chick for chicks," Adam commented, amazed.

"Ha, no. Every chicken relaxes when you put them on their back. It's their Achilles." Leaning over, Rosie set Fluffy down in a safe place for her chicken to sleep, then squared her shoulders and faced Adam.

"Look, the least I can do is thank you for your help. Why don't you come with me over to the Little Café? And let me get you a—"

"Oh yeah, let me call my girl and see if she can meet me there," Adam interjected; he was already tapping away at his cell phone. A moment later, he held the device up triumphantly, flashing a grin at Rosie as he exclaimed, "Great! She's on her way over here, and then I can take her back to The Davenport Hotel."

Rosie raised an eyebrow, annoyance flickering in her eyes. "Weren't you going to wait for me to finish that sentence?"

Adam shrugged. "I thought I'd try to be polite," he admitted, "but then I realized mid-sentence that I didn't really care what your answer would be."

"I think I should take offense to that...but I'm unsure," Rosie mused.

"Naw, just remember not to flirt with me because I'm a kept man, and all this sexual tension between us could cause a rift between my girl and you."

"There's no sexual tension."

"Are you sure?" Adam sing-songed again.

"Like one hundred and ten percent sure," Rosie responded, side-stepping over Fluffy and around Adam. "Come on, Alessandra closes at three; I need my caffeine, and you gone."

"Sheesh, yeah, you're welcome for the help. I was only just doing my duty. Oh, wait, what did you want to give me as a gift? Look, I've mentioned before, I'm a kept man," Adam rattled on, talking to himself.

"It's coffee, not a gift, dickhead. Also, stop praising yourself and get your ass out of my shop so I can lock it up."

"Fiiiiine," Adam replied as he rolled his shoulders forward, making it look like he'd been scolded by his preschool teacher.

"So dramatic," Rosie remarked with a roll of her eyes. After Adam stepped out of her shop, she firmly pulled the front door several times until she finally heard a soft click when she turned the key to lock it. The stroll to the Little Café was brief, and Rosie felt a wave of gratitude for the short distance. Rich coffee perfumes enfolded around her head, along with the lively hum of laughter and conversation echoing off the café's lofty ceilings. It was a friendly welcome that Rosie couldn't get enough of. It didn't take long for Rosie to spy Basil and Alessandra bustling behind the counter. The radiant smile that lit up Alessandra's face was downright infectious. The moment her friends caught sight of Rosie, she couldn't help but return their kindness with a bright smile of her own, despite the day she'd been having.

"Girl! Did you get that crawlspace cleared out?" Basil asked. She reached over, plucked the paper cup from the stack beside her, and prepared Rosie's usual drink. While at the same time, Rosie reached out and handed the folded-up wetsuit to Alessandra, who took it and shoved it under the counter.

"Yep, and thanks to this guy here," Rosie thumbed over her shoulder at Adam, "This guy helped remove the old, galvanized pipe, which split, and replaced it with some PEX pipes. I'm all good to go!" Rosie said, smiling.

Adam turned to Rosie and whispered, "You'll have to stop flirting with me. I'm a kept man, ya know." He shouldered Rosie.

Alessandra and Basil eyed Adam, then flicked their gaze to Rosie, their eyebrows raised in question. Rosie palmed her eyes with one hand, keeping them closed. She responded to their shocked looks with, "Numb-nuts here doesn't know the difference between a praising thank you and flirting."

Spreading his arms wide and dropping his jaw, he countered, "They are one and the same!"

"No, they aren't, dumb-ass," Rosie muttered. The friends exchanged introductions, and then a hush fell over the café like a disease. It didn't take a genius to know who had just walked in, and confirming Rosie's thoughts, she looked over her shoulder and saw Mindy. "Fuck my life," Rosie mumbled under her breath. Turning away from the disease floating towards Alessandra's counter, Rosie placed her hands on the pink granite countertop and lifted onto her tiptoes to be more at eye level with Basil and said, "Basil, could you please make a drink for Adam here. I owe him something for all the trouble he went through crawling under my shop and helping me pull all that old pipe out."

When Adam overheard Rosie talking to Basil, he cut in, "Which reminds me, I'll swing by and pick up that old pipe next week when I return to help Broccoli move into his new place."

"You mean he's moving into that building?" Rosie questioned him.

"Yeppers, it looks like the love of your life will be right next door. I give you a few weeks before you start fu-ck..." he trailed off, only to change his tone as soon as Mindy stepped up next to him. "Hello, Model-Mindy," Adam greeted, his voice slightly faltering as he attempted to smooth over his previous comment, which had purposely slipped out. He shifted his weight from one foot to the other.

"Hello to you too, and let me just tell you," Mindy replied, eyes narrowed with annoyance as she pointed her finger at Adam's chest, poking him in an attempt to assert herself. However, despite her best efforts, it was almost comical how little impact she had on him. Adam's solid physique made her seem nearly fragile in comparison, and Rosie couldn't help but chuckle at the sight of this petite figure trying to dominate someone so robust. "I don't appreciate you throwing me over your shoulder and carrying me out like some sort of alpha fireman."

Just then, the sharp sound of a ceramic mug crashing to the floor broke the moment, sending milk splashing across the floor. Rosie, Alessandra, and Adam turned their attention to Basil, who was frozen in place, eyes wide with shock.

"Please, god, tell me you recorded that," Basil whispered, her voice desperate. Rosie let out a snort of amusement and shook her head, a grin on her face as she indicated no.

Adam turned to face an angry Mindy. He lifted his finger and pressed it to her lips. "Shhhhh, it was the only way I could get you out of Rosie's shop. I needed to pave the way for their relationship to take off."

"What?! No! Are you kidding me! She's nothing; look at her and her purple mullet! And those weird eye colors she's sporting like a cartoon," Mindy cried out.

Rosie pressed her teeth into the tender flesh of her lower lip, biting back her smile. Her eyes were glued to Mindy's temper tantrum. The smug grin plastered on Adam's face seemed blissfully unaware of the storm brewing inside Mindy, a storm that her agent had warned her not to engage in. The beautiful red face blooming with anger matched Mindy's already perfectly applied red lipstick.

"And besides, who would even believe it! We recently had a GQ photoshoot! We're a power couple! I'm with Broc...he's not with her."

Rosie glanced at Mindy's chest as it heaved with each angry breath, her lips pressed into a thin line.

"Yet...shhhhh," Adam said again, plastering his cocky grin over his face; then taking the same finger he shushed her with, he ran it from his ear down his jaw.

"Did...did you just mog me? What the hell?" Mindy scoffed.

With a soft sigh, Rosie leaned closer to Adam and, her voice barely above a whisper, teased him with the words "kept man." Rosie made her way to the far end of the counter where a sign boldly proclaimed, 'Order Pick Up.' While she waited, her gaze drifted back to Adam and Mindy. "Psst, Basil, parched over here," Rosie commented, pointing to her throat and leaning forward to get her attention.

"Yep, on it! I'm sorry. Your friend is rather attractive, and I'm trying my best not to picture him naked."

"Trust me, if he wasn't a *kept man*, he'd strip naked in this café," Rosie replied.

Alessandra looked up and shuddered, but smiled. "God, I hope not. Do you know how many health code violations that would be?" She paused, placing a finger on her chin, tapping it for a second. "But it might be worth it though..." Her brown eyes were almost liquid as she stared openly at Adam, standing aloof while Mindy was seething unsightly words in his direction. Rosie snorted. If she only knew that was his bad ear.

Basil and Rosie giggled as they watched their friend Alessandra daydream about Adam, his Adonis body, and his goofy grin. Finally finding their composure, both Alessandra and Basil set to work and prepared Rosie's drink. As Rosie wrapped her fingers around the warm latte, the subtle notes of vanilla filled her nose, calming her as she stepped back to observe the people around her, engaged in various stages of conversation in the café.

The realization struck Rosie: there was a reason she spent more time with her plants than with people; it meant less time around idiots. Cutting into her thoughts, the front door chimed again, and in walked a young woman who stood out like a red rose among white flowers. Her fiery red, unruly hair framed her delicate face, and her pale skin shimmered as if touched by a sparkling vampire from Forks. *A trait that Adam and this woman both seemed to possess*, Rosie thought. She was dressed in only an emerald-green sports bra and black Nike Pro shorts, an outfit that would usually look fine in the summer months, but now, on the edge of fall? Out of place.

From behind the counter, a gasp escaped Basil's lips, and her chest and cheeks flushed a vivid shade of pink. Clearly, the heat in the café was overwhelming Basil. Adam quickly turned away from the angry Hollywood star, as if she were nothing more than a fly that needed to be swatted away from him, and eyed the little red-headed pixie as the fiery beauty walked right up to Adam and Mindy. There was no hesitation when she placed her hand possessively on Adam's chest and his fingers wrapped around her wrist holding her against him. Rosie loved watching how she squeezed in between Adam and Mindy, an act that caused Mindy to yelp and jump back.

"Excuse me!" Mindy hissed. Although Rosie suspected that she was Adam's girlfriend, the way she'd pushed Mindy aside without a second thought only confirmed that this woman would, in some way, be Rosie's best friend. Even though they had never communicated, this act was enough to compel Rosie to defend Adam's girl if anyone ever said something rude about her.

"My little wildfire, god, you're a sight for sore eyes. Come here, I've missed you." Adam's eyes crinkled as he smiled down at the woman pressing against his chest and pulled her into a tighter embrace, gently cupping her cheek before pressing his lips to hers in a tender kiss. Leaning back slightly, he gazed into her eyes before kissing her again. This time, the kiss was anything but gentle; this was a possessive kiss, his tongue entwining with hers, igniting a thrilling heat that even Rosie felt in her core. Resting his forehead against hers, he whispered, "How are you, my wildfire?" His fingers traced the damp, sweat-covered curves of her back, leaving goosebumps in their wake. Which matched the ones that creeped across Rosie's skin.

"Hey, fireman, I'm all done," Adam's girlfriend replied in a quiet voice.

"Eh-hem," Mindy blurted, not liking that she was being ignored.

"Oh, my apologies. Is that Rosie?" the red-headed girl asked.

"As if!" Mindy scoffed, then pointed at Rosie, who was at the end of the counter. "That hot mess over there is Rosie," Mindy stated, narrowing her eyes and pointing to where Rosie stood, sipping on her latte, not hiding how she was watching the little interaction she'd just witnessed over the lip of her cup.

Adam drew his girlfriend closer; his arm protectively wrapped around her waist. "Now, now, Model-Mindy, don't go picking on my flowers. This is my girl, Daisy," he declared, his voice filled with pride. "And that is Rosie over there," he said nodding towards Rosie still sipping away on her latte.

Mindy possessed a smug grin as she crossed her arms. "You were hitting on me," she seethed, clearly intent on creating a rift between Daisy and Adam.

"Not at all. I'm a kept man now," Adam refuted, nuzzling against Daisy's cheek. "This is my Red, my wildfire. She's everything to me." He tenderly traced a finger along Daisy's face, his gaze locked onto her bright blue eyes, which seemed to be fixed on him. Rosie wanted to remove this little disease from the café so Adam and Daisy could be left alone. It was painfully apparent that Adam only had eyes for Daisy. But Adam beat Rosie to it. "Okay, Mindy, it's time for us to leave. Nice chat, by the way. It's been real fun," Adam said without looking at anyone else, only at Daisy. And that was Rosie's cue as well. There was no way she wanted to stay in the café with a woman shooting daggers her way.

Before he could get his drink ordered, Basil called out desperately to Adam, “I didn’t get a chance to make your drink.”

Waving her off dismissively, Adam turned to glance over his shoulder. "No need for that," he responded with a smirk which had Basil audibly sighing. "I need to take this one back to the hotel shower and lick the water off her body," he added, giving her a slap on the backside. “I’ll just drink my wildfire.”

Daisy let out a soft giggle, her cheeks flushing slightly. "Come on, Adam! How many times do I have to remind you not to spank me in public?" she chided lightly, a smile breaking across her face despite her mock annoyance. The muffled scoffs around the café quickly faded when Adam narrowed his eyes, challenging the people sitting nearby.

He raised a finger to gently turn Daisy's chin, compelling her to meet his gaze. In a low voice, he told her, “A lot, and I’m going to keep doing it because of the way your ass bounces.” Adam visibly groaned, throwing his head back in pleasure. The eyes in the café shifted to the bulge in his pants. Most people averted their glances discreetly, while some stared openly. The flush spread from Daisy's chest to her cheeks, embarrassment seeped deep into her skin. “Come on, I need to take you back now...I’ve got things to do to you.” Adam grabbed her hand and pulled her out of the café, leaving Mindy huffing by the counter, angry that she’d just been dismissed.

Alessandra was the first to speak through the suffocating silence that enveloped the room as the door clicked shut behind them. “Dear god, Rosie, where on earth have you been hiding these friends of yours?”

“Not my friends, just accidents from the past,” Rosie replied with a slight smile, raising her steaming latte in acknowledgment as she gracefully maneuvered around a fuming Mindy, whose glare could have sliced through glass.

9

Pro Tip: Spin your plants around to allow all sides to get the sun and prevent them from being lopsided.

The biting chill in the air dragged Rosie from her bed, only to stumble into her clothes which were strewn across the bedroom floor like there had been a fashionable tornado. A complete fire hazard, but with a burst pipe that she'd had to deal with first and the mounting headaches from Orson and Broc, tidying up simply wasn't an option. Fully clothed and palming her eyes to wake up, Rosie descended from her bedroom, down two flights of stairs, then pushed through the back door to feed Fluffy.

The sun climbed higher, the day brightened, and Rosie returned to her potting room, put everything back in order, and then headed up to the second floor of her apartment. The kitchen and living room were next on her to-do list, where she spent time cleaning and washing the dishes which were stacked high. Finally, a smirk tugged at her lips as she surveyed the freshly tidied space. Time was on her side, just enough for a latte from the Little Café, a sweet reward for a morning well-spent, not to mention the caffeine boost she craved.

Alessandra greeted her with a friendly smile that Rosie loved.

"Hi-ya, Rosie!" The café was delightfully empty today. Rosie wasn't feeling sociable, and let's be honest, most days she preferred privacy. Alessandra gathered her long black hair and twisted it into some sort of hairstyle that kept it out of her face. She turned to a new barista and instructed her to whip up Rosie's latte. When she turned around, Rosie was leaning against the counter, watching how effortlessly her friend moved about behind her counter.

"Thanks," Rosie said, taking the warm mug and loving how it slightly burned the tips of her fingers while the steam of coffee filled her heart with the aroma that promised a much-needed lift of energy. "Today is going to be about small wins, like watering without fussing over buckets," Rosie mumbled into her mug, closing her eyes as she took her first sip. "Mmmm."

"And I get to avoid post-haul mopping, thank you very much." A soft giggle slipped past her lips as Alessandra shot her with a wink.

Rosie raised an eyebrow. "I thought I only spilled outside your cafe."

"That would be a negative," Alessandra replied. "It's fine really, but I can tell you, I wasn't about risking any slip-and-fall drama. Becca and Basil would back me up, though."

"Those ladies are champions," Rosie agreed, sipping her latte. A few more minutes of easy chatter slipped by before they said goodbyes.

On her way to her shop, Rosie saw an elderly man, leaning against her front door. He looked worn down by time and the harsh reality of homelessness. His outfit was an odd mix: a tattered denim jacket, mismatched shoes, one a snow boot, the other a scuffed slipper paired with a bright red dress that screamed for attention. He clutched a black plastic bag, a pitiful suitcase for his meager belongings. When their eyes met, a wave of pity washed over her. His face was a map of hardship, chapped lips parting to reveal the ugly truths of his life, his eyes bleary and distant. The unmistakable scent of alcohol wafted towards her, the lingering evidence of his struggles. "Hey...I need some weed, only got a five," he rasped with a voice made gravelly from too many nights in the cold.

Rosie's heart tightened, but she stood firm. "I'm sorry, I don't sell any marijuana here. Only house plants." She tucked her key back into her pocket, hesitating at the door, instinctively wary of inviting an inebriated stranger into her world.

"But your sign says, 'The original pot shop!'" the guy exclaimed, waving a hand at the poster plastered in the window. He hobbled out, squinting up at the faded, worn-out letters hanging over the entrance.

Rosie's gaze drifted to the tongue-in-cheek ad she'd put up; it was her little jab at Spokane's increasing popularity of weed shops. Only, the joke was on him. She was one of the few places that catered to the green life, but in the form of house plants. "That's not what I meant," she started, her voice dripping with exasperation. "It's a pun... You know, because I'm selling pla—never mind. Look, over there's the actual weed shop." Rosie gestured down the block, where a marijuana leaf covered the side of another building, the vibrant colors of a rainbow painted just behind the leaf acting like it was a pot of gold. "With the giant leaf?"

His back straightened slightly, and he leaned closer. "So, you don't sell weed?" His disbelief was almost comical, especially when he pointed back at her cheeky poster.

"Nope," Rosie replied, crossing her arms, a hint of annoyance threading through her tone.

"Just plants," he echoed, his voice skeptical. "Anything worth smoking in there?"

Her expression hardened. "Just house plants. And trust me, I don't smoke. So, that would be a hard pass."

But before she could continue, the man's gaze drifted over her shoulder, and curiosity compelled her to turn around. Broc emerged from the Little Café; one hand was casually tucked into his pocket and the other cradled a cup of coffee. The old guy took a few steps back, his eyes lingering on Broc as he sauntered up to Rosie, a tall, commanding presence that cast an imposing shadow.

"Morning, Rosie," he drawled, his voice smooth and rich, like dark chocolate. "Sorry, I didn't open the shop earlier." His arm slipped around her shoulders, pulling her into his body, a casual gesture that also felt electric. Rosie's heart stuttered as she turned to him, their eyes locking in a moment that felt much heavier than it should. A treacherous flutter twisted her insides, and she fought to stifle it. This was Broc, for heaven's sake. She had no feelings for him, right? But damn, if the scent of his cologne—a blend of bergamot, leather, and amber— hadn't sent her thoughts spiraling. *Not good.*

"I've got it," she snapped, irritation flaring in her chest as she tried to shake his arm off her shoulders. With a swift, fluid motion, she wriggled freely from his arm, creating space between them as she stepped aside, shaking off the lingering heat of his touch. Her shoulders were tense, a subtle but undeniable resistance building within her, coiling tight in her stomach. It pissed her off how she still remembered the feel of him, the ghost of his touch lingering like a haunting memory. A heat pooled low in her belly, a visceral reminder of emotions she had fought so hard to bury.

But Broc was undeterred. He turned his attention to the elderly man lingering nearby. "How's it going, sir?" he asked.

"Sign says 'Original pot shop,'" the old man grumbled. "She ain't got any." His face twisted in disappointment.

With a heavy sigh, Broc pulled a hundred-dollar bill from his pocket and held it out to the man. "See that rainbow building over there?" he continued, gesturing to the same pot shop Rosie had already pointed out. "Go get the weed you want, and maybe a burger too. You might need it afterwards."

"Alright, then," the old man mumbled. He fumbled to pull a leather strap from beneath his tattered red dress, stuffing the cash into a small pouch before tucking it away once more. A pang of sympathy swept through Rosie. Despite his rough appearance, there was weariness in his eyes, now faced with his consequences. With that, the homeless man turned and shuffled away, mismatched clothes and all.

"You know he'll be back for more," Rosie finally said, as she pulled open her front door. The echo of her footsteps bounced off the walls as she stepped inside, not bothering to see if Broc followed. The door started to slam shut, but not before Broc's foot wedged itself in the way.

"What's this?" Broc asked, bending to pick up a slip of paper that had slipped through the brass mail slot. He held up the envelope, studying it closely.

A single number, '46', scrawled in black Sharpie, taunted Rosie. Flicking her eyes up, Rosie's heart raced for a beat before she regained her composure. She snatched the paper from his grip and crumpled it into a tight ball. "Nothing," she replied, her voice tight. "What do you want?"

Broc leaned in, his piercing gaze locking onto hers. "I'm here for you, Rosie, and I'm not leaving without you." He hooked his finger under her chin, lifting her face to meet him, forcing her eyes into his. He dipped his head closer, something primal igniting between them, the sweet perfume of her presence wrapping around him like an intoxicating fog. His gaze dropped to her bow-shaped lips, the zaps going up and down his spine escalating. He just needed to taste her.

Rosie's gaze slid over Broc's sculpted muscles, the veins in his forearms standing out; he was something she shouldn't want. Her heart raced, pounding a warning in her chest. "You're delusional if you think that will work on me," she murmured, brushing her lips tantalizingly close to his. Her hand instinctively pressed against her chest, rubbing at the lingering sting that had recently become so common against her heart.

"Eh-hem." Mindy's voice instantly changed the mood in the room. Hands firmly planted on her hips, eyes narrowed like a blade aimed at the two of them, Mindy stood there. The fury on her face was undeniable. "If I didn't know any better, I'd think you were about to kiss my man, fully aware he has a girlfriend," she spat, the warning in her tone.

Broc broke their gaze like it was a fragile thread, stepping away from Rosie; the absence of her floral scent hit him like a punch to the gut. With a careful turn towards Mindy, he glanced back over his shoulder, catching Rosie's blue-violet eyes. Guilt settled on him like a heavy cloak, and he mouthed a sincere "I'm sorry."

They stood at an emotional precipice, and Rosie wasn't about to jump, but she couldn't move either, rooted in place as her lungs screamed for breath. It was only when the front door clicked shut that she finally exhaled, her body trembling, the ache in her heart drumming a relentless beat against her ribcage. She knew deep down that today was going to stretch on forever.

10

Pro Tip: If roots are starting to come out of the bottom of the pot, it's time to re-pot. Make sure to pick a pot that's at least two inches larger for their new home.

Days slipped away, and now Rosie found herself holed up in her shop a week later, wrestling with the relentless beast known as the IRS.

39 days left.

With each sunrise, the pressure spiraled, and all she had to show for it were those damned daily reminders from Orson, his unwelcome little tokens. Sealed envelopes with the countdown numbers—45, 44, 43, 42, 41, 40—scrawled across them in black Sharpie. They appeared everywhere. Some lay tucked under her front doormat; others perched on her potting rack. A few even made their way to the top landing of her staircase, only adding to the spiraling anxiety her mind was sitting on. Today's particular countdown had found its way nestled between the vibrant green leaves of her plant shelf, right in front of her shop's picture window. A cruel juxtaposition, sitting there surrounded by her plants like an evil smile on display.

These weren't mere scraps of paper. No, they were daggers that pricked at her sanity, a nonstop jab at her already fragile finances. Rosie clenched the latest piece of paper in her hand, wishing she could wrap her fingers around Orson's throat instead. She didn't just hate him; she loathed him with a fiery passion. And yet here she was, shackled between a rock and a hard place, with no way out. Just where Orson wanted Rosie. As the weekend loomed, she'd managed to dodge Orson—and Broc. But not seeing her new neighbor was starting to gnaw at her, a feeling of unease creeping where there should have been relief. A new emotion buzzed under her skin every time she thought about Broc, which was also an annoyance to her as well.

Early the next morning, as dawn broke, golden rays spilled across Spokane's quiet streets. The mail-lady delivered a hefty package that morning, her usual bright smile struggling against the box's awkward size. "Whew! What did you order from the Philippines?" she asked, her brow arching at the return address. She plopped the package onto the floor.

A squeal of delight escaped Rosie's lips as she rushed over, adrenaline sparking through her veins. Reaching for the small barcode reader the mail-lady offered, she scribbled her signature. "Orchids! They took forever to arrive. I just hope they're not frozen," Rosie replied, a grin spreading across her face as she handed the device back. She pinched at her knees, pulling up her overalls; she knelt next to the box, then riffled through her pockets for her box cutter; nothing. She stood and made a beeline for her desk, sifting through the papers as she tried to find anything that would cut tape. No luck. "AH-HA!" she exclaimed, her eyes lighting up as she finally spotted her box cutter hiding in the mess of papers. She triumphantly tore open the flap, ripped back the cardboard, and dove into the nest of shredded newspaper and organic packing material, tossing it over her shoulder in a flurry. The mail-lady stood by, adjusting her mailbag, as she watched Rosie's shameless joy.

The swift movement and Rosie's antics drew Fluffy, who strolled over to the packing material, scratching and pecking at the shredded paper. Rosie gently lifted her hand, shooing Fluffy away. When she reached into the box, her fingers pulled out a stunning white orchid. It was unlike anything she'd laid eyes on in the grocery store or even the fanciest flower shop; instead of the usual round petals resembling moth wings, this orchid flaunted feathery, narrow blooms that seemed to take flight off the stem.

Rosie's gaze lingered on the delicate flowers, her fingertips brushing against the soft velvet petals. She couldn't help but marvel at their distinctiveness, each bloom exuding a serene beauty that captured her, holding her in its spell. The petals reminded her of a white egret taking flight, perched gracefully atop slender, vibrant green stems. An absolute showstopper. Drinking in the breathtaking sight, Rosie felt as if she were holding a treasure; what had initially caught her eye online now left her speechless under its beauty and now in her possession. Setting the small potted orchid down, she unraveled another plant wrapped in newspaper. It was crucial to check the roots because traveling always took its toll on plants, especially with exposure to varying climates, such as Spokane. "Thank god the roots were in bark," she muttered to herself, a sigh of relief escaping her as she stuck her finger into the bark, only to hit something squishy.

"AHHHHH!" Rosie screamed, dropping the precious orchid, her heart lurching from shock to fury as fear ignited her senses. She kicked back like a startled crab, scrambling away from what had invaded her beautiful plant. But even in her panic, she scooped Fluffy into her arms.

"What!?" Mail-lady asked, stepping away from the plants, her brow furrowing, looking at the litter of bark, and Rosie, who was now bouncing on her toes, eyes wide, pointing at the mess.

"There was something squishy in there!" Rosie squeaked, cradling her chicken protectively while gesturing wildly. The mail-lady cast a skeptical glance at Rosie before returning her attention to the mess on the floor. Cautiously, she stepped closer, and suddenly, a green frog popped its head out from the bark. "HOLY MARY MOTHER OF JESUS! AHHHHHHHH!" Rosie screamed, vaulting onto her small desk, her heart racing. "FUCK!" She bounced with imitation, the wooden desk creaking beneath her weight.

Caught off guard by Rosie's shrieking, the mail-lady erupted into laughter, the kind that brought tears of joy streaming down her cheeks and echoed around the room. "Oh my god! Rosie! It's just a little frog!" she gasped, desperately trying to wipe away her tears. "I... haven't...laughed...so...hard in forever!" Her laughter came in waves as she bent over, only to freeze when the frog made an unexpected leap. "Absolutely not! As hilarious as this is, I'm not touching that slimy thing!" Backing away, she made her escape toward the front door.

Just then, the door burst open, and in stormed Broc, eyes wide and chest heaving. "Rosie!" he barked, hammer at the ready, poised to fight off whatever threat loomed. His gaze swept over the scene, catching the mail-lady, her cheeks still glimmering with tears of laughter, and the tipped over orchids on the floor. Relaxing his stance, he lowered the hammer, confusion morphing into a sly smile as he focused on Rosie, who stood atop her desk holding Fluffy and pointing dramatically at the orchid. Broc raised an eyebrow, a smirk creeping onto his lips as he tried to keep a straight face. He side-eyed the mail-lady, a playful smirk tugging at the corners of his lips.

She flashed a grin at him, the kind that bubbled with laughter, her cheeks stained red as tears streamed down her face. "Thanks for the laugh, Rosie! I'll catch you later!" she called out, turning on her heels and breezing through the front door, leaving an echo of giggles in her wake. Broc's gaze flicked to Rosie, whose flushed cheeks and death grip on Fluffy were practically begging for a good-natured tease. With casual confidence, he rested his tattooed hands on his hips, his eyebrow raised in curiosity, like a cat spotting something intriguing from a resting position.

"You, okay?" he asked. There was something about the moment that warranted the story behind Rosie's obvious fluster. She huffed, blowing her flyaways from her eyes.

"Frog!" The word burst from her lips before she could find her rhythm. "I touched it... It was squishy."

Broc raised an eyebrow, chuckled softly, clearly feeling amused. "Squishy, huh? You make it sound like you were wrestling a snake, not a tiny frog."

Rosie set Fluffy down on the desk and watched as the chicken flapped down to the ground, then standing, she crossed her arms, trying to stifle the grin fighting its way to the surface. "Oh, please! You have no idea how squishy it was. It was just sitting there, daring me to touch it."

He couldn't help but chuckle again, shaking his head at her dramatics. "Daring you? More like it was just minding its own business. You realize frogs have feelings, too, right? Maybe you're screaming scared it half to death."

"Yeah, right. Shut up," Rosie mumbled, shaking her head in exasperation.

"Super mature words you got there, Rosie," Broc chastised. Rosie scrunched up her nose while Broc took a step closer, peering around for the frog. "I'm pretty sure that poor thing is terrified. It probably thought you were going to fry its legs or, god forbid, kiss it." His eyes flicked back up to Rosie, a teasing grin fresh on his lips. "You really put on a show over that small frog. What's next? A dance performance?"

"I hate you," Rosie grumbled, her seriousness only fueling his playful demeanor.

"I think my heart can only handle so much drama from you at once," he pointed out, still grinning.

"I'm not Mindy. There's no drama, just a slimy frog," she replied, her impatience evident as she blew her hair out of her face. "Right there! It's mocking me!" she squealed again, pointing.

Broc followed her finger, chuckling as he caught sight of the tiny green frog, a mere speck against the backdrop of scattered bark on the floor. Its diminutive size was laughable compared to the tree bark it had tried to hide in. He leaned in closer, a genuine smile softening his features as laughter bubbled from within. "Seriously, you deal with plants and dirt all day, and a little frog makes you jump and squeal like a kid?" He shook his head, letting out another laugh. "Where do you keep your containers?"

"My what? No, throw it outside!" she screeched, her voice ringing with disbelief.

Broc slowly pushed the bark away from the little frog, cupping it in his hands. He straightened up, holding the frog between his fingers. "Seriously, Rosie? It's like, what, forty degrees out? This guy came from..." His voice trailed off, challenging her to fill in the blank.

"Philippines," she finished, taking his bait, still bouncing on the desk like she needed to use the bathroom.

"Where it's hot and humid," he added with a knowing grin. "This little guy will die out there in seconds. So, again, where are the containers? I know you hoard them."

Rosie huffed, finally sliding off the small desk. With deliberate care, she gently used her foot to move Fluffy from the orchids, who immediately began to scavenge on the ground. She brushed past Broc, keeping her distance from his outstretched hands as if he were a ticking time bomb, and hurried into her potting room. Moments later, she emerged with an old 'I Can't Believe It's Not Butter' container, her eyes wide as she set it on the table, making a wide berth for Broc.

He laughed at her disdain for the little frog, then he gently plopped it into the container. "See? All better. Here you go."

"Oh hell no. No way in hell!" Rosie exclaimed, her hands raised defensively. "Take it? Nope, not happening," she declared, retreating a step until the back of her legs bumped against the shelves just outside her potting room.

Broc's laughter rolled through the air, low and teasing. "Got it. Well, if no more frog princes are lurking around, then I guess I'll just..."

"W-wait! H-hold on..." Rosie stammered, inching forward but maintaining a safe distance from the container. "N-no, hell no...stay right there...but c-can you..." She bit her lip, the nervous energy radiating off her only amplifying her dodginess. "C-can you p-please check for any more...f-friends hiding in the b-bark?"

Broc's chuckle was irritating, a sound that made her scowl even as she felt a rush of embarrassment. "You sound like you're negotiating with a dragon," he teased, a sly grin spreading across his face. "But sure, I'll take a peek."

It took him about five minutes to scour the pots, confirming that no other unexpected amphibian guests had made their way into Spokane. With potential anarchy averted, Broc stretched, lacing his fingers and cracking each joint in his hands before rising. He walked out of her shop without another word.

"Goddamn frogs and princes," Rosie muttered under her breath. "Fucking Broc."

11

Pro Tip: Don't fertilize in the wintertime; plants need time to 'rest' in the cooler temperatures. Springtime is the best time to start feeding plants again.

The sight of her beloved plant shop, defaced and smeared with dripping white paint, made Rosie's blood boil. The anger surged through her veins, escaping as a slight sob that she quickly swallowed back. Her plans for a morning coffee had been ruined, and there it was, 38 painted across the front of her shop, a not-so-gentle reminder.

Rosie's frustration twisted in her chest, forcing her to lower her head. But wallowing wasn't an option; the paint was drying fast, and she couldn't let Orson's vandalism win. With a huff, she gathered her cleaning supplies, slipped on her rubber gloves, and threw on an old sweatshirt before getting to work with her soapy bucket of water. The paint smudged and smeared against the rough clay brick, staining everything in sight as she scrubbed.

"Damn you, Orson," she muttered under her breath, grinding her teeth and pushing harder against the wall. Her arms burned, a dull headache pulsed at her temples from the lack of caffeine, and just when she thought things couldn't get worse, Broc strolled up, coffee in hand, like he owned the damn place.

"Nice number you've got there," he said, lifting his cup and pointing at the graffiti, as if she hadn't noticed it already. Rosie narrowed her eyes, taking in his perfectly styled curls, his black sweatshirt that clung to all the right places, and those damn ripped jeans showing the artistic vine tattoos on his thighs, the same kind that peeked out from under his sleeves. He stared at her, knelt on the ground, yellow gloves and all, hair coming loose from her French braid. Broc shrugged, a casual smirk sitting there on his lips like a permanent mockery. "What? Just checking in on our little neighborhood plant lady."

"Are you just going to stand there sipping your coffee while I'm busting my ass?" she snapped, irritation bubbling over. "You look like a lounge lizard taking in the sights."

"This coffee is amazing. Basil knows how to brew the best," Broc replied, ignoring Rosie's little outburst. "I'm just seeing what you're up to. You're always in some kind of weird adventure, like you're in some sort of VR reality game. By the way," he continued, nodding toward the wall, "missed a spot."

Rosie's patience frayed, throwing her hands up in exasperation. "Oh great! Now you're a cleaning critic. What's next? Should I clean your shop too?"

Broc leaned on one foot in a relaxed stance with an infuriating smirk still plastered on his face, which aggravated Rosie even more. "Extra service? I wouldn't mind." He took a sip, the smug confidence radiating off him. "Can I pick the outfit?"

"Ha-ha! Very funny. You know what's not funny?" Rosie shot back, scrubbing the wall as if she could erase her irritation with each stroke. "Your sense of humor. It's worse than this spray paint!"

"What does 38 even mean?" Broc asked.

"Mind your own fucking business," Rosie answered.

"Come on, that can't be nothing. Looks more like a countdown, with those other numbers you kept getting. Why, are you flying to Mars soon? You'll probably freak out at the first squishy alien you see.

Guessing that's not what's happening," He chuckled then reached up, rubbing the stubble on his chin. "So, who'd you piss off?"

"Your mom," she muttered under her breath, hoping he wouldn't catch it.

"Classic. Resorting to childish burns now, Rosie? How original." His mocking tone made her grit her teeth. Ignoring him, she dipped the wire brush back into her soapy bucket and resumed scrubbing, trying to block out his annoying presence. "Try again, Rosie," he said, his voice low and steady, sending a shiver down her spine like a jolt of electricity. Her traitorous body working against her, and it caught her off guard, stirred something deep in her, tightening around her chest, leaving her head spinning with confusion. *Great, just what I need, more complications*, she thought, forcing herself to focus. But the ache between her legs refused to fade, making the air around them thick with unspoken tension as the thought of him lingered, and naughty thoughts appeared into her mind.

When she finally voiced her misery, her head hung low, arms limp by her sides, and her voice barely a whisper, "I'm gonna lose my shop." The truth hit her like a physical blow, a sting blooming in her eyes and a lump forming in her throat that made it hard to breathe. It was the ache in her chest that really rattled her, a raw pain inward, intensifying as she fought to suppress it.

Broc didn't hesitate. He closed the distance between them, his hand finding her shoulder in a silent offer of comfort. It was a simple gesture, yet it broke her. The last wall crumbled, and she allowed herself to release the pent-up stress, tears cascading down her cheeks as soft sobs escaped. He knelt beside her, wrapping her in his embrace. Seeing her cry pulled at Broc it hurt his heart in a way he'd never felt before, and he hated it. He wanted to fix everything for her, stop those tears from reddening her beautiful blue-violet eyes, take the shimmer of tears away from her cheeks.

"How?" he asked, his voice a gentle caress, while his fingers brushed the wisps of violet hair that fell across Rosie's face, tucking it behind her ear before he leaned back, taking in those bright, watery violet-blue eyes, a color he'd never seen before and felt compelled to protect. Whereas his pinkie finger traced a delicate line along her cheek, a flood of mixed signals surged through her, but the looming reality of her loss paralyzed her. She turned her face away, the weight of it all overpowering. Then as casual as the day, he took a sip of his coffee.

"Sorry," Rosie mumbled, wiping hastily under her nose with the back of her hand, then using her sleeve to dry her tear-streaked cheeks. She stood abruptly, stepping out of his hold, leaving him kneeling, still processing the moment. He watched her as she moved back to her bucket of water, grabbed the wire brush, and began scrubbing the stubborn white paint from the building. "Useless anyway," she muttered, frustration spilling out when the paint refused to budge. "Orson screwed me over," she added with a bitter sigh.

"Your ex?" he inquired, nodding toward the fresh artwork adorning her storefront. He rose slowly, another sip of coffee, attentive to her every move. The sight of her tears twisted something deep within him, anger that made him want to confront the asshole who'd made her cry, to punch him square in the face, possibly make him swallow his own teeth in the act.

Rosie nodded, her gaze drifting like leaves in the wind, unable to meet his eyes. The thought of judgment clawed at her, a fear that he would see her as a failure, just like everyone else did. "Miss Marigold's shop got a letter from the IRS months ago about missed payments, but Orson took it. I…I didn't even know; I should have. I'm just not good with running a business." She shrugged, crossing her arms defensively, her eyes falling to the ground as she wiped her nose again, the tears trickling like a slow stream. "He promised he would take care of the fine if I married him." Her voice faltered then cracked, and she turned away again, the weight of it all pressing down on her shoulders, making her ribcage tight against her heart. "If I don't, I lose my business, my home." She rubbed her chest, the grief constricting. "And I lost my last $400 on soil with rye-seed roots."

The anger coursing through Broc was like venom, igniting every cell in his body with a fierce, simmering rage that blurred his vision. In a fit of emotion, he tossed his coffee cup against the wall of Rosie's shop, the sound sharp and jarring in the air. Stalking over to her, he gripped her shoulders, pulling her into an embrace that was as much about needing her as it was about sharing the fury that burned inside him.

Rosie glanced at the splattered coffee, sarcasm dripping from her voice. "Well, that wasn't helpful. Why not just pour salt on my eyes while you're at it? Guess I'll be cleaning that mess up too."

"Damn it, no, Rosie." He ran a hand down his face; frustration etched across his features just like his tattoos. "I'm sorry. I'll clean it up." He lifted a finger under her chin, turning her face to meet his gaze. The suddenness of his touch left her breathless. "This isn't okay, Rosie. He's blackmailing you, and I can't just stand by." With deliberate slowness, Broc cradled her head, fingers threading through her braided hair, lingering just a moment too long. His hand slid down to the nape of her neck, thumbs gently guiding her chin upwards. He leaned in, pausing just inches from her lips, his voice dropping to a whisper. "Rosie," he breathed, her name inking across her skin like a tattoo. She closed her eyes, feeling the heat of his breath against her skin, her stomach twisting in a way that made her dizzy. When his lips finally met hers, it was electric. The sudden surge left her knees weak, and she collapsed into him, her body conforming to his sturdy frame. Her cheeks flamed as he murmured, "Don't hide from me, Rosie."

She scoffed, her voice shaky as she tried to regain her composure. "Maybe I wasn't hiding; maybe I just didn't want to kiss you."

His quiet laugh was low and teasing as he swept his hand down the side of her face, cupping her cheek with a tenderness that belied the heat sparking between them. "No? Because your body seems to think otherwise." His gaze traced a path down to her chest, noticing the telltale sign of her tight nipples through the thin fabric of her sweatshirt.

Rosie rolled her eyes, the defiance in her voice faltering as a breath caught in her throat. "Those damn things are treacherous bitches." Yet, despite her words, her nipples stayed hard, so hard they felt like they could cut glass.

"Marry me instead," Broc spit out. "I can keep him away from you."

"Wow, I see your ego has humbled you after all these years of fame," Rosie said mockingly. "The only thing I thought you'd ever marry was your right hand," Rosie added with a laugh, trying and failing to swallow it. His eyes lingered on Rosie's face, captivated by that violet-bright color; it was mesmerizing. Their bodies were close, his strong arms wrapped around her tightly, so tight he felt her heart beating against his broad chest. This intimate moment, something he had imagined for weeks, was alive with connection. Surrounded by the sweet floral scent of her hair, he inhaled deeply, loving the softness of her body against him.

Instantly, the swelling in his cock pressed against the zipper of his pants; the tightness had him pressing his intention into her belly even harder, trying to relieve the ache. In response to his hardened length, she let out a soft, sultry sound that completely unraveled Broc's self-control. He couldn't see anything standing in the way of his pursuit of this flower, not even Mindy. In his mind, he was already devoted to Rosie; Mindy was just an afterthought, an untied ribbon blowing in the wind, lost and aimless. He adjusted his position, leaning closer, his breath teasing her cheek as he let his nose trace a path along her jawline. Each feather-light touch sent tight shivers through her body, rendering her out of control. The only thought running through her mind was how much she longed to feel that hard cock against her body, but mostly inside her. Meanwhile, Brock was battling the internal war with his mind and cock, both losing to the will of his dick because he needed to feel her stretch around him as he impaled her. The battle they were both facing was rapidly coming to a truce.

Gone were the days of one-night stands, or friends with benefits. It felt like someone had flipped a switch, either breaking something in his head or, more likely, fixing what was long ago shattered. The thought of another woman in his bed made him feel hollow, a sick twist in his gut that was impossible to ignore. The intensity of his feelings for Rosie burned brighter than ever, an undeniable force that pulled him in. He craved her. He needed her. As she nestled against his chest, her breath hitching in a way that felt right, he knew she was right there with him. Even when Rosie was angry, she couldn't hide the truth.

Leaning in, she brushed her fingertips over his lips, her voice low and steady. "You know, I used to Google you, obsessively. All those years, I was so consumed by hate, holding onto that grudge like it was a trophy. I was furious with you then, and honestly? I'm still pissed."

"Still?" He lifted an eyebrow, tilting his head in curiosity, while he moved his thumb over her hardened peak.

"I don't know. I get so frustrated with you. I hold onto grudges longer than I hold onto anything else. It's like I'm a crow, perching on resentment." She snorted, her finger tracing the intricate vines inked on his forearm, dipping beneath his sleeve and reemerging at the collar of his shirt snaking up his neck. The slightest touch from Rosie had him hissing and his cock screaming at him with pain as it grew to an almost impossible size.

"Grudges aren't good to hold onto, you know, the stress..."

Lifting her shoulder, she smirked as the pain in her chest began to ease, rubbing it in small circles. "What can I say? I'm filled with hate. Shit always finds its way to mess me up. I was just hoping that maybe one time I Googled you, I would see a drunken mugshot or something."

Broc snorted. "How'd that pan out for you?"

Rosie rolled her eyes while two fingers walked over his collarbone, giving Broc a wake of goosebumps. "You kept succeeding. And I hated you for that." She paused and looked at him, her eyes darting back and forth as she studied him. "I don't know if I would have won a spot in that float contest, but I really thought I had a chance to win, to get me out of my hellhole. But life, and you, decided to throw me a wrench...or a football in my lap."

"Rosie," he whispered, his breath warm against her skin as he cradled her face in his hands. "You should have won, and I was a complete jerk for not standing up for you. God, I'm so damn sorry. I'm sorry about everything. For sleeping with you and then ghosting you. For making you feel less than you are. I'm really sorry."

She blinked back tears, while the back of her throat prickled and a single tear slipped down her cheek. "I should hate you; you know that?" Her voice trembled, edged with pain. "I really want to hate you. You didn't even know my name when we met at the Little Café. That killed me."

Broc ran a hand through his hair, letting his head drop back for a moment before he locked eyes with her. "God, Rosie. I'm...shit." He turned away, his jaw clenched as he stared at the threat splatter painted across her shop's wall. "I'm going to fix this. I'll pay off the debt and get someone to clean up the mess that Orson made."

"No, you can't," she insisted, shaking her head. Shame laced her words. "Orson..." Her voice dropped to a hushed tone, and he felt the heat rise in his ears with that soft murmur. "Orson is loaded. Trust fund baby and all that. He promised that if any man..." She leaned back, her arms falling to her sides, vulnerability shining through her fierce facade. "He said he'd hurt anyone who tries to help me. And believe me, I wanted to strangle you for a while, but I can't carry that on my conscience if something happens to you."

"You can't let that punk control your life, Rosie," Broc said, his brow furrowing in determination. "Listen, I have an idea. You want to get rid of him, right? I'm not afraid of Orson." He pinched the bridge of his nose, sighing as he turned back to her, searching her eyes for understanding. "I need a date for this end-of-the-year celebration in Seattle. They're filming it weeks before the new year. What if you came as my fiancée? It would benefit both of us. I need a way to shake Mindy loose, and you need to get away from Orson."

"Broc, you know that makes zero sense with the whole 'I hate you' attitude I've got going?" Rosie responded with a teasing smirk playing on her lips.

"Trust me, we can navigate through this. After the first of the year, if you still think dating me is the worst idea ever, we can go our separate ways. I'll pay off that IRS bill because, honestly? I owe you that much."

She shook her head, uncertainty flickering in her eyes. "Broc, we're talking about close to forty-five grand, and I have less than 38 days to sort it out." She gestured at the glaring reminder on her building. "Orson loves sending me those little reminders. Such a caring ex-boyfriend."

Broc didn't flinch at the dollar figure; he was ready to cover more than that. Hell, he had millions, but he wasn't about to flaunt it, not when it seemed like he'd finally gotten Rosie on his side. "So, what do you say?"

The thought of escaping Orson felt exhilarating, the idea of having some freedom lighting a spark in her. A glint of determination crossed her face. "Alright, but this is strictly a fake relationship. I'm still holding onto my grudge against you. Deep down…like a crow."

She extended her hand for a shake, but in a swift movement, Broc pulled her toward him, crashing his lips against her lips. "I don't shake. This kiss will seal the deal," he murmured against her lips. With her mouth covered again, Rosie felt her senses swirl and blur as his tongue danced with hers, and he pulled her into his chest. Every muscle in her was tense, but just as quickly, it unraveled as she melted against him. Once he pulled back a fraction of an inch, his tongue trailing down the delicate column of her neck while his hand tangled in her hair, just enough to expose her skin to his lips.

Rosie gasped and tore herself from his hold, breathing hard like a hummingbird in flight. The cool air rushed between them, shattering the haze of pleasure and tangle of emotions swirling in her head. She fought to remind herself of the grudge she held against this man, the one who'd had her pinned against him, trying to drown out the angry echoes of her past. Try as she might, she desperately needed to remember one thing: this kiss wasn't real. It was all about guilt, from actions long gone, rising again to help her out of the mess she was now in. *This isn't real; it's fake*, Rosie told herself. "Fake," she muttered under her breath.

"What?" Broc asked, head tilting slightly, searching for clarity in her words.

"This is a fake relationship, Broc," she reminded him, her voice firm and shaky all at once. "Just a reminder that this is fake. You're helping me because you owe me, and I've run out of options."

His silence spoke volumes; his tongue had done all the talking they'd needed. Deep down, Broc had no desire to let her go, to watch her wilt like a flower when their agreement came to an end. That kiss? It was more than a simple act; it locked them both into something neither of them expected. For him, it signaled a silent future. He caught his lower lip between his teeth, eyes wandering over the fierce little vixen in front of him. "Okay, fake." He couldn't quite manage anything more.

"We should have some rules, so, you know—"

"What do you mean?" he pressed, curiosity flaring. He wasn't sure exactly what Rosie was hinting at, but he wanted to know. "What?"

She waved a hand between them, "So, you don't... I mean, we don't get attached."

"Rules, huh..." That idea didn't sit right. He was only human, for crying out loud, and men had needs, especially Broc, who had a penchant for satisfying them. But he had no choice but to agree. *Just hope she understands, I don't usually play by the rules*, he thought.

Rosie sidled away, muttering softly to herself, "I'm a crow, I'm a crow, I'm a crow, I'm a crow."

12

Pro Tip: When plants don't grow, you need to adjust the environment, not the plant.

The morning felt like a slow crawl, the kind where customers trickled into the shop as if the chill outside was some road-block. No one was wandering in to buy a house plant; it seemed caffeine was the only thing on anyone's mind today. The Little Café, with its cozy vibe, made a killing as usual, while Rosie's plant shop felt more like a forgotten corner of the world. Even though it was quiet, Rosie found herself contemplating a steaming cup of coffee, just as the bell above the door jingled, heralding the arrival of a customer.

"Rosie, you around?" The voice cut through her thoughts like a blade. She emerged from the potting room to find Adam leaning against the doorframe, grinning like he was just as surprised to see her as she was to see him, even though he knew this was Rosie's shop. Many days had passed since he'd spent hours helping her, and it was hard to hold any grudges now, especially with that killer smile of his making her heart trip over itself.

"Hey, Adam, how..." she replied, trailing off. She felt her heart race not from caffeine, but from that inexplicable magnetism that drew her, like many women, to him. She fidgeted, tugging at the straps of her overalls. God, why was she acting like a high schooler in front of him? He was dressed in that same plain gray shirt and a blue and gray flannel that hung off him just right, low-hung jeans clinging to his hips, leather boots completing the outdoor model look. If he stepped onto a magazine cover, she'd seriously consider taking up hiking just to follow him into the wild. *No, he's dating someone! Stop it, Rosie!* she chastised herself. Adam shoved his hands deep into his pockets, catching her gaze with a smirk. "Broc finally got his act together and moved his stuff out of storage. And this idiot," he gestured to himself, "agreed to help him haul everything up to his new apartment."

One week. Just one long week of silence, and now it was wrapped around Broc and Rosie like a bow. A faux union that had been nothing but an irritating thought gnawing at her mind. Broc's absence since that day loomed over her like a dark cloud. Convenient, indeed.

This whole ridiculous scheme had been his idea in the first place. If he really didn't want to be around her, he shouldn't have proposed it at all. Now that she'd spent all this time mulling it over, the whole notion felt even more absurd. No one in Broc's world would ever believe he was involved with a "nobody" like her. Orson would surely see right through it, too, and the last thing Rosie needed was the scrutiny of someone who thrived on fucking up people's lives for the hell of it.

But it wasn't just Broc's lack of appearance that bothered her; she hadn't made the trip over to his building either. It was a dangerous game they were playing, one that ruined her more than him. And the longer it went on, the more she wondered if they were the punchline to some karma joke. The other issue with this charade was that it hadn't yet reached social media. No posts about Mindy's split with Broc, no updates from Mindy about their relationship status, just the silence, and that didn't sit well with Rosie. Another red flag waving in

Rosie's face was how, no matter where Broc went, Mindy was practically glued to his side. She'd made her feelings about Rosie abundantly clear; the disdain was evident. What gnawed at Rosie most was the impending fallout. Would Mindy's legion of fans turn on her? They were a wild bunch, just as unpredictable as Mindy herself.

The thing was, Mindy had two kinds of fans: those who couldn't stand her and the ones who would defend her to the death. And sadly, for Rosie, all she could do was hope Broc would navigate this delicate situation with some finesse. Because, honestly, Rosie had no clue how to manage the inevitable aftermath that would break out once Broc broke the news.

"Oh," was all she could manage, her wide eyes betraying the weight of everything she had been juggling. Adam caught sight of her, a playful chuckle slipping from his lips as he took in the carousel of emotions flaunting themselves across her face. He planted his hands on his hips, his chest flexing, biceps subtly bulging under his fitted gray t-shirt, all too aware of the effect he had on her.

"Ro, I can see the sadness all over your face. Has it been a while since you've slept with your beau?" he teased, a hint of amusement on his lips as he winked. Not in the mood for his antics, Rosie shot him a pointed look, silent but loaded, as she scrutinized him. It was ridiculous how easily she flushed around him; Adam was practically a magnet for her embarrassment. The worst part? Did he know about the kiss she and Broc had shared? The thought made her cheeks prickle with heat.

They're close friends, Rosie reminded herself. *Adam probably knows.* That realization only deepened the flush creeping up her neck. It felt like an accident waiting to happen. Adam was either already clued in or somehow bound to find out soon enough, just like the rest of the world. And knowing Mindy, she would blow up that secret the moment she had the chance.

Before Adam could dig himself deeper, his phone chimed, breaking the tension. With a playful huff, he fished it out of his pocket and held it up for her to see. "Looks like Broccoli needs me next door! I'll catch you later, Ro. And hey, my Red loved the little flower we picked out for her." Rosie couldn't help but smile back, words escaping her as he reached behind him for the door. "Good talk, Rosie. Good talk," he added, giving a mock salute before disappearing through the doorway, leaving Rosie alone in her plant shop and still without her much-needed cup of coffee.

13

Pro Tip: Planting a seed too early means more time for trouble to develop from pests and diseases.

The breeze rushed past Adam as he slipped into Broc's empty shop; the sharp scent of fresh paint and wood shavings filled his nose. Broc stood there, tension radiating off him, with Mindy beside him, her arms crossed tightly, brow knitted in irritation. What had begun as a quiet conversation quickly erupted into a full-blown argument, the kind that set off fire alarms. Adam could feel it in his chest, a simmering anger. It was clear that whatever spat they were tangled in was far from trivial, and he couldn't help but hope this drama was the last chapter in their "relationship." Adam had plans, damn it; plans that included double dates with the duo of Broc and Rosie.

Not one to tiptoe around their bubble, Adam leaned against the wall, a casual facade plastered over his curiosity. His fingers wrapped around his cell, and he tapped away, sending text messages to Daisy. Even as he stayed quietly in the corner, he couldn't resist sneaking glances at Mindy as she spoke, her voice climbing higher, a pitch that felt meant for the dogs. Mindy likely wanted to keep their spat private, but Adam had never been one to read between the lines of an uncomfortable situation. "Hey, guys! Don't mind me; I'll just be over here, listening to everything like a glorified tape recorder," he interjected, a wry smile forming on his lips as he tried to make himself present for them to see.

Mindy had her back to him; the tightness of her posture was sharp with anger spilling from her mouth. "Why do you always bring her up?" she hissed at Broc, her voice rising despite her attempts to rein it in. "It's like you're just trying to prove I'm not enough! I'm right here, Broc!" Her irritation seeped out, frustration that swirled around them, causing a puff of drywall dust to rise as she stomped her expensive flats against the concrete floor. Every meticulously manicured finger she pointed emphasized her rising ire, and Adam couldn't help but snort, proving his point. Mindy's head snapped over her shoulder, glossy hair flying across her face as she fixed a fierce glare on Adam. He quickly returned his focus to his phone, but the arched brow he tried to hide betrayed his intrigue. A front-row seat to the unfolding drama.

"Seriously, Mindy," Broc said, irritated. "It's not like that. Rosie's just a friend. You know we've known each other forever." His words were steady, but Adam could hear the strain, the rasp of a half-truth hanging out on the line.

"Friends? You never mentioned her before coming back to Spokane. That's rich! You think I'm just supposed to sit back and watch while you two bond over whatever plant or fucking flower shows up at your door. You seriously want me to believe that dirt-girl was scared of a frog? I don't want that stupid aquarium in this shop! That frog habitat makes this place look cheap! It's not a pet store. God!" Mindy stomped her foot again. "There's already a fucking chicken next door; this isn't a farm!" And for a split second, Adam couldn't help but think how much she looked like a little toddler throwing a fit over being denied ice cream. "It feels like you're keeping me at arm's length! What's really going on, Broc?" Her face flushed, anger amplifying her jealousy, Adam knew she had a point. And at the same time, he couldn't care less.

"How many times does she text you?" she snapped, her tone sharp. "What is she, your safety net? You think you can just string me along while you entertain her?" Mindy was fierce, and if Adam didn't know better, he'd swear she was practically glowing green with jealousy. Broc, for all his nonchalant charm, didn't seem fazed by the swell of her anger at all.

Here's a little-known fact in Hollywood: Mindy was a walking tornado, all circus and no confidence. Adam stood there. It hit him that this confrontation was only the beginning of the end for them, and despite his best efforts to suppress it, he couldn't help but smile. Gloating was just part of his DNA.

"Mindy, look, I'm glad you got that audition call. I really am. I know you were waiting for that director's call, but this is our end. We've run our course. This has nothing to do with your audition. It's over," Broc finally said, his voice steady.

"There it is," Adam mumbled, his eyes lighting up with excitement as a broad grin spread across his face. He leaned in, completely engrossed in the moment, savoring it like the climax of a blockbuster movie.

"You knew when we hooked up, we both agreed we didn't want attachments. I made that clear from the start," Broc added, running a hand through his curly black hair.

Mindy sighed dramatically, throwing her arms up. "That's what all girls say when they want to fuck someone hot! I figured you'd just keep fucking me into a relationship!" she cried out, waving her arms in exasperation. "Broc, this is just shit timing. My agent said that settling down with one guy is what directors and the backers want to see. You and I together have boosted my followers on social media," she pouted with that familiar mix of adorable and infuriating charm that Hollywood producers loved.

"Don't take the bait..." Adam whispered under his breath.

Broc ran a hand down his face, frustration evident.

"Besides, I liked waking up to your head between my legs," Mindy whined, catching Adam's attention instantly. That admission made him drop his cell, but he caught it right before it smashed to the concrete floor. Broc shot Adam a look, knowing that they had an audience for this little drama, though it was Broc who'd texted Adam to come over in the first place. *Or maybe he needed to have a witness*, Adam thought.

"Mindy." Broc sighed deeply, tilting his head back for a moment. He placed his hands firmly on his hips, a gesture of exasperation, before lifting his gaze back to Mindy with laser intensity. "That was ages ago when we first got together. We got busy; we were both pulled in different directions."

Huffing in frustration, Mindy crossed her arms, her mind racing like a chess player plotting her next move. "Look, I'll be gone for a while. I have two auditions and a few must-attend events to keep my sponsorships. Take that time to think because you and I are good together." She pointed back and forth between them.

Broc sighed, pinching the bridge of his nose. "Mindy, no, we aren't going to work."

"Why? Are you already fucking her behind my back?" The words shot from her lips like a bullet, her eyes narrowing to slits that could slice through steel. "How many times have you fucked her?" Mindy's glare was directed fiercely towards Rosie's plant shop, her arms crossed so tightly against her chest that it seemed like they could explode.

Broc shook his head. "No, I'm not sleeping with anyone. I've got my flower shop opening to deal with," he muttered, gesturing vaguely at the space that was supposed to be his sanctuary. Adam, who was unabashedly reveling in this incredible showdown, crossed his arms and leaned back. "You're busy refining your social media empire," he pointed at Mindy, "and possibly juggling two movie deals on the side," Broc added, holding up two fingers.

"And hopefully driving business away from that crap hole next door," Mindy whispered with a sneer. Her inappropriate mumble was just loud enough for both Broc and Adam to hear. Adam's jaw tightened in response as he fought the urge to defend Rosie. His eyes flickered towards the plant shop. Broc already had a feeling that rushed through him, his protection toward Rosie that he didn't quite understand. He shoved his hands into the pockets of his ripped jeans, masking his fury at Mindy's venomous remarks.

Mindy shifted her weight, her chin jutting into the air with an air of faux confidence. Uncrossing her arms, she tapped her finger against her chin, studying Broc like he was some kind of puzzle she needed to solve. "I don't believe you," she declared, scrutinizing him. "But I'll post about your opening, and you're welcome." Leaning closer, she jabbed a finger into Broc's chest. "So don't cross me because just like the Swifties, I have my Mindys. When I'm sad, they're miserable. When I'm mad...well, you catch my drift."

"Oh, fantastic! Nothing like showing love with a mid-morning threat," Adam quipped, his sarcasm rolling off his tongue like honey.

Broc took a deep breath, tilting his head ever so slightly as he steeled himself against her relentless gaze. Mindy scoffed, and Broc decided to shift the stakes. "I've got my own following, Mindy. All I need to do is flash..." He paused, the moment stretching like a taut rubber band before he ripped his shirt off in one smooth motion. Mindy gasped, her expression suddenly shifting from anger to desire as she took in the intricate tapestry of floral tattoos sprawling across his chest and up to his neck. His bare skin, chiseled and perfect, was a masterpiece in its own right.

"That's so hot." Adam couldn't resist the grin that spread across his face, appreciating the view despite his loyalty to Daisy. Broc pulled out his cell phone, capturing the moment with a broody selfie and quickly uploading it to Instagram.

"See what I mean?" Broc challenged, holding the screen out for Mindy to look at the flood of likes pouring in. Frustration filled Mindy's eyes as she stomped her foot like a child yet again, sending more puffs of sheetrock dust into the air.

Adam whipped out his cell and tapped onto his Instagram, finding the post Broc had just made and responding cheekily:

@Fireman_are_bigger: Mine are still bigger.

"Over 18k, Broc!" Adam shouted, his gaze fixated on the screen, dismissing the look on Mindy's face. She scrunched her features, clearly miffed at the rising numbers. Both Adam and Broc tossed her knowing smirks, enjoying her little outburst more than they should have.

"I've got my own following," Broc continued, cocky as ever, "so no need for your Mindys to boost my game." Mindy, unimpressed, turned her focus to Adam. With a sly grin, she raised her phone, aiming the camera at them. She leaned into Broc, her hand boldly rested on his chest before she planted a quick, chaste kiss on his tattooed pectoral muscle. But when Broc caught on, his hand shot out to grab her wrist, yanking the camera away. "Cut it out, Mindy."

"Just a little reminder..." she sang, thumb grazing his nipple, relishing the way it reacted to her feather-light touch. A smirk, while she snapped another photo and uploaded it to her social media, giggling at the immediate response. "The Mindys are fierce." She winked back at him, reveling in the moment.

Adam opened her Instagram, his eyes widening at the photo. The angle and their proximity made it look scandalous, her caption reading, '**Nothing like skin to skin before I leave.**' He exhaled sharply, glancing at Broc, whose expression turned dangerously serious as he noted the flurry of likes flooding in.

"Shit," Broc cursed under his breath. "Delete that."

"Not happening. My fans love our vibe," Mindy replied, playfully booping his nose. "Thanks for the photo op, babe. This'll help when I land in Hollywood. Catch you later." Planting a teasing kiss on his chin, she turned and sashayed past Adam, completely unfazed by the wreckage of their relationship.

Once the front door clicked shut, Adam strolled over to Broc, picking up the shirt he'd discarded. He tossed it back to Broc while mid-sigh, and he slipped it on. Adam glanced back over his shoulder, a grin creeping onto his face. "Gotta hand it to her, she knows how to make an exit."

"Fuck, that pic is gonna bite me in the ass," Broc muttered, palming his eyes.

Adam raised an eyebrow, studying him closely. "How?"

"Seriously?" Broc's head dropped back, arms flailing before he resigned to a dramatic turn away. "Fine, fine! Okay." He spun around, hands clasped behind his head. “Rosie...” he said, gesturing toward her shop, and Adam couldn’t help but smirk, an all-knowing grin spreading across his face. He waggled a finger at Broc playfully, only to have Broc swat it away, irritation flaring. “Shut it, man. It’s not like that. Look, Rosie’s got some messed-up drama with her ex.”

That made Adam stop, the playful smirk vanishing in an instant, replaced by a furious intensity that could’ve rivaled a racecar taking off.

“What the hell do you mean? Can you just spit it out? That flower? She’s probably one of the sweetest... She was already fucked up by you years ago...now what?” Adam snapped, his eyes narrowing.

“Thanks for that, asshole. Look, she’s holding it together for now. But damn, she used to be the sweetest. I take full responsibility for that horrible shit. But she’s not the same girl we knew in high school.”

“Seriously, man. What were you thinking?” Adam punched Broc on the shoulder, his face flushed as he clenched his jaw. “Why’d you screw her over? I’ve been dying to know.”

“Greed, I guess. Back at that competition, I saw Rosie walk in with that floral masterpiece. She was already a winner. And even though I didn't mean to ruin her work, I think I did it subconsciously. Even worse, that was the same day I...well, I took her virginity.”

“DUDE! Oh my god,” Adam groaned, throwing his head back, his eyes wide with disbelief. “You’re a total jerk. I should hit you! What the hell happened to our rules in school?” He threw his hands up, trying to reason it all out. “BROC!” he shouted, his voice echoing. “WHAT were the rules?” He pointed emphatically at the ground as if it were the source of all their problems.

Broc rubbed his face, then tilted his head back, taking a deep breath. Shifting his stance, he finally said, “Don’t sleep with virgins. They get attached too fast.” Adam hit him again on the shoulder. “Ow, damn it.” Broc winced. “Wait, you said Daisy was a virgin!”

“Damn right she was!” Adam replied, a wide grin spreading across his face. “Best thing ever. I have no clue why we even had that rule; it felt like trying to shove a square peg into a round hole. And god, she was tight; it felt amazing every second."

"TMI, dude! Then why are you yelling at me?" Broc shot back.

Adam was lost in thought, his nostalgia shining through. "Yeah, knowing I was her first makes me want to knock out any guy who even glances her way. I've turned into a full-on alpha. Touch her, and you die," he laughed, slapping Broc's chest. "So let me get this straight. You took Rosie's virginity and then really messed her up at the competition thingy back at Ferris? Jesus, if I were you, I'd be careful around her. She probably knows how to use those plants to poison you!"

Broc scratched his head. "Nah, I don't think she's like that. But Mindy? If she had more than just 'hearts and likes' in her head, maybe. Anyway, back to the point. Rosie's ex either withheld her tax refund or turned her in to the IRS. Now she's buried under forty-five grand in debt. I told her I'd help her out; I totally owe her that. But I asked her to be my fake fiancée to keep him off her back and Mindy off mine."

"Speaking of Mindy." Adam held up his phone and flashed her post. "Doesn't look like you two just ended a relationship...you know?"

Broc's eyes darted to the post. Seeing the photo with over a million likes made him groan, running his hands down his face. How the hell was this supposed to work, with Mindy sharing everything and Rosie drowning in her ex's mess?

They both stared at the photo and said in unison, "Shit."

14

Pro Tip: Seeds should not be planted deeper than twice their width.

An hour later, Broc and Adam had successfully unloaded and carried most of the boxes up to Broc's new apartment. For weeks, Raymond had worked on the living space upstairs first. Now that the apartment was finished, Broc had a completely remodeled kitchen, living room, and a main bedroom with an adjoining bathroom, as well as two spare rooms.

Adam lifted his shirt and wiped off his forehead. "Okay, let's get that dresser."

Broc sighed, then wiped the back of his neck with a towel that was slung over his shoulder, then said, "I hate saying this, but my arms are tired."

A smile broke out on Adam's face. "Pussy."

Broc snorted. "Wrong, you should be saying *balls.*"

"Why the fuck would I say that?" Adam asked, following Broc down the stairs and into the back of his building, where the moving truck was parked.

"Because our dicks pound pussies like they are a lump of meat to be tenderized, and women keep coming back for more. Not to mention, they can deliver babies, and you, of all people, should know because you've delivered babies and seen them stretch as they push a baby out. Hell, when someone touches our balls, and not tenderly, we collapse on the floor like a baby."

Adam roared with laughter. "Okay...okay..." he said, bending over and clutching his waist, laughing uncontrollably. "Shit, touché, yeah, you have a point." He stood up and used the palms of his hands to wipe away the tears that were streaming down his cheeks. "Balls it is, fucker."

"Come on, dip-shit, let's get going," Broc encouraged, feeling justified; he then begrudgingly stepped up into the truck, ready to pull out the dresser.

Closing and locking her shop's front door, she walked down the block to the Little Cafe. Once she pulled open the front door, she pocketed her cell phone in her overalls. Two bright, welcoming smiles greeted Rosie as she stepped up to the counter.

"Hey, Rosie!" Basil greeted, waving her free hand in the air. Today, her green spiky hair was slicked back, and she wore a cute white folded scarf and a bright blue A-line dress with yellow tights. Alessandra wore an adorable cream-colored sweater with red cherries knitted into the design, complete with her red apron wrapped around her thin waist. Her long black hair was tied back in a loose braid, slung over one shoulder.

"Hey, you guys," Rosie said with a half-smile.

"Wait, what happened?" Basil immediately asked, pointing one finger directly at Rosie, quickly placing the shot glasses under the espresso machine to make Rosie's vanilla latte. "Your aura is messed up; there's..." She looked at Rosie again, raising her hand and moving it in a circular motion, gesturing over Rosie's body. "...something going on with you. Spill the tea now, or no coffee," Basil said, popping out her hip and setting the latte on the countertop for Rosie, but keeping her palm over the lid, not ready to give her the liquid of love.

"You're a monster. Uh, fine, how'd you know? It's so creepy that you know shit like that," Rosie mumbled, scrunching up her nose. Alessandra smiled and leaned on her elbows at the end of the countertop, watching her two friends talk.

Basil smiled and responded, "I don't know, it's just how you carry yourself, Rosie. It's really not hard at all."

"Fine, but I'm coming behind the counter to talk to you," Rosie relented, walking around the counter to her usual moping spot.

"Just don't sit this time because the floor is filthy. I'm mopping and spraying down the mats after I close up," Alessandra cut in.

"Totally ruining my sulking session, you know," Rosie told her, rubbing the side of her nose.

Alessandra and Basil both smiled and said at the same time, "We know."

"Gah. Fine. Okay. So...Orson," Rosie started.

"Hate that douche," Basil added.

"He's a dick," Alessandra said at the same time as Basil.

"Glad you two told me how you felt when I was dating him!" Rosie snapped.

Both girls looked at Rosie and then at each other, each lifting one shoulder. "We did," they once again said in unison.

Narrowing her eyes at her friends, Rosie crossed her arms. "Orson had been keeping some important mail from me, and I even think he might have made an anonymous call to the IRS. They now claim I owe them about forty-five thousand dollars in back taxes."

"I'm calling Becca," Basil announced as she reached under the counter for her cell phone.

Rosie placed her hand on Basil's arm. "Wait, there's more," she said. "He told me that he would pay it off if I married him at the end of the year."

"Are. You. F-ing. Kidding. Me," Basil hissed. Her face went from normal to red in a flash. She pointed at Rosie and stepped forward, crowding her space, finger about an inch from Rosie's nose. "Does he think he can get away with that?! Does he even know who I'm married to?" Basil rubbed her hands together. "My wife is going to rip his balls off."

"There's more..." Rosie sighed. "Because I never agreed to his ludicrous threat, he's been leaving me a countdown in or *on* my store. Annnd to make matters worse, Broc saw it in living color. He was walking back with a cup of coffee from your place and saw me trying to scrub off the latest threat painted on my shop. You know, a *gentle* nudge, telling me I have only a certain number of days till the fines start to accrue. I'm scared that if I don't pay, I'm going to jail." She groaned, collapsing in on herself. "In a moment of weakness, I agreed to the proposition that Broc proposed...hold on, it gets better," Rosie continued, raising her hands to settle her friends down, then pressing her lips together with her hands up to keep Basil and Alessandra still. "Broc told me that if I act like his fake fiancée till the New Year, he would be happy to pay off my debt."

Alessandra clapped her hands together as a giggle slipped from her lips. "Oh my god, it's happening! It's really happening! You get to live in a real-life rom-com trope! I am so jealous!" She squealed, fisting her hands into a ball as she raised her knees and ran in place with her hands under her chin.

"I'm still calling Becca as backup. When you get back to the shop, give me all the letters you have. If Orson has them, then I'll have Becca get them from the IRS," Basil said.

"Fan-fucking-tastic," Rosie mumbled.

15

Pro Tip: If buds fall off stems before they bloom, try moving them.

The only thing Rosie wanted after dumping her soul—what she liked to call "spilling her guts"—to Basil and Alessandra, was another cup of coffee. It was a two-cups-kind-of-day because she believed that dark steaming liquid could somehow resolve all her problems. With a sigh, Rosie surveyed her empty shop; she decided coffee was definitely the answer. Locking up, she strolled down the sidewalk, her mind blank, too stressed to think, when she passed Broc's building and froze mid-step. The unexpected shouting drifted from the Broc's unfinished floral shop.

"Hey! Lift your end! What the hell are you doing, Adam?" Broc barked, irritation straining through his voice. Rosie couldn't help but peek around the door, a grin creeping onto her face at the familiar banter.

"I am lifting! My hands are raw, Broc, damn it!" Adam yelled, his voice strained and cracked a little as he grunted while readjusting his grip. The playful argument sent Rosie stifling a laugh as she watched from a distance.

"Fuck'n-A! Then stop giving yourself a five-knuckle shuffle all the time, and your hands won't be raw! God...it's like you're scared your dick will fall off if you don't do it daily!" Broc grumbled, frustration edged in his voice.

Adam retorted, "At least I'm rubbing them out, instead of pining and wishing I was rubbing them out like I do! Now lift the stupid dresser!" Rosie couldn't see Adam, only his shoes and lower legs awkwardly maneuvering as Broc struggled to push the dresser around the corner of the stairwell. "Would you just pivot and lift the damn thing? It's caught!" Adam yelled, exasperated.

"You're not my friend right now," Broc said through gritted teeth, clearly over the whole situation. "And I am pivoting! Shut your mouth and lift it over the banister."

"I. AM! FUCKING. PIVOTING!" Adam shouted out, his voice rising with frustration. Rosie chuckled quietly, the scene resembling a scene from *Friends* as Adam's flair for dramatics took over.

Groaning, Broc lifted one thigh, resting the dresser on it, trying to haul it up and over. "You are NOT *Rossing* me right now, Adam," he pointed out, barely holding it together.

Rosie burst out laughing. "I'm sorry, it's just, oh geez...this is amazing, please do continue..." Rosie chuckled, placing her hand on her chest.

"Hey, Rosie," Broc called, turning to her with a weary grin. "Sorry, you have to witness this idiot over here with his *Friends* Tourette-syndrome. I swear, it's a rare disorder."

"PIVOT!" Adam yelled again, the word transforming into a frantic chant, half annoyed, half amused. "PIVOT it, you fucker!" His voice dipped, the demand losing its edge as chuckles slipped through. "PI... V..." But before he could finish, Broc shoved the dresser over the banister, pushing against Adam in the process, causing him to tumble with a loud thump as he landed on his ass. "Ow!!"

"Shut the fuck up, you dick!" Broc growled. "Move your fat ass up the stairs so we can call this a day!"

"I'm hurrying!" Adam laughed. "And you love this ass," he replied, grabbing the dresser again. Rosie doubled over, tears of laughter streaming down her cheeks as she fought to contain her giggles. "Pick it up, Broc! I have to poop! All this laughing and your weak ass is making it touch cloth!"

"Ew, that's fucking disgusting!" Broc mumbled, clearly losing patience.

"It's touching cloth! Hurry, because it's trying to turtle out! Let's move!" Adam bellowed, laughter bubbling in his voice.

Rosie could hardly breathe as her own laughter pulled at her sides.

"Fuck, Broc, I can't hold it!" In a panic, Adam dropped the dresser on the stairs and bolted up to the apartment, his footsteps pounding the floor like a race against time. A door slammed, a groan followed, and the unmistakable sound pure relief. The bathroom door creaked open, and Adam's voice rang out triumphantly. "Oh my god! Broc! You have to come see how long this is!"

Rosie snorted, her hand flying to her mouth as if to hold back the retching laugh that bubbled inside her. Broc just groaned, dropping his head onto the dresser, lifting it and banging it a few times. "Seriously, he's gross. Like, still in the frat house or he's an adult toddler, take your pick." He rubbed his face. "FLUSH THAT TOILET! And if you clog it, use the plunger! And for the love of all that's holy, OPEN A WINDOW AND WASH YOUR HANDS!"

"Killjoy!" Adam's voice echoed from the bathroom. "Broc, I just snapped a pic. Andy is gonna eat this up!" Laughter followed, mixing with the sound of a toilet flush. "Ha! No pun intended! Damn, I was sweating through that! Thought I'd have to borrow a pair of your boxers to get home." His footsteps grew louder as he made his way back to the landing, freshly washed hands wiped on his pants. When he spotted Rosie beside Broc, his face lit up. "Rosie! I just emptied my lower intestine. Took a photo, too, if you're interested."

Shaking her head, Rosie rolled her eyes. "Definitely not. But hey, proud of your achievement. Want a star on your poop board?" She smirked, biting back another laugh.

He planted his hands on his hips, striking a ridiculous pose. "I like you, Rosie. You get it. Daily bowel movements help prevent colon cancer! Now, Broc, quit standing there and help me get this damn dresser upstairs. My cock misses my wildfire back in Seattle."

"Oh my god, Adam," Rosie lamented, rubbing her forehead. "Are you always like this?"

"What? I'm just honest!" His signature grin melted her annoyance; his arms lifted as if he were completely innocent.

"Pick up the fucking dresser, Adam," Broc growled, irritation spilling over.

"Fine, you're such a killjoy," Adam groaned then rolled his eyes with juvenile flair.

THE SUN DIPPED below the horizon, and the cold crept in, biting skin and fogging up the front windows of Broc's new shop. Rosie was sticking around, helping him move the last boxes. The irritation with Broc opening a floral shop right next door had slipped away when she'd learned he wouldn't be selling plants, just floral arrangements instead. He had kept quiet about Mindy's desires to sell plants purely to put Rosie out of business. The plan was to avoid, well, a lot of things about Mindy, which made sense.

Afterwards, the two of them settled onto the new floor of Broc's upstairs living room, digging into pizza. Rosie couldn't help but admire the transformation; his space was striking compared to hers. Everything in her shop still screamed Miss Marigold: old, peeling linoleum floors in nauseating yellow and brown, a pink bathroom that felt like a time warp with its ceramic tiles, and a tub that matched all the tile.

Leaning forward, she lifted the pizza box, grabbing another slice. Broc, being the considerate guy he was, had guessed she wouldn't want meat, landing on the safe choice of cheese. He'd figured she didn't eat chicken, and she had to admit he was spot on.

"Hey," he began, his tone shifting, a seriousness flooding in. "We need to talk about Mindy. She...didn't take the breakup well." He turned to look at her, his expression pensive.

Rosie snorted. "Funny, because from her Instagram post, it looks like you two are still pretty chummy."

Broc kept an eye on Rosie, searching for any flicker of jealousy in her gaze, but he didn't find anything. He let out a heavy sigh and leaned back against the wall, closing his eyes for a moment. "No, that's not how it went down at all. And just so you know, Adam was there."

"Eww, gross." Rosie grimaced, setting the pizza back in its box. "I knew you were close with Adam and your friend group, but..."

Broc raised his hands in mock surrender, a laugh escaping him. "No, no, no," he said, shaking his head with a smile. He shifted to face her, lifting a knee and resting his arm on it. "Adam was in the room while I was telling Mindy that our time had run out. To prove my point, I took my shirt off and snapped a selfie to show her that I didn't need her support on social media for my floral shop."

Rosie listened, watching the way his muscles flexed under his tattooed skin as he gestured. A warmth blossomed in her chest as she sat next to him, studying the way he spoke. There was something about his explanation that made her want to believe him. The photo of Broc with Mindy had hit her like a lightning bolt, stirring up feelings she'd rather have kept buried. Confusion swirled within her; if this was going to work, she needed to distance herself from Broc's world. It was all too easy to get swept up, and sitting here with him felt like a gamble she couldn't afford to take.

"Rules!" Rosie blurted, raising her hand as if counting them off on her fingers.

"Listen...Rosie." He reached out, grasped her hand gently, then pulled it to rest in his lap, rubbing her arm with the other hand. His touch sent sparks through her, igniting her skin and leaving her breathless. "You need to trust me," he said, his voice steady and soothing. "Mindy caught me off guard, took her own photos. I asked her to stop, to leave. But I want to be honest with you, so you don't have to worry about anything." He tugged her closer, his fingers threading through her braided purple hair, trailing down her back in a way that made her shiver. Intense and unyielding eyes stayed on her.

"Broc, I'm not yours," she whispered, trying to sound resolute. "You don't need to answer to me. I'm not going to get attached or feel…anything." But her voice faltered, betraying her.

"That's where you're wrong, Rosie." His tattooed fingers glided down the side of her face, following the curve of her jaw before cupping her chin gently. "If you're going to be my fiancée, fake or not...I promise to respect us." His sincerity rang true, but he didn't voice the deeper feelings swirling within him. All he wanted was for her to feel the same way he did. Because he was in this for the long game. He was already falling for this captivating woman, his thumb tracing the curve of her full, bow-shaped lips, lingering at her lip ring. A soft gasp escaped her, sending a thrill through him as if the tattoos on his skin were alive, intertwining with her own tattoos. His words brushed over her, a gentle whisper that fanned the flames of her attraction. "There won't be anyone else because I don't want anyone else." The softness of his voice wrapped around her like a warm embrace. In that moment, Broc made her feel sheltered, safe in a world that usually felt so sharp-edged; it was then when her defenses crumbled even further still, leaving her heart exposed over an open pizza box.

Rosie was teetering on the edge of falling for Broc, and that thought sent a flutter of panic racing through her veins. She had hoped that by the time the New Year rolled around, the ache of the past would fade, but as the sparks flew between them, she realized it was becoming harder to hold the line. Doubts clung to her like a shadow, the devil's advocate whispering questions in her ear. How could she even consider forgiving him after all the hurt he had caused? After winning her affection, he'd ignored her, pushed her away, and tossed her aside like a weed on the side of his path.

Yet, even with all those reservations clawing at her, a part of her wanted to trust him. When Broc leaned in, closing his eyes, Rosie followed suit, their lips meeting in a collision. The scent that encircled her was a concoction of something uniquely his, mixed with bergamot and a hint of cedar. It filled her lungs, igniting a warmth that surged through her, flipping her stomach and squeezing her heart tight against her ribs.

It hurt.

She reached up, instinctively rubbing the dull ache between her breasts, but Broc caught her hand, coaxing it to rest against his chest. With a teasing nip at her lower lip, he pulled back just enough to gauge her reaction, his gaze lingering on her swollen mouth. She bit down on her bottom lip, a nervous twitch, before Broc's hunger got the better of him. His hands slid up her arms and gently cradled her neck, fingers tangling in her braid as he pulled her into a kiss that was tender and but held so much persistence.

Rosie tried to resist, to protest against the heat of his lips, but the moment the tip of his tongue sought entry, her resolve melted away. A soft moan escaped her, swallowed by him as he rolled her onto her back. *What was she doing?* a voice screamed inside her head. She wanted to say no, to beg him to stop, but the fire igniting between them stifled her voice.

Broc moved swiftly but with a grace that sent shivers through her. He settled over her, pressing himself against her belly, making his intentions painfully clear. The way his hand moved across her body, along with his lips and tongue, kept Rosie's mind from allowing what was happening to sink in. The way he touched her body was the only thing she was focused on. And the feel of how Broc rocked his hips into her body, and how his cock rested at the apex of her thighs, was nothing short of perfection. With sweet abandonment, he continued to thrust into her, both fully clothed; he watched as she started to come undone under his body. A series of kisses lined over her jaw, as Broc licked and sucked her chin, while his hands pulled her head back, exposing her neck for his slow assault on that delicate, exposed skin. The heat that unfurled inside her core had Rosie meeting his grind, with the same movements, matching his hip pushes. The feeling had him growing to almost an impossible size, a thickness he'd never felt before, pressing against the zipper of his jeans, making an indentation on his dick.

"Broc," she gasped, his name floating in the air like a prayer from the heavens. And that was all it took for him to cum in his pants like a teenager. The impossible girth was still begging to seek entrance into her wetness, the heat of hers which could be felt through her clothes. His grinding was relentless. The beautiful show before him, Rosie's back arched, her neck straining as Broc pulled it back, wrapping his fingers firmly around her thick purple braid. The way her mouth fell agape as her legs trembled, gasping for air, her lungs pleading for relief—it was a beautiful sight. Broc plunged his tongue inside her mouth, swirling it, helping her to breathe as she worked her way down from her climax. Their kiss was wet and messy as his free hand slipped down and unhooked her overall bib, palmed her breast. The guttural cry that escaped her throat hit him hard again in seconds. His body shoved into Rosie with such great force that her breasts shook with each thrust until she cried out, hissing, "Broc, Broc... ahhh, yes...harder..." Her nails biting into his shoulders as he pushed her through another orgasm.

Doubts clung to her like a weight, the devil whispering all the things she dared not say. How could she ever think about forgiving him after he'd shattered her world? He was the man who had picked up her heart and tossed it aside like yesterday's news after winning her over.

But god, he feels so good, Rosie argued with herself.

16

Pro Tip: Don't forget to water weekly; spray when the air is dry in between waterings.

"What the hell happened to my dignity last night?" Rosie muttered under her breath as she wrestled with her tangled thoughts. Today, she threw on her favorite chunky cream cardigan over a purple t-shirt emblazoned with the words "I'd propagate that." The IRS papers in her hand were a damn reminder of all the confusion she'd let spill over her desk and into drawers. She was on a mission to get it all sorted out, heading to the Little Café to drop off the paper trail. Becca was stepping in to handle Rosie's legal case pro bono, and that alone helped ease some of the tightness in her chest, though it still lingered like an unwanted guest.

Mixed in with the paperwork was a sly little note, just a plain white scrap of paper with the number 36 scrawled on it. The childish threat annoyed Rosie, but there was a silver lining: at least she didn't have to see his face while he played these games.

A flush spread from her chest, a warm rush that tingled under her skin as it worked its way up to her cheeks, heat flooding her ears in embarrassment. She could practically hear her heartbeat pounding against her ribcage, just thinking about the night before—with Broc, and his very sexy cock, and that feeling. What was even more embarrassing was how Rosie had handled herself after that mind-blowing sex. She'd bolted from Broc's apartment, leaving him to wonder what the hell had just happened because it was the same thing she kept asking herself. The phone kept buzzing with his name, and she couldn't find a way to answer his calls. She couldn't shake him either. Broc was never hers; she'd never belonged to him, not really. Their little charade, that carefully constructed façade of a relationship, was bound to crumble after the New Year. She knew, deep down, that it was all set up to end in heartbreak. Who would walk away without a scratch or a broken heart? One thing was clear: it would never be her.

This was why she had to keep him at arm's length, shield her heart from further damage, especially after last night. Yet here she was, drawn to him like a moth to a flame, battling the familiar ache he'd left in her chest, staring at her cell as another call went to voicemail. Was it attraction? Hormones? A reckless combination of both? Whatever it was, she needed to get it under control before it consumed her entirely. It was probably already too late, the way her chest was aching.

Lost in thought, head down and eyes glued to the crumpled paper in her hand, Rosie didn't notice Broc stepping out of his shop until he blocked her path. "Whoa there, Rosie," he said, wrapping his long fingers around her shoulder and halting her mid-step. "Where are you off to?" The thoughtful intensity of his presence made it hard to breathe as he leaned in, searching for her gaze.

"Oof, Broc, what the hell?" Rosie grumbled, irritation bubbling beneath the surface. He was the last person she wanted to deal with right now, but somehow, he was the only one that she wanted to be around; a conundrum to say the least.

"What's got you in such a hurry?" His eyes were full of that damn curiosity she couldn't shake, like he was the one trying to dig into her thoughts. "You left so fast. Are you okay?" He lifted his hand, fingertips trailing down her cheek. Without thinking, she leaned into his touch, warmth flooding her despite her intention to pull away.

"Please, stop," she whispered, eyes fluttering shut as she turned her face away, her eyes burning. *Yep, this has got to be hormones*, she thought.

Broc's hand froze, his fingers gently cupping her face as he leaned closer, studying her eyes. "Rosie, tell me what's going on." His thumb traced the line of her jaw. When silence lingered, he glanced down at the papers she clutched tightly in her grip. Instantly, recognition flashed through his eyes, and the weight of unspoken words pressed heavily between them. "Did he come back this morning? Did Orson threaten you? Please tell me," he growled, frustration spilling over as he snatched the paper from her hand. All Rosie could do was shake her head, a lump lodged firmly in her throat. All her spite flew out the window. "He slipped this into your shop?" he pressed. She nodded slowly, and he pocketed the threat, carefully taking the stack of papers and gripping them tightly away from Rosie. Each finger walked over the envelopes and letters, flipping through them, his lips pressed into a tighter line, anger simmering with each clench of his jaw. "Shit, Rosie, this is insane," he muttered, shaking his head in disbelief.

Panic gripped Rosie like a vise, the chill of winter creeping into her bones as stress flooded her veins. Everything felt insurmountable, all of the unpaid bills which were piling up, and the lack of customers; they seemed to be nowhere. She had known long ago that she'd need to manage her finances better, often choosing between food and utilities. How many times had she put off luxuries, leaving her apartment cold to save on bills? How often did she stop at the food bank, prioritizing chicken feed over basic needs?

"I'm taking these to Basil; her wife offered to help me, pro bono." Her voice trembled, the fight draining from her as the weight of it all pressed down hard. The tightness in her chest intensified, urging her to rub her sternum to soothe the pressure. The biting air cut through her, and she stepped forward, eager to escape the chill that was making her skin freeze. When she pushed past Broc, her hand reached out, snatching the stack of envelopes and papers he held, tucking them securely under her arm. "Sorry," she mumbled. "I'm cold, and I really need to get these to Basil before she leaves." Then slipped by Broc but came to an abrupt halt when he seized her upper arm and spun her around.

"Rosie, you're my fiancée." His eyes seemed to say things, but the words that escaped his lips were far more complicated.

"Fake," Rosie interjected.

Those words didn't sit well coming off her tongue, the same tongue he felt swirling with his in a messy kiss, but he ignored her comment. "I'll take care of this. I don't want you fighting a battle that could drag on for months. I've got the money, so let me handle it because I said I would."

"Broc, that's not what you said. You promised that after the New Year, once I acted like your fiancée and went to that end-of-the-year party in Seattle, you'd pay for it."

"I know what I said, but I want to pay this off now. I don't want Orson's threats hanging over your head, and it wouldn't sit right with me to stroll through Spokane, knowing you've got this burden weighing you down." He lowered his firm voice. Rosie felt every nerve in her body scream to argue, but she was tangled in a secret agreement with Broc. The stress was creeping in, manifesting like a storm inside her, physically and emotionally, and it settled in her heart because the ache was creeping back. No words came to counter him, only action: she rubbed her chest, walked down the sidewalk, pushed open the door to the Little Café, and surrendered to the warmth and aroma of fresh coffee.

Basil and Alessandra greeted her with bright smiles, but Rosie didn't need to look back to know Broc was right behind her, invading her personal space. She could feel the heat radiating from him, the intoxicating scent of bergamot and cedar wrapping around her like a shroud. Every cell in her body vibrated with an unwanted temperature, wishing for his hands to skim her skin, while heads turned and phones came out to capture their intimate moment. A wave of unease washed over her at the thought of all those invasive clicks, knowing the social media world beyond the café would eat up their moment. She froze, and Broc, sensing her discomfort, lowered his hand to the small of her back, guiding her forward as strangers filmed them.

Rosie felt trapped, aware that this moment would soon go viral, its fallout and an impending Mindy-storm to be bracing for. The backlash was hers to bear, and the thought of it made her chest tighten. Broc, on the other hand, seemed unfazed by the phones pointed at him; his world long since hardened by the spotlight. But the way he turned to the teenagers, his voice smooth and steady, sent a small rush of tingles through her. "Please, no more," he said, and their flushed faces told her they were as starstruck as anyone could be.

Broc leaned closer, his fingers brushing against Rosie's shoulders, catching her long purple braids and tucking them back over her shoulder. When he wrapped his arm around her, pulling her close, everything else fell away. Instinctively, she leaned against him, resting her head on his chest as she breathed in his scent and let the tension slowly dissipate. It felt like he'd peeled away the weight of the world, allowing her to exhale, to sag against him as the pressure lifted from her shoulders. Broc drank in this moment, wanting to savor it, to pack it tight and lock it away as his secret. He took the papers from her hands, moving closer to the counter where Alessandra beamed at them like a kid on Christmas morning. Her smile was wide, bordering on giddy.

"Rosie said she needed to bring these to Basil," he said, pulling the papers from Rosie's grip. "I'm paying them off now. Just to tell Orson to shove it."

Basil crossed her arms, a mischievous grin spreading across her face, and pointed at Broc with a playful glint in her eye. "I like him," she declared, leaning forward as if she'd just found a treasure. "Ever think about a threesome?" Broc's eyebrows shot up at the same time as he cleared his throat, and Rosie groaned with embarrassment.

Being as smooth as he could without raising a scene, Broc recovered quickly, shaking his head with a grin. "Maybe a long time ago, but not now." Finishing as he looked down at Rosie and kissed the top of her head. An act that a true fiancé would do.

"Bummer. There could still be time," Basil teased back with a wink.

The weirdness finally broke when Broc's phone chimed in his pocket, but he brushed it aside, focusing on Basil once more. "I've got this, so tell your wife she's not needed." He shot a glance at Rosie, whose fingers were once again rubbing the tension over her chest, before she looked back to him.

"Fine, but don't hold it against her," Basil replied, her sympathetic eyes narrowing with resolve. "You'd be no better than Orson, and I'll get my wife to be all over your ass...and not in a good way."

"Never," Broc responded with sincerity, the kind that left no room for doubt. Rosie's debt was about to vanish, slipping away in the next 7–10 business days, along with the looming threat from Orson. Broc had made sure of it, quietly slipping into Alessandra's backroom to make that fateful call to the IRS. Payments would be extracted straight from his personal checking account, leaving Rosie debt free.

Alessandra cleared her throat. "Well, that was fun!" She clapped her hands together, a spark of mischief in her eyes. "Alright, Rosie, I'll grab your usual."

17

Pro Tip: Calculate the maturity dates for when you need to plant seeds in the season.

For the rest of the day, Rosie felt a lightness she hadn't felt in weeks; the weight in her chest had lifted, and genuine smiles crept onto her lips as she settled into a sense of normalcy. A chill danced through the air as the Spokane weather shifted. After securing the shop's front door behind her and letting Fluffy explore the back room, she immersed herself in the plants, watering and pruning, finding her happy place once more. Lost in her routine, a knock echoed against the glass front door. Peering through the window, she was surprised to see Broc standing there. The playfulness in his eyes ignited a flutter in her stomach, and he lifted his hand in a casual wave.

"Hey," she called out as she unlocked the door, pulling it wide enough for him to step inside.

"Hey, come over. I need your opinion on something," Broc requested, gesturing her closer.

Rosie's brow furrowed. "Me? Why?"

"Just trust me," he insisted, reaching across the threshold to grab her arm, gently pulling her along after ensuring her shop was secure. "Okay, look...which one do you think?" He pointed at a wall draped with three stunning shades of deep blue-gray.

"Paint?" she questioned, her curiosity piqued.

"Yep. Mindy picked these out and mentioned they're trendy or whatever. I was only half listening. So, which do you prefer? I've got the painters coming in tomorrow, and all the floral fridges, tables, and countertops are set to arrive this week. This place will be up and running in no time."

Rosie surveyed the stark space, disbelief etched on her features. "How? There's nothing here." She spun around, taking in the exposed brick and the sheetrock leaning against the walls like abandoned dreams. "There's no way."

Smirking, Broc pulled her into a hug, their bodies colliding seamlessly, igniting sensations that rippled through her. Leaning in closer, he whispered in a low, teasing tone, "If you throw enough money at people, things get done."

"Bragging about your wealth in front of someone who can barely imagine that kind of spending is a bit rude," she replied.

His expression softened. "That was rude of me." His breath, hot and tantalizing against her skin, sent a shiver coursing through her. They stood there, breaths mingling, a heady heat spreading through her core. "Tell me, fiancée, which one do you like?" Teasing each heartbeat until words escaped her. Instead, she nodded toward the deepest blue-gray sample on the far right. "Excellent choice," he said, wrapping an arm around her waist and spinning them to face the swatches. "That color matches your eyes perfectly," he mused, pressing a gentle kiss to her temple. A new feeling that Rosie decided she liked.

Slowly, Rosie looked over her shoulder to glance up at him, her heart racing as he studied her. His dark eyes traced her features with an intensity that made her pulse quicken, memorizing each freckle and dimple as a secret map only he could read. With a swift motion, Broc gripped her narrow hips, turning her in his hold. His long fingers squeezing her sides sent a thrill racing through her. Stepping closer, he pushed her back against the wall, their bodies aligning as he held her firmly. "Fiancée," he murmured, his hands gliding from her hair to the sides of her face; every touch sent a pulsing throb between her thighs and made her stomach flip. His lips descended again, brushing against hers, catching the soft gasp from her lips. The kiss, unhurried, sent his mind spiraling, igniting a hunger that was almost unbearable. Rosie knew, today would not be the day that she needed to set more boundaries; today would be a day to simply feel. Rosie knew she shouldn't. She knew it was wrong, so when Rosie heard her own voice say "yes," she surprised herself. The cry from the back of her throat matched his heady desire as his hands slipped down her body, unhooking her overalls and watching them drop to the floor. He grabbed under her knees, forcing her to wrap her legs around his waist once more. Pressing her tight against the wall, Broc slipped his hand between their bodies and made quick work, unzipping and unbuttoning his pants and pulling her thong to the side.

Slipping his fingers into her heat, she was unbelievably slick, making his cock grow to an uncomfortable size. Now that it was free, its velvety length jutted up between their bodies. Broc's strong fingers wrapped around his cock, pulling it with a few tugs as he aimed his tip, crowning her pussy. She inhaled and, in a swift movement, he plunged deep inside her. The only sounds in the room were the echoes of her cries, his heavy breathing, and a long-winded moan from the fullness of his body stretching Rosie wide. The delicious stretch had her throwing her head back, hitting the hard wall. The pain in her head was nothing to her because she loved how stretched she felt, and his gyrations had Rosie's mind in a mess of feelings while his slicked cock slid in and out with every thrust rocking against her center. Her hands slid down his neck, Rosie gasping and matching his grunts. That's when she peered over his shoulder and caught a deep glare from a man on the other side of the window—Orson.

His beady eyes pinned Rosie down with a predatory intensity, like a hunter sizing up his prey. The way Orson's chest heaved, a menacing rhythm fueled by anger, was all too familiar, a dark mark of hatred etched deep across his features. He absentmindedly swiped at his nose, the telltale gesture that sent shivers down her spine. Yet another sign that he was slipping back into his old ways.

Rosie's smile wavered, the realization crashing over her like ice water;: she'd stoked the fury within him, the beast she dreaded. But within that fear, a flicker of hope ignited; maybe, just maybe, he would finally understand that she was done playing his games. The thrill of his unfiltered gaze didn't repulse her; it exhilarated her. She wanted him to know she was free, unbroken, and refused to be caged by his darkness.

His lips curled back in a snarl, teeth bared as he pushed his sunglasses off, the grip around them tightening to the point of cracking. He hurled the shattered pieces onto the cement, his eyes still locked onto hers, a silent battle raging between them. And Rosie? She met his glare head-on, unflinching, daring him.

Broc slid his hand under her shirt and palmed her breast, pinching her nipple, causing her to cry out. "More, Broc, harder," Rosie begged, gasping for breath while staring at Orson, challenging him. The tightness in Rosie's body intensified, waves of pleasure rippling through her as Broc assaulted her in the best way, fucking her hard against the wall. Rosie met him, stroke after stroke, her pussy welcoming his thick cock, till he slipped his hand between them and rubbed at her bundle of nerves, sending her off into the stars. A whirlwind of emotion within Rosie's body lifted her to euphoric heights as he kissed her eagerly, igniting a fire within Broc's body; he was not far behind her.

The swell of his cock made it almost impossible to fuck her tight pussy, but he continued to grind into her. Inhaling deeply with each grunt and sob, her scent invaded his body, a smell he'd memorize. Broc slammed a hand against the wall next to Rosie's head, his tongue licking up her thin column; the sweet sweat tasted like honey as he lapped it up. The embers burning his core erupted as soon as Rosie lost all sense of time and space. The same feeling inched to engulf him, sending a flame coursing through his veins, tears threatening to fall over the edge of his eyes as he cried out his pleasure.

Blindness crept over as he strained his neck, lifting his head, exposing the strength of his body as he exploded inside Rosie, filling every inch of her with ropes of cum, coating her like the paint on the wall.

Slowing down, with his renewed determination, he pushed harder into her again, his knuckles white as he forced all his willpower to slowly fuck through their shared orgasm. Leaning his forehead against Rosie's, his breath caught in his open mouth, and he tenderly lowered her legs and withdrew his cock from her body. His fingers traced soft patterns on her face, exploring every feature as his eyes drank in the moment of her post-sex flush on her skin. With each passing second, he found himself falling that much more deeply, unable to resist the magnetic pull of her presence.

She rested her head on his shoulder as he pulled her close, wrapping his strong arms around her, a sense of safety. Peering over Broc's shoulder, all Rosie saw was the sun sinking slowly into the scenery through the front windows of Broc's building. A smile spread across her face, relieved to see that Orson had finally caught on and walked away, leaving her to bask in Broc's hold.

"I think we need new rules," Rosie declared with a snort.

"I think if you don't put your pants back on, I might fuck you again," Broc warned.

Rosie snorted again, rubbing her face into Broc's shoulder.

18

Pro Tip: Use sticky paper to kill the fruit flies that are attracted to the nectar.

Throughout the week, Raymond and his construction crew worked on the floral shop, putting in long hours. At the same time, Broc had been up late most nights, actively promoting the launch of the floral shop on his social media account. He even reached out to Kerry, his former mentor, inviting him to stop by for a brief meet-and-greet during the grand opening. But the best news that Broc had received so far? An email from Netflix Productions. They wanted to use his floral shop as a promotional location for the upcoming release of their historical romance movie. A happy coincidence for the two of them. The best part was that this would be simple for Broc, as he was the lead florist on set during the filming of said movie.

"Wait, Raymond," Broc said to Raymond as soon as he entered his floral shop. Raymond was packing pallets, ready to toss them into the dumpster. "Don't toss out those pallets; let's put them up on the wall. I have this cool idea I saw on Pinterest, and I found these hooks; we can attach them to a couple of them," Broc explained, walking over to the counter and picking up the small brass hooks. "I want the pallets to be a feature wall, so don't break them down. Just hang them." With a nod, Raymond got to work placing them on the wall.

The floral shop was coming together quickly, and standing in the middle of the shop, with Broc's hands on his hips, a smile finally broke over his face. The bank of refrigerators was front and center upon entry, waiting for the flower deliveries. In the center of the shop, Broc's floral-cutting counter stood proudly, and the vases and other floral containers were already waiting for his creative touch. Floral foam, tape, and wires were packed into every cupboard under the countertop, and the green recycle bin was ready. To the right in the shop, where the wall of pallets was being hung, was a new seating area. A golden-belted Moser couch was the centerpiece, flanked by two elegant wingback leather chairs. On the sleek, modern coffee table, stacks of floral magazines rested. While soaking in his shop, and the guys walking about, Broc's cell phone pinged. Reaching for his back pocket, he pulled it out and tapped the screen. The alert was another photo Mindy had posted on her social media, tagging him. It was of him wrapping his hands around her shoulder as they'd walked together on the beach months ago. Seeing this was an instant annoyance. These little posts she'd been doing had been aggravating, a tactic that Mindy was using to keep their relationship looking alive and well. And also, a passive-aggressive way to make Rosie look like she was a wedge between Broc and Mindy's loving relationship. The worst part was that Broc had no idea how many of these old photos she had stockpiled on her cell, but knowing her, she probably had a lot.

Broc lifted his hand, rubbing the bridge of his nose, and shaking his head as he dialed Mindy's number. Per usual, she picked up instantly because her cell was glued to her hand. "Remove it," Broc said without saying hello.

"Oh, baby, I miss you too. I'm glad you loved the photo," she purred into the speaker.

"No, not missing you. Our time ran its course; I've already told you so. We're done. Stop dragging out this shit. Stop posting, just stop," Broc said through gritted teeth, balling his free hand into a fist.

"Aw, baby. Don't worry. As soon as I finish a few things, I'll be on the first flight back." In the background, Broc could hear the chatter of a group of people standing around Mindy; he knew she was acting for them, keeping up the charade.

"No, fucking no, Mindy. Isn't happening—" he tried to say, but Mindy cut him off. It wasn't until Broc heard the clicking of her heels on the sidewalk that he knew she was walking away from the group of people she had been standing near.

Mindy's true personality came out once she was away from her audience. Then she seethed into the phone in a hushed tone, "No, you listen to me; remember the importance of appearing in a stable relationship to secure movie roles? You have no idea the influence in the movie industry that my ex, Colin Peters, has; he's all but blacklisted me, after I tried...never mind." She sighed. "Our *dating* has been helping me to get back into the directors' good graces again. So, no. I. Will. Not. Stop." She huffed. "And if I were you, I'd stop touching that dirt-girl because I keep getting fucking DMs from my fans asking if I know about your little side-cunt!"

"Watch your mouth, Mindy. I won't have you talking about Ros—"

It didn't matter what he was about to say because Mindy cut him off again. "You're mine, Broc. End of story. I'm coming back to claim what's mine. And trust me, I have no qualms about ruining anything that means something to her. Keep your fucking paws off that dirt because the *Mindys* are watching." With that, she hung up.

Tossing his head back, he yelled, "FUCK!

"Something wrong?"

Broc turned as he was greeted by a melodious voice; his gaze met the most captivating woman—his purple-haired vixen. With his eyes softening, he approached Rosie, delicately caressing her face with the back of his hand, then stepping closer and wrapping his other hand around her waist, pulling her closer to his body. Needing to feel her, touch her, and kiss her.

“Rosie,” he said, dipping down to kiss her on her forehead. “I’ve missed you.”

With narrowed eyes and a subtle head tilt, she considered her response carefully before speaking. “Perhaps, but that doesn’t explain why you cursed to the ceiling just now. Is something wrong with the room?” she questioned, her gaze sweeping across the floral shop with curiosity. “Because from what I see, this room looks like it's from a magazine.” With a smile playing on her lips, her finger tapped her upper lip as she turned slightly away from Broc. “You were right; if you throw enough money at people, things happen,” she quietly whispered.

Broc studied her, his eyes roaming her body; soon every bloom in his shop would match the intricate designs of her tattoos, which twisted and coiled gracefully around her legs, spiraled up to her breasts, and wrapped elegantly around her shoulders, draping over her arms like a tapestry of nature's artistry. He loved how she looked like a forbidden garden. It was something he’d thought of after their amazing sex the other day. He loved the ink that she had, and he wanted something that would remind him daily of her pretty pussy and gorgeous ink.

“No, vixen, everything is perfect; you’re just as perfect. This room is you. I was dealing with some work stuff, trying to clear it up,” Broc responded. He gently slid his hand down her arm, tracing her tattoos until he interlocked his fingers with hers.

She smiled back at him as she stepped away from his hold, but the coldness between them was unsettling to Broc. “You know, we don’t have to pretend when no one is around,” Rosie said, lifting her hand as she tried to pull away from his. Instead, he tightened his hold as he stepped forward, cupping her face. Using his thumb, he captured her earlobe and gently rubbed it.

“Rosie, I can’t pretend anymore, and when I’m in front of people, I won’t be pretending because what I feel is real. I've told you that I don't want to see anyone because you're my everyone." His eyes studied hers momentarily, allowing her to drink in his words. “Standing by you, holding your hand, is what I want. What I need is all of you, every inch, and I don't usually step away from something I want. I know we had a rocky start, but I want to straighten out our future and see how it grows."

Rosie's eyes widened in surprise as the weight of his words sank in, stirring a flurry of emotions within her. "But it was fake... For Orson, and you wanted a way out for Mindy." As she attempted to say the words, they felt hollow even as they left her lips. Deep down, Rosie knew that nothing about Broc was fake, and she no longer wanted it to be. She was like a crow, her grudges were strong, but the confusion settled in her thoughts because she liked that he had a dream—and really liked how he hated Mindy, a shared hatred to bond over. Maybe slightly unhealthy, but she reminded herself that she'd never really followed the rules. And there, standing right in front of her, a little closer now, Broc shifted on his feet, and she realized she wanted to be with him too, regardless of their past. Because that past still sent her down the same road and into his arms, even if it had been a little bumpy along the way.

"I don't think I'm really a crow," Rosie whispered as she wrapped her arms around his neck, pulling him closer, brushing her lips against his.

"I'm glad because you're much more beautiful than a crow," Broc murmured against her lips before pressing his lips onto hers, taking hers fully and feeling the weight of her body fall into his hold completely.

"But I can hold grudges like a crow," she said between kisses.

"I can deal with that."

19

Pro Tip: Always check the soil's moisture before filling it with water.

The look on Broc's face says everything as he steps forward and rests his hands on either side of Rosie's neck, sending a shuddered breath from her mouth. The sound makes his cock rock hard in mere seconds. The tumult in her chest beat against her ribcage. At the same time, the beginnings of a squall twisted and flipped inside her belly, swirling and winding throughout every part of her, sending waves of pleasure throughout. Wetness seeped out of her center, the telltale sign that she also couldn't do fake anymore.

"Nothing is fake to me, Rosie. Nothing. My life is surrounded by one of the most beautiful shades of purple..." His eyes dropped over Rosie's lips and then back up as his thumb and finger rubbed a small strand of violet hair that fell across her blue-violet eyes.

A quiet whisper, so silent that Broc almost missed the words, the admission that confirmed what was happening between them. "Not fake, this isn't fake."

Broc didn't hesitate to shake his head before leaning closer to peer into Rosie's eyes. Prickling needles danced at the back of Rosie's throat, but she remained transfixed by the breathtaking view before her. His gentle breath rustled her hair, sending it drifting across her nose in gentle tendrils.

She wanted him.

For Broc, the feeling inside his chest was an intense, primal energy that surged through his body, awakening a visceral carnage. It was a feral feeling of obsession, a feeling of possession. He wanted to taste her, devour that sweet nectar on her lips. Seconds later, his mouth slammed down onto her lips, his tongue pushing past that perfect bowtie, locking in a deep, slow, passionate assault. It was his breathing that calmed Rosie's heartbeat again as he pushed more of Rosie's stray hair out of her face. He then brought his thumb to the corner of her lips, softly rubbing her cheek, then brought it to his mouth, sucking it like you would after a meal.

His heated stare held Rosie frozen, and then something pulled at every inch of her clothes-covered skin; her mind was begging for something. It was begging for his hands, his rough, calloused fingers to pull her tighter against his chest. She took a deep breath, then leaned back into his kiss, crushing her mouth to his, while he sucked on her tongue. A deep whimper filled her throat, but he kissed her back and continued to attack her while his hand wandered over her breasts. Saliva dripped from his lips, as he sucked and licked, nibbing and kissing around her mouth. Their kiss was messy, but it was everything to both of them.

Taking her waist in one hand, he dipped his forehead to hers, only to stare deep into her uniquely colored eyes. Every inch of Broc's clothing touched his skin, reminding him that there were too many layers on between the two of them. The room began to spin, but the only thing Rosie could see was his dark eyes. The scent of her made his eyes darken further, and his nostrils flared with an aromatic need. The taut muscles under his shirt, the thin layer that hid his tattoos as they crept up his tanned skin before disappearing back under the sleeves of his shirt, had Rosie wanting him to remove that shirt, and quickly. Rosie's mind was spinning with so many thoughts, but the most prominent one was how badly she wanted to be under his body. She wanted to be draped in a beautiful display, his personal canvas, solely by the ink etched on his skin. Broc's dark eyes filled hers as he dipped down and nipped at the shell of her ear while his hands roamed and cupped her breasts. His thumbs rolled over her nipples, forcing them to pebble. Those calloused hands then cupped her between her legs, rubbing his palms over her pussy, readying it for his thickness.

"Broc, please," she whispered. All cognitive thoughts left Broc's brain, leaving him to be a sex slave to the siren who stood before him, pulling Broc deeper into the caverns of lust. And any thought she'd had of a crow flapped away in the winds.

Rosie lost her footing, and in an instant, Broc scooped her up in a bridal-style embrace, swiftly ascending the stairs to his bedroom. Kicking the door open, he dropped her down on the mattress and watched as her long braids recoiled and landed over her shoulders while her breasts bounced. A growl erupted from Broc's throat as he watched every soft curve of Rosie's body move under his penetrating stare. Reaching down, Broc lunged forward, wrapping his fingers around her ankles, and pulled her down to the edge of the bed. His warm hands seeped into her skin, causing her to gasp while her eyes fluttered closed, and a tingling sensation shot up her legs.

"Take off your clothes," Broc growled; he was already unbuttoning and unzipping his black, ripped jeans. The leather belt slid through the belt loops, loosening with each tug till it broke free and whipped out with a *snap.* The ripple in Rosie's tummy churned with an unsatisfied feeling that coursed through her body. This force gripped her across her abdomen as her body craved the feel and stretch of his cock, reminiscing on how it once burned with a delectable intensity years ago, then again, the other day. Catching her breath, she watched each muscle flex as his broad chest leaned over her body, snapping the belt in his hands. "Ready, for me again?" His breath resonated loudly in Rosie's ears. "I'll make you feel good." Her lungs momentarily forgot to draw breath, leaving a burning sensation across her chest, begging for air.

The dark glint in his eyes warmed her stomach, while he locked his hands around her wrists, and a harder irritation crawled under her skin. At the same time, she gently rubbed her thighs together, trying to relieve the ache in her center. The leather strap tightened around her thin column, oblivious to her struggle as she tried to regulate her breathing. His eyes were almost impossible to read under the shadow of his brow, making Rosie's heart skip a beat. Broc cinched the belt tighter, not to the point of choking her, but enough to evoke euphoria, which he knew would wash over her. Desperate to relieve the pressure building in her pussy, to release the cord that was tightening around her stomach.

"Trust me, vixen, trust me to make you feel things you've never felt." He pressed a kiss against her lips, forcing her to open for him; their tongues met, his chest pressed against her breasts. And then with a lower growl he said, "I'm not going to hurt you; I'm just going to drink in your sweet nectar." He unbuckled her overalls and pulled them down her body, allowing them to pool on the floor, exposing her black lacy thong. Hooking his thumbs under her panties, he slipped them down her legs. Socks and shoes were next, tossed across the room. His eyes followed along the contours of her fine-line floral and berry tattoos, how they snaked up her slender, pale physique. "You're perfect."

Hands skimmed up her legs while his kisses made their way to her pussy, his fingers digging into her thighs, leaving faint bruises in the shape of fingerprints as he spread her thighs open for him, making room for his broad shoulders. Bathing in her arousal, her pussy, tight and beautiful, ready for the taking, he bent his head, inhaling her honeysuckle aroma. Flicking his tongue out, he dipped into her slickness while taking a deep inhale. The beating of his heart went into arrhythmia from the intensity of this woman's slippery, wet cunt. The pheromones flooding from her center were enough to knock him out, but instead, they unfolded and tugged him into her body; pleasure roared inside his own center, sending his cock to an uncomfortable size. Rubbing his lips over her throbbing wet pussy, he buried his face between her folds as he lapped from her anus to her little bean. She gasped and let out a moan as his tongue nibbled around that bundle of nerves. The moan from her lips was loud; she loved it when he did that, and he did it again, feeling her tightness, tasting her sweetness. His cock seeped pre-cum when he continued to eat her pussy as he undid his zipper, releasing the pressure from his hardened cock. Her hips shot off the bed as Broc dipped his tongue back into her center, and then with a long lap, he sucked at her slick lips.

His hands held her inner thighs down, pressing and opening her pussy wide as she tried to wiggle away from the beautiful quiver Broc was forcing onto her. Holding her open, he skimmed his hands up to her folds; opening those lower lips, he plunged his tongue back inside her. Inhaling once more as the perfume of her sex spilled into his bedroom, he spat on her pussy, the string of saliva coating her with his warmth. Using his fingers, he swirled her clit, mixing and coating her heat, pushing his finger inside, a small taste of what his dick would be feeling in just a minute.

"More, please," Rosie pleaded. A smile lifted on the side of Broc's lips as he plunged two fingers deep inside her, while his tongue lapped the wetness that leaked down her ass. Sucking her clit while his fingers pushed against to where his mouth was hungrily feasting from, slipping his long finger inside her body, Rosie started to rock her hips.

"Greedy little vixen," he chuckled, his voice a playful whisper. Looking down her slender body, as it was lying open for him, Broc smiled as he watched her eager little pussy suck his finger in as if it were devouring its final meal. Thrusting his finger deep and hard inside her, he forced a cry out of her from the back of her throat.

"Ahh, oh my god." And then she settled into the sweetest moan as she arched her back, echoing off the walls. A blinding white liquid heat coursed throughout her body, and she couldn't contain her writhing under Broc. The sounds of his hand thrusting inside her wetness filled the room, tightening her core to an impossible rigidity, along with that feeling of the impending climax she was about to reach.

His hair tickled her thighs, but her groans and moans were the only sounds she uttered; her fingers clutched his dark curly mop as she wrapped her legs around Broc's head while he devoured her heat. His mouth conquered her, bringing her closer and closer to her precipice with every sweep of his tongue. Two fingers methodically pushed deep inside her wetness, moving them in and out again, while his lips sucked, pulling her small bundle of nerves into his mouth. The taunt, coiling cord within Rosie's body started to build and intensify as all the blood rushed from all her limbs, sending a shiver down her spine, a sensation so intense it made her toes curl, a delightful numbness filling every inch inside her body.

"Please, Broc, I need more," Rosie begged. "Please." She squeezed her eyes shut, struggling to contain the sanity, a force to be reckoned with, ready to burst free from her skin.

"Come on me, come on my face, fill my mouth, coat my tongue, because I'm a hungry bastard." Broc's voice dropped to a low, commanding tone, so deep that it caught her off guard, sending her off. Head tilted back as the sparks exploded behind her eyelids. "Look at me," Broc demanded, leveling with her as their chests rose and fell. The sheets started to pull up as Rosie's fists squeezed the sheets while she gasped for breath.

"I can't! I can't! I'm coming!"

"I need to see those gorgeous eyes of yours." Slowly, she lifted her head, locking eyes with his dark irises.

"Don't stop, I'm there...please don't stop. I-I need you to stretch me."

Broc chuckled because this was the woman he wanted, one who begged for him. The woman who knew what she wanted. "That's it, baby girl, keep your eyes on me." With his two fingers in her cunt, his pinkie teasing her tight ring, he lowered his head and sucked on her clit, while his other hand snaked up her body and began to pinch and roll her peaked nipple. Her pretty little breasts bobbed back and forth, and Broc ran his free hand up and down her body, squeezing her tit, holding her face, and wrapping his arm around her neck. Rosie's body took everything Broc was giving her. It had been a long time since he'd felt this way for another woman. She wasn't just a hole to fill and spill into, not Rosie. He wanted more with her, and feeling that meant something a lot more to him.

The rise of her lungs was faster, shorter, stronger. She breathed through her teeth and, with a slam of her hands on the mattress, she arched her back and tightened that pretty pink pussy around Broc's fingers, her tight ring squeezing his pinkie as she screamed, gasping for air.

"Oh my god," Rosie gasped as she relaxed back onto the mattress, and Broc worked her through her orgasm with slower strokes from his tongue. Now his two fingers pushed deep inside her body, turning and curling onto the rough patch in a 'come hither' motion. Just a subtle movement that would keep her on edge.

“Rosie. You did so well.” Broc ran the bridge of his nose down and over her slit; dipping to inhale her aroma and to taste her once again, he lapped at her wetness. Struggling to find peace, she squeezed her eyes shut, allowing her head to fall back onto the bed, seeking a moment of something she didn't have a name for but needed. Broc didn’t wait for her to catch her breath. Instead, he pushed his fingers back inside her; using his thumb, he gently rubbed circles on her clit, forcing a gasp from her lips. Her legs tried to lock Broc’s head between her thighs.

A chuckle against Rosie's pussy, his fingers pulled out of her greedy pink lips; the hollowness left Rosie unhappy with a disapproving moan. But then his broad shoulders rose as he crawled closer, causing Rosie’s eyes to widen in surprise, caging her head in between his arms. Glancing down at her, he locked eyes, and she focused on his dark, feral stare. A smirk crept across his lips before he licked his mouth. The spark in Rosie’s eyes only resonated for a second before Broc reached down, fisting his own cock between their bodies; crowning against her swollen pussy, and with one swift movement, he shoved himself inside Rosie.

Her cry could be heard everywhere, and it wrapped Broc in the most sexual of songs. The pressure and fullness left her lips in a blinding scream as she arched her back and tossed her head onto the mattress. Broc’s fingers clenched around the belt still wrapped around her neck, pulling it tighter, constricting her breathing in a startling grip of dominance. With a small gasp and a choked sound, his gaze swept over her face as he maintained his firm hold.

The sparkle of lights flashed across Rosie's face; the pinks and silvers spread across her eyes as Broc slid his cock and sank back into her with such force, her breasts shook and bounced under his body. The flush of redness under her pale skin illuminated the artwork inked on her body, making her skin resemble stained glass, with vibrant hues dancing beneath the surface. Broc slid his hand away from the belt and up to her jaw, then down to the silky feeling of her sensitive skin at the base of her neck. Only to then drop his mouth to her, kissing her with worshipful demand, lips melting together, intense, violent; his hurried kiss took more than Rosie could offer. Internally claiming this vixen, he vowed to love, reveling in the twisted possession he held over her. He needed more of her.

"Don't." *Thrust.* "Stop." *Thrust.* "Looking." *Thrust.* "At." *Thrust.* "Me," Broc demanded. Each syllable carried a form of idolization. Rosie raised her hands, intertwining her fingers in his dark, curly locks, a tender gesture. Gently grasping his hair, she pulled his face back towards hers, their kiss fiery and disorienting; she loved it. Everything he was doing to her body had her wanting more; the fire was lit, and his touch sent sparks through her and fanned the embers under her skin. While his fingers danced across her exposed breast, he gently rolled his fingers over her nipples, keeping them as hardened beads under his touch. Their hips kept rolling in sync. "Take me, Rosie, come on my cock again because I can't hold on any longer." Broc's mouth watered with hunger as he drank her kiss. "Rub yourself," he growled into her neck, and her slender tattooed hand worked its way between their bodies until she found her wetness and started to rub small circles, working her body back up to another masterpiece. His body hummed as his own embers started to burst into flames; his pounding became erratic as he began to chase his own dragon, his body straining over hers, wet and slick, perspiration dampening their skin. Pressing up onto his hands, he slipped one arm under her lower back and lifted her as he thrust hard into her pussy, causing her to cry out with the new angle, each thrust causing her breasts to bounce. Dropping his forehead to hers, squeezing his eyes shut, his own saliva dribbling from his lips and falling onto Rosie's face before he lifted his head and cried out his own pleasure. The strength and sex that was flowing through his veins scalded his skin, and the taut corded muscles in his chest and neck screamed as he reached his peak. His wordless final grunt had his body collapsing on top of Rosie's.

Their bodies glistened with sweat while Rosie continued to struggle to capture a full breath. Slowly, Broc loosened the belt around her neck, kissing the slight redness around that perfect pale skin, slipping it out from around her. The red necklace she wore was a sight, and to Broc it was beautiful. He licked and soothed her marred skin, offering a riot of soft kisses, his tongue touching and kissing away the redness like he had special healing powers.

Throughout the night, Broc and Rosie exchanged kisses, laughter, and slow heated sex; it began to strengthen their bond as they learned more about one another.

Once he was her enemy; now her ire was quickly blossoming into affection.

Every crow left her body at that moment.

20

Pro Tip: Just don't kill the plant.

Broc couldn't look away from her.

The early light brushed over her skin like it had been waiting for the moment to paint across her creamy skin. Rosie lay tangled in his sheets, her breathing soft and even. Something in his chest pulled tight. Before he could talk himself out of it, he reached for his cell on his nightstand, lifted it, and snapped a photo—quiet, stolen, but a very necessary moment for him. He hovered above her for a moment, caught in the pull of her, and pressed a slow kiss on her lips. She didn't stir, but the familiarity of her warmth unraveled him. He lifted his phone again, sliding closer, capturing the two of them in the same frame, his past and present colliding in one impulsive act. He was happy.

Staring at the picture, he felt it, an old ache deepening, stretching, becoming something new. Falling for her again hurt in all the best ways. "I love you, Rosie," he breathed, barely audible, like saying it too loud might break whatever spell had brought her back to him. Before he could reconsider, he posted the photo. The caption read:

Finding my past love again.
Falling for her all over.
Nothing has ever felt more right.

The fallout from this post was going to be big; he would most likely need to brace himself, protect Rosie, but ripping off the band-aid now was the best course of action. For him, it barely mattered what would happen on social media because he was in love. He was done hiding. Done pretending. He'd already told Mindy the truth. There was nothing left between them. Hadn't been for a long time—or ever; she was just a way to relieve stress. But she kept trying to resurrect something dead, posting old pictures like they were current, clinging to a version of him he'd never really given her. A relationship built on convenience and distraction, never love.

This vixen, his Rosie, was what he wanted. What he'd always wanted. And he wasn't going to apologize for it.

The winter sun was barely awake, a thin sweep of pale gold slipping through Broc's bedroom window when he rolled onto his side. Cheek resting in his hand, he propped his elbow on the pillow, just as Rosie's eyes fluttered open.

"Hey," she whispered, her voice still filled with sleep. The way she smiled, a soft, unguarded tilt of her lips, sent something bright and unsteady spiraling through his chest. Lifting his hand to brush aside a strand of purple hair that had fallen over her eyes, he smiled back. His fingers drifted down the length of her braid until he reached the rubber band at the end. With a slow, deliberate tug, he freed her hair. It was wild, silken, impossible not to touch; her hair fell over her shoulder, spilling everywhere.

She was...breathtaking. Effortlessly. Painfully.

"What?" she murmured, eyes narrowing a little as though she could feel him staring straight through her.

Broc shook his head, a quiet laugh escaping him. "You're just so damn beautiful," he said. "Stunning. Like an orchid that decided to bloom just for me." Thumb stroking along her cheekbone, he kept his hand on her cheek.

Rosie arched a brow. "Is that what you say to all the women you wake up with?"

He heard it, the tremor, the slight jealousy under the tease. The vulnerability she'd never admit aloud. So, he let his hand trail down her shoulder, following the inked strawberry vine that curled around her arm. When he reached for her hand, he took it gently, threading his fingers through hers before lifting it to his lips. He kissed each finger, slow enough that she could feel every intention behind it. "I've never said that to anyone else," he whispered, his gaze flicking from her eyes to her hand as he worshipped every delicate inch. "Because I've never attached myself to anyone, not like you. I want you, Rosie; I want us." Color flooded up Rosie's chest, blooming across her neck; she couldn't hide it even if she tried. His voice dropped, rough and low. "I love when you blush for me. Makes me want..." His breath hitched against her skin. "...to ruin you all over again."

The sound of a light burst of laughter escaped from Rosie's lips as she turned and buried her face in the pillow, then yanked the sheet up to hide her face. "We should brush our teeth first," she said through a giggle, peeking her violet-blue eyes at Broc. "We both reek," she insisted, but her eyes were earnest, sparkling, absolutely giving her away for feeling the same stomach-flips that Broc also felt.

Broc's grin shifted with a wicked hunger. "Good thing I'm planning on kissing something else."

Before she could reply, he dipped beneath the covers, sending the sheet up with a bellow, while he slid down her body. His fingertips skimmed every sensitive spot he knew by heart, dragging laughter and soft gasps out of her until her sounds melted. With a nudge of his shoulders, opening her wider for him, Broc settled between her thighs, his mouth finding her with slow laps, but it was the beautiful sound of her breath catching that made his cock rock hard. Slowly, her knees bent, falling open for him, the sheet discarded as his dark curls fell over his forehead, his gaze locked on her—like she was the only thing he'd ever worship.

And then she wasn't laughing anymore. Just breathing his name.

Broc's hand slid up her torso, his palm finding her breast,

squeezing it in a soothing rhythm. Rosie gasped. The morning blurred after that, the two of them drifting between soft laughter and lazy kisses, whispering secrets they hadn't meant to say out loud. It felt like time folded around them, like they were the only two people awake in the world. Eventually, they peeled themselves out of bed and wandered down the block to Alessandra's coffeehouse. Their fingers stayed laced. Their eyes stayed soft, unfocused, still lost in each other. They didn't even notice the cell phones turning their way the second they stepped inside.

"Well, well, well, look who finally crawled out of bed," Basil called from behind the counter, one hand popped on her hip, her red lipstick making her grin look wider than usual. "Anything you two want to...share?"

"Hi, Basil," Rosie greeted, still fighting the smile she couldn't seem to get rid of. "My usual, please. Broc?"

He pressed a kiss to her cheek, casual, like it was already a habit. "Americano. Hot."

"You got it." As Basil turned away, the kitchen door swung open, and Alessandra emerged balancing a tray of fresh muffins. The smell hit first: warm cinnamon, butter, sugar.

"Rosie!" she squealed. "Your hair! It's so wavy and cute! Wait—" Her eyes flicked from Rosie to Broc. To their hands. Back to Rosie's eyes. "Oh my god." Her grin stretched. "You two totally had sex. Tell me everything. Was it what you thought? Was he—I love tropes!" She squealed again.

"Alessandra!" Rosie choked. "He's right here!"

She waved Rosie off like she was being dramatic. "Please. It's not like his...equipment is a secret. Internet, remember? Right, big boy?"

Broc only lifted a brow, amused.

Rosie's face went scarlet. She covered it with both hands. "I'm so sorry," she muttered to Broc. "She's usually shy. Quiet. Respectful. Something that I miss right now."

"No, I'm not," Alessandra replied proudly, hands on her hips.

Rosie inhaled sharply. "Not that it's any of your business, which it isn't, but yes, we may have had a moment."

"Or five," Broc added, holding up his hand. Rosie groaned and buried her face in his chest.

A small thunk could be heard as Basil set their drinks on the counter. "Don't panic, Rosie. Alessandra didn't use some mystical sex-detecting power. She just saw the post Broc put up on Instagram."

Rosie froze.

Then she slowly peeled herself away from Broc and walked toward the drinks. She questioned, "You did what?" But before she could finish, someone bumped into her.

"Oh—sorry," Rosie began to say, but a splash of ice-cold water hit her straight in the face. She gasped, jerking back, pushing the girl's hands away. "Oh my—! That's freezing!" She yanked her drenched shirt away from her skin, shivering. Her once-lavender wavy hair hung dark and soaking, dripping onto the floor. Water slid down her jaw, down her neck, and her expression went from bewildered, to furious, to stunned before hardening into something sharp. "What the hell?" Rosie breathed.

"Hey!" Broc's voice cut sharp through the café as he rushed toward Rosie. Basil darted out from behind the counter with a tea towel, already blotting Rosie's dripping hair, wringing out the ends as cold water streamed down her shirt.

Another girl brazenly lifted her phone, snapped a photo of Rosie in her soaked humiliation, and bolted out the door.

"Stay here," Broc instructed, jaw snapping tight. "I'm gonna—" He didn't bother finishing before he spun on his heels and sprinted out of the coffee shop.

"Oh my god, Rosie," Alessandra breathed. "Shit. Why would someone do that?"

Rosie stared at them both, her chest rising and falling, clothes clinging wet and cold to her skin. Basil and Alessandra worked frantically with towels that were already damp, trying to soak up what they could. Then she swallowed hard. "You want to guess who put them up to it?" Her voice shook not with fear, but fury. "Basil, check her account. I'm probably already uploaded."

Basil rushed behind the counter, dug through her purse, and

snatched out her phone. Fingers flew across the screen, tapping fast, so fast. Then she froze. Her face went pale. "Rosie...you're not going to like this."

Rosie stepped forward and gently took the phone. One glance. One heartbeat. "Jesus Christ."

The door chimed as Broc stormed back inside. "Those girls had a car waiting. They're gone. Did anyone get a look at them?" He scanned the café. "Alessandra, do you have cameras? Anything?" Then he was at Rosie's side again, pulling her into his arms despite the cold water soaking through his shirt. His eyes dropped to the phone in her hand. "What the fuck?" He snatched it lightly, staring.

"Tell me this isn't real," Rosie whispered.

But it was. Too real. Mindy's post. No, her lie was everywhere.

Rosie's stomach curdled. The room grew too loud, too bright. Cell phones rose around them. People gasped. Some recorded her like she wasn't a person, just content for their feeds. Heat crawled up her throat, panic clawing at her, and the ache in her chest returned with vengeance. She needed to get out. Away from all of it. She couldn't breathe.

So, she ran.

By the time she reached her shop, her clothes were stiff against her skin, her hair heavy and cold. She spied Fluffy, who was scratching outside her shop, not a sight she'd been expecting. She scooped down and pulled her chicken tight against her chest with trembling hands, staring at the ruins in front of her. Two windows shattered. Glass everywhere. The winter air poured inside.

Tears stung her eyes, begging to fall.

Now Rosie stood frozen in place, staring at the gaping holes punched through her storefront. Thousands of dollars of plants, all fragile, tropical, impossible to save in the cold, they would be dead within hours.

Even Spike her desert cactus. Miss Marigold's last gift.

But everything else...her mind stalled, thoughts frozen like the air on her face.

"Rosie!" Broc's voice carried down the block. He jogged to her, breathing unsteadily. "Rosie—" He reached her and grabbed her arm softly but firmly. When he saw the broken windows, his mouth fell open. "Jesus fucking Christ. What happened?"

She turned her head but barely looked at him. "You know I'm not a detective, but I'm guessing it was something to do with what you posted on social media. I'm not exactly liked by most of the country right now. I'm sure this was her doing."

"I swear she'll pay for this. And that post of hers...Rosie, it's a lie. It's all a lie."

Rosie's throat squeezed tight as she stared at the shattered windows; the irony wasn't ignored. The lump in her chest felt like it might explode from the inside out. Fluffy clucked softly against her arm, reminding her how cold it was. Rosie needed to bring her in. Needed to do something, anything so she didn't completely fall apart. She stepped toward the door, then slightly turned. "She called me a homewrecker, Broc." Her voice cracked. "She said I took you from her." Carefully and slowly her hand reached out, one still cradling Fluffy as the other pushed open the store's door. "She's pregnant, Broc. And now the world thinks I tricked you into sleeping with me; they think I pulled you away from her. From your unborn baby."

"It's not mine," he said quickly, voice rough, while Rosie scoffed, allowing her head to fall; hearing his denial out loud sounded so pathetic. "I used a condom every time. I swear, Rosie. It's not mine." A desperate plea in his gaze. Rosie paused in the doorway, slowly turning enough to look at him. Really look at him. The man she'd finally let back in. The man she'd let her guard down for. And the man whose past was now tearing her apart.

"I can't do this right now," she whispered. "You have a child to think about. I can't compete with that. And no matter how awful

Mindy is, that baby didn't ask for any of this." A tear slipped down her cheek while her voice cracked. "I won't let that kid end up like I did. Lost in the system, forgotten. Unwanted." Another tear slid down her cheek. "I'm sorry." She slipped inside the dark shop. Her chest tightened brutally, making it hard to breathe. She clutched her shirt over her heart as she set Fluffy down. Broken glass crunched under her feet. Plants lay overturned. The cold bit her skin.

Everything swayed.

Her vision darkened at the edges. "Breathe," she begged herself, trying to suck in air. But her lungs seized, giving her nothing. The world tilted, then she dropped to her hands and knees, sharp stings of glass cutting into her palms, but gasping for air failed her like a fish out of water. Her body folded in on itself as panic and heartbreak crashed inside her ribcage. The darkness swallowed her before she even hit the floor. A loud thud was heard as her head struck the glass; it was deafening.

"ROSIE!" Broc's scream sounded like it came from miles away. It was distant, echoing as everything faded to black.

21

Pro Tip: Plants will die if you don't water them.

Mindy's pregnancy announcement on Instagram sent a chill down his spine. Alongside the post was a photo showcasing a blissful embrace between Rosie and him at the Little Café, and the caption:

> ***'This little home-wrecker is destroying my future; if only I could destroy hers.'***

It was a bomb. The implications were clear. Mindy didn't need to spell it out for her followers, but they took her hint and ran with it.

Broc ran down the sidewalk, following Rosie as he bolted from the cafe, trying to catch up to her, his heart pounding. The memory of having sex with Rosie crashed into his heart. *"I don't want kids,"* Rosie had said. She'd explained how the trauma of her upbringing was nothing she wished on anyone. He was not ready for fatherhood. Not even close. And for their shared bond, it only drew them closer.

"Rosie," he called after her, "Mindy's baby can't be mine," he insisted, urgency flooding his words. "I always used protection. The only time I didn't...was with you..." Rosie didn't move; it was like she couldn't hear him, and then he saw why. There was glass shattered across the sidewalk and into her shop, the front door glass panel destroyed, and all her plants inside dumped out and pulled apart. All sponsored by Mindy's fanatic fans.

The look on Broc's face as he tried to deny the rumors only deepened the confusion in Rosie's mind, but she still pushed him away because it was just too suffocating. Being near him had already cost her everything. Her shop lay in ruins, and as she stepped through the warped door, hanging by the frayed remnants of a hinge, shards of glass crunched beneath her shoes. Each step was a cruel reminder of their ruse—this was supposed to be fake, to keep Mindy and Orson away from them; never was a destroyed business part of the plan. The pounding in her chest made it hard to draw in air, and she stifled small coughs, desperate to inhale a full breath.

Slowly, she sank to her hands and knees, the rough ground pressing against her, slicing into her skin. An ache bloomed deep in her chest, sharp with the unbearable pain that had a flame igniting where hope used to reside. It coiled around her heart, squeezing it mercilessly, making every breath feel like a struggle against the fire consuming her. Strong hands grasped her shoulders, gently turning her over, but even as she tried to rise, the pain pinned her down like a rock she couldn't roll off her chest. She winced and gasped, her hair falling around her face, vision blurring. She pressed her fingers to her heart, as if she could rub away the burning agony.

"Jesus, Rosie! Oh my god!" Broc shouted.

The bitter cold of Spokane would have hit him like a slap, but all he could see was Rosie on the floor, shards of broken glass littering the scene.

"Can you open your eyes for me?" He pulled her against him, cradling her like she was the most precious thing in the world. A tender touch, brushing down her face. "Shit, baby, you're bleeding." Pain melded with confusion as Rosie fought through the fog, slowly coming back to the present. "Careful, don't move too much," he murmured. Urgency fueling his movements, his fingers skimmed her face again. "I'm calling 9-1-1." Kneeling beside her, Broc pressed a gentle kiss to her forehead before yanking out his phone from his back pocket.

"9-1-1, what's your location?" a calm female's voice crackled on the other end.

"I'm at Miss Marigold's Plant Shop in downtown Spokane. My girlfriend, she's hurt," Broc blurted out, unable to complete a sentence. "There's something wrong with her...I don't know. Please hurry."

"Sir, is the area secure?"

"Yes, I think. I don't know."

"Sir, do you need police presence?"

"It's freezing outside, please hurry," Broc begged, clutching Rosie closer onto his lap.

"Please hold, sir. Let me send out the call to the first responders; don't hang up."

"Okay." Broc waited anxiously; minutes felt like an eternity, though it was only a short while. Fortunately, the fire station stood at the end of the street. A moment after the phone call was placed, sirens wailed.

"I'M HER FIANCÉ!" Broc barked, his voice cutting through the already bustling nurses' station. Tension etched across Broc's face, and his agitation only served to heighten it. A nurse sat behind the desk, reading some sort of book, ignoring his rants. Broc's eyes flicked to the name tag on her scrubs: RN Diana Slaughter. She glanced up from her book, locking eyes with him. Her deep brown gaze softened for a moment, but the firm set of her mouth hinted that she knew how to deal with unruly family members. This was clearly not her first rodeo.

"Sir, it seems like you're looking for someone. How can I help?"

Almost as if daring him to let his frustration spill over, her tone was steady. Slowly, she placed a bookmark deep into her book, setting it aside as her attention shifted completely to Broc, who was falling down a rocky emotional slope.

Broc inhaled deeply, pinching the bridge of his nose. "My fiancée was brought in by ambulance. I was told to come to this hospital," he explained, voice strained as he leaned over the countertop, jabbing a finger down as if trying to etch 'this is where I need to be' in stone. Panic clawed at him, and he brushed it away with a flick of his eyes, still desperate to hear news of Rosie. "I can't find her! She's not answering her phone or my texts."

"Sir, please," Nurse Slaughter interjected, her voice cutting through his thoughts. "Why don't you tell me her name? Let's see if we can find her. How does that sound?" She tucked her fiery red bob-cut behind her ear, a simple gesture that barely masked the steely edge in her gaze. With a slow exhale, Broc tilted his head back; his heart was racing at the edges of his sanity.

"Thank you," he finally murmured, resting his forehead against the countertop. "Her name is Rosie Clark; she was just brought in by ambulance." The words repeated once more.

Nurse Slaughter scrutinized him, assessing whether he was on the verge of breaking down. "I didn't even put on my lipstick today, and it's already clear this shift is going to be a nightmare," she muttered to herself, placing her book on the desk and finally shifting her focus to her computer. Catching his gaze again, she looked up, pinning him in place. "You said Clark, right?"

"Yeah, Rosie Clark." Each word felt heavy. A moment later, her fingers danced across the keys. After only a few seconds and a couple of "mmms," her lips pressed tightly together, swallowing her real response, turning on her professionalism. "Okay, got it. She was brought into the ER. They're moving her to the Heart Unit."

"Heart unit? She just fainted from shock!" Broc replied incredulously.

"Uh-huh, honey. Listen, bodies can faint for a variety of reasons. The doctor is probably just covering all bases. But if you want to see your fiancée, I suggest you rein in your emotions." Nurse Slaughter leaned in closer to Broc. "I'm the only nurse on duty right now, and there's a rule you don't want to ignore..." She rose from her chair, glancing back at him with a glint in her eye. "Never tick off the nurse taking care of the one you love." Her warning was heard. Broc couldn't help but let out a hum of laughter, shaking his head. "She's in room 1452," Nurse Slaughter said, and with that Broc pushed past her and sprinted down the stark hospital corridor.

"Hey! You'd better not run into my patients or scuff up my floors! I might not clean them, but I'll certainly be upset if I have to wipe up bumps and scrapes, so slow your roll!" The nurse's voice followed him as he ran, forcing the roar of panic down to his toes. He skidded to a halt and clutched the doorframe, momentarily steadying himself before entering. Inside, there were two doctors, a young one and an older one, and a nurse's assistant tending to the IV and the tubes strapped to Rosie. They were deep in conversation until they caught sight of him. Their heads turned in unison. The young nurse with a long blonde ponytail gasped, instantly recognizing Broc and his Hollywood status.

"Can I help you, young man?" the older female doctor asked, an eyebrow raised.

"Yes, that's my fiancée," Broc responded, pointing at Rosie, who lay awake and wide-eyed on the bed. He leaned over, hands on his knees, desperate to catch his breath. "I'm sorry I wasn't here sooner... There was a nurse...and a thick book, then a long hallway..." Broc's voice trailed off under the doctors' indifferent gazes. The older doctor dismissed him with a wave, turning back to Rosie. "Ma'am, do you know this man? If not, I'll have to call security." The young nurse exchanged glances between Rosie and Broc.

Nurse Slaughter breezed into the room, her hands on her hips. "Looks like you found the room," she said, eyeing Broc beside Rosie's bedside. "Dr. Hammond, this is Ms. Rosie Clark's fiancé. He's been looking for her, and it seems he found her."

"I see, Nurse Slaughter. So, Rosie, is he allowed to stay?" Dr. Hammond rephrased, shifting his attention back to her patient. Rosie pressed her lips together and nodded. “Very well, sir, and your name?” the doctor asked Broc.

At the same time, the young nurse stated, “It’s Broc Chase.”

“Broc,” he echoed, shooting her a quick smile before focusing back on Rosie and reaching out to Rosie's hand to entangle his grasp with hers. “Broc Chase.” He leaned down to place a gentle kiss on her forehead.

The young nurse, frozen with her hand on the machine next to Rosie’s bed, stared at Broc, her mouth dropping as she stammered. “Oh...my god, d-do you...think I can g-get your autograph?”

With an air of authority, Nurse Slaughter stepped forward. “Sorry, Dr. Hammond. Shelby only knows Mr. Chase from his social media presence and his Netflix shows. I trust she’s aware of the HIPAA regulations and her role here as a nurse; otherwise, she’ll be looking for a new job.” She shot a glance at the young nurse.

With wide eyes, Shelby nodded fervently. “Yep!”

Nurse Slaughter then leaned closer to Broc and whispered, "I might be married, but I'm not dead. I know who you are, Mr. Chase." She paused and smiled at Rosie, and then straightened to look directly at the young nurse. “Great. Ms. Shelby, I believe you have other patients to attend to. I’ve got it from here; she’s my charge anyway.” Nurse Slaughter waved her hand dismissively, ushering Shelby out of the room.

“Eh hem. Okay, Rosie. Mind if I call you Rosie?” Dr. Hammond’s eyes were focused on Broc, who held her hand tightly. But Rosie couldn't tear her gaze away from the doctor's stare. “We did a quick ECG in the ER and noticed some abnormalities. I just consulted with Dr. Michelle Hart about your results. We ran a few blood tests, and until those come back, both of us believe you’re experiencing a form of Broken Heart Syndrome. It’s similar to a heart attack.” That little tidbit sent Rosie’s pulse racing; her heart leapt in panic, causing the machines beside her to beep more erratically, and the pain in her chest to reappear.

Dr. Hart, the younger doctor, stepped closer, her hand warm against Rosie’s leg. “There’s nothing to panic about. Just breathe.

We're checking your blood enzymes, and given your medical history and healthy diet, we don't think it's a heart attack. But yes, your stress levels could have triggered your fainting spell. With a few lifestyle adjustments, I don't see any reason why you can't live a vibrant, full life."

Broc, his protective instinct raging, leaned closer. "Reduce stress? Is that really all? What else can I do to help her?" His voice was low, almost desperate. "Does she need a new heart?"

Rosie wanted to echo the same question, but the words twisted in her throat, a heavy weight lodged in her beating chest. Easing her stress felt impossible—laughable, almost—hiding away seemed her only option. The relentless scrutiny from the Mindy fans had put her on the map. And if that wasn't enough, fall in Spokane had its icy grip wrapped around her, with the broken windows of her shop likely going to cost a fortune to replace. Taking a deep breath, Rosie turned her gaze to the window, her heart wrapped in a heavy veil. "Thank you," she whispered.

"Alright, I'll talk to Diana—er, I mean Nurse Slaughter. She'll check on you now and then, and once we have your results, one of us will be back to update you. In the meantime, focus on breathing through your stress. Maybe consider yoga to help balance things out? Sound good?" Dr. Hart said. Rosie nodded through her fog, avoiding the doctors' eyes as they made their way to the door.

"Thanks, Dr. Hart, Dr. Hammond," Broc said, quickly releasing Rosie's hand to shake theirs. He ushered them out, then shut the door softly before turning back to her, closing the distance with a few long strides. "Hey, Rosie," he said softly, rubbing the back of his neck nervously. "You, okay? God, you scared me." But Rosie was retreating into herself, pulling away. The news of Mindy's baby, the attack on her shop—it all spun her thoughts into a frenzy. "Rosie, look at me," he urged, stepping closer to her bed. "Rosie, we can get through this. What happened with your shop, well, that was out of line. I promise, I won't let Mindy do anything to you again." Broc's gaze darted around the room until it landed on a chair in the corner. He grabbed it, pulled it beside Rosie's bed, and settled in, reaching for her hand as if it were his lifeline. Tilting her head towards him, his thumb grazed her arm, then she slowly met his gaze with unshed tears. "Don't cry. I've locked up Fluffy; she's safe in her coop. I've dealt with the IRS, so that's one less thing for you to worry about."

She leaned back against the pillow, turning to fully face him. "I can't do this anymore. It's tearing me apart, and I don't even know if I still have a business left." Fresh tears spilled over as she blinked, allowing them to cascade freely. "Mindy's pregnant with your baby, and that child deserves two loving parents."

"Rosie, listen. I don't believe she's really pregnant. Call it a hunch; it feels off. And I refuse to just dive into this without knowing the truth. We weren't fucking for a long time...I mean, sure, she did give me a blow-job—"

"Stop talking."

"Yeah...um...what I mean is, I haven't slept with her for a long time," he said, holding her hands firmly, his forehead resting against them. "But even if it turns out I'm the father, I'll still step up. That's because of you, Rosie." He pressed his lips against her hands, his eyes earnest as he spoke. "You've shared how sad it was in the foster care system, being shoved around like trash in a plastic bag. No child should have to go through that, mine or not." And just like that, Broc pulled her from the depths of her mind and back into his heart.

She nodded, eyes closed, squeezing his hands as she rested her head back on the pillow, startled by the creaking door and a familiar silhouette. It sent her pulse racing. "Orson," she gasped. An ominous alarm blared as he moved closer, his gaze locked onto her, ignoring Broc completely, who sat protectively between them. Broc straightened, his eyes darting between Orson and Rosie. With every step closer, the alarms grew louder. Rosie placed a hand on her chest, feeling the pressure of his presence crushing her breath.

"Looks like I arrived just in time, Rosie. Broc's got his hands full with the news about Mindy. And when I stopped by to see how you were doing, well, to my surprise, I saw your destroyed shop. Thought since he'll be on daddy duty, you might need my help to get things back on track," he said, scratching at the stubble on his chin. Leaning over the footboard, he casually swiped at the remnants of white powder on his nose. Confirmation confirmed. He was back to using.

Alarms were getting louder, and the rock that fell off her chest rolled back on her ribcage. "Get out, Orson. You're stressing her out," Broc snapped, then turned back to Rosie, cupping her cheek. "Just breathe, Rosie. Focus on me, not him. I've got you."

Orson turned on his heels, his fingers lacing behind his back as he rolled his head and turned in a circle, living in his own little drugged world. "Oh, me? What about you? Because it looks like Mindy has figured out a way to trap the most eligible bachelor. But I got to hand it to her!" Orson smirked and then pulled out his cell, thrusting his hand out to show Rosie the latest post. "Checkmate." A picture of her ring finger with the biggest engagement ring Rosie had ever seen. The air rushed from Rosie's lungs, the rope lassoed around her heart tightened.

Just then, Nurse Slaughter stormed into the room with her pink matching scrubs wrinkled from running. "Who the hell are you?" she demanded, her hands popped on her hips as she glared at the intruder.

"Get him out of here!" Broc shouted simultaneously. He turned back to Rosie, pulling her face close, their noses almost touching. "I didn't ask her, Rosie. I didn't ask her to marry me," he said softly, cupping her cheeks with unsteady hands as the tears finally crested, cascading down her cheeks. "FUCK!" Broc roared, and in that moment, Rosie opened her mouth to whisper before darkness enveloped her, stealing her away from everything, leaving the words frozen on her tongue.

22

Pro Tip: Keep shade plants out of the sun.

The hospital room was shrouded in a heavy silence, the shades drawn tight as if to shield the world from Rosie. Nurse Slaughter, with her no-nonsense vibe and unwavering composure, had swept in and out of Rosie's space throughout her grueling 12-hour shift, acting as the steadfast captain. When Rosie's heart rate monitor had jumped into a frenzy, it was Nurse Slaughter who had managed to remove Orson, leaving him to fight his own demons in his head while the drugs worked their way through his veins. Twilight cascaded over the city, and Broc sat hunched in the corner, his face buried in his hands, grappling with his mind.

This wasn't the best time for shit to hit the fan, with the grand opening of his floral shop just around the corner. Guests were already traveling from all corners of the nation to Spokane. Netflix's staging team had already been dispatched to set up the shop for the movie preview, transforming it into an enchanting botanical garden to mirror the historical romance premiere they were about to unveil.

Yet, no matter what, Broc wasn't about to leave Rosie alone in the hospital.

After ending a tense call with his contractor, Raymond, his heart lifted slightly. Broc took it upon himself to make sure that Rosie's shop was secured, and Raymond was just the guy to get that done—and quickly. His crew had painstakingly secured the shop with plastic to keep the chill at bay, removed the dead plants, and cleaned up the shattered glass. He'd even ordered custom double-paned windows to replace the broken ones. The thought that Rosie's beloved plant shop would be back on its feet by the year's end provided a glimmer of hope. With his phone feeling like a weighty anchor in his hand, Broc opened a new group chat with his friends, desperate to offload some of the heaviness.

BROC:

Rosie's not doing well.

ADAM:

I told you I'd only hold your balls that one time!

ANDY:

What's going on, man?

DAVIS:

Hey, dude, what's up?

BROC:

Jesus Christ, Adam.

ADAM:

I'm more worried about your ball support situation...

DAVIS:

Where are you, Adam? Seriously, are you hiding out in the basement again?

ADAM:

Just got out of the shower, on my way to see Red.

ANDY:

Our bro Broc needs us! Let's put an Air Tag on Adam and get going!

BROC:

Rosie's in the hospital.

ADAM:

What? Is she going to be okay?

ANDY ADDED LIZ TO THE CHAT

ANDY:

Liz, Broc's girl is in the hospital.

LIZ:

Is that the only reason I got added here?

ANDY:

Nope, because you're smarter than all of us combined.

DAVIS ADDED SAMMY TO THE CHAT

ADAM:

Liz, because Broc needs support from a banana hammock.

SAMMY:

What's happening? Why am I here? Banana hammock? Seriously?

DAVIS:

Broc's girl is in the hospital, remember the girl from Ferris Horticulture?

SAMMY:

Oh no! What happened, Broc? (I remember—socializing wasn't my thing in high school.)

ADAM:

Thank you, Sammy. Who do I need to break for you, Broc?

BROC:

Mindy Harper.

SAMMY:

The actress?

ADAM:

Yeah, no. She's the only one I won't touch—too much drama.

DAVIS:

Oh man, she's brutal.

ANDY:

Yeah... uh, not exactly a fan here.

LIZ:

Sammy told me she's a pill. Caused a lot of issues with Carla's friend Poppy and Colin.

BROC:

What's happening? Why the hell didn't anyone tell me you all knew her... while I was sleeping with her!

SAMMY:

My friend Carla is friends with Poppy Peters, who's married to Colin Peters.

BROC:

Jesus Christ... what?

SAMMY:

Colin Peters worked with Mindy, and she tried to pull some stunt to make it look like they were a thing on set. Nearly wrecked his relationship with Poppy.

BROC:

Some of that sounds familiar. She kept whining about being blocked in Hollywood.

ADAM:

For good reason. Tier-climbing is her middle name.

ANDY:

Says the guy who "networked" his way through a sorority.

ADAM:

I'm a unicorn! What can I say? I'm a kept man! My loyalty – AKA my dick - only swings for Red.

SAMMY:

Ewww.

DAVIS:

For the love of all that's holy, Adam! Please tell me you don't pull out the helicopter move.

LIZ:

If you do that again, I might burn my eyes. Seriously—that's a feat from a medical standpoint.

ADAM:

See? It's practically medical!

SAMMY:

Dear god, Adam... Broc, why was I added? I can't deal with this dick-swinging nonsense —I'm barely surviving Archie!

ADAM:

My boy discovered his anatomy??

DAVIS:

Don't you dare teach him anything!

ADAM:

OMG, I'm not a monster!

SAMMY:

Please don't—pedophilia is no joke. Crime doesn't suit you.

ADAM:

I wasn't going to show him! Jesus! But if he runs up to me when he's in puberty, I'm going to be real! It's all natural! I had no guide growing up, and honesty is key.

DAVIS:

I'm right here; he's my son. And your dad was still part of your life in HS!

ADAM:

Do you really think I wanted to talk to him about that? HA, not happening! That's why I vented to you idiots back in the day.

BROC:

Yeah...that was not fun...Bring it back to me – this is my text!

LIZ:

Thank you, Broc – back to Rosie – spill the tea.

BROC:

Mindy posted some shit on IG – and her fan base took it into their own hands – threw water on her face inside her friend's coffee house – then threw bricks inside her shop, breaking the windows and tearing up all her plants in the shop.

ADAM:

Just getting my pants on and coming over...

SAMMY:

You can't leave! You promised to babysit for us, and Daisy was coming over!

ADAM:

Damn it! Andy, get your ass over here and take my spot.

ANDY:

Can't, man, I'm on call, and Liz is at the hospital.

ADAM:

Fine, leave the car seat.

SAMMY:

You're not taking Archie to Spokane.

ADAM:

Who says I am?

DAVIS:

Adam, WTH, man...settle down, let Broc finish.

BROC:

She fainted but was complaining about chest pain before she did.

LIZ:

Panic attack?

BROC:

I wish! The blood and the EKG or ECG, whatever, showed she has Broken Heart Disorder because of the rise of some enzyme.

LIZ:

Interesting. Let me read it. I can also talk to the cardio doc here about it...BRB.

ADAM:

Davis, where are your keys? Asking for a friend...

DAVIS:

All my friends are in this text stream, you fucker! In my pocket – but no...sit your ass down on the couch.

BROC:

Her crackhead ex came into her room, and it caused her to faint, again-her nurse kicked him out-we now have police presence outside her room.

SAMMY:

Who's there? Which department? Need me to call and check on them? I've got some connections...

BROC:

No, it's okay – but I have that grand opening this weekend, and I'm not sure I can make it.

ANDY:

Want me to see if I can get my shift covered and come over?

BROC:

Maybe

ADAM:

Hey, you said you won't cover me! But you'd go over this weekend? WTF man!

SAMMY:

Let me call my friend Carla and see if she can help. Davis, can we drop Archie off at your mom's and head to the grand opening?

DAVIS:

Yeah, I'll text my mom. She'll be thrilled to babysit him.

BROC:

Carla? She fooled around with Adam, right?

ANDY:

It was me.

LIZ:

How long ago?

ANDY:

So long, the only vagina I know is yours, babe.

ADAM:

I heard it looks good, too.

SAMMY:

Seriously, Adam?

ADAM:

Fine, I loved yours too.

SAMMY:

OMG YOU PROMISED TO FORGET

DAVIS:

Do I have to punch you, Adam?

LIZ:

It did look nice.

SAMMY:

I hate you all. I was pregnant! I didn't care who saw my Hoo-Ha at the time!

ADAM:

Watching my best buddy slide out of your Hoo-Ha was the most fantastic thing ever.

SAMMY LEFT THE CHAT

ADAM:

Rude

DAVIS:

I'm going to kill you, Adam. If Sammy is pissed, you'd better go somewhere else tonight – Broc, keep us posted.

ADAM:

Sammy would never — she loves me too much.

ANDY:

Who is her doctor?

BROC:

Dr. Michelle Hart

ANDY:

Oh, I know her! (Not romantically, Liz.) She worked at UW for a while, so I'll call her.

LIZ:

Okay, I talked with cardio over here at UW. She should be okay if she keeps her stress low and practices more yoga and breathing exercises. She's too young to undergo any surgical procedures.

BROC:

Yeah, that's what they said. Thanks, guys. Gotta go. She's waking up.

ADAM:

See you soon, man.

DAVIS:

No! Sit your ass down...Hey, Red is here! Get your ass upstairs.

ANDY:

Saved by the redhead.

ADAM:

RED!!!! Later dick heads.

ADAM LEFT THE CHAT

ANDY LEFT THE CHAT

Tossing his phone onto a chair, Broc walked over to Rosie's bed, his fingers brushing against her cheek in a gentle caress. "Hey there, sleepyhead."

"Hey," she murmured, blinking against the early light streaming in. Bolstered by a mountain of pillows, she sat up, rubbing the remnants of sleep from her eyes and running her fingers through her tousled hair. "Did the nurse say anything about me being discharged? I really can't stay here much longer."

Broc studied her before he leaned down to place a soft kiss on the top of her head. "Don't worry about it. I've already called Raymond. He's fixing your windows and dealing with the mess. Custom orders because, of course, your building has to be difficult. And I had his crew clear out the dead plants. Some survived, but not many." He sighed, sitting on the edge of her bed, his hand resting possessively on her thigh. "Basil and her kids are taking care of Fluffy for you, and I had her move your stuff over to my place. There's no way I'm letting you stay there alone with Orson out of his damn mind. You deserve to be safe."

The way he had taken control of the situation should have irritated her, but instead, warmth spread through her. At this point in her life, she was grateful for Broc. She knew she needed to reduce the stress weighing on her heart. This nurturing side of him was something she had to learn to accept. Allowing people in, letting them help, was foreign but somehow essential now.

"Can you grab me a piece of paper?" Rosie asked.

"Sure, what do you need?" Broc replied, hopping off the bed to rummage around on the counter for a pen and paper.

Shaking her head, she settled back into the pillows. "I need to prioritize. I have a shop to run. You said it'd be ready by Christmas, right?" Panic prickled at the edges of her thoughts as she realized how much a month's worth of lost work could cost her. The machinery around her began to beep more urgently, reflecting her rising stress.

Broc was back in an instant, crossing the room to sit beside her, cupping her face in his hands. "Stop. Rosie. You can't stress yourself out like this. Just breathe," he instructed, his voice steady. He held her gaze, his thumb brushing lightly across her cheek as he cradled the back of her head. "I've got you. You don't need to worry about anything."

"Broc..." she murmured, leaning into his touch. "This is so hard for me. I'm not used to...any of this." She waved her hands around, feeling lost.

He let out a low chuckle, glancing away briefly. "I know. I messaged my friends in Seattle, and you should have seen Adam's reaction. He practically threatened to teleport here; he's furious about everything with the opening this weekend for my shop..."

"Oh my god, Broc! You have to go!" Rosie shouted, panic creeping into her voice. The machine's beeping quickened, stirring the air around them like an electric charge.

Before Broc could say a word, Nurse Slaughter breezed in, papers tucked under one arm and a small box clutched in her hand. "Well, well, look who's rejoined the land of the living. How're you doing, Ms. Rosie?" she asked, her tone concerned as she stepped closer. Broc slid off the edge of the bed, making space for the nurse.

"Good, mostly," Rosie replied, her voice a tired whisper.

"Your stress levels were off the charts, and my little alarms were going wild in the nurses' station. So let's try again. How are you really doing?"

Rosie leaned her head back against the pillow, eyes fluttering closed as if blocking out the world. "Honestly? I feel like I got run over by a bus."

"Putting it mildly, aren't we?" Nurse Slaughter chuckled softly, then dropped her papers and the box onto the end of the bed and began taking Rosie's vitals. "Everything looks decent. I have your discharge papers ready, and Dr. Hart sent this along: a portable heart rate monitor. It wraps around your chest and syncs with an app on your phone. If your levels hit a danger zone, you'll get an alert. Instructions are all here, along with your discharge paperwork."

Broc leaned in, curiosity piqued. He opened the box, revealing the sleek strap. "Could I connect it to my phone, too? Just in case?"

Nurse Slaughter shot him a knowing smile. "Why not? Better safe than sorry, especially until she gets a grip on her stressors." Her gaze narrowed playfully. "You're not one of them, are you?"

"Absolutely not. And don't believe everything you read online."

She waved him off dismissively and sashayed over to the window, pulling up the shades. Darkness loomed outside. "You can stay the night and leave in the morning, or head out whenever you're ready. And Mr. Chase, about the online nonsense? Just remember, what's on the internet is often trash. I trust what I see with my own eyes." She stepped closer to Broc, her voice dropping. "Looks to me like a scorned woman is trying to drag down whoever she can. Classic move, really." She strode over to the closet, retrieving Rosie's arrival clothes. Shaking them out, she frowned thoughtfully. “I’ll bring you some scrubs; these overalls are a mess, and your shirt? Well, let’s say it didn’t survive.”

Broc’s expression softened, a gentle smile breaking through. “Let’s get you home, Rosie.”

23

Pro Tip: If you plan a multi plant pot, ensure the plants you select bloom in the same conditions. Example: Plant sunloving plants together, don't add those plants with shade-loving ones.

The ride back to Miss Marigold's Plant Shop was a welcome reprieve; it was swift, easy, and soothing for Rosie, less stressful too. The real comfort came from Broc, no longer a pretend fiancé, more than just a trope. Broc had become fiercely protective, like a knight found in a fairytale. Rosie had never tasted this kind of emotional stability before, and it felt good. A feeling she could get used to. Whereas Orson had made the relationship with her all about him, using her weaknesses against her while promising to make things better, and she'd fallen for it every time. But the recent assault on Rosie was a nightmare she couldn't shake. Plus, after the destruction of her little store, it was Broc who'd stepped in, hiring Raymond to clear the damage left by the Mindys, replace the shattered windows, and install a security system. Concern for Rosie's safety had driven the two of them into a new trope: forced proximity.

Inside Broc's place, Rosie let the moment catch up with her mind. Her stuff was already in his apartment.

"Should I be worried?" he teased Rosie, holding up a small potted cactus, the name 'Spike' Sharpied across the rim of the terracotta pot it sat in.

Rosie giggled and shook her head at his hint of jealousy. She took the small pot from him and held it close, treating it as something special. "No, no, Spike is just a little cutie. He's just my pet cactus. Miss Marigold gave him to me before she passed. She planted him around the time I was born, apparently. I love him." She checked to make sure Spike was settled in his pot, then looked up at Broc through her lashes. He smiled, stepped closer, gently touched her cheek and kissed her nose.

Broc's fingers slid between hers, the warmth sending butterflies racing through her stomach. "So, what do I need to do for *Spike,* your little buddy?"

"Just remember, he loves dry heat. And he's not winter's friend. Sometimes I read to him, and you have to keep him updated on your daily activities. He's a sucker for gossip. And trust me, sometimes I have to remind him to dial down the dramatics. He can be a bit of a diva." She laughed softly.

Broc tilted his head, a playful glint in his expression. "Got it. So, when we want to...you know, will I need to put him in another room? Just to keep the drama to a minimum?"

She only smiled back, her heart racing at the implication.

"We can put a pot over his head to muffle your screams," Broc suggested.

Rosie stifled a laugh, covering her mouth as she fought to suppress a grin. "Or we could just bring in Betty; she could keep him company with her chicks. They're practically dating," she whispered, her tone dropping conspiratorially. "Honestly, she's a bit of a loose hen, if you ask me, with all her babies and their fathers. But you know how it is with a Hen & Chick...they just breed like rabbits." A soft giggle escaped her lips. She took a steady breath, her hand resting against his chest, locking eyes with him as he trailed his fingers down her arms. "So, what about Mindy? Orson, for that matter? Things really spiraled out of control," Rosie pointed out, turning the lighthearted conversation into something a little more serious.

"There's nothing to discuss. I don't love Mindy. Can't trust anything that comes out of her mouth. The only person I want in my life, the only one I want to remember, is you, and apparently that will also include Spike as your wingman, but I'll let it slide." The slight tip of his lips and his gaze held hers for a heartbeat before he turned away. "I've said it before; I can't change the past. I wish I could," Broc admitted. "The women I've been with mean nothing... It's always been you. The one that got away."

"Another trope," Rosie murmured. "Alessandra says we're living in a romance trope."

A scoff escaped him as he kicked at nothing on the floor. "I'm enjoying our little tropes." Then walking back to stand before Rosie, he raised her hand to his mouth, pressing a gentle kiss against her skin. "You're not just beautiful; your passion for plants bleeds through the artwork on your skin." His admission left Rosie breathless, vulnerability crashing over her like an unexpected wave.

"Broc..." she whispered, her voice barely breaking through the rush of emotions. "Broc, how will we deal with the world after you leave Mindy?" Uncertainty filled her voice.

"I've already left her, Rosie, and I don't care what the world thinks of us," he swore, steel in his tone. "Look, as far as I'm concerned, it's only us. If Mindy really is pregnant, we'll face it together. I won't abandon the child or you." Grazing her cheek with the back of his hand, he added, "It's just us, Rosie. No one else; you and me against the world." He pulled her face toward his and kissed her without warning, without asking for permission. Pressed into her deeply, she felt as if she were both flying and falling at once, her mind a whirlwind of emotions. He pulled back slightly, crooked his finger under her chin, and kissed the tip of her nose. The rise and fall of Rosie's chest instantly had Broc's cock swelling and hardening to steel. Carefully, Rosie lifted her hand to her chest, but the pain in her heart wasn't the same blinding pain; this was something very different. Healing almost. "Don't ever doubt that I care about you, Rosie, because every cell in my body aches for your touch. Without you near me, I feel homesick."

Pressing a finger under her chin to lift her face to his, he leaned in, his voice low.

"Remember this, Rosie: my mouth is yours, now and forever. Every kiss that falls from my lips belongs to you. Nothing will change that. I swear to you, not even Mindy can push me away. Let Orson do whatever he thinks he can because your taste is mine, and I'll defend it with everything I have. I'm yours, period. Understand?" Those eyes held her heart, and it pounded with a fervor that gripped her throat tightly.

All that pent-up hatred needed time to simmer, to bring them to this pivotal moment in their lives. It was renewal, pure and simple. A perfect collision of past pain and present. Words failed her, so she simply nodded in understanding and smiled back at Broc. He pushed back her long, wavy purple hair behind her ear, then placed a ghost of a whisper against her lips. Falling in step with Broc, Rosie nestled up next to him, his arm wrapped around her lithe frame, and they walked downstairs, all the while, Spike nestled in her arms.

"Coffee?" Rosie asked, setting Spike down on the counter.

"Coffee," Broc agreed. Their eyes were only on each other as Broc opened the front door and pressed a soft kiss on her head, his hand guiding her outside. But the moment was shattered as blinding flashes erupted around them. Rosie instinctively raised her hand to shield her eyes, but Broc was faster, enveloping her in his arms and protecting her from the relentless click of the cameras encroaching on their moment.

"Hey, what the fuck!" Broc shouted.

A man's voice cut through the flashing lights. "How does it feel to leave your pregnant girlfriend for someone who doesn't care about breaking up a relationship?" the man called out as he held his camera up to his face. Broc moved to swipe at the camera, but Rosie pulled him back, forcing him to cover her face again with his hand in a protective manner. "Wouldn't try that, Broc. It could be a lawsuit," the man taunted.

"I'm going to give you a lawsuit!" Broc growled back at the man. "You're on my private property!"

"Naw, man, I've checked; this sidewalk is community property. So, I'm good." The man lowered the camera for a second to show his knowing smirk. *Prick*, Broc thought. His eyes landed on the intruder, and the realization hit him in the gut: it was Diesel. One of the most ruthless paparazzi in the industry, he was good at what he did, and someone Broc had always hated. This was the same man who'd hunted Mindy during her exile from Hollywood. A photo like this would bring in a lot of money to TMZ. It wasn't something Broc usually had to worry about in Spokane, but learning that Mindy's former co-star, Colin Peters, was living here full-time with his new wife and his family, it made sense that Diesel would lurk in the shadows. Broc flexed his jaw, grinding his teeth while he surveyed the street. Coupled with Mindy's talent for manipulation on social media, Broc should never have let his guard down. "Tell me, Rosie, what makes you so special? What makes you think Broc won't leave you for someone else?" Diesel heckled Rosie.

Ready to respond, Rosie's back stiffened as she snapped her head up. She was already on edge, anxiety filled her lungs, pushing through her body and settling on her chest like a heavy boulder.

The pain was back.

Breathing became more difficult as she pressed a hand against her chest. This movement caught Broc's attention; he swooped down and lifted her, one arm under her legs and the other behind her back, carrying her in a bridal-style back into the floral shop, readying his foot to shut the door behind him. Looking over his shoulder, he shouted, "If she faints because of your recklessness, you're going to face a lawsuit for harassing us!"

"I'm well within my rights, Broc, and you know it," Diesel replied, lifting his camera again, snapping more photos of him and Rosie. "Is there a medical reason she's going to faint? Your fans would want to know! Is she also pregnant?"

"You're perpetuating the situation; get the fuck away from here!"

"What's the medical condition? Rosie dying? Does she have

cancer? Come on, Broc, spill her medical history!" *Click, click, click.* Diesel's voice echoed as Broc turned his back to him, grunting in irritation before slamming the door with his foot.

"Rosie, slow your breathing, close your eyes, and focus on my voice," he instructed, his eyes locked onto her as she struggled to steady her heartbeat. He walked straight to the Mosier couch, laying her down gently on the velvet cushions, his hand resting over her hand, which was still over her heart, both feeling the frantic thumping under her skin. Leaning down, he pressed his forehead against hers. "There, that's better, Rosie, just look at me."

Broc settled back on his heels, fingers trailing down the side of Rosie's cheek, pausing to trace the curve of her lower lip and the glint of the silver ring that adorned it. Her gaze softened, a calm slowly replacing the fear that had filled her. Lifting her hand, she rested her palm on Broc's cheek, the connection sparking familiarity even in the heat of her anxiety.

Her breath caught as she took in not only Broc's beauty, but also the finished floral shop's cozy interior. Rosie sat up on her elbows and looked around him. Every nook was filled with vibrant floral arrangements, the colors of late-blooming peonies, Pieris mountain fire, and alstroemerias in hues of white and pink. Fresh flowers filled the floral refrigerators, tall English ferns framing the scattered arrangements like sentinels. Above the Mosier couch was a pink neon sign placed over the pallet wall; it glowed with a soft hue, casting a warm light that read, '*She loves me, she loves me not.*' It was breathtaking; his entire shop was a sight that would make even Thomas Kinkade envious.

"What's that?" she gasped, pointing to the light above her.

A playful smile tugged at his lips. "That's the name of the store."

"*She loves me, she loves me not*, where did that come from?" Her voice held intrigue.

Broc slipped a hand beneath her lower back, helping her to sit up. "You. It's all you."

"Me?" She raised an eyebrow, skepticism in her tone.

"Yes, you." He brought her hand to his lips, starting to kiss each finger. "She loves me," he said with a kiss, moving to the next finger.

"She loves me not," he continued, kissing another. Then he flicked his eyes up to meet hers, looking over her hand as he remarked, "Just make sure you pluck the last petal while saying you love me." He pressed gentle kisses along each of her fingers, his gaze intense.

A smile bloomed across her face. Rosie pulled her hand from his, cupping his neck. Leaning closer, she whispered, "It said she loves you."

"Thank God," he breathed, the words barely formed before his mouth crashed into hers.

The kiss wasn't gentle. It was relief and Broc's desperation of every fear he'd had while she was unconscious pouring out all at once. Rosie melted into him, letting him take what he needed, giving just as fiercely back. Clothes disappeared between frantic hands, fabric tugged and torn aside as if neither of them could stand another barrier. With the large picture windows papered up, they had their privacy in the little nook. Her fingers fumbled at his jeans, pulling at the zipper, breath shaking as they kissed like they were trying to climb inside one another. Their teeth knocked, their mouths fought for control, Broc's tongue sweeping into her with a hunger that made her knees weaken.

"Christ, Rosie," he growled against her mouth. "You have no idea what you do to me." His hands framed her jaw, kept her right where he wanted her as he kissed her deeper, harder, claiming her mouth the way he always touched her, like he needed proof she was real and alive and *his* for this moment.

"I think I do," Rosie breathed. Heat tore through her, sharply and suddenly, her body arching into him as a sound broke from her throat; it was half moan, half surrender. Broc swallowed it like it belonged to him. Then he sank back onto the Mosier couch when she pushed, letting her take control, his chest rising and falling in quick, uneven breaths. She slid between his legs, hands gliding up his thighs, her touch slow as they trailed over his ripped jeans to his center, where he was already hard with his intention.

"Rosie..." His voice cracked; it was rough, warning but pleading, bleeding from his voice. She looked up at him with her violet-blue eyes, pupils blown wide, her lips swollen from his kiss. The sight alone made his breath stutter, his fingers curling hard against the edge of the cushions as if holding himself back took effort. But he didn't attack her the way he wanted to throw her on the couch, rip her clothes away, and suck on her pussy. Instead, he shuddered and closed his eyes, feeling her touch him. Another shudder escaped his lips as her hand moved to rub over his cock. Made him curse under his breath as his head tipped back, throat exposed, the muscles in his abdomen tightening in response. The connection between them snapped like a live wire. "Come here," he rasped, reaching for her, needing her closer, needing his cock inside her sweet, pretty pink pussy. "I want—" His voice broke off as she rose, her hands sliding up his torso, her mouth trailing after them. He was already shaking under her, already fighting for control he didn't have anymore. And when she settled on top of him, her center knew what she needed, and it hardened his cock to an impossible size, to the point of pain, like her touch rewrote his willpower, and there wasn't any left. Broc dragged her up along his body, kissing her until she gasped into his mouth, his hands firm on her hips. "Rosie," he whispered, voice low and dangerous, "I'm not done with you. Not even close."

Running his hand over her face to trace the dips of her cheek and jawline, his hand found her breast, roughly, rolling her nipple between his fingers until a sharp gasp escaped her. Heat surged through Rosie, tightening low in her belly. Broc shoved the coffee table back with one sweep of his arm, the scrape of metal on the floor barely audible over their ragged, desperate breathing. He dragged his mouth down her torso, slow enough to taunt, greedy enough to brand her. Little bites. Soft lips. A pattern he knew would undo her. Pants down, clothes removed, both were bare to each other in a flurry of seconds.

"Broc..." Her voice broke, and he smirked against her skin because he loved the sound of her losing control. Stroking himself once...twice...before settling the thick crown of his cock against her slick entrance. The sight of her opening for him, wet for him, pulled something primal straight out of his chest. Her pussy wrapped around him, and the growl that tore from him was wild, while she hissed as he rocked his hips, thrusting up into her pussy, trying not to fall apart too soon.

"Jesus, Rosie..." His voice cracked. He dipped his head, kissing her with such assault while his fingers found her clit, flicking slowly, then hard, then slow again; she moaned around their kiss, and the vibration punched straight through his spine. His balls tightened instantly.

Rosie slid her hands up his abs, then around, grabbing his ass as she laid back on the couch and his thick body hovered over hers; she kept kneading his ass, spreading him open just enough for her thumb to press against his back entrance.

Broc froze mid-lick. "Fuck, Rosie, don't tease me," he ground out.

"You like that?" she purred, easing his cock partly out of her cunt, wanting to watch his reaction.

He did like it.

Too much.

It made his breath stutter, made his tongue work frantically against her mouth as if he could outrun what she was doing to him. Her thumb breached him, slowly, and he was tight; the feeling had him hissing with a new pleasure. He choked on a moan, almost a plea, and thrust deeper into her cunt, hitting his hilt.

"Rosie—fuck—Rosie, I can't...I'm gonna—" His voice broke apart, hips jerking, any rhythm gone. He was lost, undone, his cock devouring her pussy like a man starved while she swallowed every desperate kiss as he pulled her tongue into his mouth. She pushed her thumb all the way inside him and wrapped her other hand around the back of his neck. His whole body locked. "Fuck, fuck, fuck —" His cry was hoarse, raw, as he came hard, spilling into her pussy. Filling her up, pushing deeper, forcing each pulse and every ounce of his seed into her, needing her to take every drop.

Her moan was low, strained, and rippled over him as she climaxed, her body arching. Still shaking, Broc shoved three fingers inside her, sliding in around his cock that was already stretching her wide. Rosie cried out, bracing her palms against his chest as he fucked her with his hand and cock, the wet sounds between them obscene, addictive.

Her breasts bounced with each thrust, her body rocking under his urgency, possession, and hunger all tangled into one. And then he tore himself away from her, breath ragged, pupils blown wide, like he couldn't decide whether to devour her again or fall apart at her feet.

Turning her over, he slid down between her legs. Pressing his hands on her inner thigh to open her legs wider for his shoulders, he attached his lips back to her clit and sucked while thrusting his fingers deep inside her. With her on all fours, Broc used his free hand and reached up, tracing delicate patterns along her skin and igniting sensations that danced like wildfire beneath her flesh. Palming her breast, twisting, and pinching her nipples, he kneaded her skin like bread, his touch firm, molding to her.

"Broc, I need you inside me again. Fuck me, push into me, stretch me wide," she begged with bated breath, words almost incoherent as she pleaded.

Within seconds, Broc's cock thickened again, licking her back as he situated himself behind her, notched his thick mushroomed head at her entrance, and with one single push, he forced inside her body, making her scream as he did exactly what she'd asked him to do. Broc dipped down, crashing his lips to the delicate skin at the nape of her neck, sucking her harder. Forcing a dance of heat between them, their bodies moved in a rhythm. Over and over again, her pussy surrendered to the primal rhythm, lost in the timelessness.

"Rosie, Rosie, I've got to cum, fuck..." He stumbled on his own words. Reaching between their bodies, using two fingers, he started to rub her clit, sending her off the precipice and into the abyss. A silent scream echoed in his heart as he reached his climax, hitting her with every thrust. Then he slowed his movements down as they both floated back into their bodies. The man was a pure masterpiece, and Rosie was done for.

24

Pro Tip: Sometimes worms are necessary when making compost.

The days leading up to the Netflix premiere felt like a whirlwind, but not as crazy as the grand opening of Broc's floral shop, She Loves Me, She Loves Me Not.

Rosie was trapped inside Broc's building, unable to escape to her own space thanks to the relentless construction. Her special-order windows had finally arrived, and now the crew was working on her shop. Also, it was cold. Rosie wrapped her cream cable-knit sweater tighter around herself; even her wool socks couldn't keep out the chill as Spokane slipped into winter, with the freezing temps proving autumn was no longer around. The only silver lining in her otherwise monotonous days was Raymond—the contractor who had worked his magic on Broc's remodel.

Once the windows were finally installed, Raymond waved goodbye, a small salute followed by a wink. Alone in her shop, she felt a familiar body slide behind her, wrapping his strong, tattooed arms around her waist, pulling her close. He dipped in, kissing the sensitive skin at the nape of her neck, igniting sensations that shot through like fireworks.

"Do you plan to make my tummy flip like this forever?" she teased.

"God, I hope so," he murmured against her skin, a deep growl rumbling in his chest. "Because knowing I make you shudder drives me wild, and my cock hard." His body pressed into hers; an unmistakable message wrapped in his jeans.

A soft moan slipped from her lips as she leaned back against him, letting her head fall onto his shoulder. "You know exactly what you're doing, don't you?"

"Mm-hmm," Broc mumbled through his kisses, his hands sliding up her torso and slipping into the front of her bib-overalls, fingers kneading through her bra in a teasing, torturous way that left her breathless.

Pulling away slightly, Rosie turned to face him, his hands resting on her hips. "Hey, can I say something without you getting upset?"

His gaze softened, the corners of his mouth lifting. "Of course."

"I get that you paid Raymond, and I truly appreciate it. I do. But it just feels important for me to handle the bill... You have to understand." She paused, taking a deep breath, the weight of her past creeping in as she looked away. "Orson used to do this, and he always held it over my head..."

"Rosie, I'd never..." Broc interrupted, a hard-edge creeping into his voice. "Listen to me. You don't have to worry about that with me. I'm not Orson, and I don't do things with strings attached." His promise was felt.

Patting his chest with a determined smile, Rosie said, "I know you aren't him, but I need to handle this myself." She took in the tight lines of Broc's jaw but continued. "My problems aren't your burden. I want to be with you without the constant urge to lean on someone else for support. I might even have to rethink my entire business because I'm realizing how lost I truly am." She lowered her gaze, tucking a stray purple strand behind her ear before meeting his eyes again. "You have to let me try. It takes courage to let go, you know?"

"Rosie," he replied softly, sorrow etched in his expression. The weight of their situation pressed down on him, the looming shadow of Miss Marigold's Plant Shop possibly coming to an end. He knew what she was saying, but most of it was his fault because Mindy was out to destroy Rosie's dreams, twisted by her own false narrative that Rosie had broken up a relationship that had never even existed. Lifting her chin with gentle fingers, he let his gaze roam over the delicate features of her face before settling into her violet-blue eyes. "I don't want to see you fail..." The words hung between them, then he swallowed hard, refusing to push her away, knowing that allowing Rosie down this path alone was the only way for her to grow. He had to stand by, watch her, and let her find her footing, even if it meant watching her fail.

Teetering on her tiptoes, she pressed a soft kiss to the underside of his chin. "Thank you." A pause, then, "Thank you...um..." Concern flashed across her face, and she frowned. "Do you smell something?"

His hands found her shoulders as he instinctively pulled back. "Is that smoke?" The urgency in his voice cut through the moment. Strides quickening toward the back door, once he turned on his heels, thick tendrils of smoke coiled around them. Rosie was right on his heels, her instincts kicking in; the back alley was saturated with suffocating plumes. Broc fished his phone from his back pocket, dialing 9-1-1 in a hurry. Sirens were already wailing in the distance. A fire licked at the small chicken coop, flames dancing hungrily over the wood, weakening its structure. Rosie rushed toward the door, her breath quickening, sending alarms ringing in Broc's thoughts. All he could think was, *It's too late.*

The ache was back, Rosie pressed her palm against her chest, desperately trying to soothe the pain. Panic surged through her as she searched for a way to open the chicken coop door and rescue her beloved Fluffy. But the flames raged like a monstrous beast. Rosie lifted the collar of her shirt, pulled it up around her nose and mouth, and held it in place with one hand while trying to pull open the door with the other, but the heat was searing. It wouldn't budge, which didn't make any sense to her. She glanced around to see what was blocking the door and noticed the problem: five nails had been driven into the door, sealing it shut.

Sirens blared as they came closer. Then Broc wrapped his arms around Rosie's waist, lifting her effortlessly and carrying her away from the inferno that threatened to consume everything she held dear. "NO! Stop! Put me down! Get Fluffy! Put me down!" Rosie screamed, kicking at Broc, trying to pull herself free from his hold. Once they were against the back of her shop, he dropped her, ran to the outside faucet, and pulled the hose out with the other.

"YOU STAY THERE!" he barked back. With the hose in hand, Broc moved. Water poured from the hose as he ran up to the coop, determined to protect what little he could before the firefighters arrived.

Sirens shrieking, the firefighters rolled up; one of the older firefighters, built like a wall, shoved Broc back, redirecting his focus to the flames that engulfed Rosie's heart. She sank to the frozen ground, hands trembling as they covered her mouth, tears streaming unchecked down her cheeks. Her heart was heavy with grief as she stared at the smoking remnants of what had once housed her joy. Words failed her; the fire was contained in minutes, but the devastation within her was anything but contained.

"Anyone inside?" the older firefighter asked Rosie, but her only answer was silence. Just then, Alessandra and Basil burst onto the scene, breathless, their expressions painted with disbelief as they took in the remains of the fire. Without hesitation, Rosie's friends dropped to the ground beside her, grabbing and pulling her into a trembling hug. They stroked her hair, trying to soothe the silent tears in Rosie's eyes.

"It'll be okay," they whispered, but those words felt like a cruel joke. Deep down, Rosie knew that losing Fluffy would never be 'okay.'

Broc was standing off to the side, his gaze fixed on Rosie, his heart aching for her. He was angry about all the shit she'd been dealing with in such a short time. There was anger in his heart, such hatred towards Fate; they were being unfair to her.

"Sir, was this your shed?" the man asked, standing before Broc. He gave a swift nod over to Rosie.

"It was my fiancée's chicken coop, but I can talk to her," Broc added swiftly. Sadness washed over Broc as he lowered his gaze, kicking at the ground. "Shit," he murmured. When he finally looked back up, he forced a grateful smile at the firefighter. "Thank you for containing the fire," he said.

"I have to ask, but do you know what started the fire?" the firefighter inquired.

"No, we were inside her shop when we smelled something," Broc stated.

The older fireman took off his helmet and scratched his forehead. "Okay, the city will be in touch, and we'll look around to see if there is anything out of the ordinary. In the next couple of days, an investor will come out; it's all pretty standard. We'll be in touch." Nodding, Broc walked over and shook the man's hand before he walked over to the men standing around the burned-up coop.

"Broc..." she whispered. And that's all she needed to say for Broc to hurriedly walk to her side. Both Basil and Alessandra stepped away from Rosie, allowing Broc to wrap his arms around her waist and pull her close. His hand rested on her forehead, then slid down to her cheek.

"Rosie, I'm sorry about Fluffy..." Broc's voice cracked.

She fought the pain deep in her chest and bones, the feeling of loss incomparable to anything else. Now, the last remaining thread connecting Rosie to Miss Marigold had been severed. Rosie's eyes drifted to the wisps of smoke swirling up to the heavens, carrying the memories of Miss Marigold.

"Goodbye, Fluffy," she whispered before resting her head on Broc's shoulders, allowing the tears to slide down her cheeks.

25

Pro Tip: Coffee grounds are rich in nitrogen, which is beneficial for plant growth. Sprinkle them around your plants or mix them into the compost heap.

When Rosie opened her eyes the following morning, the sunlight streamed through her window, making Spokane golden under the rays. But in the distance were dark, foreboding clouds, a storm that would soon cover the city. Rolling back onto her pillow, the grief from the night before was an unwelcome guest, gripping her heart with sharpness. She pressed her hand to her chest, just as her cell phone beeped the alarm from her monitor, which she'd finally set up last night. A few calming breaths, and the beeping subsided. Despite the lingering sadness, Rosie resolved to stick to her routine. The only reason she rose out of bed was the need for coffee, her liquid courage at the moment. But first, a hot shower was calling her name. After stepping out of the shower, she glanced over at her cell on the dresser and saw that it was speckled with unread messages.

BROC:

I'll be back soon. I need to order flowers for the premiere.

BROC:

Saw Alessandra – she's waiting for you with your coffee.

BROC:

I'm sorry I'm not there for you this morning. Just know I'm thinking of you and that gorgeous smile of yours.

ALESSANDRA:

Stop by this morning – Basil and I miss you.

UNKNOWN:

(GIF of a KFC bucket)

Her heart raced as she flung the phone across the room. Taking a deep breath, she steadied herself, releasing the tension in her shoulders before tossing the towel aside. She pulled on her favorite overalls over a long-sleeve blue shirt, layering it with a cozy Irish cable-knit cardigan. With a flick of her wrist, she twisted her hair into Viking-style braids. Once she finished her makeup, her reflection in the mirror wore a punk-inspired flair, edgy, just like her spirit. Rosie stepped into the hallway. A sudden impulse took her back to grab her phone, slipping it into her back pocket before making her way downstairs from Broc's apartment to the main floor.

Two guys loitered in plain black sweatshirts and jeans, trying hard to blend into the floral shop. Red caps emblazoned with 'Netflix' rested on their heads, as they set up lighting and cameras for Broc's upcoming film premiere. They looked up briefly, giving her small smiles, and Rosie returned their nods before slipping past, the blur of floral arrangements around her feeling oddly comforting. Plants and flowers were her love language.

Rosie knew that if she didn't open her shop's doors soon, she would lose it. Forward was the only direction she could afford to move. Today, she would have to suck it up and open the doors, see if anyone would be interested in her "vandalism sale," which would hopefully help her buy a few new orchids.

A gentle fog settled over the frosted sidewalk, a sign that Jack Frost had danced through the night, touching every building, road, and walkway in Spokane. The sun began to hide behind the dark, low-hanging clouds, keeping the city under a blanket of chill. Carefully walking down the block, wearing Birkenstocks was probably not the best choice for this particular morning. Wrapping her Irish cardigan around her body tighter, Rosie was about to step inside the Little Cafe when something caught her eye across the street. There, leaning against the old brick building next to the wedding dress shop, was Orson. In his hands was the trademark bucket of fried chicken. A smirk spread across his face, and he lifted a chicken leg to his lips, taking an exaggerated bite while his eyes remained fixed on Rosie.

Her heart must have stalled because little alarms beeped on her cell, once again telling her to relax and take a calming breath. But then Orson lifted the little chicken leg, nodded with a smirk, and slinked back into the shadows like a bad dream. Rosie stood there, staring, her stomach churning at the horrific display he had just presented. A disturbing realization flashed into her mind: *He killed Fluffy*.

Rosie took two deep breaths, repeating the process until the ache in her chest subsided, and she regained control over her Broken Heart Syndrome.

The bell above the door chimed softly.

"Hey there!" Alessandra's voice was a melody of familiarity. Rosie rounded the corner of the counter, and in one fluid motion, Alessandra closed the distance, pulling Rosie into a tight embrace that made it feel like the world was melting away. "Let's get you something to drink, shall we?" she suggested, her fingers gently weaving through Rosie's long, purple braids.

"Rosie!" Basil's voice sliced through the comforting hum of the espresso machine. "Guess what? I've already started your drink, made it a 16oz this time, not a 12oz. Tomorrow's event is going to be a marathon; you'll need the fuel." The grin on Basil's face could light up an entire city. "And hold on to the straps of your overalls because Broc invited Alessandra and me! Can you even believe it? Me! I'm pairing this adorable pearl dress from Vida Lux Boutique with a chunky vintage white-and-gold flower necklace. Becca's my plus-one, and you know she'll bring down the house in her signature pantsuit. With those killer heels, she's downright irresistible." Basil leaned back, her eyes fluttering shut for a moment of pure bliss. "If forbidden fruit were real, she'd be it, and let me tell you, I'd eat that all day long," Basil said while Rosie giggled. "I've missed that smile of yours, honey," Basil commented.

Alessandra pulled up a chair beside the counter. "Alright, spill! You doing okay?" The late morning flew by in a flurry. She told them what Orson had done and also about Broc's premiere at the flower shop. Rosie explained the whole naming of Broc's shop, 'She Loves Me, She Loves Me Not.' That revelation sent both friends into a swoon. "I knew it! I knew it! Forced proximity! Fake dating never stays fake!" Her joy was infectious.

The three friends wrapped up their celebratory muffin treat when the door chimed again, and in walked Broc, a living work of art, his skin adorned with mesmerizing tattoos. The moment his gaze found Rosie's, the world spun in slow motion. He walked to her with purpose, positioning himself between her legs on the stool, his hands gently resting on her shoulders. He leaned in, placing a tender kiss on her forehead, then dipped to press another soft kiss against her cheek. "Rosie, I've missed you. Did you have a good morning?" he asked while he scanned her face.

Rosie met his gaze, returning his smile. "Yes, they really helped me through a rough morning."

Basil tossed her tea towel aside, her expression twisting into a scowl. "I'll take care of that," she declared. With a swift movement, she rounded the corner toward a table of girls, each with their cell phones out, some recording and others snapping pictures. Before Rosie could see what would happen, Broc gently turned her face back toward his with his long, slender finger.

"Don't worry about them, Rosie. I'm here. Nothing is going to take me away from you." Broc's voice had that deep, soothing undertone that made her feel safe. Just as that warmth settled in, a loud clap shattered the moment, and Rosie turned to find Alessandra standing there. "Ignore me. I'm just here to witness the miracle of my friend actually being interested in someone. I mean, after that creep, Orson, who could blame me? That guy had a vibe that sent chills down our spines," Alessandra remarked, brushing off the thought like it was an annoying bug. "But now look at you! You've got this walking masterpiece!" Her eyes sparkled as she slapped the countertop and straightened up, alternating her gaze between Broc and Rosie. "Did you fill him in on that Orson incident from this morning?"

"What happened?" Broc's immediate concern was focused on Rosie.

Taking a deep breath, Rosie recounted the morning's events. The truth hit her hard. Orson's possibility of harm was more chilling than she wanted to admit. If he had it in him to be so cruel, what else was he capable of?

26

Pro Tip: Don't punch a cactus.

Anticipating a high rating on the Netflix premiere, Broc decided to reach out to the last person he ever expected to speak to: Colin Peters, Mindy's ex. Despite their past, Colin and Poppy agreed to attend Broc's soft launch and the Netflix premiere, with the assurance that Mindy would not be in attendance.

Exiting the shower, Broc smiled as he watched Rosie standing with her hands on her hips, watching him with a strong glare, a look that made Broc chuckle as he walked closer. There was a buzz in the air with the preparation commotion downstairs. Broc watched as Rosie scrunched up her nose at the dresses laid out on his bed.

"Rosie, is something wrong with the dresses I ordered for you?" His voice was low as he toweled off, the damp fabric swishing against his skin. Rosie stood at the foot of the bed, hands shoved deep into the pockets of her overalls, her eyes glued to the two pristine dress bags sprawled across the bed.

Tossing the towel aside, he chuckled softly while he slipped into a pair of black boxer briefs. He moved closer, a confident stride that closed the distance between them. Resting his chin on her shoulder, his front to her back, he inhaled deeply, letting her sweet, floral scent wash over him, a blend that seeped into his veins and sparked a hunger he couldn't ignore.

His body reacted instantly, desire pooling low in his gut as he pressed himself against her back. But Rosie scoffed, shrugging him off with an exasperated roll of her head. "Broc, we don't have time. I need to get ready for tonight. Your shop opening is a big deal, and it's broadcasting live," she reminded him, her tone filled with annoyance.

"Relax," he replied, kissing her shoulder and then the nape of her neck. "I've got a makeup artist lined up...Sage, I think her name was? The Netflix producer mentioned she's worked with Colin Peters. And when I called Colin, he even recommended Sage."

"Wait," she said, twisting around in his hold, his chest vibrating from her touch. "You talked with Colin Peters? Like *THE* Colin Peters? Hold on, wasn't there a rumor that he slept with that makeup artist somewhere on the internet?" The heat of her breath fanned across his skin, making his core pulse. He was not even thinking about what she was saying. "Sometimes I forget what circles you run around in. And if that rumor is true...I don't think I want you to be alone with her," Rosie commented, tapping her lip with her pointer finger. A broad smile graced her lips as her hands skimmed over his abs, causing him to hiss, hooking her thumbs in his boxer briefs and tugging them from his body. A low, almost growl-like rumble emanated from his throat. His shaft bounced up, trapped between him and Rosie's fully clothed body. Broc rolled his hips as he ground himself against her pelvis, slamming his mouth to hers, kissing her deeply.

He reached up, his fingers finding the back of her neck, tangling themselves in the rich cascade of her long purple hair. With a gentle twist, he pulled her head back, exposing the delicate floral tattoos that danced across her collarbone and coiled around her throat like a seductive noose. Leaning in, he traced the ink with his nose, inhaling, tasting her on his tongue, appreciating the liquid heat seeping from her body. When she pulled back slightly, a soft gasp escaped her lips, a flicker of disappointment flashing in her eyes, and Broc couldn't help but smile.

"It's possible, but only before Poppy came around. Those two are inseparable; Colin would never cheat on her. He's completely in love with her and their kids."

"Is it terrible to admit I want you to stay away from Sage?" Rosie asked, brushing her lips with her pointer finger as she tried to regain her composure.

"I have to say, I kind of dig this possessive side of you," Broc responded, a smirk stretching across his face, enjoying the playful back-and-forth. He shifted closer, his body pressing into hers as he let his hand slide down her cheek, locking eyes with her electrifying violet-blue gaze. "Trust me," he breathed, his lips teasingly brushing along her ear. "No one will come between us. If it helps, I can wait downstairs when Sage comes upstairs; no need for you to worry about me lurking around." Then he pulled her into him, their bodies fitting together like pieces of a puzzle. He added, his voice dropping low, "I should be there to greet our guest anyway..." His gaze held hers, feeling her concern.

Nodding, she wrapped her arms around Broc's neck, a cheeky smile forming as she admitted, "Sorry, my green-eyed monster just leaked."

He lifted his hand to trace her cheek, tilting his head to rest his forehead against hers. With a feather-light kiss on her nose, he murmured, "I love seeing that fire in you. Seriously, if anyone touches you, I might just lose it." His breath danced across her skin, igniting a heat that overshadowed her earlier jealousy, leaving only an insatiable need for his thick cock.

There was a fervor in her kiss as she slammed her mouth to his, his tongue teasing, sweeping into her mouth, meeting every demand, searching for more of her sweetness.

"Mmm," he groaned against her. "I think we have a few precious minutes, but we'll have to be quick."

In a swift motion, she reached for the clips on her overalls, unhooking them and letting the fabric fall away in a cascade at her feet. Rosie was wearing a thin scrap of fabric as she pulled it down her thighs. Broc reached for it and ripped it off her, allowing her to kick it away. Exhilaration rushed through her veins as Broc cupped her cheeks and lifted her effortlessly, her legs instinctively wrapping around his solid frame. Their mouths collided in a fiery dance, each kiss more frantic than the last. He pressed her against the wall next to the door, a whirlwind of hunger crashing as their teeth smashed in a messy kiss, his lips nipping her lower lip. Slowly, with barely any control, Broc lowered his hand, slipped it under her shirt and her bra to palm her breast, kneading it while he rubbed his thumb over her hardened nipple. Rosie's hair cascaded around her shoulders as Broc slipped his hand away from her breast down to her pulsing wet need, running his thumb around her wetness in slow circles.

"Mmmm, you're already so wet for me. Tell me, Rosie. Do you want me to fill you with my seed?" Rosie moaned, her eyes shut as she nodded. "You ready for my hot cum to coat the inside of your body?"

"Please, Broc," she begged.

"I want to see my cum dripping from your pussy. I want every man to smell our sex dripping from you," he growled into her ear, his breath lightly tickling her flesh, his hips rolling against her body. "I want other men to know that your cunt was already filled tonight and will be for the foreseeable future—only by me."

"Yes," Rosie gasped as he thrust a finger into her wetness. Moving her hips, she met him thrust by thrust. "Oh god, that feels like I'm in heaven." She moaned before her tongue flicked out to lick her lip, and then she bit down, pulling her lip in her mouth with a hiss. Broc adjusted his hold for a split second; his shaft remained trapped between the two of them. He removed his hand from Rosie's sweet cunt as she cried out her disapproval at the lack of his touch. His hardened, thick cock leaked cum from its mushroomed slit. Rosie rolled her hips again, wiggling down to allow him to notch his swollen head against her slick, wet folds.

"Greedy little thing." He chuckled.

"I need you inside me," Rosie pleaded. She let her head fall back against the wall once more. "Please, Broc, push inside me."

With one pump of his hips, he penetrated her, his cock filling her halfway, "Fuck, Rosie. Goddamn, you're so tight!" he groaned. "I don't think I could get any bigger, fuck. This is what you do to me." Thrusting aggressively, he shoved his cock all the way inside her, then he gasped. "Never mind, I was wrong, Jesus fuck Rosie, I might embarrass myself. I'm about to cum all over you...fucking hell, give me a sec." Her pussy coated his cock with even more of her wetness. The inner walls of Rosie's cunt rippled as he seated himself to his hilt.

Breathing ceased in Broc's lungs as he started to ascend into heaven with his cock buried deep. His neck muscles tensed, his lungs demanding air, and he emerged from the fog of passion as if breaking the ocean's surface with a final, audible gasp. Slipping his hands down on the round globes of her ass, he swung around and carried her to his bed, shoving the dresses onto the floor with one swipe.

Lowering her while still inside her body, he somehow managed to kneel on the bed as he adjusted his grip, his eyes locked onto her with a cautionary intensity. A grin spread wide while his fingers skimmed down her legs to her knees and gently pressed her legs against the mattress, forcing her pussy to open wider for him. Broc watched his cock push inside her tight cunt. He leaned forward, spitting on her pussy, watching the slickness of her moisture and his spit mix for only a second before he rubbed her clit and began to pound into her tight wetness.

Blinding white light and stars exploded behind her eyes as she cried out, her hand muffling her sobs. Chasing after his own pleasure, he held himself on top of her body, rhythmically quickening his pace. Sweat glistened down his forehead, his face subsequently turning a shade of red as his passion reached a precipice and flooded her cunt full of his seed. With a few rugged pumps, he collapsed down over her body. His lips connected to her neck, licking his way to her lips until he claimed them with his kiss, forcing his tongue inside of her in a deep, passionate kiss. His cock jumped inside her pussy, which had her chuckling.

"As much as I want to fuck you again, we have to get ready, Rosie."

27

Pro Tip: Regularly prune your plant to encourage growth and remove dead or diseased parts. Deadheading flowers can promote more bloom and keep your garden looking tidy.

"Hey, numb-nuts! Get over here!" Adam called, striding past the swarm of press and paparazzi gathered outside the entrance of She Loves Me, She Loves Me Not. The usual dance of smiles and angled shots didn't interest Adam one bit. He was all about that carefree swagger, as he crossed the threshold without a backward glance.

Davis and Sammy, on the other hand, took their time as they walked in. Each was impeccably dressed to support Broc for the opening of his floral shop. They approached the front doors, and the cameras snapped away, uncaring that they weren't part of the elite world, as the paparazzi still yelled and called out for their names. Davis didn't even flinch. Instead, he placed a hand on Sammy's lower back, steering her into the shop.

Inside, Broc was deep in conversation with the Netflix director and producer for the premiere of their historical romance, casually talking about the evening's agenda. But when he caught sight of his friends, a genuine smile broke across his face. He patted the shorter, older man on the shoulder, stepping aside to seek out Adam. Once their hands met, Adam pulled Broc into a bone-crushing hug, two friends reunited as if it were second nature.

"Dude, the place looks great! But I wanna know, where's your girl? How's she doing? Where is Rosie?" Adam's eyes scanned for Rosie, barely looking at Broc.

Davis moved in next, extending his hand for a firm shake. Broc accepted it, and then he turned to Sammy, his smile softening as he took her in. "Wow, it's been ages, and you're even more stunning," he said. Davis instinctively wrapped an arm around her waist, pulling her in closer against him. A shielding gesture that didn't go unnoticed. Broc leaned in, planting a light kiss on Sammy's cheek, and then he whispered just loud enough for her to hear, "Don't worry, I won't steal you away from my best friend." Sammy's cheeks flushed a shade of pink that was hard to ignore.

Spinning in a full circle like a kid in a candy store, Adam planted his hands on his hips, his eyes wide as he took in the vibrant décor of Broc's shop. "This place is incredible, Broccoli! I absolutely love it!" he shouted, giving Broc a slap on the back. Just then, he spotted a passing waiter, the tray garnished with herb-melba toast. Without a second thought, he lunged forward, snatching one in each hand. Leaning into Broc, he whispered conspiratorially, "What the hell is this?"

"Just eat it and shut your hole," Broc responded. Adam's smile grew broader as he spotted champagne flutes being carried toward him on trays and quickly shoved the canapes down his throat.

Sammy's eyes widened as she spotted another tray with melba toast decorated with nasturtiums. "Oh, Adam! Can I have one?" she chimed, pointing to the other toast in his free hand.

"Sure, take this rabbit food," Adam teased, passing the one he hadn't eaten to her. "Any ribs or something with real meat?" he asked, casually swiping another glass of champagne from a waiter who wove his way through the crowd.

"Adam," Davis warned.

"What?! I'm starving!" he said over his shoulder. The group exchanged knowing glances, watching Adam's quick strides to yet another champagne glass.

"Where's Rosie?" Davis shifted the conversation.

"She'll be down," Broc assured. "So, what do you think?" he questioned, throwing his arms wide. He was wearing his stunning blue paisley blazer, matching the floral decoration in the room. The room buzzed with a sea of A-list Hollywood personalities, the industry's elite.

"Andy and Liz couldn't make it," Davis said, a sympathetic lilt to his voice. "They wanted to be here, but let's be real, they're drowning in test prep. Some fellowship...or maybe it's an internship, honestly, I have no idea how that whole doctor tier works." He chuckled softly. "But Liz? She's on the brink of a meltdown. The idea of the two of them being separated into different hospitals? It's driving her insane. And Andy? He's doing everything in his power to keep her from spiraling completely out of control. He sends his love, though."

Broc couldn't help the smile that spread across his face at Andy's concern for Liz; it struck a chord deep within him. He got it. "Thanks, man. I'll shoot him a text later; let him focus on what's really important," Broc replied. "But...what about Daisy? Is she coming?"

Adam's grin turned infectious as he sauntered back to Broc with a fresh flute of champagne in his hand and a flash of that familiar panty-dropping smile he and Broc had perfected in high school. "Shit, she's got my life in a chokehold. Seriously, though, I love that wildfire. She's working hard in her training. There's a major indoor meet soon, and I'm headed to Virginia Beach for the Diamond League. It's a big deal," he explained, his smile dimming slightly as he pushed his hair back from his scarred brow. "But you've still got me, motherfucker!" He burst into laughter, delivering a light punch to Broc's chest.

Another waiter glided through the room with a tray of pink champagne flutes. "Well, why not? Two for me!" Adam called out, snatching the drinks and downing them like a champ. "Frat life had its perks!" he declared. Davis raised his own flute in a toast to Adam's "talent," while Sammy hid her smile with her hand. Davis just shook his head, bemused.

"Broc, is Rosie going to show up tonight?" Sammy asked softly. Broc lifted his glass and nodded.

"She's on her way," he confirmed, gesturing toward the back of the shop. Moments later, she swept down the final steps into the room, dressed to dazzle. Sammy gasped, and Broc's heart raced as Rosie glided into the room, the camera flashes bursting like fireworks all around her. She wore a fitted chiffon dress in a delicate pink, adorned with pearl-like accents that caught the light and teased the eye. The daringly high slit showcased her strong, pale legs, and those strappy heels elevated her height, leaving every onlooker breathless, and all her artwork on display. Broc was already a goner for her.

Sage's artistry came alive; she'd wielded her brushes and sponges on Rosie perfectly, showcasing her artistic tattoos that snaked around her skin like a living work of art. Her eyes were a mesmerizing blend of deep pink shadow, entirely edged with bold evening eyeliner. A touch of translucent powder kissed her skin. He felt that familiar surge of possessiveness coil around his heart, a feral warning to any man who dared let his gaze linger on her for even a second too long.

When Rosie met Broc's intense gaze, an electric jolt of gratitude flowed through her. She moved closer to him, seamlessly melting into his embrace. He pulled her tight, pressing a tender kiss to her cheek before burying his face in her long purple cascading hair, breathing in her post-sex scent.

Adam tilted his head, his grin wide as he tapped his finger with the hand still holding onto his flute. "You fucked." It wasn't a question. Adam just knew. A chuckle slipped from Broc's lips before he leaned in and kissed Rosie again, causing her cheeks to flush as red as the strawberry buds drawn on her skin.

Sammy squinted, her gaze sharpening. "Seriously, Adam!" she scolded her friend.

He lifted his shoulders. "What? I can tell! Only stating the truth; I had to knock out the five-knuckle shuffle before I came here because I missed my Red."

Sammy slapped her hand to her face and then took a deep breath. "God, Adam, your filter needs to be adjusted."

"What? No, it's perfect!" He flashed his characteristic sly grin, tilting the flute of champagne back and draining it in one smooth motion. "And I know you and Davis just fooled around, too, because there's a broken seam on your strap right there." Adam gestured towards a loose thread on Sammy's little black dress.

"Okay, that's enough, Adam. Walk over there and be good," Davis instructed, pointing to the other side of the floral shop. "Broc, it was great to see you, but I need to take Sammy for a bite to eat. I really need to take full advantage of my kid-free time with Archie at my mom's place," he said, shooting Sammy a playful wink. She chuckled softly as they strolled away.

"Honestly, I kind of wish I'd spent more time with them back in high school," Rosie mused, watching them go.

Broc leaned closer, his thumb lingering beneath her lower lip ring. "I can't shake the feeling that I wasted so many years not begging on bended knee to claim you as mine," he admitted, his voice low. "But I'm just grateful that you're here with me now."

"Hey, I'm back," Adam announced with two more flutes in his hands. "Look who also showed up," he mentioned, tilting his head. "Carla and her bartender-dude."

Turning his gaze to Rosie, Broc asked her, "Did you ever hang out with Carla in high school?" Rosie peered over Adam's shoulder and then shook her head.

"But I think I remember that you might have dated her?" Rosie questioned Adam.

Standing beside Rosie, Adam leaned into her. "Naw, Andy dated her. But shit, look at her cute button nose and that dress she's wearing —look at her fucking rack. Check them out! They're perfect. I love boobs. I...love...RED! I'm a kept man, Rosie! How dare you point out another woman's boobs to me, and my god, with her man right there!"

Rosie laughed at the ridiculousness behind her own hand. Broc's head fell back briefly before he pinned Adam with a narrow gaze. He was just about to shut him up when Carla walked over and stopped right in front of Adam, placing her hands on her hips. "Adam, I swear to god, I'm going to punch you in the face if you keep talking about my boobs in public. I swear...I shouldn't have to tell you for a third time. It's like you're a toddler or something. And it's total harassment too, you idiot. You don't see me walking around saying, 'God, check out Adam's cock.'"

"I wish you would! It's pretty amazing," Adam cut in, his smile widening.

Carla shook her head, switched her expression to a pleasant smile, and looked at Broc. "Hey, Broc, long time no see! Is that Rosie?" she asked, her gaze narrowing as she smiled.

Broc stepped forward, wrapping his arm around Rosie's waist just as another waiter wove through the crowd behind him, nodding in acknowledgment. "Yep, Rosie Clark graduated in the same year as me, one year behind you though," he replied.

"I can totally picture her in that tiny floral shop at Ferris High School," she reminisced, squinting her eye and tapping her finger against her lips. With a glance over her shoulder, she caught Samuel, AKA bartender-dude. Dressed in a blazer over his black Santa Cruz t-shirt, new black jeans, and Vans, he looked effortlessly cool. "So, were you going to say something to Adam about his comment on my...assets?" she interrogated him.

Samuel shrugged. "I mean, he's not wrong. You've got incredible boobs," he added, then turned his attention to the waiters walking around the shop.

"Thanks for that, bro!" Adam chirped, giving Samuel a slight slap across his chest, then lifted his hand for a high-five, one that Samuel readily returned.

"Oh, for fuck's sake," Carla exclaimed, throwing her hands up in exasperation. "Can you just get me some champagne?" she demanded, rolling her eyes.

Reaching into his pocket, Samuel pulled out a silver flask, unscrewed it, and offered it to her. "Eww, seriously, Sam? I meant from the waiters walking around with champagne!" she said, disgust evident on her face.

Shrugging, he tilted the flask to his lips with a devil-may-care attitude. "I just prefer having my own. You never know if they'll have the good stuff."

"If I didn't know you better, I'd think you've got a problem. But with Carla around, I guess you're just an aficionado trying to avoid a beatdown." Broc laughed, shaking his head.

"Something like that," Samual agreed.

Carla cut in, "Broc, he owns a bar on 57th, up on the hill. You know that place Sammy and Davis met?"

"Oh, the one with the pool tables? Morty's?"

"Yep, that's the one," Carla confirmed.

"Cool," Broc said, smiling.

Carla shot Broc a playful smile, hands on her hips, confidence radiating from her. "So, Broc, listen up. This big doofus and I are tying the knot soon. Think you can fit us in for the flowers at our wedding?"

Broc's face illuminated with a grin. "Absolutely! Just shoot me an email next week, and we'll hammer out the details."

Samuel leaned back, taking a long swig from his flask. "See? All settled. But honestly, hitting the Hitching Post in Coeur d'Alene would be way easier." He turned his gaze toward Broc. "Thanks, man. Carla was stressing over the flowers, but I told her that anything she picked would be fine. I just want to marry her, not the damn flowers."

Carla huffed and gave him a playful smack to the stomach. "I'm only getting married once! Broc is one of the best florists out there, at least the most popular. And let's be real, he's pretty cute, too."

"Not sure how I feel about that..." Samuel replied thoughtfully. Then he chuckled, taking another swig before his attention shifted to Colin Peters and his wife stepping into the floral shop. A grin broke across his face as he closed the distance in brisk strides. Colin pulled Samuel into a bro-hug, clapping him on the back, while Carla wrapped her arms around Poppy, squeezing her tightly.

"Broc, you remember my good friend Colin and his wife?"

Samuel asked, his voice light. Broc's and Colin's handshake was firm, the nod meaningful, with a unity against the manipulative force that once sought to drive them apart. Yes, they knew each other. Broc was sure he was only about 5 degrees from Kevin Bacon...which made him smile. He couldn't wait to meet him one day.

"Great to see you, and you look as radiant as ever, Poppy. How are the twins?" Broc leaned in, pressing a soft kiss to her cheek. Drawing closer, he introduced Rosie to Colin and Poppy, effortlessly sliding into conversation about their four-month-old twin girls and their toddler Aiden, who was the son of Poppy's late husband. Once the world had caught wind of Colin's love for Poppy, everyone learned how he'd stepped into the role of fatherhood without hesitation, even officially adopting him.

Their conversation quickly turned to scheduling plans for a standing order through Poppy's non-profit organization to provide flowers for families facing hospital challenges. But just as they began to delve deeper, their conversation was sliced through by the sudden, jarring swing of the shop's front doors. A cacophony of cameras and chatter swept into the room, all eyes snapping to the spectacle.

Mindy Harper strode in, a calculated predator, her gaze unkind as she walked through the crowd with a chilling glint that sent shivers crawling up Rosie's spine, like an army of spiders skittering over her skin.

28

Pro Tip: Adequate air circulation is critical for photosynthesis and waste disposal. It helps in the removal of harmful pollutants from the air.

Rosie felt her heart clench as her breathing grew shallow. Her posture stiffened, and her palms grew clammy. At the same time, Broc couldn't help but notice the concerned look wash over Poppy's face.

Colin leaned forward. "I think Poppy and I should check on our babies. Rosie, it was a pleasure meeting you, and I hope your plant shop is back up and running soon. I know Poppy would love to come in and see your plants," Colin said, shaking Rosie's hand, then turned to Broc and adding, "Broc, thanks for the invite, and..." He nodded towards Mindy as she approached the group in a skintight silver cocktail dress. "Be careful." With that, Colin guided Poppy away just as Mindy closed the distance with her stilettos clicking on the cement floor. She shouldered Rosie aside, her fingers curling tightly around Broc's shoulders. Without a second thought, she pressed her lips against his, while the cameras clicked away, immortalizing the stunned expressions on both Rosie and Broc's faces.

"Hey, Broc, we've missed you." Mindy placed a hand on her flat stomach, gesturing towards her supposed pregnancy. Turning her gaze to Rosie and making sure she'd stepped between the two of them, she slipped her hand through Broc's arm and nestled up to him. "Looks like I arrived just in time," she remarked, turning her attention back to Rosie. "Thank you for being there for Broc during our challenging time apart. It was especially tough for him knowing he couldn't witness his little bean growing." Her voice had a sickeningly sweet, affectionate tone as she rubbed her cheek against his arm, staking her claim.

With a slow, resigned nod, Rosie pressed her lips into a tight line. There was nothing else she could do then; all eyes and camera lenses were on her and Broc, watching their every move like a hawk. She tried to inhale and calm down as she watched Mindy step closer into Broc's body and say, "Broc, your friend is really starting to draw attention. I think she needs to go. After all, this is an invite-only party, and there's no reason for her to be here when I'm carrying your baby."

Rosie's mouth opened, ready to speak, when a hand enveloped her shoulders, drawing her close to another warm figure. She turned her head, catching a sideline glance at Adam, who pulled her snugly against his chest. The sudden onslaught of flashing cameras intensified Rosie's anger, each burst echoing the ache in her chest, making it harder to breathe.

Instinctively, Rosie lifted her hand, rubbing her chest in a futile attempt to ease the pain now radiating throughout her body. Broc's gaze flickered from Rosie's hand rubbing against her chest right over her heart, to Mindy's hand on his chest, a tactic that she was proudly using to display the engagement ring for the cameras to capture.

"Mindy, what the hell?" Broc snapped, his voice low. He pulled away from Mindy's grip, stepping closer to Rosie, an action that made her heart flutter more rapidly. Cupping her cheeks, Broc forced her to meet his gaze. "Breathe, Rosie, just take a deep breath." His eyes flickered to Adam, urgency creeping into his tone as he leaned in. "Can you help her? She's going to pass out; there's a faint blue tint on her lower lip." Rosie struggled to draw a breath, her chest constricting as the rope cinched tighter. Adam cleared his throat, a discreet attempt to mask the moment from the prying eyes of the press and the crowd swirling around them. Drawing Rosie close, Adam turned her away from the cameras, his voice a soothing murmur in her ear, guiding her to focus on his breaths and calm the wild racing of her heart.

Concern in deep lines formed on Broc's face as Adam whispered, "Rosie, you're looking a little bit pale. Steady your breathing." With an arm around her, Adam slid his hand down her arm, searching for her pulse, seeking nonchalance while urgency beat beneath Rosie's skin.

But Rosie was lost in a frantic spiral of thoughts. "She's not supposed to be here," Rosie whispered, her voice so small that Adam could barely hear it. And the idea of leaving Broc alone with Mindy made her heart race even faster, a fire igniting in her chest. Her other hand flew to her throat, clawing desperately, gasping for air. Each breath became a struggle, every gasp a desperate plea against her own body. Though her cell phone wasn't on her, no doubt the alarm was ringing upstairs where she'd left it.

And just when it felt like everything was closing in around her, Broc's cell phone erupted with an alarming ring. Several people nearby, close friends to Broc in the Hollywood world, turned their heads, their curiosity piqued by the sound emanating from Broc's back pocket. With a swift movement, he retrieved his cell phone, tapping a few keys to silence the persistent alarm. "Adam, she needs to calm down before she faints. Take her," he instructed. Then, his gaze shifted to Mindy with a firm resolve. "And, Mindy, you need to leave right now because, as you said, this is an invite-only event." She scoffed at the remark, crossing her arms over her chest and stomping her dainty foot. Broc ignored her, keeping his attention on Rosie.

Adam nodded briskly, enfolding Rosie. His hand glided down her back as he leaned in close, his voice a gentle murmur in her ear. "Shh, try to calm down, Rosie. Feel my heartbeat, focus on its steady rhythm." Lost in her struggle to regulate her breathing, Rosie hardly noticed as Adam guided her away, leading her to the alley behind Broc's building, shielding her from the prying eyes and the clamor of the crowd inside Broc's floral shop.

The chill in the air jolted Rosie back to awareness, and she rested her head against Adam's chest, finding his heartbeat. Minutes passed as Rosie's eyes searched Adam's. There wasn't anything intimate hidden behind his gaze; there was more concern. Slowly, the ache in her chest subsided. "Thank you," Rosie murmured, her breath a puff of white that swirled around between her and Adam's face. A smile tipped Adam's lips as he tugged her back into a hug, then pulled back and cupped her cheeks.

"You feel okay now?" Adam's gaze swept over Rosie, a silent assessment of her well-being, before focusing on her neck. With a soft touch, his fingers sought her pulse once more. Satisfied, he shifted his touch to the back of her head, tilting it forward with a tender gesture and gently kissing her forehead. "Come on, let's go back inside. You're getting cold out here."

Taking a slight step back, she touched his chest. "You go back in and tell Broc I'm okay. But I don't think it's a good idea for me to go back inside with Mindy there still." Just the mere thought of Mindy touching Broc had the ache in her chest returning, searing into her heart. The jealousy gnawed at her, igniting a liquid rage through her veins. The realization hit her like a thunderbolt; her heart belonged to Broc. The truth echoed louder: she was in love with Broc.

Adam's hands settled on Rosie's shoulders, his gaze probing as he wrestled with his medical training and his own emotions, his jaw clenching. Rosie's reassuring pat on his chest prompted him to relent. "Alright, but as soon as Mindy leaves, one of us is coming back for you," he declared.

"I wouldn't expect anything less," Rosie replied with a smile. She remained rooted in place until she watched him disappear inside. Missing out on the party saddened her, but knowing she could still watch the movie premiere from the comfort of her own bed was just as good. She'd have to text Alessandra and Basil to let them know she wouldn't be there when they arrived. With a sigh, Rosie rubbed at the lingering ache in her chest, allowing her head to fall back as she exhaled deeply, watching her breath swirl into the night sky above. Life had been a whirlwind of stress lately, each day feeling like a new roller coaster ride. She longed for a reprieve, a moment of respite, but it seemed that tonight was not the night for it. *Be a crow, be a crow...*

29

Pro Tip: Be aware for seasonal changes and adjust your care routine accordingly. Some plants need protections from frost in the winter, while others may require extra watering during the summer months.

When the premiere event finally ended, reality took a sharp turn. Mindy's presence had caused drama, leading to her being escorted out of the premiere by Netflix security. It was only a matter of time before she was considered a washed-up actress. If it hadn't already happened by tonight.

Only Adam remained beside Broc as they watched the Netflix crew pack up their cameras and bundle the wires. A cleanup crew was scheduled to arrive in the morning for a final once-over, guaranteeing the shop would be ready to open in a few days. Now that Mindy was no longer in the picture, it seemed like a small weight had been lifted from his chest, at least for now.

"Adam, did Rosie go back to my apartment?" Broc asked.

"She wanted a few outside, to calm herself." Adam shook his head, a bottle of champagne monopolizing his attention and his grip firm around the neck of the bottle. Raising the bottle to his lips, he took a long swig. "This is exceptional," he complimented, staring at the bottle. "Fucking love the expensive shit." After another swig, he drew in a deep breath, exhaling with satisfaction. "Shit, man, I'm drained; gotta call up Red, make sure she knows I wasn't hanging all over Rosie, and fill her in on the little situation. The last thing I want is a breakup over a stupid misunderstanding."

"Alright, man." Broc nodded, placing his hands on his hips. He nodded towards the stairs. "Head up to my place there and take the couch or the spare bedroom. I think there's an air mattress in the closet."

"Couch it is! I'm too fucking drunk to fill that mattress with air," Adam said, and placing the champagne bottle down on the floral-cutting island, he strolled over to Broc and gave his shoulder a single slap. "Turned out pretty well, considering things nearly went sideways. Proud of you, dickhead. Don't let the years slip away again; this time, stay in touch, man. We've all missed your hairy ass."

"I will, man," Broc replied, smiling back as he watched Adam stumble up the stairs. "You really must be drunk if you didn't make a *that's what she said* comment."

Adam paused at the stairs in the back of Broc's shop, looking over his shoulder. He added, "Just wait till you fall asleep; I'll be spooning that ass like it was covered in chocolate. Leave the condoms out," Adam stated, winking mischievously.

"There it is..." Broc said, chuckling to himself.

"Night, little spoon," Adam called, chuckling, as he ascended the stairs.

Broc turned his back on Adam, shrugging off his blue suit jacket and tossing it over the Mosier couch as he collapsed onto the cushions, his body sinking into it. He crossed one leg over the other and let his head fall back, eyes fluttering shut.

Even with Mindy not by his side at the premiere, her relentless social media posts were wearing him down. It was an unending cycle of reminders like a chain he couldn't break. The latest was fresh from a few hours ago, showing her wrapped around him, solidifying the illusion of their perfect relationship. The engagement ring in the center of the spotlight, designed to calm the Mindys.

He rubbed the bridge of his nose as a man cleared his throat, jolting him from his thoughts. Broc reluctantly opened his eyes and lifted his head, forcing a smile.

"Sorry, sir. Just wanted you to know we finished packing up the cameras and will be out of here soon. There's a cleaning crew scheduled to come in probably around 8:00 AM."

"Thanks, I appreciate it," Broc replied, trying to muster something more genuine as he offered a hint of a smile.

"Of course, and hey, congrats on the new business." The guy nodded respectfully. "Take care, man." He reached out, and Broc shook his hand.

The door clicked shut with a finality that echoed in the space. Broc watched the two men exit the back of his shop, but just as he prepared to lock up and hunt down Rosie, the door swung open again. "Did you forget something—" Broc began, but his words trailed off as a young woman stepped inside. Her camera hung around her neck, a sling cradled her arm, and a badge clipped to her shirt read "PRESS."

Without a second thought, Broc replied, "Sorry, the event is over." His tone brooked no argument.

The woman, with dark features and hair that shimmered like midnight, pressed her lips together, her expression tight. "I know, sir. I'm sorry. There's something I need to tell you. I hope that's okay."

Broc's patience was already wearing thin as he waved her off. "I don't need anything. Netflix will handle the photos and distribute them to the media," he said, gesturing toward the door.

"It's about Mindy, sir." Her voice quivered slightly as she held her ground. "I...I think she's trying to trap you. I've sorta been tracking her, following her patterns, and..." She cleared her throat, her eyes darting around the room. "I just wanted to let you know she's lying about her pregnancy. My friend, he's a photographer down in Hollywood, and he caught her in some...compromising positions," the woman explained, twisting her fingers over her camera.

Broc raised an eyebrow, skepticism etched across his face. "What exactly are you saying?"

"She was after my younger brother. He was working on one of the sets in California. He's young and dumb, and they slept together. But it was what happened afterward that led me to consider her patterns with men. Mindy, um...she warned him that if he said anything about sleeping with her, she would accuse him of rape. I know it's our word against hers, but my brother was infatuated by her stardom. Me not so much...but you have to believe me."

Anger surged through him, every muscle trembling with suppressed rage. How could she! To use the boy as a weapon. The threat of labelling him a rapist ignited a fire in Broc's veins. How could she be so cold, so manipulative? *What the hell is wrong with her?* he thought.

The woman studied Broc for a moment before continuing. "My friend has some pictures of her recently getting drunk in a strip club and giving head to a bouncer. I have the proof right here." She reached into her back pocket, pulled out an SD card, and offered it to Broc.

"What do you want in return?" Broc questioned the young woman. Glancing at her badge on her shirt, he read her name, "Aisha T."

"Nothing, sir, I just don't want anything to happen to my brother. He's a good kid. And trust me, he already got an earful from me." Fidgeting with the strap around her camera, she glanced at her hands before looking back into Broc's eyes. "I followed her after she was escorted out of the premiere. She took an Uber to the Blue Spark downtown, where she danced and took shots with some of the regulars there. One of the guys eventually led her out back. She was on her knees, while he...um..."

Broc interrupted her, raising his hand to halt her words. "You don't need to elaborate further. I understand," he said, cutting her off gently.

"Well, I did manage to snap some photos of it. You can compare the dress she wore tonight, and there's a clear shot of her engagement ring, too. She posted herself on Instagram in the same dress. And you know she never wears the same dress twice, so this would be concrete evidence you can leverage. I mean, if she were truly pregnant, I doubt she'd be slamming shots like she was or shoving someone's cock down her throat," Aisha explained, offering her insight.

"You did all this for nothing?" Broc questioned her.

"Not for nothing; for my brother," Aisha whispered. "This wouldn't work out in his favor, unfortunately. Any tear that Mindy cries, and the world cries with her."

"God, this just makes me sick. I'm sorry, Aisha. I really am." Broc sighed. He couldn't shake the truth of her words. Mindy was America's sweetheart, capable of using a situation to her advantage, even if it meant falsely accusing an innocent man. Her eyes widened briefly when Broc addressed her by name, but she quickly realized he must have seen it on her ID badge. Then she reached up to her camera, released the latch, and pushed the SD card, which popped it out.

"Take it and keep my brother safe," Aisha said, passing the SD card to Broc. His fingers closed around it tightly as he nodded.

"I promise," he stated firmly.

"She's a bad seed," she murmured.

"A rotten seed," Broc echoed. He clutched the SD cards like a lifeline, the cold plastic, the upcoming freedom from Mindy. Stowing them carefully in the floral island drawer, relief washed over him. Just as he reached for his phone to message Rosie, an insistent alarm began to beep loudly.

Broc bolted from the workstation, his heart racing as he ascended the stairs to his apartment. With a forceful shove, he flung the first living quarters door open, eyes wide with panic. All he found was Adam, bleary-eyed and groggy, slumped on the couch.

"What's going on?" Adam grumbled, the haze of sleep thick in his voice.

"It's Rosie," Broc gasped, each word tumbling out in a frantic rush. "Her heart rate alarm is going off. I need to find her and calm her down."

"She said she was going to bed," Adam told him, using the palms of his hands to rub at his eyes.

Broc's heart dropped like a stone. "She's upstairs?" Broc asked, rushing over to the bedroom stairs.

"No, she's back at her place...maybe?" Adam responded. The damn alarm screeched from his cell phone. Time stretched, each second desperate to reach Rosie.

Bolting out the back door, Broc skidded to a halt, Adam close on his heels. Their gazes locked onto the third-floor window, where flames licked the building in the night, casting an eerie glow that illuminated the swirling smoke.

"Fuck! Rosie!" Broc gasped, his heart lurching with fear.

Adam didn't hesitate, not for a second. He yanked out his cell phone, fingers moving with determination as he dialed 9-1-1 before Broc could even think of giving the order. The fog of grogginess evaporated from Adam's mind, adrenaline pumping through him like wildfire. With a swift motion, he dashed into Broc's shop, yanked the fire extinguisher from its place by the back door, and charged back outside.

They raced into Rosie's building, the urgency had their hearts pounding, and Broc scanned the potting room until his eyes landed on the fire extinguisher, hidden under the sink. He snatched it up and bolted for the narrow stairs. Once Broc ascended the stairs, the space around him transformed into a suffocating haze of thick, black smoke that clawed at Broc's throat and seared his lungs. He instinctively covered his mouth with his hand, then pulled his shirt up over his nose in a desperate attempt to filter the thick black smoke. Tears filled his eyes, blurring his vision and stinging his eyes. He had to get to Rosie. She was all that mattered in that moment.

In only a matter of milliseconds, Broc reached the third floor, and he didn't hesitate. He kicked the door open with force and rushed into the room, with Adam right behind him. Adam pulled the pin from his fire extinguisher and aimed the foam at the hottest part of the flames. The fire flickered dangerously close to the edges of the rug, already consuming the curtains. This time Broc aimed his fire extinguisher nozzle at the blaze and unleashed a flood of foam.

30

Pro Tip: When transplanting a cactus, use tongs to protect your hands from spikes and wear rubber coated gloves.

Rosie's gaze lingered on Adam as he slipped back into the premiere. A dull ache settled deep within. Instead, she made herself inhale slowly, desperately trying to ease the hurt from Mindy. For her, the evening had started with mind-blowing sex and a makeover that had now gone to waste as she stood outside. The makeup did little to mask her disappointment, and the biting cold that hugged her did little to soothe her frustration.

Rosie flicked her eyes to the back of Broc's shop, and with Mindy still inside the building, returning felt impossible. Instead, Rosie pushed past the destroyed remains of Fluffy's chicken coop, straight to the back door of her shop. She swung the back door open, stepping inside. No longer did it feel like the tropical haven she'd once adored. The chill that greeted her was like a slap in the face, a reminder that her old building wasn't as weatherproof as she'd thought. Just another bill, another problem that was quickly adding up. Empty containers sat on the shelves like ghosts of what had been. Reality hit hard. This would likely be her last year at Miss Marigolds

Plant Shop, and knowing that felt like a knife twisting her soul. Closing her eyes, she brought a hand to her chest, pressing her hand down against her ribcage, hoping to stop the pain. With a heavy sigh, she let her head drop and made her way up the stairs to the third floor.

Alone. Cold.

A retreat into her bedroom was all she wanted. Ascending the final steps, she kicked off her heels and yanked a blanket from the hall closet, then collapsed onto her unmade bed, pulling it snugly around her. Most of Rosie's personal items had already been packed up and moved into Broc's apartment, courtesy of Basil, which pushed Rosie into a new phase of her story: the forced proximity trope.

Just as she began to find sleep, the sharp sound of a lighter flicked her into alertness, her heart racing, beating an anxious rhythm in her chest. She pulled the sheets up to her chin, eyes darting to the flickering light that cast eerie shadows across the room. A faint flicker illuminated Orson's face, his features dancing in the shadows as he cupped the lighter in one hand, lighting his cigarette. Another vice.

"It's about time you woke up, little petal." Orson's voice was polluted with malice. A tone that made Rosie's skin crawl. He took a deep drag from his cigarette, the ember flaring before he casually flicked the ashes onto the floor, watching the tiny sparks flare and extinguish beneath his heavy boot.

The pounding of Rosie's heart thrummed against her chest, each beat like a drum, but her voice so soft it wouldn't even lift a feather. "Orson, what are you doing here?" A suffocating fear washed over her as she met his gaze. The familiarity in his eyes was gone, replaced by a darker version of a man she used to know, and a glimpse of someone she'd dealt with from the past, the face of addiction. His pupils were dilated, void-like, his sallow skin clung to his bones, making him look like a shadow of the man she once knew. Drugs had spiraled back into his world and filled his veins.

"Rosie, Rosie, Rosie," he taunted, his voice oozing disdain as he rolled her name over his tongue like a bitter pill. "Did you really think you could just have Mr. Fancy Pants pay off your debt and be rid of me? You still owe me a wedding. Tsk, tsk, tsk." He took another drag from his cigarette, the glow brightening as he inhaled deeply, a flicker of wild in his eyes, stepping closer to her bed. "You forget..." He straightened, smoke billowing out with a slow, deliberate breath. Rosie instinctively recoiled as he leaned in closer, his weight pressing down as his hands gripped the edges of the bed. "You're mine. Always have been," he stated, his tone possessive.

A glint of metal emerged from his free hand which had slid behind his back; it was a hunting knife, and Rosie's breath caught in her throat. "And if you don't want to be with me..." His voice trailed off. "Then you can't be with anyone else."

Each inhale was sharp and jagged. Rosie's eyes widened. The pain in her chest pressed tight against her heart. The glint of the knife pulsed a new fear through her, knowing that Orson was high on drugs, his mind could not be met with reasoning. A smile twisted into something sinister, stirring a primal dread deep within her chest, causing her to withdraw, moving away from him. Orson lunged across the bed, his fingers grasping her hair like a sin, pain blooming at her scalp as he yanked her off the mattress.

"AHHHH! Stop! Orson, please, you're hurting me!" Rosie's scream tore through the room. She fought against the sharp pull, instinctively trying to inch closer to him, hoping that maybe, just maybe, he'd ease his grip. But he was relentless, dragging her along as if she were nothing more than a rag doll. With a brutal shove, he tossed her into a chair in the corner of her room, her body hitting the wood hard, trembling from the impact. Her head throbbed as she struggled to focus on him, hovering over her, that twisted grin etched on his face.

Before she could gather her thoughts, he swung the handle of the hunting knife down against the side of her head. The world erupted into blinding stars, and for a moment, all she could do was gasp, temporarily frozen. Seizing the opportunity, Orson whipped out zip-ties from his back pocket and worked quickly and efficiently. He zip-tied her ankles to the chair legs and her wrists to the arms, leaving no chance for escape. Rosie's head lulled back, blacking around her vision, leaving her to feel nothing, to say nothing.

Time stretched out in that room, the silence occasionally broken by the dull *plunk* as cigarette butts hit the floor. Orson lounged at the edge of the bed as he flicked yet another spent butt into the corner. The ember sizzled against the fabric of the curtain, a small flicker of flame dancing dangerously close. His impatience grew, swirling with the smoke that smoldered against the fabric. He sauntered over to Rosie, nudging her foot with the toe of his boot. She didn't stir. Undeterred, he reached into his back pocket, pulling out a small plastic bag filled with a fine white powder. The crinkle of the plastic filled the quiet space as he unfurled it, dipping his finger into the little baggie, watching it cling to his long, slender finger. He brought it to his lips, licking it off slowly, the bitter taste that ignited the craving.

With a deep inhale, Orson poured a small amount onto the back of his hand, crumpling the bag in the palm of his hand as he pinched one nostril closed with his finger. Leaning down, he sucked up the powder in one swift motion, gasping as his head tilted back, waiting for the high to wash over him. The edges of the room blurred as the drug took hold, igniting the demon within, wrapping him in a cocoon of adrenaline. Nerves sparked like electricity, and a wild hunger flickered in his dilated pupils. He could hear colors, taste the sounds, and feel a shiver dancing across his skin. Voices swirled in his mind, urging him to do things to Rosie, whispering dark temptations as he eyed his prey, his obsession.

Orson's gaze ensnared his petal, who slumped lifelessly in the chair. He dipped his finger into the baggie again, the white powder. Once more, his boot nudged Rosie's foot, but she offered no response. With viciousness simmering in his gut, Orson grabbed her long purple hair, yanking her head back to the slackness of her jaws. He pressed his powdered finger against her gums, smearing the drug in a way that had his cock hardening.

The rush of control curled through him as he repeated the ritual. Again and again, he plunged his finger into the bag, taking hits for himself in between. Finally, Orson released Rosie's head, a careless act that lolled her head back in its previous position. Stepping away, he crossed to the dresser and dumped the rest of the powder. He pulled out his wallet, the worn leather creaking softly in his grip. From within, he fingered a credit card and began to methodically carve the powder into pristine lines. He leaned over the first line, nostrils flaring as he sealed one off with a flick, and in a single, fluid motion, he inhaled deeply, the powder igniting a searing trail that tore through his sinuses and blasted through his bloodstream. A gasp escaped his lips, his head falling back in utter surrender as the euphoria wrapped around him like a familiar lover. His hands dropped to his sides while a twisted smile curved his lips.

The drug surged through him, clouding thought and reason, every heartbeat pounding wildly against his ribcage. The persistent buzzing in his ears melted into a distant hum as the drug insulated him in a haze. But even as the initial high peaked, the craving for more sat on his frontal lobe.

More, more, more, Orson thought. With urgency, he bent over again, greedily snorting another line, the powder vanishing into his nostrils like a lifeline to a world beyond. His gaze flickered towards Rosie, who remained motionless. With a dismissive sniff and a flick of his thumb, Orson leaned forward, swiping the last remaining line of powder into the palm of his hand. Crossing the room, he approached Rosie and stood before her. Kicking her foot once more and receiving no response, he seized her by the hair, tilting her head back to expose her slack-jawed mouth. With his thumb, Orson pried her mouth open, then sprinkled the remaining powder into her mouth.

With a final, indifferent glance, he released her, allowing her head to fall back against the chair with a dull thud before retreating once more into the embrace of his own addiction. The blood flowing to his cock had him on edge. He watched with fascination as the powder delicately settled upon Rosie's tongue. Despite its initial reluctance, he knew the intoxicating transformation would soon consume her. With a quick sniff and a casual swipe of the back of his hand, he leaned closer over Rosie's parted lips. Rosie's drug wasn't dissolving fast enough, so Orson spit saliva into her opened jaw. To him, it was her initiation for they were about to share. The powder quickly turned liquid, and the heat in his core overtook him as his cock began to press against the zipper of his jeans. The awareness that she would soon taste fear, hear colors, and see sound turned him on.

Nervously, he glanced over his shoulder; he felt the shadows closing in on him. In the subdued light, the glint of metal caught his eye—his knife laying on the floor. Orson wrapped his fingers around his knife, his grip firm. Then, with a fluid motion, he turned the knife around, and he guided the blade along the side of Rosie's face, starting from just beneath her temple. Dragging the blade across her skin, leaving behind a faint but noticeable trail as the sharp edge made contact with her skin. Blood oozed from the thin gash, a meandering path down her cheek, lingering momentarily before descending further to her neck. Each droplet seemed to hesitate in its descent, clinging briefly to her skin before succumbing to gravity, leaving tiny, scarlet spots on her shoulder, then on her dress.

In a deft motion, Orson slid the blade beneath the straps of her dress, slicing through the fabric, leaving matching gashes on her shoulders. The bodice of Rosie's dress slid down her body, revealing the flesh-colored bandeau beneath. Orson's gaze lingered momentarily. With another swift stroke, he maneuvered the knife beneath the expensive fabric of the bandeau, delicately peeling it away from her chest. The material yielded to the sharp edge of his blade. The flimsy fabric was free from her body; it unveiled more than just bare skin. Beneath her small chest lay a slender, black heart rate monitor; a sense of confusion flashed across the folds of Orson's mind.

With another jab from the toe of Orson's boot, Rosie stirred, a low moan slipping past her lips, echoing in the shadows of the dimly lit room. Slowly, as if wading through a thick fog, awareness began to claw its way back to Rosie's mind. She rolled her head upright, squinting through the stupor at Orson, who stood before her with an unsettling aura, his features shifting and blurring like a mirage in the dark. Confusion spiraled in her mind, the drug coursing through her veins warping her sense of reality. Orson seemed to glow, his very skin liquefying and merging with the shadows.

Panic flowed as realization crashed over her. Thoughts filled her head, but she was strapped down, arms and legs firmly bound to the chair, her heart beating rapidly against her chest. A sharp breath snagged in her throat as her heartbeat quickened, each pulse hammering like the beat of a hummingbird's wings, its frantic echo drowning out everything else. The constriction of her restraints tightened with every jerk of her limbs. The adrenaline coursing through her, merging with the drugs, had her eyes wide, her heart pounding, and her breathing hitched. Staring at Orson's face and the way it seemed to melt was too much for her, and the pain was almost too much for her, causing her eyes to burn.

"Orson..." she whispered, "my heart..."

31

Pro Tip: Too much sun on shade plants will burn their leaves.

Everything around Rosie shimmered in a dizzying haze, the world blurring as she slowly turned her head. Orson stood above her, his melting presence unsettling and confusing. In one hand, he wielded a knife, the blade gleaming as it caught the sparse light. The sharp tip traced along her skin, leaving a line of pain, while Orson's eyes held a coldness that penetrated her very core, examining her every reaction through the haze of his own addiction. At the same time, she remained paralyzed, not understanding why her body felt light and dizzy yet confined, unmoving.

Orson leaned in closer, his breath brushing against her neck, prompting involuntary shivers that danced down her spine. "I loved you once. How tragic that was," he growled. The smoothness of his nose brushed against her neck, just below her ear, drawing in a hiss as if he were trying to savor the remnants of a love-obsession that had turned to ash.

And so, the drug coursed through his veins, taking over his mind. Orson's breathing quickened at the frantic rhythm of Rosie's panicked breaths. The tightness in her heart was pounding against her ribcage, begging to be set free like a bird in a cage. The fear on her skin looked delicious to Orson; the little drug-uninhibited voice in his head willed his tongue to lick her neck, *"more, more, more."* This delicious taste shot straight to his core while his hand reached down to palm the pain of his thickness. Orson tilted his head back, drawing in the heady blend of her scent and the assault of smoke that curled through the room. Both aromas twisted around them as the tiny flame flickered ominously at the back of her apartment. The struggle for control was relentless; he needed to fuck her, but he wanted her to feel pain. The small voice was persistent—*"lick her, lick her"*—the thought exacerbated by the drug coursing through every inch of his body.

For Rosie, the walls of the room began to close in, the air thick with blackening smoke, her lungs begging for air, her eyes watering and stinging with each blink. Terror tightened its grip around her throat, each breath becoming more constricted as if an invisible hand was clawing at her neck. The restraints felt like iron chains. She spiraled deeper, her heart pounding, making her cough along with the smoke that coiled around her body like a rope.

Orson's movements were distorted as Rosie watched him, darkness shifting in liquid form. Shadows followed him, fell from the walls, crawled on the floor, darted around her body causing her to slink into her chair. His sudden lunge caused Rosie to jump. His laughter was cold. "You think..." He paused, bringing his free hand to the back of her head with such force that her head swiveled to the side. He inhaled deeply, wiping his nose with his thumb as he held his knife, sniffing. "Do you think you are part of his life?" His arm swung again, and he struck Rosie's cheek with a heavy hand. A cough erupted from her chest, gasping for air, while her head twisted violently, sending shockwaves of pain down her back, the impact causing an agonizing whiplash. "You're not my broken petal, not even close." Rosie's gaze stretched and warped as she watched the words spill from Orson's lips, not making any sense. But the words formed letters lifting from his mouth like a cartoon. Each letter swirled and bounced in vibrant colors. She felt like the alphabet was oozing out, dancing in the air like a psychedelic creature. The drugs twisted her thoughts into a kaleidoscopic graphic novel, where everything was exaggerated and surreal, like a bizarre dreamscape unfolding before her wide, unblinking eyes.

Orson's frantic search through his pocket was almost manic. His fingers finally grasped the object of his preoccupation, a glimmering ring shaped like a laughing skull, catching the light with a mocking sparkle. Wild eyes lit up his gaunt face as he held up the ring.

Rosie's heart raced as dread crept in, and she coughed some more. "Orson, I can't breathe." Orson lunged forward, seizing her wrist with a grip that bordered on madness, a motion the Joker would make.

"Stop squirming, darling...my little petal." He sneered at her. Rosie's breath caught in her throat. With a savage jerk, he claimed her wedding finger; he dug his grip into her flesh, leaving Rosie trapped in a nightmarish performance of this wedding ceremony.

"Aaaaaahhhhh!" A sharp cry tore from Rosie's lips as pain shot through her finger down her arm as her joint was being wrenched back. For a moment, everything seemed to blur together: the sound of the chair crashing to the ground, the swell of blood on her tongue, the acid taste filling her mouth.

And then it was the sound of Orson's labored breaths, his chest heaving with the effort of his words. The wooden chair creaked ominously as Orson pulled her upright, her restraints digging into her skin. He stood, his slicked-back hair glistening with sweat, and sniffed sharply again. Dipping his finger into another baggie, he rubbed the white powder onto his gums, a manic grin splitting his face. This time, he dipped again before shoving his finger into Rosie's mouth, smearing the powder across her gums with a grotesque sort of tenderness.

"Do you..." he rasped, every syllable punctuated by shallow breaths, while words swirled around his body like a boa. Dilated eyes locked onto Rosie, a psychosis teetering at the edge, battling invisible demons. "Take Rosie to be your wife, to have and to hold from this day forward?" The words burst forth from him in a muddled torrent.

His gaze was fierce as he waited for an answer. "I do!" The words exploded from his lips, ringing through the smoky room. Using the back of his hand, Orson wiped away the spittle gathered at the corners of his mouth. And then, without another word, he began to pace around the back of Rosie's chair with little giggles that erupted from his lips.

"No, stop it, Orson, stop it," Rosie demanded in disbelief.

The smoke writhed in the room like a living thing, wrapping around Rosie's throat and choking her every breath. Heat surged, prickling her skin as the flickering flames crawled up the wall, seeming to hiss like demons from Hell. Dizzy and disoriented, Rosie's eyes flicked around in search of clarity. Orange shadows danced across Orson's features as he slipped a wedding ring onto his finger. Beads of sweat glistened on his brow as he ran a hand through his slickened hair; his once-solid form shifted into melting wax. Rosie blinked in disbelief, her vision swimming as she watched Orson's face contort and morph before her eyes, the lines of reality blurring.

A feral glint hardened Orson's features and went straight to his veins. His hand shot out, fingers tangled in her hair, yanking her closer, pain sparking a gasp from her lips. "Shit! Orson, let go!" Fear wrapped around her, and she felt herself teetering on the precipice of the dark and ominous. Hades himself seemed to be lurking just beyond reach.

"C'mon," he growled. His grip tightened, jerking Rosie's head back like the tolling of a bell. "You still don't get it, do you?" With a desperate shake of her head, Rosie carried a silent plea in her eyes, but Orson only responded with violence. A guttural roar escaped him as he lunged, his fist a thunderous storm crashing down on her. Blow after merciless blow landed with precision, each strike turning the world into a whirl of pain and confusion. Her body convulsed, her skull meeting the unforgiving ground, and her chair tipped over, sending stars dancing in her mind. "This is your fault! If you'd only stayed with me! Not him; this is all on you! You need to be punished! You need to get your priories in place because, *WIFE*, this is not the behavior I will allow in our marriage." Sprawled on the cold floor, where the air was cleaner, Rosie saw the smoke swirling upward, lifting just enough for her to gasp for breath.

"St-stooop, Orson...p-please," Rosie whispered.

Kneeling beside her, Orson appeared again, a dark figure straight out of her nightmares. He leaned in. "Why do you always have to push me, Rosie?" he hissed. "Why do you make me show you what a proper wife should be like?" Slowly, his hand reached out, and Rosie flinched involuntarily. But the drugs in Rosie's mind turned his body into something out of a dream; he was twisted and misshapen like the tentacle of some ancient sea creature. With eyes as dark as the ocean's depths, Orson traced a chilling path down Rosie's cheek. Before she could react, his fingers invaded her mouth, probing deeper and deeper until her throat constricted with the need to gag. "Just need to train that mouth of yours because soon you'll be giving me my wedding gift with your lips wrapped around my cock."

A radiant glow filled her eyes as reality morphed into her drug-hazed mind. The carpet beneath her seemed to warp and liquefy at her touch, casting patterns that danced before her while Orson's wicked laughter echoed through the room like a mocking taunt. The fibers beneath her chair sparked, sending waves of heat that curled around her bound legs. Sweat trickled down her temple. Every second stretched into an eternity as the flames inched closer, their orange tongues licking hungrily at the edges of her prison, threatening to engulf her in a fierce, fiery embrace.

"Free me..." Rosie whispered, her voice trembling. Panic tightened her throat as she watched Orson's once solid features begin to melt once more. Those tentacle fingers pressed against his thighs, and he stood tall, surveying her with amusement, that same grin stretching wide across his face like the Cheshire Cat. An unsettling shiver raced down Rosie's spine as Orson circled her bound body. Another ominous hiss echoed from the walls, making Rosie's instincts scream for escape. "Cut me FREE! Orson!" She squeezed her eyes shut.

With no warning, Orson's foot lashed out, striking Rosie squarely in the chest and expelling the last vestiges of air from her lungs. Her heart lurched as her world stalled, questioning if his attack was real. The orange glow enveloped Orson, devouring him as the darkness of Death's cloak slithered into Rosie's sight, a stalker. Another vicious blow struck her belly, leaving her gasping for air, her body faltering like a fish flailing out of water, her heart bound tight at the loss of air.

Just as the shadows threatened to swallow her whole, the door to her room burst open with a violent crash. Rosie's eyes flew wide, the sudden intrusion yanking her from the brink of her fading consciousness. She stared at the door in disbelief, her mind racing to comprehend the twisted reality before her. Four identical doors spun in a dizzying merry-go-round, their forms blending into a maddening whirl, each one taunting her with the question of escape or more confinement. The white rabbit's disturbing tease.

Shaking her head in disbelief, Rosie's eyes remained fixed on the door, where a bizarre sight greeted her: tall penguins marching into the room. The contrast of those winter-loving creatures entering Hell sent her synapses ablaze with confusion.

Fury found its way through Orson, knocking him on his ass, while Rosie tried to understand the scene playing out in front of her eyes. She watched as Orson swung at the penguins, his liquid legs propelling him forward in a display of aggression. He attempted to drive the bewildered arctic birds back through the door, away from the fires and where she lay on the floor. The heat from the fire demons licked around her limbs, ensnaring her in its embrace as she remained trapped in the chair. Rosie's heart raced as Orson dissolved before her eyes, his form transforming into a shimmering pool of liquid.

A crimson glow brushed against her feet, and a terrified scream escaped her lips. "AHHHH! Help me!" The frantic movement of a taller penguin caught her eye as it sprinted toward her. Fear gripped her, and she instinctively recoiled into the wooden chair, her breath quickening as the giant penguin loomed over her body.

The penguin's voice shouted back over its shoulder, but the crackling fire and the whirlwind of confusion swirling in her mind drowned out the words. Rosie squeezed her eyes shut, but when she finally opened them, a new nightmare greeted her: dragons loomed overhead, their massive forms looming like ancient mountains. Their jaws gaped wide, unleashing gushes of white clouds that fell around her, filling the room with a chill that quieted the fire demons around her legs and hushed through her very core.

32

Pro Tip: Pruning is an essential gardening practice that promotes the health, aesthetics, and productivity of plants. Done correctly, pruning encourages stronger growth, improves air circulation, removes diseased or damaged parts, and can even enhance flowering and fruiting.

The coolness of the white foam slathered across Rosie's body momentarily dulled the heat searing her skin. It felt like the dragon's breath had wrapped her in a soothing lick, its magic coursing through her veins, cooling the orange heat of the demons crawling up her legs. But that serenity began to slip away as she sank deeper into the shadowy corners of her consciousness. At the same time, distant sirens wailed through her foggy thoughts, a melody that floated through the open window of this funhouse. Just when she thought she might float away entirely, a sharp tug at her ankles and wrists yanked her back to a harsh reality. Her eyes shot open at a pull around her bound wrists and ankles, which caused her to bump her finger. "OWWW! Agh!" Her dislocated finger throbbed, a wave of pain radiating up her arm, but the drugs held her in a half-dream state, a place where the agony danced just out of reach, all while still feeling achingly real. "The dragons cooled me," Rosie mumbled incoherently.

“Shh, Rosie, I’ve got you, I’ve got you. Orson can’t hurt you anymore,” a voice, devoid of discernible features or identity, filled Rosie’s ears.

“He married me,” Rosie slurred.

“Stay with me, babe, I’ve got you now.” Another distinctive yet strangely familiar voice drifted into Rosie’s ears, affirming that her hearing remained intact despite the static distorting its tone, as if someone were chatting through a CB radio.

“Broc, you got her? Shit, her finger is dislocated. Want me to fix...”

Rosie struggled to home in on the voice cutting through the fog of her drug-laced thoughts, but it felt like it was walking through a waterfall. Just then, a firm hand closed around her injured finger and wrist, anchoring her in place. In an instant, the searing agony that had been a dull throb morphed into a piercing scream that erupted from her lips.

"AHHHHHHHHH! Oh my god!"

Her vision blurred, and for a moment, the sharp gasp echoed in her ears, mingling with the pulse of pain in her heart. The searing heat radiating from her finger pulled her closer to where the shadows whispered oaths and Death's cloak beckoned her into unawareness.

“GOOD MORNING, sleepyhead! It’s time to wake up and welcome the day.” A woman's cheerful voice filled the quiet room. Rays of sunlight peeked through the curtains, casting gentle patterns on the walls. “I have some wonderful news: your doctor is considering releasing you in the next few days.” Her words carried on as if she couldn’t wait to share the update. But for Rosie, still caught in the grasp of sleep, the interruption grated on her. Letting out a tired groan, Rosie reluctantly surfaced from her slumber. With a slow, deliberate movement, she pulled the sheet snugly over her shoulders. Turning away from the source of the cheerful voice, she longed for uninterrupted rest. But the incessant cheer encouraged Rosie to shift position and sit up. Nurse Slaughter stood at the edge of her bed, her fingers touching buttons on the machines and tapping on screens. "How about we let in some natural light? It might help you wake up and start the day feeling refreshed," she suggested kindly. Rosie didn't like that idea because she wanted nothing more than to be left alone.

Instead of agreeing with the friendly nurse, Rosie shot Nurse Slaughter with a warning glare. "Don't touch those blinds." Despite the firmness of Rosie's tone, Nurse Slaughter responded with a chuckle and a knowing smile, seemingly undeterred by Rosie's struggle. Resisting the urge to roll her eyes, Rosie remained stoic; all she wanted was for the nurse to leave so she could wallow alone in her room.

Days passed, the police came and went, and when she finally had a clear head, she understood the gravity of what she had gone through. The cuts and bruises were slowly beginning to heal. There were scars on her shoulders and down her face from Orson's knife; thin as they might be, nonetheless, they served as a silent witness. Of all the scars she bore, the ones on her face haunted her the most. Every time she caught her reflection in the mirror, the memories of her unpleasant time in the house of horror rushed back. She loathed every last mark that Orson had carved into her skin. But beneath the unease, a flicker of determination simmered. Rosie was ready to take control. Soon, she'd be sitting in front of her trusted tattoo artist, prepared to turn those scars into something stunning, something that would not just define her, but empower her. She would wear them like armor.

With a grimace, Rosie painstakingly maneuvered herself into a seated position despite the sharp twinge of her fractured ribs. Nurse Slaughter's disapproving click of the tongue echoed in the room as she watched Rosie's discomfort, prompting her to set aside the clipboard in her hand and offer her assistance, then carefully arrange the pillows behind Rosie's back. "The good news is, your cuts are healing well. Your bruises will fade, and those cuts will hardly be noticeable," she chirped to Rosie as she peeled back one of the bandages on her cheek.

"I'm going to cover them with tattoos," Rosie murmured. She carefully shifted her left arm, wincing slightly at the discomfort it stirred. "And when can I bid farewell to this?" she inquired, gesturing towards the bulky cast.

With a sympathetic smile, Nurse Slaughter offered a smile. "Not much longer, dear. Once the swelling goes down, I'm confident they'll give you the green light," she explained. "Oh, your friends called the nurses' station to let me know they plan on visiting soon. You'll have some company to look forward to," she said, winking at Rosie. "Do you need any help getting ready?" Rosie shook her head and watched the nurse leave the room.

The rest of the day dragged on, and Rosie found herself sitting in silence. No matter what the nurse had told her, the swelling on her face was still painted with red blotches, and one eye was nearly swollen shut, while her cuts were hidden under bandages. She felt disgusting.

"I've got a latte for you, darlin'," Basil said from the doorway; her eyes were filled with sadness, and Rosie hated it. Snapping out of her vacant gaze, Rosie wrestled her mind back to the present moment as she watched Basil and Alessandra saunter into her hospital room. Gratefully accepting the latte, Rosie sank back into her pillows, determined not to let the pain show on her face. Basil leaned down and planted a gentle kiss on the top of Rosie's head. Meanwhile, Alessandra dragged a chair across the room with a loud squeak, positioning it directly beside Rosie's bedside. She settled in, resting her elbows on the bed and cradling her head in her hands.

"So, how are you doing?" Alessandra inquired.

Basil let out a derisive snort before striding across the room and sinking into the small couch, crossing one leg over the other and intertwining her fingers, resting them atop her knee. "Rosie, Broc wanted us to tell you that he will be by soon; he had a meeting to attend."

When it was finally time for visiting hours to end, her friends had slipped away, and Rosie was easily pulled into the darkness and fell quickly asleep, finding that even talking took a lot out of her.

Rosie's eyelids fluttered open, greeted by the dim glow from the hospital hallway. It was late, and the moon hung high in the sky. But when she finally found her bearings, she felt a weight on her legs. Broc was nestled close to her hospital bed; his head lay on her thigh while his fingers intertwined with hers in a delicate linking of hands.

Despite the late hours and the strict visiting policies, it was clear that Broc had steered the bureaucratic maze of the hospital policies, perhaps slipping a subtle floral arrangement to the nurses' station.

What Rosie and Broc had going on was more than just a fake engagement and forced proximity trope; it was love. Rosie gently lifted her good hand, running her fingers through Broc's curly black hair. A contented sound escaped Broc as he nestled closer to her. With a soft sigh, Rosie continued to stroke his head, feeling him drawing her nearer by wrapping his arm around both thighs. The embrace eased Rosie's mind, allowing her to drift back into sleep, finding peace from the nightmares of her attack.

33

Pro Tip: Digging the right hole is crucial when planting. The size of the hole depends on the height of the plant and the size of the pot. As the pots and plants get larger, so does the hole.

"I've got coffee!" Adam's voice called out, assaulting Rosie's ears as she groaned with disapproval.

"Whhhhy?" Rosie moaned. "Adam, I was sleeping." Rosie groaned again, throwing her arm over her eyes to cover the sun as it filtered through the windows; another reminder that the sun gave two shits if you wanted to sleep in, because like a rooster's call in the morning, the sun rose like clockwork. *Both are fuckers*, Rosie thought. Still feeling Broc on her thighs, Rosie lowered her arm and pushed on Broc's shoulder. "Broc, make your friend leave," she grumbled.

"Hey now, I brought yummies!" Adam feigned a broken heart, but his wide grin told otherwise.

Peeking through her arm, she opened one eye slowly to see that Adam was carrying a muffin from the Little Café and a latte, which meant he had stopped by to see Alessandra and Basil before rudely waking Rosie. "Fine! But I want whatever Alessandra gave you." She pretended to pout. A smile spread across his lips as he crossed the room and dropped the bag on Rosie's lap; she quickly pulled out a double chocolate chip muffin, still warm. With a swift movement, she pushed the muffin into her mouth, emitting a contented moan as its delicious flavor enveloped her taste buds, and her stomach growled with acceptance.

Broc, hearing her moan, lifted his head. "I love waking to that sound." He let out a yawn and rubbed his eyes with his palms. "Fuck, Adam, I didn't see you there; warn me next time," Broc said yawning again.

Adam stood tall and proud with his fists on his hips next to Rosie's bed, clearly impressed with himself. "I did, dickhead!" he responded, moving over to the small couch in the room, plopping down on it. "Check this out!" he said. leaning to one side of the couch to pull out his cell phone from his back pocket. Tapping the screen, he fiddled with his cell for a second before he cleared his throat dramatically. "There's a review about your shop and the Netflix premiere...it's pretty bad, probably shouldn't read it...it says..."

Following the recent debut of a major romantic holiday film on Netflix, the launch party provided all the drama reminiscent of Hollywood itself. This event coincided with the debut of set designer and florist Broc Chase's new business venture in Spokane, Washington—a flower shop named "She Loves Me, She Loves Me Not." Broc's creates exquisite floral arrangements for the A-Listers in Hollywood, but his touch of beauty can be seen in the Blockbuster film recently released on Netflix.

During the grand opening, speculation arose about the significance of the shop's name, rumored to be a dedication to Broc's tumultuous relationship with Mindy Harper. Rumor has it Mindy was not on the guest list but came to confront Broc amid his apparent closeness with another woman. Mindy still wore her engagement ring Broc had recently given her after her pregnancy announcement. She was trying to dispel rumors that they had recently broken up. Despite Broc's attempts, the other woman

whom he was seen with departed with another man while Mindy was escorted out of the shop.

Among the Netflix premiere attendees were Spokane's own celebrity couple, Colin and Poppy Peters, who hastily exited upon Mindy's arrival due to prior personal conflicts. Notably, the Hollywood elite and the film's cast distanced themselves from Mindy, leaving Broc to manage the fallout of his romantic entanglements.

With Broc's infidelity now exposed, skepticism looms over his ability to uphold the values of love and sincerity upon which his business is founded.

"Oh, and check this out; Mindy even posted a photo of her ultrasound and a photo of the two of you...but your hair looks shorter here. Huh...how can you cut your hair longer?" Adam questioned, scratching his head.

"I didn't, fucker; she's been using old photos of me to uphold this false façade about our *supposed* relationship," Broc uttered with clenched teeth. "This has to stop. It's fucking absurd." Rising from his seat, he leaned in to plant a kiss on Rosie's forehead, his hand tracing down from her crown to her neck. Rosie's gaze filled with frustration as she took in Broc's fatigued expression.

"Rosie, this Mindy shit ends today. Will you be okay with Adam while I take care of the mess she's stirring?" Broc asked. Adam casually crossed one leg over the other, his posture relaxed as he leaned back on the couch. With a nonchalant gesture, he draped his arm over the backrest, exuding an air of ease and confidence like a sage professor, waiting for the kids to turn in their assignments.

"I've got her, plus that sweet Nurse Slaughter has already called in hospital security to keep watch outside if you haven't already noticed. You being here instead of by Mindy's side clutching her pregnant tummy has caused a few people to hate the two of you," he said, lifting a shoulder. "Did you check out the photo of—hey...hold on?" Adam uncrossed his legs and leaned forward. His attention was fully captured by his cell phone screen. Tapping away for a few moments, his expression suddenly shifted. With a gasp, he looked up, his eyes filled with amusement before erupting into laughter. "Fucking Christ, Broc, get over here and check this shit out! I think you got something over her now!" Closing the distance between them, Broc rushed over to Adam. Wordlessly, he extended his hand, offering Broc his cell phone.

There was a silent stare between the two men, and Rosie's gaze shifted between them as she sipped on her latte. With one eye impaired and her movements restricted by the pain radiating from her ribs, she shifted cautiously on the bed, wincing at the protesting ache. A hiss escaped her lips involuntarily, prompting Broc to move towards her. However, Rosie lifted her hand, signaling for him to stay back, calling him off with a gentle gesture.

"Rosie..." He lowered his voice, adopting a tone that disagreed with her.

"I'm fine really, just moved too fast." She shifted slowly again, smiling back up at Broc. With a quiet determination, Broc returned to Adam, though his gaze remained fixed on Rosie with an intensity bordering on obsession.

Adam thrust his cell phone back towards Broc, his gesture punctuating the tension between them. "Look at the upper left-hand corner, and then when you enlarge it...look, what do you see?"

"Holy shit, Adam! This is exactly what I needed!" Broc held on tight to the cell phone, walking over to the bathroom, only to be stopped by a hand wrapping around his upper arm.

"Slow down, dickhead, my cell isn't going into the shitter with you. That's super grody," Adam said laughing. "Yeah, and while you're in there, brush those grinners because...damn," Adam added, chuckling as he pulled his cell out of Broc's hand, then punched him in the shoulder.

"Are you going to tell me what's going on?" Rosie questioned Adam as soon as the bathroom door shut.

In mid-sit, Adam looked up. "Uh...sure, guess this also involves you; okay, look at this photo Mindy just posted of her..." Adam held up his hands and air-quoted, "pregnancy." He stood up and walked closer to Rosie. Taking hold of the small device, Rosie scanned its contents, only to feel her heart sink as she realized she was looking at an image of a small human being inside Mindy's body. "No, seriously, look...here," Adam said, placing two fingers on the screen and then spreading them to enlarge the photo. Lifting the cell closer to Rosie's face, he pointed to a small circle with the letter 'c' in the middle of it. "That is a copyright symbol. So, either she took this photo right off the internet, or she stole it from iStock, because there's no way that she needs to use a photo like this if she had the real sonogram print-offs. This means that Broc was right; this was all a ruse to put you and him through hell so she could get the upper hand." A proud grin spread across Adam's face, and Rosie couldn't help but smile back at him. Before she could articulate her thoughts, the bathroom door swung open. Broc, with freshly washed face and 'grinners,' appeared more alert than he had been mere moments ago and stepped closer to Rosie's bed.

"I used your toothbrush. I'll bring you a new one when I get back." Before he kissed Rosie goodbye, his cell chimed, and a smile spread across his face. "Perfect," he commented, pocketing his cell phone once more. With a gentle touch, he placed his hands on either side of her cheeks, mindful not to apply too much pressure given her swollen and blotchy face. "I'll put a stop to this, I promise, babe. I'll see you soon."

34

Pro Tip: Starting seeds inside with a grow light is the best way to start a garden without the fear of seeds rotting.

Broc approached the Little Café under a threatening sky. He was ready to end the irrational charade. But as he reached for the front door, Broc's cell phone chimed. Retrieving it from his back pocket, he tapped the screen to read a text message. A smile spread across his face as he glanced up and spotted a man across the street. Halting mid-step, Broc turned around and hurried across the street to the narrow alley beside the bridal shop. Casting a wary glance around, he stepped into the alley. "Diesel?"

From the darkness, and coughing a few times, Diesel stood leaning against the brick wall, rubbing his hands against the cold. Despite his black knit cap and heavy leather jacket, he had a pink tinge on his nose; his eyes narrowed at Broc. "Why are we meeting, Broc? You know Mindy is in that café. If you're thinking of trying to buy me off from your little love triangle, you can just fuck off," he said, his fingers twitching restlessly on his camera hanging around his neck. "My family won't be happy if I miss the mortgage payment."

"Which family?" Broc retorted, tilting his head with a knowing look.

Diesel's eyes widened in shock as Broc hit a nerve. Swiftly recovering, Diesel regained his composure, but Broc new he had gained the upper hand; the man had two wives on either side of the country, and neither of them new about the other—but Broc did. And that was because Colin Peters had told him a while back. A smirk spread across Broc's lips.

"I have something for you that could cover a year's worth of mortgages for both your homes," Broc said. He reached into his front pocket and pulled out the USB he had copied from the SD card Aisha had given him.

"What's this?" Diesel asked, eyeing Broc warily. His gaze was hesitant. Diesel's long fingers hovered over the USB drive for a moment before he wrapped his gloved hand around it and quickly stowed it away in his pocket.

"It's something that will end the facade Mindy is lying about on her social media. You can quote me." Diesel tapped his cell and held it out for him to speak into it. "We haven't been together in a long time, and the time we had was short lived. Mindy needed a clean slate to secure leading roles again, but I want to clarify that our relationship has long been over," Broc asserted, glancing briefly towards the café before refocusing on Diesel. "I'm in love with someone else, someone who's been on my mind for years." Broc cleared his throat, his hand nervously moving to the back of his neck as he locked eyes with Diesel.

"That purple-haired beauty you were with at the premiere?" Diesel asked.

With a sharp nod, Broc confirmed his question. "That woman has been kicked when she's been down. The shit she's been dealing with is all because of individuals like Mindy, and she certainly doesn't deserve any of it. I've even hurt her in the past, and that will haunt me. But the difference between me and Mindy's is, I knew when to apologize, whereas Mindy's comments put a target on something she has tirelessly tried to preserve for Spokane."

Diesel questioned pointedly, adjusting the cap on his camera, "What about the fire? Does the USB have proof that Mindy started the fire?"

A gust of wind that followed caused both men to tighten their jackets against the sudden chill, and Broc shook his head. He absent-mindedly wiped his nose with his thumb before addressing Diesel directly. "No, that fire wasn't started by Mindy," Broc clarified. "It was her ex who caused it. If you want his perspective on what happened, you'll need to visit him in the Spokane jail. As far as I know, he's still in custody and undergoing detox."

"But you were there," Diesel pressed.

Broc nodded. "Yes, I was. I helped put out some flames but was more concerned about getting her out."

"Is it true you fought her ex, broke his nose, and forced drugs on him?" Diesel asked, a sly grin spreading as he readied his camera. And that's when Broc knew that Diesel had already interviewed Orson and knew about him. Because that would have only come from Orson, desperate to spread lies.

Broc narrowed his eyes, clicking his tongue. "So, you've done your homework then, and know about Orson." Broc pulled his lower lip between his teeth and shook his head. "No, that's not true; the rest I can't comment on because it's an ongoing case."

But the sneaky man pushed on, ignoring Broc's comment. "I heard *your friend* was high on drugs too. Did you interrupt her little soiree?" Diesel continued, lifting his camera and taking a few photos.

Broc remained impassive, showing no visible reaction on his face. "Your source is unreliable."

With a shrug of indifference, he said, "My source was from a sweet little nurse who blushes when you compliment her. She was quite chatty once I had my face buried in her cunt," Diesel remarked casually.

Broc eyed Diesel for a moment, contemplating how to respond. He lifted his hand, using his thumb to wipe his nose again, a gesture to dispel the chill that had settled into his bones and the annoyance on his skin. "Wait for the official report before making accusations,"

Broc snapped, his patience clearly wearing thin. "I've got a date with Mindy to put an end to her games."

Diesel considered Broc's words. "Need me?"

"Follow me, take a photo of me entering the café, and then wait for Mindy to post it on social media," Broc suggested with a shrug. "You're a pro. Figure it out from there." Another gust of wind whipped up, pushing against the two men as they crossed the street. Broc lowered his head against the chill and strode purposefully to the front door. Not waiting for Diesel, Broc stepped inside and scanned the room. It didn't take long to spot Mindy; she was seated at a table, engrossed in her phone. Her camera doubling as a mirror while a group of teens nearby stole glances in her direction. When they noticed Broc, their eyes widened with excitement. Almost reflexively, they lifted their phones and began recording, caught up in the moment as if they were filming a scene for reality TV. Broc slid into the booth opposite Mindy and patiently waited for her to snap the photo of him, knowing she would promptly post it on social media. Quietly, Diesel entered the café.

Quickly reacting, Diesel lifted his camera and captured several shots of Broc and Mindy sitting across the room. Turning his attention away from Broc, Diesel settled back, fixing his gaze squarely on Mindy. "Mindy, America's sweetheart no more," he mumbled.

Plastering on a forced smile, Mindy glanced around the café, fully aware of the eyes fixed on her. She shifted in her seat to draw Broc's attention, and anyone else's who might be watching. Her demeanor was composed. "We've been missing you, Broc," Mindy replied in a tone that carried a veneer of innocence, her voice soft and sugary.

He had a serious expression laid across his face when he leaned forward slightly, his hands folded on the table between them. His eyes bore into her eyes, never blinking. "Mindy, your posts are a lie. And it's those lies that will ruin your career."

"I don't understand. I'm pregnant with your baby; we're going to be a family." Mindy's response was a subtle squint of her eyes, a coy gesture accompanied by running her tongue over her lips, a tactic often used to flirt.

Broc, however, wasn't swayed. He maintained his focus, ignoring Mindy's flirtatious ploy. With a calm tone, he laid down his ultimatum. "If you don't remove those posts and quietly disappear from my life and Rosie's, I can make your life very embarrassing." The clearing of a throat drew Broc's attention, prompting him to turn his head. "Hello, Basil," Broc greeted calmly.

Basil eyed him cautiously, uncertain of the situation unfolding before her. "Can I get you a drink? Since you didn't order at the counter, I just assumed you wanted me to come over and make sure that woman wasn't trying to ruin my dear friend's name or what's left of her business."

"I'll have water, please, with light ice. And also, a strawberry milk tea with Lychee boba toppings," Mindy rattled off, not fully paying attention to what Basil said, then turned her attention back to Broc, gesturing for him to place his order.

"Basil, just one Americano, and don't worry, she won't stay long," Broc replied calmly.

"Hey!" Mindy objected. Basil glanced at Mindy and then back at Broc, her lips pressed into a tight line, clearly holding back what she wanted to say. With a stiff nod, she acknowledged his request and walked away. Once Basil had left earshot, Mindy turned her attention back to Broc with frustration, then her eyes focused in on him. "Broc, what the hell?"

"Listen, all this talk about us being engaged and you being pregnant needs to stop, Mindy. Your lies are already catching up to you. I can walk away from this without being tainted by the nonsense you've concocted," Broc asserted firmly, jabbing his finger on the table.

"It's not a lie," Mindy hissed, her voice dropping.

"Fine, let's see," Broc challenged, leaning to one side. He pulled out his cell phone and tapped the screen several times, opening Mindy's social media account and clicking on the sonogram photo. Zooming in, he examined the image closely. "You see here, I must admit I missed it, but my friend pointed it out. I could easily contact a good friend who's a forensic expert to verify this...without involving the police. But this is clearly a stock sonogram to support your fake pregnancy claim." Broc glanced back up at Mindy; he saw the blood drain from her face, leaving her paler than a ghost. He knew then that he had her. Setting his phone down, he patted the inside of his jacket and pulled out a white package just as Basil approached with his coffee. It was a pregnancy test.

The girls recording the scene gasped and lowered their heads into a flurry of whispered conversation. Basil gestured towards Mindy with a slight brush of her hand. "Yeah, just put the rumors to rest. Take the test, simple as that," she suggested calmly. A smug smile spread across Mindy's face, a knowing grin suggesting this wasn't the end for Mindy. She was digging her heels in, refusing to let this go.

"I can't," Mindy responded defiantly, her chin jutting. "I...I have some bad news." Her eyes welled up with unshed tears in an instant. "I lost the baby," she declared, crossing her arms defensively.

Basil snorted. "Was that before or after you posted another photo of your supposed pregnancy?" she retorted sharply. "What was the fruit shape you compared it to?"

She narrowed her eyes, glaring at Basil momentarily before shifting her gaze to Broc, attempting to regain control of the situation through sympathy. "It's...it's just too hard to accept," Mindy insisted in a stiff voice, her words tinged with desperation.

"Mindy, here's the thing," Broc began, his voice low and serious as he leaned closer. He gestured subtly towards Diesel. "He has copies of interesting photos. There are numerous compromising images of you with different men in various situations...on your knees...in alleys, elevators, bars supposedly while pregnant with my baby. Not very faithful of you. If medical professionals and nurses in the NICU saw how much cum you swallowed, they'd have serious concerns." Mindy's expression shifted from defiance to realization. Broc had struck a nerve. "This needs to stop, Mindy."

"You need me, this is good for us, we can..."

"Mindy, I warned you," Broc continued, his voice more forceful. "This is not how you climb in this world. You mess with me; I mess with you. Your little game is over. Whatever you thought was between us never existed and never will, and I told you that. I suggest you walk away, salvage whatever dignity you have left, and return to Hollywood."

EPILOGUE

Pro Tip: Calcium-deficient plants can lead to weak stems and limp leaves. Take crushed eggshell powder and sprinkle it on the soil. This will help promote healthy plant growth.

"Alright, Broc, just lean a little more into Rosie. Wrap your hand around the back of her head. Rosie, can you lift that chin? Yes, just like that. Push that chest out, okay, perfect. Hold it. Now, take the shot!" the creative director's voice instructed. A flurry of rapid clicks echoed in the floral shop as the woman in the snug black jacket and form-fitting leggings started to clap. Her round black glasses sat just right on the tip of her nose, accentuating the playful smile across her lips; her fingers, adorned with large, chunky rings, clicked when she clapped.

Broc leaned in and kissed Rosie's neck, whispering against it, "I'm so hard for you right now. Don't think I won't do something about this hard-on as soon as they leave because, babe, I'm about to ram my cock so deep inside that wet pussy, you won't be walking by tonight." With a playful nip on the nape of her neck, Rosie couldn't stifle her giggle.

"I think I'm all in on that plan," she teased, leaning in close while

Broc pulled her into his chest, her head resting comfortably on his shoulder.

The creative director for GQ sauntered over, hand outstretched for a handshake. "Thanks for this. Let's say the editor was about to lose his mind over the last story being pulled, but this, this is so much better." She paused, waiting for Broc to shake her hand before her gaze shifted back to Rosie. "Never hold back, alright? You've got this incredible vibe. It's rough around the edges, just captivating. The camera loves you, and those tattoos are just as stunning. You need to tip that artist of yours. I can already see a tide of women rushing out to flaunt their own green thumbs if it means scoring a guy like him," the creative director stated, then tossed a thumb back at Broc, a smirk on her face. Rosie couldn't help but stifle a snort, snuggling closer against Broc while her heart was racing. "Alright, we're done for today. Thank you once again. I'll have the lawyer talk to the CEO, and we'll pull the lawsuit in exchange for this shoot. If I need anything more, I'll call you." The woman turned on her heels, the photographer trailing closely behind her.

Once the back door closed with a soft click, Broc's hands slid up Rosie's arms. He wrapped one hand around her neck, his thumb brushing under her chin, tilting her head back to expose her long, elegant neck, creamy pale skin adorned with twisting vines and delicate flowers drawn over her skin. She was breathtaking, everything Broc craved and far more than he needed.

He locked on Rosie's violet-blue eyes; he was about to devour her. Without a moment's hesitation, he crashed his lips against hers, the urgency of the kiss igniting a fire within him. A scorching blaze mirrored his heat as she licked the seam of his lips, begging for entrance. He obliged, surrendering to the moment. Their kiss was wild and unfiltered, hunger spilling over as their teeth clashed, every suck and lick frantic; it was wet, it was messy, it was everything to *them*.

Broc craved her while stealing her breath, then bit down on her lower lip, tangled his fingers in the mess of her hair, still twisted from the photo shoot. In that moment, nothing else mattered; it was just them, and Broc was devouring without reserve at his feast.

One hand slid down the front of her overalls, unhooking the buckles with effortless precision, letting the bib fall away to reveal her bare chest beneath. The creative director was chasing a sultry vibe, and Rosie was more than ready to deliver. With the front of her overalls falling forward, her tattoos were now fully exposed. Broc's possessiveness had flared when this was first brought up, a flicker of jealousy igniting within him at the thought of others seeing what belonged solely to him. But in his current moment, with easy access to her soft curves and her nipples already peaked with excitement, all he felt was gratitude. Each curve was a treasure he could admire, each tattoo a story that made her even more irresistible. And she would look delicious with his cum dripping from her nipples.

Needles pricked the back of Rosie's throat as she locked eyes with Broc. The tease of his dark curls fell just right across his forehead, and his cologne wrapped around her like a second skin. It was the deep blend of bergamot and cedar that hit her senses hard. She couldn't help but close her eyes, surrendering to the rush, feeling every electrifying touch from Broc sear into her memory. Broc slid his rough, calloused hands over her exposed breast while his kiss nipped down her neck, biting, sucking, biting again, all the way to her nipple, where his warm lips pulled her nipple into his mouth, while his other hand massaged it up while kneading her heavy breast.

A breathy moan filled the space between her and Broc as she arched into his kiss. "More, Broc...please..." she moaned again, listening to the sucking sounds as a feral growl erupted from the back of his throat.

It was the way that Broc's hips moved against Rosie while sitting on top of his floral cutting board that made him harder than concrete. The need to fuck Rosie into a stupor was the only thing he was thinking about, like a damn caveman with the need to breed. The floral shop grew smaller as he continued to press into her core, while her leg wrapped around his torso, using her bare feet to pull him closer to her body.

A lazy half smile split across Broc's lips as he tipped his head up, then moved to her other breast, switching places with his hand, then with his tongue. He gave a long lap, feeling Rosie shudder under his touch. "I need to fuck you, Rosie," Broc stated.

The front door chimed, and then Adam yelled from the front, "Hey, Broc! You're late! Poppy, Colin, and Davis are waiting for you." He walked towards the back room. Once he saw how Rosie and Broc were positioned, he started chuckling and placed his hands on his hips, popping them out, as if he were enjoying the show. "Nice. You know how much I love voyeurism, but as much as I would like you to keep fingering Rosie—"

"Shut the fuck up, Adam," Broc shot back, growling at him. Rosie leaned into Broc's body; his hands protectively wrapped around her bare back as she reached between them to secure the bib back in place. Since she was still topless under her overalls from the seductive GQ photo shoot, Broc reached over his head, removed his black "She Loves Me, She Loves Me Not!" sweatshirt, and helped her slip it over her head for coverage.

"Well, tell me I was wrong!" Adam countered defiantly, frowning as Rosie covered herself, ignoring Broc's earlier command to 'shut the fuck up.' Rosie rested her head on Broc's shoulder while he gently cupped her jaw, lowering his head to kiss the side of her face.

"You were wrong," Rosie stated matter-of-factly.

"Fine, palming your breast then," Adam replied as he threw his arms up in a motion of 'I don't really care.' "Look, press came, ribbon cutting happening. Poppy is worried. Davis is annoyed. Colin is pissed. And now you'll have to deal with blue balls. Get your ass over there, dude."

"Alright, we're coming." Broc's voice was steady, but the way he stepped away from Rosie, still holding her hands, sent a spark of electricity through both of them while their hands were still connected. Rosie jumped off the floral cutting island, her heartbeat quickening as he led her out of the shop, the two of them following Adam like a pair of shadows.

The crowd was buzzing outside Rosie's old building, their

applause washing over Colin Peters' voice. But when Colin caught sight of Rosie standing behind the crowd, his eyes lit up, and he gestured for her to come closer, pulling her into the spotlight.

"Go get 'em, babe," Broc murmured, his thumb grazing her cheek, igniting a heat that spread through her. He tipped her chin slightly, his lips brushing against her forehead. It was a simple gesture.

Rosie flashed a playful smile, her fingers resting lightly against his chest. "You owe me a *to be continued*, sir." The grin that spread across Broc's face was wicked. He definitely wanted to pick up where they'd left off. But this time, he thought, he'd like to strap her to their bed while he plunged deep into her pussy.

Colin lifted his hand and pulled Rosie close to him as he spoke into the microphone. "This wouldn't have been possible without the incredible generosity of this woman right here, Rosie Clark. A true Spokane-ite, Rosie didn't just donate her building; she gave my wife's non-profit, The Richard Snow Foundation, a lifeline. Along with the Jensen House, which serves as a retreat for families in need of a free place to stay during medical visits, The Richard Snow Foundation now has Miss Marigold's Home. This newly renovated building will welcome six families, offering them a smooth transition from the clinical confines of a hospital to the comfort of home. This building will host an on-call nurse and physical therapists."

The crowd erupted in applause, and Broc could see Rosie's cheeks flush a deep crimson. Just then, Rosie felt a warm hand wrap around hers. Turning her head, she found Poppy stepping beside her, beaming like a superstar who had married her. The camera flashed, and Colin glanced behind him, spotted the enormous scissors, and handed them to Rosie and Poppy. Together, they turned and snipped the large red ribbon.

Once the ribbon fell, applause erupted again, and Colin stepped forward, swinging open the front doors. Rosie stepped inside for the first time since Orson's reckless fire had reduced everything to ashes. The upper floor had been unrecognizable, now rebuilt from the studs up. Rosie's mismatched shelves and haphazard plant arrangements were replaced by a spacious seating area, a playroom off to one side, a welcoming reception desk in the center of the room, and, on the other side, a fully equipped physical therapy area complete with a massage table. The room was painted in a dull beige, but Rosie's heart fluttered at the transformation.

A new lift had been constructed outside, designed to accommodate wheelchair users. While some guests opted for the elevator, Rosie trailed behind Colin, Davis, and Poppy, ascending the stairs to her old apartment.

"This floor has three rooms with a shared bathroom and a kitchen, just like the third floor," Poppy explained, her excitement barely contained. Colin opened the door, and Rosie stepped into the freshly minted space, absorbing every detail. Each room, tight but functional, featured a bunk bed, a pull-out couch, and a double bed. The closets were designed outside the bedrooms to maximize space. A tiny dining area sat adjacent to a small TV nook, and despite its compactness, the area felt fresh and airy.

Rosie turned to Colin and Poppy, her smile radiant. "Miss Marigold would have loved this," she said, a wave of nostalgia washing over her. Poppy clapped her hands and directed her attention to Colin.

"I've got a little thank-you gift," Poppy said, her eyes sparkling. "It's not much, but I spoke with Broc, and he thought you'd love it." She hurried into another room and returned moments later with a small basket. "Here!" she exclaimed, thrusting it into Rosie's hands. Inside was a tiny black-and-white hen. Rosie loved how unique it looked; without a single white feather on its head, though she was fully grown, it was about the size of Rosie's palm. "It's a Bantam Hen."

"You got me a hen?" Rosie sank to her knees, setting the basket down before lifting the hen into her hands. "Oh my goodness, she's stunning." She glanced up at Poppy, then turned to Colin, who had just stepped into the room with his hands shoved into his jeans, his proud stance telling her he shared in her joy. "This is incredible!"

"Knock, knock!" Adam called out as he breezed into the room, followed closely by Sammy. "Oh, you like the cock!" he teased, grinning.

"It's a hen, Adam," Broc shot back, kneeling beside Rosie, "What do you think?" he asked.

"I think I'm already in love with her," Rosie replied, her voice soft. "Looks like we're going to need a whole new coop for her.

Broc winked, reached out, and stroked the hen on her head, which caused her to close her eyes under his touch. "It's already done. Raymond will be stopping by later tonight with it. This time, the light is mounted to the ceiling and equipped with cameras and alarms. And I also asked Raymond to hook it up to a sprinkler system in case of fire."

"Broc," Rosie murmured, her voice barely audible as her hand pressed against his chest; a blooming heartbeat thrummed under her hand. "Thank you."

Broc's lips curled into a smirk. He reached up, his fingers threading through the soft strands of hair at the nape of her neck, pulling her closer until their mouths met. Her lips were perfectly kissable.

"Oh, great, kissing while I'm here," Adam chimed in, mockingly placing his hands on his hips. "While you know Daisy isn't here with me! Rude." With a swift flick of his wrist, he slapped Davis playfully on the chest. "You feel me, right? Rubbing it in and all..."

Davis rolled his eyes, pushing Adam off him in a half-hearted gesture. "Yeah, we get it. Seriously, how the hell does Daisy put up with you?"

"Not entirely sure, man, but she's a keeper," Adam stated with a wink.

Davis stepped forward, extending his hand to Colin. "Thanks for giving me the bid on the remodel. If anything pops up or you have more projects, know I'd love to pitch another proposal for you again." Davis pulled back, then reached for Sammy's hand. "My mom has Archie tonight; you know how rare it is having a kid-free night? No time to waste. Time for date night, sans kid."

Colin shook Davis's hand, a grin spreading across his face. "Absolutely, but we should head back too. The twins are probably terrorizing Carla, and I can't imagine Tate and Aiden are up to anything good, especially when dinosaur toys are involved."

"Yeah, me too, thanks for asking... *Davis*, but Daisy will actually be meeting me at the Davenport later, and trust me, I'll be having a great time!" Adam called out as he followed the two couples slipping away, leaving only Broc, Rosie, and their new hen in the room. Then Adam stopped and looked over his shoulder before turning and leaning against the doorframe, crossing his arms and saying, "So will it be her tits or ass? You two going to finish where I interrupted?"

The glower from Broc's eyes said it all, and all Adam could do was raise his hands and back out. "Alright! Alright, I get it; don't ask about tits or ass around Rosie. God, such a baby. Here, let me take that off your hands," Adam offered, walking back over to Rosie, leaning over to lift the hen from her before dropping it back into the basket. "Go on, I've got the hen. You two should really stop eye-fucking around me; it's uncomfortable because I don't know if you're inviting me or ignoring me... Go take care of it before she explodes," Adam said, pointing to Broc. A smile spread across Broc's lips, and Rosie exchanged a knowing look as soon as Adam was gone.

Broc wasted no time; his hands were steady as he scooped Rosie up into his arms, cradling her against him as he descended the stairs and then into their apartment next door. His feet couldn't move fast enough to their shared bedroom, but once he was there, standing against his bed, Broc lowered Rosie gently to the floor, his fingers brushing against her cheek, tucking her vibrant purple hair behind her ear. The sizzle from his hand traveled down the delicate curve of her neck. He couldn't ignore the way her pulse quickened under his gaze. With a smirk that hinted at mischief, he let his hand drop, tilting his head slightly as his teeth toyed with the corner of his lip.

"Show me how wet you are, babe. Take off those clothes," he murmured, his voice a low growl that sent a liquid heat raging through both of their veins, as a smile tipped the corner of Rosie's pink bowtie lips.

BONUS EPILOGUE

Pro Tip: Starting seeds inside with a grow light is the best way to start gardens without the fear of seeds rotting.

Mindy Harper Seeks Treatment Following Breakup.
Broc Chase's Floral Business Thrives In Drama

In a surprising turn of events, actress Mindy Harper has checked into a private facility for treatment following the abrupt end of her high-profile relationship with Broc Chase and the failure of her career. This follows the release of scandalous photographs that have put her personal life under intense scrutiny. Mindy's publicists confirmed that she is addressing her personal issues related to exhaustion and a sex addiction, though they declined to comment further.

The fallout from these photos has also affected other planned media. GQ Magazine has pulled its much-anticipated article featuring Mindy and Broc as 'Hollywood's Power Couple' from the January issue, and the publication has filed a lawsuit seeking damages.

With Mindy's future uncertain, questions remain about the once-beloved star, who was hailed as America's Sweetheart.

On the flip side, Broc Chase is succeeding professionally. His floral business in Spokane, Washington is blooming thanks to his partnership with Rosie Clark. The duo has gained attention for their innovative floral arrangements and has maintained a relatively private life.

However, not all has been calm for Broc and Rosie. Rosie's ex-partner, Orson Ryes, who remains incarcerated, has been linked to a series of alarming incidents, including allegations of possession of controlled substances, administering drugs to another person without consent, multiple arson charges of 1st and 3rd degree, reckless endangerment, kidnapping, false imprisonment, unlawful restraint, battery, coercion, and aggravated assault. The case is still with the courts as investigations continue.

Rosie rolled over, swishing her arm back and forth on the mattress, only to feel the chill of cold sheets. She pushed up her fuzzy eye mask, but Broc wasn't there. She squinted at the bright morning light streaming through the window and, with a dramatic sigh, stretched her arms overhead, reluctant to abandon the bed. But today was a big day. Valentine's Day was just around the corner, and the floral shop was already busting at the seams with orders. Sliding out of bed, Rosie dropped to her knees and riffled through the scattered clothes on the floor until she found her favorite overalls and a cozy cream-colored cable-knit sweater. Tossing on a green and pink tie-dyed shirt underneath, she paired it with her cream wool socks and Birkenstocks.

Downstairs in the kitchen, she snagged a bagel, slathered it in cream cheese, and headed to the main level to open the shop. The lower-level door to the shop was slightly ajar, lights were already on, and the music was playing one of Broc's favorite stations. Upon entering the shop, bagel in hand, Rosie was met with a sight that always made her heart flutter—in a good way. Broc stood behind the cutting table, carefully arranging a dozen roses into a crystal vase, complete with greenery and baby's breath. He wore gray sweatpants that hung low on his narrow hips, and the outline of his glutes was mouthwatering. With his snug black shirt on, the one with the *"She Loves Me, She Loves Me Not!"* logo and petals cascading down one side, handsome didn't even begin to cover it. Broc's sharp jaw and messy black curls teased Rosie's core, and the memory of what his tongue had done to her pussy last night made her thighs press together. The scene was a slice of heaven as she walked over to the Mosier couch, completely content watching him work his magic.

With each bite of her bagel, she soaked in the moment, her own thoughts quiet for once. Placing her half-eaten bagel between her teeth, she pulled her hair into a messy bun, her gaze traveling to the floral vase, noting a few odd placements of roses that could use a little tweak. She would have arranged them differently, but that thought stayed locked away while she watched Broc work on the arrangement.

The moment Broc caught sight of Rosie moving through the floral shop, his heart kicked up a notch. She was a rare bloom, impossible to ignore. Last night, he'd poured every ounce into her, and, hell, he was ready to do it all over again.

"Morning, babe." His gaze lingered as she bit down on the bagel, her purple hair swept back in a carefree mess. He felt a sizzling heat under his skin as he snipped another rose, placing it in the center of the vase and rearranging the others to make them look just right. "I've got this order to wrap up today. Next week's going to be chaotic, and I might need to order more roses. Oh, and your plants are here." He nodded toward a box resting on the floor beside the coolers.

"Yay!" Rosie cheered with her mouth full of her bagel. She squealed with delight as she raised one fist in the air.

"Wait! Before you open that, can you take care of Kermit? He needs some veggies." Broc pointed to a small dish of cut fruit by the narrow aquarium in the corner of the floral shop.

Rosie shot him a glare that could rival an MMA fighter. "You did that on purpose," she huffed. "I can't stand that thing! It's squishy, and it literally tried to eat me." She crossed her arms and leaned away from the aquarium.

"It's just a little tree frog, babe. It's more scared of you than anything. Just open the lid and drop the food in. I promise it won't bite your hand off." A teasing grin broke across Broc's face, loving how much she hated this chore. It was his favorite game.

"I really hate you," she grumbled.

"Admit it, you love me," he shot back, lifting an eyebrow. He turned back to the vase and spun it around for a 360-degree view.

"That's up for debate. And seriously, why did it take so long for that ugly little thing to come back to you? I thought you gave it away... Don't Basil's kids want it?" Rosie challenged.

"Nope. And Basil's wife gave me an *'immediate no'* anyway." He snorted a chuckle. "He's quiet. Just feed him, and then you can check out your new orchids." Broc nodded towards the front of the store. "There's plenty of room over there." He pointed to the display window already bursting with plants. "Just mix them in with the Valentine's décor and those funky stuffies you ordered."

Rosie cast her gaze toward the window, where her jumbled collection of plants thrived. The orchids would bring the perfect flair, mingling effortlessly with her plucky succulents and those alluring trailing violets. It was her corner of happiness: 'Miss Marigolds Corner.' The mismatched chairs surrounded her small wooden desk, while baskets overflowed with different varieties of plants. A smile tugged at her lips, and without missing a beat, she crossed the room and planted a quick kiss on Broc's cheek before snatching the box cutter from the floral table. Seven orchids awaited her; some were petite, and the others were standard, but some were unique in color.

"What did you get?" Broc asked. He rested his palms on the floral cutting island, looking at her as she sat on her heels.

"I don't know; I should have a few boxes, but I guess only one came. I think..." Rosie paused and pulled the box's flaps back. With excitement in her eyes, she reached into the box and pulled out a small potted orchid. "This one's called 'Minki Black.' It's just a Phalaenopsis," Rosie explained. The petals resembled watercolors, swirling with deep blacks and purples, splashed with delicate bits of white. "It's even more breathtaking in person," she confessed, trying to rein in the thrill as she wiggled on the floor. Broc moved around the island, pinching the knees of his worn black jeans as he knelt beside her. She handed him the pot, grinning. "Check for stowaways, will you?" He snorted. After Broc found it was amphibian-free, he set the pot down and pulled out another.

This miniature orchid was about the size of Broc's palm and was wired to a sturdy piece of elegantly twisted bark, showcasing tiny blooms the size of his fingernail. Rosie squealed when she saw the orchid in Broc's hand. "Oh, shit! Look how tiny those blooms are! That's a Cleisostoma arietinum. It won't get any bigger than that, and look at those bright green stems, they're so—Jesus Christ, what the fuck is that!" Rosie hissed and pointed to the upper right-hand corner; there was a cluster of stems and tiny leaves. Broc pulled the bark closer, and clutching to the small branch was the tiniest camouflaged chameleon Broc had ever seen. It was so little that he almost missed it. It stayed frozen, trying to hide amongst its surroundings, but its small eyes were searching as if planning an escape...extremely slowly.

"He's so tiny! I'll put him in with the frog," Broc declared and stood up.

"NO! That thing tried to eat me! And this new thing, no bigger than those fucking crickets you put in there, you'll kill it if you feed it to that alien!" Rosie said, grabbing a hold of Broc's jeans.

"Do I sense a love for this creature?" he teased.

"Eww, no! I just don't want to add an 'executioner' to my resume. I'm fine with co-owner of the floral shop for now," Rosie admitted.

"Okay, well, I need to put this little one somewhere safe and warm. I'll just hang it on the pallet boards till we can get another aquarium."

Rosie rubbed her nose. "You're keeping this one, too?"

Looking over his shoulder, he smiled. "Yep!

"Why can't you just get rid of them? This isn't a pet store," Rosie grumbled.

"The kids love it when they come in, and it keeps them busy while I talk to their parents. I also like the quirkiness it brings," Broc confided. "Plus, it distracts Adam; he's basically a kid himself. I'm not sure how Daisy puts up with him."

Rosie let out a soft sigh, pushing herself up from the floor. "Can you please check the rest? I don't think my heart can take much more of this." She rubbed her hand gently against her chest. Broc's expression softened. A tender kiss pressed against her forehead along with a wink from Broc as he slipped his hand up her waist and palmed her breast.

"I swear, the next time we have stowaways, they're going straight to a pet store," he promised, the corners of his lips lifting into a reassuring smile.

ABOUT THE AUTHOR

Shannon is an experienced youth cross-country coach who, alongside her husband, has directed and coached teams across the nation, guiding young athletes to compete at national championships. She skillfully balances these responsibilities with her passion for writing contemporary romance.

During the challenging COVID-19 years, Shannon not only taught and parented her three children but also made a significant impact in the literary world.

A lifelong reader and writer, Shannon often found herself writing in the rare moments she could carve out between piloting her family full-time, and coaching her youth running club. Despite struggling with spelling and grammar, which earned her the nickname "Shammar," she pushed past these fears and completed her first novel, *Broken Luck*. The positive reviews from her debut inspired her to revisit *Fairytale in a Big City*, a manuscript she wrote in 2009. She edited and refined it to become part of her Pacific Northwest Love series.

Shannon has been happily married for 18 years to her Air Force husband, serving as the core of their family dynamic as they traverse the nation with each new military assignment.

Never be scared to be yourself.
-Shannon Morse

instagram.com/shannonmorseauthor

tiktok.com/@Shannonmorseauthor

ACKNOWLEDGEMENTS

I need to express my ever-growing gratitude to my older sister, who has been the inspiration behind this book. Your passion for all things green has influenced my daughter, who is now obsessed with plants, and has led me to bring around 500 plants into my home. You are like Rosie, but with purple hair, piercings, and tattoos. (For reasons we all know - I HAD to change your appearance.)

I must send a thanks to my amazing editors, Samantha and Ramona. Your expertise consistently impresses me, and I can't thank you enough for everything you do.

A special shout-out goes to my PA, Kalie Gerwig, at Good Girl Author Services. You have saved my butt countless times, and I deeply appreciate your help and friendship.

Lastly, I want to thank Alesandra Lopes at Lopes Designs for the stunning cover. I am so grateful to be working with you and to trust your creative vision. Your talent is truly remarkable.

www.ingramcontent.com/pod-product-compliance
Ingram Content Group UK Ltd.
Pitfield, Milton Keynes, MK11 3LW, UK
UKHW041634190726
13854UKWH00006B/2488